Author and screenwriter Simon Booker writes prime-time TV drama for BBC1, ITV and US TV. His UK credits include *The Inspector Lynley Mysteries*, *Holby City* and *The Mrs Bradley Mysteries*. He has written many plays for BBC Radio 4, worked extensively as a producer in television and radio, and as a journalist. Simon lives in London and Deal. His partner is fellow crime writer Melanie McGrath. They often discuss murder methods over breakfast.

Also by Simon Booker

Without Trace

KILL ME TWICE

SIMON BOOKER

ZAFFRE

First published in Great Britain in 2017 by

ZAFFRE PUBLISHING
80-81 Wimpole St, London W1G 9RE
www.zaffrebooks.co.uk

This is a work of fiction. Names, places, events and
incidents are either the products of the author's imagination or
used fictitiously. Any resemblance to actual persons, living or dead,
or actual events is purely coincidental.

A CIP catalogue record for this book is available from the British Library.

ISBN: 978-1-785-76078-5

also available as an ebook

1 3 5 7 9 10 8 6 4 2

Typeset by IDSUK (Data Connection) Ltd
Printed and bound by Clays Ltd, St Ives Plc

Zaffre Publishing is an imprint of Bonnier Zaffre,
a Bonnier Publishing company
www.bonnierzaffre.co.uk
www.bonnierpublishing.co.uk

For my mother, Edna Tromans,
and all single parents.

PART ONE

One

Someone is watching.

She can feel his eyes.

But there's no one in sight.

No one down on the shoreline or in the woods up ahead.

Morgan and her daughter have had the cliffs to themselves since the rain died away and the sun began to shine. No sign of another soul since leaving the beach and climbing the steps to the windswept path looking over to France. Once you get past the golf course (the ugly clubhouse, the manicured green) things get rougher.

Wilder.

Lonelier.

The track dips into a wooded hollow then rises towards a kissing gate. Looming on the horizon is the memorial to those who kept the Channel open during two world wars. On a normal day the obelisk is a beacon spurring Morgan towards coffee at the White Cliffs Café. This is not a normal day.

Her instincts are right.

Someone is watching.

The savage blow to the back of her head comes out of a clear blue sky. One minute she's trying to talk twenty-year-old Lissa out of getting breast implants, the next she's face down in a puddle, crying out in pain. Her first thought is for her daughter.

Is their assailant a mugger?

A rapist?

Worse?

Sprawled in the mud, she doubles up in agony as a heavy-booted kick connects with a rib. The pain is white hot, obliterating everything except Lissa's cries.

'No! Leave her alone!'

Another kick, this time in the stomach. Then, blinded by pain, face half submerged in a puddle, Morgan can hear the struggle as the attacker goes after Lissa. The thud as she is hurled to the ground. The sound of blows to her body. She tries to struggle to her feet, to protect her daughter.

NOBODY HARMS MY CHILD.

But she can't move.

Can't speak.

Can't see.

Seconds before she blacks out, she's aware of a metallic sound: the unmistakable *clink* of a Zippo lighter, the *rasp* of its flint. As she drifts towards unconsciousness, her nostrils detect a distinctive smell.

Human hair.

Her daughter's hair.

Burning.

Two

Clink-rasp.

The sound of the Zippo haunts Morgan's dreams. For forty-eight hours she refuses to leave Lissa's bedside, sleeping fitfully in a hospital chair, trying not to weep at the pain searing her ribs despite the powerful painkillers. She must stay strong. For her daughter's sake.

'Did you see his face?'

'No.'

Detective Inspector Neville Rook has kind eyes but Morgan fears he'll never trace the maniac who set fire to Lissa's hair. Neither woman saw their assailant. There were no witnesses.

Clink-rasp.

Morgan's ribs are bruised but not broken. She's been told she's lucky. Lissa has lost most of her hair but is deemed 'lucky' too. Shocked and bruised, but otherwise unharmed. At first, Lissa wept uncontrollably, which the doctor said was normal – a natural reaction to violent trauma – but she seems to have calmed down, settling for being moody instead. Just for a change.

Clink-rasp.

After two days of sympathetic police officers and brusque doctors, Morgan is allowed to drive her daughter home, to the converted railway carriage on Dungeness beach. The sun is shining – an Indian summer day in mid-October – but a stiff wind is blowing in from the sea, singing in the power cables strung across telegraph poles. A couple of miles to the west, she can make out the shape of the prison. To the east lies the vast nuclear power station, dominating the landscape for miles around. And in between, the abandoned fishing boats, derelict shacks and piles of rusting scrap that make the desolate shoreline resemble the location of a post-apocalypse movie.

In the cluttered kitchen, setting the kettle to boil, she picks her moment to ask Lissa if she wants to move away from this bleak but beautiful place. Perched on a windswept spit of shingle half a mile from the nearest neighbour, the quirky, ramshackle house with its rickety lean-to is no one's idea of a safe haven. Clusters of wild flowers and sea kale soften the rugged shoreline and the wildlife is breathtaking – stoats, weasels, badgers, dragonflies – but wouldn't it be more *sensible* to live somewhere less isolated, somewhere ordinary?

'Fuck "sensible",' says Lissa. 'It was just a random attack.' Then, less confidently, 'Anyway, if we leave because we're scared, he wins. We can't let him win.'

Clink-rasp.

Morgan wonders if the reason for her daughter's determination to stay in the area has more to do with unrequited love than defiance. She hasn't been allowed to meet Pablo and knows little about him except that he's older (Lissa scorns men her own age) and lives in a camper van. He doesn't seem to have been around for at least two weeks. Lissa has taken to sleeping at home, surviving on Weetabix and Haribo and checking her iPhone every few minutes – a sure sign of a break-up. Any hope of cosy mother–daughter chats ('what is it with *men*?') was dashed long ago. Both are lousy pickers.

No offence, Mum, but your exes? Including Dad? I'd be, like, yeucch! Swipe left.

It's true – Morgan's love life is a joke, a fact underlined by last year's fling with a fellow hack now known as 'The Shit'. When she discovered that he was married she deleted his number, burned the tacky lingerie he'd given her and ignored his messages. He retaliated by awarding her book a one-star review on Amazon.

Despite his petty gesture, *Trial and Error: a History of Miscarriages of Justice* has paid off her overdraft. Its surprise bestseller status has rescued Morgan's career from the doldrums, allowing her to reinvent herself as an expert in the controversial field of wrongful convictions. The *Guardian* dubbed her 'full of fury and passion, a one-woman Innocence Project'. Editors now respond to her impassioned emails concerning verdicts she believes require urgent re-examination. So far, however, no newspaper will hire her to champion the hapless souls who fall foul of the British criminal justice system.

Sorry, Morgan. All down to money.

She doesn't take it personally. She understands the reality of what remains of the newspaper industry: dwindling circulation; staff cuts; slashed budgets. Why fund a fishing expedition when you can fill your pages with TV tittle-tattle for free? Adapt or die. Ask the *Star* or the *Sun*.

Pro Bono seems different. The webzine start-up has offered to publish the next investigation Morgan undertakes which, if today goes according to plan, may be fast approaching.

As well as rejuvenating her career, *Trial and Error* has prompted a flood of letters from prisoners protesting their innocence. Morgan's kitchen is littered with Jiffy bags bulging with mail forwarded by her publisher. She reads every letter. A few have the ring of truth but many more reek of lies and desperation. Nine times out of ten she has no choice but to reply 'there's nothing I can do', or, at best, forward the letter to *bona fide* innocence projects. Their volunteers – idealistic law students – are overzealous and under-resourced, but once in the bluest of moons there's a chance they can offer greater hope than Morgan's solo effort.

Amongst the letters, one protestation of innocence has captured her interest.

Anjelica Fry.

Twenty-seven years old, a care home cook serving a lengthy sentence in HMP Dungeness for the murder of her ex-boyfriend, the father of her baby. A line from one of her letters has stayed with Morgan.

Please help me. This is the one place you can die of hope.

The prison is on Morgan's doorstep. More importantly, she feels an affinity with a fellow single mother. And there is something about the way Anjelica was demonised by the tabloids.

Cold-blooded killer.

Arsonist Anjelica.

Mum murdered ex-lover while baby slept.

Morgan remembers the story well: a late-night arson attack on a flat in Dalston, east London. Anjelica is said to have driven across the city in the small hours to torch the home of her ex-boyfriend, Karl Savage. After their bitter break-up, he'd threatened to abduct their three-month-old son and take him abroad.

Morgan recalls her own doubts about the guilty verdict. On the night in question the baby was running a temperature. Anjelica had taken him to the doctor. She was told to come back the following day if he was still unwell. To torch Karl's flat at 3 a.m. she would have had to leave the sickly infant alone for hours or take him with her, driving across London without being caught on CCTV. Nothing at the trial or in the press raised any doubt about Anjelica's devotion to her son.

Something wasn't right.

Intuition has its place, but before Morgan will commit time and energy she needs solid evidence that the system has messed up. The tone of Anjelica's letter – desperate, impassioned – has prompted her to take a crucial first step. A prison visit is set for lunchtime.

Now, her ribs are aching. She downs two more painkillers then picks up her keys.

'Will you be OK on your own? Couple of hours?'

Slumped on the sofa, Lissa nods, eyes not straying from her phone.

'Yep.'

'Heard from Pablo?'

'Nope.'

'Are you staying home all day?'

A roll of the eyes.

'No. Going to Piccadilly to show off my new hairstyle.'

Morgan takes the bolshy attitude in her stride. Why wouldn't Lissa be stroppy? She was attacked in broad daylight. If she hadn't doused herself in a puddle her burns would have been much worse. As it is, her hair is mostly gone, but at least her scalp and face are virtually unscathed.

Her psyche is another story.

Violence changes people.

And she's already been through more than any twenty-year-old should endure, thanks to a misguided fling with another Shit.

The worry keeps Morgan awake. For some time, her daughter has shown signs of being borderline agoraphobic: anxious about leaving the house, except to see Pablo; wary of strangers; panic attacks. The cliff-top assault has done nothing to help her state of mind.

'Pizza tonight?'

Lissa shrugs.

'Whatever.'

Morgan heads for the door. Outside, on the deserted beach, the wind has died down and the sun is warm. She winces in pain, clutching her ribs as she eases herself into the Mini. Lissa hurries out of the house, holding her mother's old leather jacket.

'You forgot this.'

Morgan frowns.

'It's too warm for a jacket.'

Lissa looks away.

'Might rain. Take it, just in case.'

Frown deepening, Morgan places the jacket on the passenger seat then drives off.

The sky is blue.

Not a cloud in sight, no hint of rain.

Why is her daughter so insistent?

Three

The question soon assumes fresh urgency. The drive to HMP Dungeness takes four minutes. Morgan could walk it in fifteen, but not today. Not with aches and bruises that make her feel twice her age. Parking the Mini, she dons the leather jacket, despite the heat. Not long ago the car was broken into and her belongings were stolen. Once is enough.

Entering the prison building, she shows her visitor's order and leaves her phone at the gate, exchanging small talk with the officer designated to escort her along the brightly lit corridors and through a series of locked gates. They know her here. Not long ago she was a regular, running the men's reading group on C-Wing.

Today she's heading for A-Wing. The Mother and Baby Unit, aka MBU.

One of a handful of unisex prisons in the UK, HMP Dungeness has acquired a fearsome reputation thanks to its new governor, Ian Carne. Inevitably nicknamed 'Genghis', he was parachuted in to replace the previous incumbent whose early retirement 'for personal reasons' took everyone by surprise. 'Genghis's' regime is tough for prisoners and staff alike. Spot checks for drugs and phones. Zero tolerance for violence. No second chances.

At the MBU gate Morgan resists the temptation to stroke the sniffer dog, a black Labrador. These are working dogs, not pets. She's instructed to sit on the Body Orifice Scanner, then receives a brisk rubdown from an unsmiling female officer who could use a mint.

'Open your mouth.'

Morgan does as instructed. The woman moves closer, peering under her tongue.

'Wait here.'

The officer leaves. Morgan sits on a bucket chair, scanning the rules and regulations.

Aiding and abetting an escape will lead to imprisonment.

No photography. No drugs. No bullying.

Only yesterday she read about new, metal-free plastic mobiles in the shape of tubes of lipstick, designed to make them easy to hide inside a prisoner's body. Or a visitor's. Little wonder there's a clampdown.

After a ten-minute wait another officer arrives, keys jangling on his belt. Morgan has met him before. Knocking sixty – maybe older – probably close to retirement. Beefy, bald, stubbly chin. His name is Trevor Jukes. He gives Morgan a lopsided smile.

''Morning, Miss. I need you to put your jacket in a locker.'

Morgan raises an eyebrow.

'Because?'

'Can't take anything onto the wing, not even coats.'

'But I've been searched.'

His smile thins.

'Problem, Miss?'

Morgan remembers Lissa pressing her to wear the jacket. She feels a frisson of anxiety then dismisses it straight away. She has passed the checks. The sniffer dog showed no interest. Slipping off the jacket, she puts her hands in its pockets and feels around. Empty.

'No, no problem.'

Jukes places the jacket in a locker. He hands her a numbered plastic tag.

'I'll take you to Miss Fry.'

He unlocks the gate. Whistling the theme from *The Archers*, he leads her through an AstroTurf exercise yard bordered by fencing topped with razor wire. Two female prisoners in their twenties are approaching from the other direction. One has a port wine stain on her right cheek, the other has pink hair.

'Where are you ladies off to?'

'See the doctor, Sir.'

Sir. Miss. Mister. Morgan finds the formality comical, but it's designed to foster respect between staff and inmates and seems to have the desired effect. Except when things kick off. Which can happen at any time.

Unlocking the gate to A-Wing, Jukes ushers her inside. The hubbub is raucous but not menacing, the way it can be on a men's wing. Dozens of women queue for microwaved baked potatoes and a thin brown sludge that might be chilli. Almost all wear tracksuits and trainers. A few glance at Morgan, mildly curious, but most are focused on their lunch.

She signs in at the wing office then follows her squeaky-shoed escort along a corridor and through another set of locked gates, the babble of canteen conversation receding into the distance.

'I'm reading your book,' says Jukes over his shoulder.

Surprised, Morgan says nothing, waiting for more.

'I borrowed it from Anjelica Fry. Thought I'd see what all the fuss is about.'

'I'd be interested to know what you think.'

'No, you wouldn't.'

'Excuse me?'

'I have to work with these people, Miss. They're innocent, apparently – all hundred-and-twenty-two of them. Trust me, you don't want to know what I think. Especially of Anjelica Fry.'

Morgan is nonplussed. As a rule, prison officers stay poker-faced in front of civilians, remaining non-committal about inmates in their care. It's rare for an old hand like Jukes to drop his guard. She's tempted to argue, to cite cases in her book.

Are you suggesting there's no such thing as a miscarriage of justice? Hillsborough? Timothy Evans? Derek Bentley? The Birmingham Six? The Guildford Four? And don't get me started on all those mothers wrongly imprisoned for killing their babies because some egomaniacal 'expert witness' got it wrong. Can you imagine a worse agony?

These thoughts flit through Morgan's mind, but that's where they'll stay. It's never smart to alienate a prison officer, not if you're considering resuming your status as a regular visitor.

Jukes leads her up a flight of stairs then stops at a door and punches in a four-digit code. Entering the MBU, Morgan is immediately aware of a change in atmosphere: calmer, more like a nursery than a prison, primary colours on the walls. Occupying the entire landing, the unit is open plan – a dozen cubicles separated by low partition walls. Each woman has a bed, a locker and a cot. The peace is disturbed by a couple of crying babies at the far end of the landing, but most are sleeping or occupied by their mothers. A couple of women are breastfeeding, others tend to their babies, chat to each other or nap. One stands at the communal changing table, struggling to put a nappy on a newborn.

Morgan spots Anjelica Fry straight away. Apart from two officers, hers is the only black face on the wing. Newspaper photos showed a plump woman, but the transformation is shocking. Gaunt. Dark circles under puffy eyes. Thin to the point of emaciation. The convicted murderer is twenty-seven, but could be mistaken for forty, maybe older.

She's sitting on the floor of a playpen staring dully at a baby boy who prods at a stack of plastic bricks. Registering her visitor's arrival, the woman blinks slowly then gives a frown, as if trying to work out the answer to a puzzle. Morgan makes a quick assumption: Anjelica is on powerful medication, her brain addled by a cocktail of chemicals designed to dull her emotional pain and, above all, keep her quiet.

Morgan smiles, holding up a wait-a-moment finger as she shows her visitor's order to the prison officer, a borderline-obese woman in her thirties. She can see Anjelica getting to her feet, lifting her baby from the playpen and handing him to one of the other mothers.

Looking around for Trevor Jukes, Morgan sees him muttering in the ear of another screw. She overhears the words 'Care Bear' and stifles a flicker of irritation. Prison visitors, art therapists, social workers – all are damned as 'bleeding-heart liberals' or 'busybodies'. That people think this way makes

Morgan seethe. Is it just a British thing? Do other countries and cultures use 'do-gooder' as a term of abuse?

She's relieved when Jukes leaves without saying goodbye.

'Miss Fry – visitor.'

The overweight officer beckons to Anjelica who plants a half-hearted kiss on her baby's forehead then leaves him with her fellow prisoner and shuffles towards the wing office. Everything about the woman is in slow motion – the way she walks, blinks, swings her arms. She has bruises on her forearm, cuts to her cheek and her forehead is bandaged. If asked, she will say she 'fell in the shower'.

Visits usually take place in the visitors' centre, but thanks to an initiative by 'Genghis' Carne, mothers have dispensation to receive people on MBU itself, so they can show their babies to family and friends without disrupting other visits. A baby can stay till he or she reaches the age of eighteen months. After that, 'the system' takes over. Fostering. Adoption. 'Care'.

The officer nods the two women into a side room. A circle of chairs. Posters offer tired homilies.

Change your thoughts, change your world.

Forgiveness means giving up all hope of a better past.

'Your baby's gorgeous,' says Morgan.

As icebreakers go it's far from subtle, but has the virtue of being true. Something approaching a smile crosses Anjelica's face.

'Yeah.'

Her voice is barely audible, a croak. She fingers a gold crucifix around her neck.

'What's his name?'

'Marlon.'

'As in Brando?'

Anjelica shakes her head.

'It was Karl's dad's name.' She frowns. Blinks. A thought fights its way through the cocktail of drugs. 'I keep thinking they're going to take him away, put him in care.'

She refocuses her gaze, as though seeing her visitor for the first time. Her eyes flicker towards the guard stationed outside the door then back to Morgan.

'I'm not a strong person. I can't stay in here. Please?'

Morgan keeps her voice steady. Firm but gentle.

'I need to be honest from the start. I can't promise anything. Are we clear?'

A nod.

'So, tell me your story.'

Anjelica blows her nose. She clears her throat then tucks the tissue into her sleeve, like a little girl.

'Where do I begin?'

Anjelica Fry met Karl Savage in a Starbucks near the care home where she cooked two meals a day for thirty-five elderly residents. He spilt her coffee, paid for a replacement and made her laugh so much she thought she was going to wet her knickers. A week later he charmed her into bed – her first white boyfriend, her first big love. She got pregnant almost immediately, even though they were scrupulous about protection.

One in a billion, Karl called it, but with hindsight she wonders if he might have pricked holes in the condoms.

'He made a joke about it once,' says Anjelica. 'Looking back, I think he was being serious. He was desperate for kids. "I want hundreds of mini-mes", he said. "Karl Savage is prime daddy material".'

Morgan raises an eyebrow.

'Did he often talk about himself in the third person?'

'Sometimes. Why?'

'Never mind. Go on.'

As the pregnancy progressed, Karl persuaded Anjelica to move in to his Dalston flat, above a Vietnamese restaurant. Only then did the 'charmer' slowly reveal his true nature: a control freak, obsessively jealous, incapable of passing up any chance to bed other women, sometimes two in a day. He told Anjelica he'd worked for years as an electrician but now dealt in second-hand cars. A week after Marlon was born she discovered the truth: her baby's father was a drug dealer. Karl specialised in what he called the 'ack drugs' – crack and smack – and was full of grandiose ideas. Had she heard of Pablo Escobar? Worth thirty billion dollars? Karl was going to be bigger than Escobar.

Anjelica pointed out that the drug lord had died in a hail of bullets, but he'd shrugged, retorting that 25,000 people had turned out for Escobar's funeral, and you didn't get a Netflix show about your life if you were a nobody.

He'd flashed the tattoo on the soft, white flesh inside his forearm.

Rather die on my feet than live on my knees.

She spent months plotting her escape, getting herself fixed up with a housing association flat back in her old manor, Croydon, to be near her widowed father, but he'd died of lung cancer before she could make the move. The day after the funeral, while Karl was 'at work', Anjelica took Marlon to the park. She never came back.

Cue Karl's charm offensive. Tearful apologies. Doggerel copied from greetings cards and written in red biro. Flowers stolen from the local cemetery. When these tactics failed, the harassment began. Stalking. Yelling in the street. Obsessive messaging. Nearly three hundred texts in one insane forty-eight-hour period. Standing outside her flat, staring up at her bedroom window, finger pressing on the buzzer.

Buzz. Buzz. *Buzz*. BUZZZZZZZ.

Anjelica tried to reason with the man she'd loved. She borrowed books from the library and, after reading widely, told her ex that he had abandonment issues, a legacy of having lost his father at a young age and being maltreated by his mother. She also told him that he had a borderline personality disorder and exhibited many of the tendencies associated with being a sociopath. He called her a bitch. And worse. But she didn't sever all ties.

'Why not?' says Morgan.

A shrug.

'He could be sweet. And he was good looking, sexy, exciting.'

'Exciting in what way?'

Anjelica screws up her eyes, thinking hard.

'He picked me up one night in a taxi. Not a minicab, a proper black taxi. I asked where we were going. He wouldn't say. Told the driver to go to the West End and keep driving around Knightsbridge, Park Lane, all these posh places. Then he gave him a hundred quid cash so we could do it in the back of the cab, outside Buckingham Palace.'

'Classy guy.'

The sarcasm is lost on Anjelica.

'Yeah.' A slow smile plays on her lips. 'But crazy.'

'What kind of crazy?'

Anjelica stretches her arms above her head.

'Sometimes good crazy, like the taxi thing. But bad crazy too. Like the night with the ambulance.'

'Ambulance?'

The woman cracks her knuckles then puts her hands in her pockets.

'We were driving home. He'd borrowed a flash car – a red Porsche – and we got stuck in rush-hour traffic. Total gridlock. And this ambulance was trying to get through – siren blaring, lights flashing. All the cars were desperately trying to get out of the way, clearing the road, but Karl didn't move a muscle. Just kept looking in his rear-view mirror, with the ambulance stuck behind us, trying to get past, honking and flashing its lights. And he was laughing, happy as Larry, blocking the road.'

Morgan's eyes widen.

'Deliberately?'

The woman nods.

'I said, "Someone's in that ambulance. They need to get to hospital." He told me to shut the eff up.'

'So what happened?'

'The other cars managed to manoeuvre out of the way, so the ambulance could get by. Then the gridlock cleared and he drove me home. I told him he had a sick soul. He told me not to make a fuss. Then he came up with one of his sayings: "Keep all the rules, miss all the fun."' The woman sniffs. 'He had all these stupid *sayings*.'

'Like?'

Anjelica thinks for a moment.

'Like, "Whatever you do in life, you need to go up like a rocket, even if you come down like a stick."'

'That's the first thing he's said that makes sense,' says Morgan.

'That was Karl. One minute he was smart and funny and kind, the next he was like Jekyll and Hyde. After I had the baby, it was all flowers and lovey-dovey stuff at first. But then we had a mega row and he told me I was a terrible mother. Threatened to snatch Marlon and take him out of the country.'

'Was he being serious?'

'Absolutely.' She takes a breath. 'So that's why I did what I had to do.'

'Which was?'

'I told the police he sold drugs.'

Anjelica's voice has taken on a steely edge. Morgan holds her breath. She's forgotten the ache in her ribs.

'He had another saying: "What Karl Savage wants, Karl Savage gets",' says Anjelica, shifting in her chair. 'It was true. He wanted me, he got me. He wanted a baby, he got a baby. He wanted other women, he got them. So if he wanted his son . . .' She tails off, tugging the tissue from her sleeve and blowing her nose again. 'Then the fire happened.'

Morgan remembers the newspaper accounts. Karl's body was so badly burned that he was identifiable only through dental records.

'Where were you the night he died?'

She's read the accounts in the papers but wants to hear Anjelica's version. To look into her eyes. Watch her body language. Searching for a tell.

'At home. Marlon was sick. His temperature was so high I was terrified. The doctor said it probably wasn't serious, just a fever, but I stayed up all night. I phoned NHS Direct around 2 a.m. They said to take him to A & E if he got worse, otherwise leave it till the surgery opened in the morning.'

'And?'

'I stayed awake all night, taking his temperature every hour and praying like I never prayed before. I didn't leave the flat. I swear on the Bible.'

Glancing at the crucifix dangling from the woman's neck, Morgan feels a pang of guilt. Assuming Anjelica is telling the truth, she succeeded where Morgan failed. The most important job of all. Keeping her child from harm.

Pushing the thought away, Morgan recalls many sleepless nights with Lissa, often a sickly baby. Obsessively checking her temperature. No one to turn to. She may not have been the world's best mother but she could never have left her baby alone for hours. Could Anjelica Fry?

'Tell me about the petrol can. The one the police found in your car.'

'Dad's old car.' Anjelica is twisting her tissue in her fingers. 'He left it to me when he died. I was going to sell it, but—'

'Forget the car. Tell me about the petrol can.'

Anjelica has told the story many times. To police. To lawyers. To the jury. Maybe that's why it sounds rehearsed.

'I had a bad experience when I was eighteen, just after I passed my driving test. I borrowed Dad's car one night. Ran out of petrol in the middle of nowhere. This guy offered me a lift in his van. Made me laugh for a couple of miles then pulled into a lay-by and raped me.' She takes a deep breath and falls silent for a moment. When she speaks again her voice is barely audible. 'After I inherited the car I kept petrol in the boot so I'd never run out again.'

Morgan leans forward.

'The police said the can was empty. The prosecution said it contained traces of the brand of petrol used by the arsonist.'

Angelica nods, rolling her eyes.

'The whole additives thing, yeah.'

The whole additives thing is what did for Angelica, along with the Spanish matches found in her flat. Fire investigators identified distinctive molecules from additives used by BP. The police retrieved CCTV of Angelica filling the can on a BP forecourt. So far, so unexceptional: hundreds of BP stations, millions of gallons of fuel. But the investigators also managed to identify diatoms from matches in Anjelica's kitchen – a Spanish brand with which she shared her name. She admitted bringing the 'Anjelica' matches home from a holiday in Lanzarote – just a quirky souvenir, but without it she might be at home now, or taking Marlon to the park.

Her solicitor said the evidence against her was purely circumstantial. No jury would convict.

But here she is. And here she'll stay, unless someone champions her cause.

'They said I'd have done anything to stop Karl taking my baby, which was true.' Angelica checks herself, swallowing. 'But not that. Not setting fire to his flat . . .' She swallows again, eyes brimming with tears.

Morgan lets Anjelica sob. She scans the woman's bruises, the cuts on her cheek. She doesn't need to ask how they got there. The woman is unpopular. Weeks of hostile press coverage cemented her reputation as a callous killer. A heartless mother.

Mum murdered lover while sick baby cried.

Devil woman.

'Time's up.'

The overweight prison officer is in the doorway, hands on her hips.

Morgan checks her watch.

'Still got twenty minutes.'

'My shift's over. There's no one to supervise.'

Anjelica looks panic-stricken.

'We don't need anyone to supervise.'

The officer rolls her eyes.

'Two minutes – make 'em count.'

She steps outside. Anjelica starts to babble, running out of time.

'The good Lord knows I'm telling the truth but he's testing me every day. I need you to believe me. There's no CCTV of me driving across London, the car doesn't show up on the number plate recognition thing – the ANPR . . .'

She knows all the jargon. But still Morgan isn't convinced.

You could have taken a friend's car. Or a night bus. Or a minicab.

'I need to review everything,' she says. Her ribs are aching now.

Anjelica fixes her with a glare.

'Easy to write a book, make money,' she says. 'Harder to help people.'

Morgan forces half a smile. The woman is short on charm, but has a point.

'I'll give you an answer as soon as I can.'

She gets to her feet. Anjelica follows suit, fear in her eyes, panic in her voice.

'I can't lose my baby. I can't be in here. Not for something I didn't do.' She pauses, her voice falling to a whisper. 'God forgive me for saying this, but if you don't help me, I'll kill myself.'

The threat makes Morgan bristle with anger. The words harden her heart.

'You know I'll have to report what you just said.'

A steely stare.

'Just being honest.'

The officer is back, tapping her watch, lips pursed.

'I'll be in touch,' Morgan says. But Anjelica isn't finished.

'I read your book. It says you have a daughter.'

'Yes.'

The woman stares Morgan in the eye.

'Think about me tonight, when you're trying to get to sleep. Picture me here. Imagine I'm your daughter.'

'I'll do what I can. I promise.'

Morgan follows the officer onto the landing. She turns. Anjelica is watching, twisting the tissue in her hands, a picture of anguish. Behind her head is a poster.

Today is the first day of the rest of your life.

On the landing, Morgan relays Anjelica's threat to the officer. The woman gives a weary sigh then produces a form. Morgan completes it, recording Anjelica's desperate attempt at emotional blackmail. Across the landing, the two prisoners are returning with Jukes. Morgan hears Port Wine Stain whisper to her fellow inmate, the hefty woman with pink hair.

'I'll hold the bitch down, you kick her tits.'

Little doubt who she's talking about. Morgan scans Jukes's face but he remains impassive.

'Did you hear that?'

'Hear what, Miss?'

Morgan considers her options. She could make a fuss, but knows it would be counter-productive, especially if she needs to see Anjelica again. She has yet to make a decision, but the fact she didn't warm to the woman is irrelevant. She's not looking for friends, she's looking for justice. And maybe an investigation for *Pro Bono* with a decent pay cheque attached. But she needs to be sure of her ground.

Trevor Jukes escorts her back to the exit, his jaunty whistling echoing along the corridors. In reception, he retrieves her leather jacket from the locker. Feeling in its pockets, she gives nothing away, but her heart is galloping, her brain racing.

Reaching the safety of her car, she scrutinises the jacket carefully, turning it over in her hands.

The lining has been slit open.

Then sewn up again.

Four

'What am I? Your drug mule?'

Morgan is trying to keep her temper, but the throbbing in her ribs is doing nothing to improve her mood. Sitting cross-legged on the sofa, her daughter has assumed a defensive posture: arms crossed, shoulders hunched, lips pursed.

'Fuck's sake, Mum. You're acting like I'm a criminal.'

'Well? Are you?'

They've been arguing since Morgan got home. She began the inquisition gently, mindful of her daughter's fragile state of mind, but things are getting heated.

'You insisted I take the jacket into prison,' says Morgan. 'I need to know what's going on.'

A toss of the head, a tremulous lower lip. Time for a softer approach.

Morgan reaches for her pouch of tobacco and begins to roll a cigarette. 'I'm your mum. I'm on your side. Whatever you're hiding, the first step towards making it better is to *let me help you*.'

The sympathetic tone of voice clinches it. Her daughter's resistance crumbles, her eyes brim with tears.

'It's all so messed up. I don't know what to do.'

'Is it something to do with Pablo?'

No eye contact. A deep breath. Time to come clean.

'Maybe.'

Morgan maintains her gentle tone. She has yet to lay eyes on Lissa's latest boyfriend, but is fearful of what she'll do if they ever meet.

'OK, I'm listening.'

Another breath, then it comes out in a rush.

'I mentioned you were going to see that woman in prison – Anjelica Fry – and he suddenly became really interested. He tried to get me to put a package in your jacket. Said it was just a laugh, for a mate, but I figured it was drugs so I said "no way". But he swore it wasn't drugs and he wouldn't stop hassling me, so eventually I gave in.'

Morgan is stunned by her daughter's naivety, but this is not the time to pick a fight.

'What package, sweetheart?'

'Like a little pouch, made of plastic? Light, so you wouldn't notice.'

'Do you know what was in it?'

A shrug.

'Something hard, like a glass tube. It felt cold. I think it had, like, ice in it?'

Morgan remembers the shaven-headed prison officer's insistence that she leave her jacket in the locker.

'Has Pablo ever mentioned a man called Trevor Jukes?'

'Who?'

'Never mind. When did he give you the package?'

'This morning, after we got back from hospital.'

'You saw him here?'

Lissa shakes her head.

'He phoned me. Said he'd left the pouch outside and the timing was crucial. I fetched it when you were in the shower. Then I sewed it into your jacket while you were in the kitchen.' A whimper escapes her lips. 'I'm sorry.'

'What did he mean by "the timing was crucial"?'

'I've no idea.'

'Where is he now?'

The whimper turns into an angry sob.

'I don't know, OK? When I try his mobile it says number unobtainable. I think he's gone now that he's got what he wanted. He's dumped me and disappeared.'

'Where can we find him?'

'Nowhere.'

'What does that mean?'

'He doesn't have, like, a house. He travels around in his camper van.'

'Do you know the make? Registration number?'

'Do I look like a copper?'

'This is important.'

'It's just a shitty old van, OK? White. He calls it "The Love Shack".'

A prince among men.

Morgan's daughter had dated Pablo for seven weeks over the summer, sometimes sleeping in his van, but never discovered his surname, only that he wasn't Spanish or Latin American, as

'Pablo' might suggest. His parents had simply liked the name. Lissa has no idea where he might be and took no photos, not even a cheesy selfie. He told her that being photographed was like having your soul stolen.

Puh-lease.

Morgan wonders if a penchant for bad guys can run in the genes. With her own track record, and now her daughter's, the idea seems more than plausible.

She lights her roll-up, plucking a strand of tobacco from her tongue, and studies Lissa's beautiful face, remembering what it feels like to be young and in love with a bastard. Been there, done that, got the broken heart.

'Are you OK, Lissa?'

'Not really.'

'Need a hug?'

Her daughter's voice is a whisper.

'I don't deserve one.'

'Have one anyway.'

Lissa rises from the sofa and folds her slender frame onto her mother's lap, taking care to avoid her ribs.

'Am I forgiven?'

'Ask me when you're eighty.'

'You'll be *so* dead.'

'Nicely put.'

A pause.

'Mum?'

'Yes?'

'What are we going to do?'

'You know the answer to that.'

'Tell the prison? Or the police?'

'Sure. If you feel like spending your twenties behind bars.'

A pause. Lissa coughs, waving away a cloud of cigarette smoke.

'I thought you were going to quit smoking.'

'So did I.'

The visit from DI Neville Rook comes as a surprise.

'I was on my way to the Anchor. Thought I'd pop in, see how you're both doing.'

Morgan isn't convinced (she clocked the softly spoken man checking out her cleavage at the hospital) but decides to take him at his word. Making tea, she experiences a flash of paranoia – has he discovered her unwitting role as a mule? – but quickly gets a grip. She renews her determination to remain silent about the plastic pouch. Assuming it contained drugs – 'spice' or some new chemical cocktail the sniffer dogs can't detect – she sees no reason to confess to something guaranteed to land her and Lissa in serious trouble.

Possibly prison.

There's no news on the man who attacked them on the cliffs. Even so, Rook manages to sound quietly confident.

'We'll get him sooner or later. We're like the Mounties: we always get our man.'

Morgan isn't so sure. Eighteen months ago she exposed two corrupt coppers; her faith in the police has yet to recover. All the same, she's relieved that someone is taking her seriously. No victim-blaming for DI Neville Rook.

Finishing his tea, he gets to his feet, glancing out of the window at the deserted beach, the vast power station looming in the distance. When he turns, Morgan notices him checking out her breasts.

Again.

His gaze travels upwards to meet her eyes.

'Sure you'll be OK out here?'

Nice-looking guy. Kind face. No wedding ring. Another place, another time in her life, she might have given him a smile. Instead, she folds her arms.

'We're used to it.'

For Lissa's sake, she forces herself to sound braver than she feels. Other people call Dungeness weird; she calls it home.

'My fiancée's a police officer too,' says Rook.

Engaged? Sweet old-fashioned thing . . .

'She says you wrote a book. About police cock-ups?'

'Not exactly. It's about mistakes across the criminal justice system.'

Morgan braces herself. That *Trial and Error* is resented by the forces of law and order is not surprising. The book chronicles miscarriages of justice dating back to 1679. Robert Green. Henry Berry. Lawrence Hill. Hanged for the murder of Edmund Godfrey. All three convicted on false evidence.

'Mind if I ask why you wrote it?'

Where to begin? With her father, unjustly accused of rape? With her first love, wrongly imprisoned for the murder of his stepdaughter?

'I saw too many movies when I was a kid,' she tells Rook. 'The world is meant to work a certain way: the bad guys get their comeuppance; the good guys don't suffer for things they didn't do. When the system messes up, we can't just look the other way.'

Rook holds her gaze.

'My fiancée says you're anti-police.'

Morgan gives what she hopes is a friendly smile.

'Not remotely. Most coppers are decent people doing a tough job under difficult circumstances. But the rotten apples make life worse for everyone. If people like me lose faith in people like you, we're all sunk.'

She can see Rook digesting her words. Something to tell his *fiancée*. Morgan visualises a gym-fit woman. Pursed lips. Short hair. No sense of humour.

The man clears his throat. Flips to a blank page in his notebook.

'I'm not supposed to do this, but could I have your autograph?'

Morgan feels a blush steal across her face. Is this what happens when your book makes the *Sunday Times* bestseller list?

'Of course.'

Rook clears his throat. Embarrassed.

'I meant your daughter. I told my nephew I'd met the famous Lissa. Now he won't stop pestering me.'

It's the first time Morgan has seen her daughter smile since the attack on the cliffs. In the aftermath of her fleeting brush with fame, people regularly stopped her in the street. Those days are gone. Unwitting 'star' of a sex tape, she was a tabloid sensation, albeit briefly. Her particular brand of celebrity (famous for being famous) led to a couple of tacky reality shows before her career as a 'celebutante' fizzled out. No modelling contract. No *Hollyoaks*. No footballer boyfriend. Last month *Celeb* magazine mentioned her in a 'Whatever Happened To?' round-up, misspelling her name as 'Lisa'.

Lissa sacked her agent and stayed in bed for three days. Morgan loves her daughter with every fibre of her being, but she's not always easy to like.

'What's your nephew's name?' says Lissa, reaching for a pen.

'Danny.'

The smile falters. Danny was the name of Morgan's first love – the original Shit. Lissa scribbles a signature, then sinks back onto the sofa, jabbing an angry finger at her iPad.

The police officer leaves. Silence descends on the house on the beach.

Stacking the dishwasher, Morgan tries to imagine how it feels to be twenty years old and adrift in the world. Her own twenties passed in a blur. Single-motherhood. Low-level panic. Stress. Now Lissa is struggling too, but in her own way. PTSD has her in its grip. According to psychologists, 'freezing' is a common response to traumatic events. The word describes Lissa perfectly.

Frozen. Lost.

Darkness is falling. Outside, the waves are choppy and the sea mist is rolling in. It's not yet seven thirty but Morgan longs for bed. Already woozy from the painkillers, she swallows two more then heats up the chicken soup she made earlier, while her daughter was sewing contraband into the lining of her jacket.

Morgan needs to decide what to do about Lissa, how to help her find her way in the world, a sense of purpose, but not tonight. Tonight she'll deadbolt the doors and knock herself out with Zopiclone.

'Soup and *EastEnders*?'

Lissa gives a wan smile.

'Thanks, Mum. Love you.'

After supper, Morgan leaves Lissa to watch TV while running the vacuum cleaner over her daughter's room. She chances upon an empty Smirnoff bottle stashed under the bed. She stares at it for a full minute, debating whether or not to take Lissa to task.

The discovery is disturbing. Drinking is one thing – *secret* drinking something else altogether. She decides to say nothing. For now.

Two hours later, brushing her teeth, she hears her daughter's voice.

'Mum? Phone.'

Emerging from the bathroom, wrapped in a towel, Morgan grabs her mobile. A familiar name flashes on screen. Nigel Cundy, resident psychologist at HMP Dungeness. He sounds smug, thrilled to be the bearer of bad news.

'Thought you should know, in case the media get hold of it.'

'Hold of what?'

'Anjelica Fry. She tried to kill herself, an hour after your visit. She sharpened the edges of her crucifix, managed to slash her wrist.'

'Jesus . . . Is she OK?'

'She's on the hospital wing. Under sedation.' He pauses before delivering the *coup de grâce*. Words to guarantee another sleepless night.

'She left a note – blaming you.'

Five

The pills aren't working. The bedside clock shows 2.06 a.m. – the night seems to be lasting for ever. Morgan has been lying in the dark, staring at the cracks on the ceiling, replaying her conversation with Anjelica.

Think about me when you're trying to get to sleep. Imagine I'm your daughter.

Nigel Cundy's mealy-mouthed attempt at reassurance has only made things worse.

You probably shouldn't blame yourself. The woman is clinically depressed, highly unstable.

A creak from the iron bedstead as Morgan gives up on sleep and gets out of bed. She pads barefoot into the kitchen, careful not to wake her daughter, asleep in the next room. Waiting for the kettle to boil, she smokes a roll-up while gazing at the clouds scudding across the night sky. The sleeping pills have made her thick-tongued and groggy, but failed to induce oblivion. She shouldn't have mixed them with painkillers. Two large glasses of wine have compounded the error. But however desolate she's feeling, it's nothing compared to Anjelica.

Sedated. Bandaged. Banged up.

She makes a mug of camomile tea and boots up her MacBook. Distraction is required. Something to reset her mind, to calm the 'monkey brain'. Anything will do, even videos of cats. But the internet is insomnia's partner in crime. Despite her best intentions it's only a few clicks before she's listening to a podcast about life behind bars.

Women make up fewer than five per cent of the prison population but are responsible for a quarter of all incidents of self-harm. Three-quarters go through detox and eighty per cent are jailed for non-violent crimes. They commit more assaults than male prisoners and are less inclined to blindly follow rules.

Surprisingly, they're also more violent.

I'll hold the bitch down, you kick her tits.

Turning to coverage of Anjelica's case, Morgan scrolls through newspaper accounts of the investigation into Karl Savage's death.

According to evidence given by the Met's Senior Investigating Officer, DI Brett Tucker, there was no time to investigate Anjelica's allegations against her ex before the fire that killed him. DI Tucker took the statement that incriminated Karl in large-scale drug dealing on Friday morning. By Sunday night the man was dead.

According to Anjelica's testimony, the father of her child had been selling class A drugs for years, working with a long-time crony known only as Spike, rumoured to be lying low.

Brett Tucker had planned to question both men on the Monday, after taking Anjelica's statement, but never got the chance. Assigned to investigate the Dalston blaze he worked alongside a fire scene investigator to establish probable cause, which was deemed to be arson. Anjelica was arrested four days after Savage's death.

The petrol can had been discovered in her car.

The Anjelica matches were in her kitchen drawer.

Morgan finishes her tea and checks her watch. Nearly 3 a.m. Time to give the pills another chance. Rinsing her mug, she glances out to the beach. The light is spilling from the window.

Parked fifteen yards away is a van.

A white camper van.

She's certain it wasn't there earlier. Are the pills and alcohol playing tricks with her mind? Was she too immersed in reading about Anjelica to hear the engine? Either way, there's no mistaking the van.

Or the outline of a man sitting behind the wheel, his face obscured by shadows.

Hairs prickling the back of her neck, Morgan moves to the door, checking the bolt. Now the back door. The windows. She grabs her mobile, on the verge of dialling 999, then glances out of the window again. The van is still there, the driver's face hidden from view.

The interior is illuminated as he lights a cigarette.

Morgan can't hear the sound of the Zippo but she can imagine it.

Clink-rasp.

For two seconds – perhaps less – his face is visible. Morgan can feel the blood thudding in her ears, her heartbeat racing. The face she is staring at is in some respects different from the face she's seen in the papers – full beard, shaved head – but it is unmistakably the face of a dead man.

Karl Savage.

'Lissa!'

Her voice shatters the silence.

'*Lissa!*'

She hears her daughter stumbling out of bed. The bedroom door opens, light spilling into the kitchen.

'Mum?'

Outside, the van's engine is revving. A crunch of tyres spurts shingle against the clapboard house. Morgan looks out of the window. The van is no longer in sight, the sound of its engine receding into the distance as tyres hit tarmac.

'Was that his van? Did you see him?'

'See who?' says Lissa.

Morgan knows she's not being clear – the pills and booze are making her woozy – but she can't stop babbling.

'I don't understand . . . That man . . . he wasn't your boyfriend . . . It wasn't Pablo . . . It was Karl Savage.'

Her daughter frowns.

'What are you talking about? Who's Karl Savage?'

'The man Anjelica is supposed to have killed.'

Morgan unbolts the front door, flings it open and peers out into the night. No headlamps, no lights, no sign of the van. Straining to hear, she catches the distant echo of what might be an engine but could just as well be waves hitting shingle.

Her daughter takes a step closer.

'Mum, are you OK?'

Morgan is hit by a wave of giddiness and nausea. Bolting the door, she leads Lissa to the kitchen table and reawakens the laptop. The article on Karl's murder reappears on the screen. She points to his photo. No beard. A full head of hair. But it's the same man. The man in the van.

'Who is this, Lissa?'

She doesn't want to put words in her daughter's mouth.

Lissa glances at the photo. A shrug.

'No idea.'

'Look closer.'

Lissa leans over the laptop.

A gasp escapes her lips.

'What the fuck? Why is Pablo in the paper?'

The next hour passes in a blur. Sitting at the kitchen table, Morgan studies her daughter's tear-stained face, her dismay growing by the minute. Lissa has been keeping more than one secret. The stash of vodka is the least of it.

'I thought he'd gone, so I wasn't going to tell you.'

'Tell me what?'

A long pause. Lissa shakes her head, closing her eyes.

'About the attack on the cliffs.'

She swallows, wiping her nose on the back of her hand.

'Go on,' says Morgan.

A deep breath. Lissa opens her eyes and meets her mother's steady gaze.

'It was Pablo.'

Morgan tries to sound calmer than she feels, but her heart is racing.

'You're sure?'

A nod.

'You saw him?'

'Yes.'

'Why would he do such a terrible thing?'

Lissa bows her head. Her voice is a whisper.

'I refused to plant the pouch in your pocket. So he did this.' She points to what's left of her hair. 'I was terrified he'd do something even worse. That's why I caved in when he hassled me after we got back from hospital.'

Morgan exhales a slow breath, reaching for her pouch of tobacco.

'Why didn't you tell me before?'

'I was so ashamed. I *keep* messing up.'

Torn between sympathy and anger, Morgan feels a rising surge of fury but bites her tongue. Gripped by a sense of foreboding, she tries to roll a cigarette but her hands are trembling. The tobacco spills onto the table. She gets to her feet and walks into her bedroom, resisting the temptation to slam the door. She lies on the bed and closes her eyes. For twenty years she has raised Lissa on her own. No partner. No parents. There are nights when the urge to share the burden feels overwhelming.

This is one of those nights.

*

Dawn is breaking as she parks outside the gates of HMP Dungeness, listening to the distant sound of the waves as she waits for Nigel Cundy. At first she was mystified by Lissa's failure to recognise Karl Savage, to realise that he and 'Pablo' are one and the same, but her daughter has been quick to set her straight.

'Why would I recognise him? I don't read the papers and I don't watch the news.'

Lighting a roll-up, Morgan's eyes rove the beach that surrounds the enormous prison complex. For almost four years the Dungeness peninsula, formed from hundreds of shingle ridges and valleys, has been her home. She shares her habitat with seabird colonies and a wildlife population that includes weasels, newts, badgers and stoats. Over by one of the derelict fisherman's shacks that give the landscape its air of eerie abandonment, a mangy fox picks at the remains of a dead seagull. Morgan watches for a moment, considering the efficiency of the scavengers – foxes, cats, rats – that ensure dead birds are an uncommon sight, then drags deeply on her cigarette and checks her watch.

A man who has told her many times that 'punctuality is the politeness of kings', Cundy appears at precisely seven o'clock. He's riding his bicycle, the stiff wind making a mockery of his comb-over as he removes his helmet. Morgan steps out of the Mini, watching the psychologist chain his bike to the rack. When he speaks, his voice is nasal, thick with cold.

"Morning, Morgan. To what do I owe the pleasure?'

Flicking her cigarette, she suppresses a surge of irritation. If the man didn't say things like *to what do I owe the pleasure?* she might find him easier to tolerate. But his conversation is peppered with *lovely ladies* and *footloose and fancy-free* and *it's not rocket science*. He invited her on a couple of dates *back in the day*, refusing to take no for an answer and forcing her to make it clear that she'd rather eat her own feet than sleep with him.

'You shouldn't smoke,' he says. 'It's bad for you.'

'Now you tell me.'

Squinting against the early-morning sun, Cundy scans the horizon. A fishing boat is returning to harbour, surrounded by shrieking seagulls.

'What can I do you for?'

'Can you get to see Anjelica Fry?' says Morgan.

'Why?'

'I need you to give her a message. Tell her I'm on the case. Tell her I believe her. Tell her I'll do everything I can to help.'

Nigel takes a grubby handkerchief from his pocket and blows his nose.

'I'll see what I can do.'

'The woman tried to kill herself, Nigel. Give her the message.'

'If you insist.' A sniff. 'But I'm not sure it's wise to give someone as unstable as Anjelica Fry hope where none exists. As the saying goes, "She's got no hope and Bob Hope, and Bob Hope's dead".'

'Hilarious,' says Morgan. 'You should have your own show.'

Cundy sighs.

'I take it you're an admirer of Saint Jude?'

She pretends not to understand.

'I've never been good at saints.'

She gets into her car and starts the engine. He taps on the window.

'Saint Jude. Look him up.'

Driving away, Morgan has no interest in learning more than she already knows about the patron saint of lost causes. She has more important things on her mind. More urgent questions.

Like what to do about her daughter.

And why a dead man was outside her house.

Six

He's walking on the pavement, holding Daddy's hand. Daddy's got his birthday present under his arm – the big tin of biscuits. Guy Fawkes on the lid.

- *When will I be dead, Daddy?*
- *Not for a long time.*
- *But when?*
- *Not for years and years and years. You're only four. Four today. My big lad.*
- *When will you be dead?*
- *Not for a long, long time. But we all die, son. And we're a long time dead. That's why you need to go up like a rocket, even if you come down like a stick.*

Karl doesn't know what this means but he thinks about fireworks while Daddy stops to talk to the man outside the pub. Today is Karl's special day. People organise fireworks displays to celebrate *his* birthday. Daddy says so. Rockets are Karl's favourite – they're loud and scary, but in a good way. He likes sparklers too because Daddy lets him hold them in his hand.

There's that dog again, on the other side of the road. *Maisie*. Sniffing a lamppost. Karl has seen her before. Black, friendly, waggy. Last time, the lady let Karl stroke her.

– *Daddy?*
– *Hold on, son, I'm talking.*
– *Can I stroke Maisie?*
– *In a minute.*

But Karl can't wait a whole minute. Daddy always talks for ages and *ages*. The dog will be gone soon.

He steps off the kerb.

Hears a car horn.

Daddy yells.

– *Karl!*

Daddy's shoving him, hard. A screech of brakes. A loud thud. The dog lady screams. Maisie barks.

Now Daddy's lying in the road. Blood is coming from his head.

Karl looks at Daddy. There's more blood now. And the biscuits – *his birthday biscuits* – are scattered all over the road. Karl starts to put them back in the tin. Then he puts the lid back on and sits on the kerb, waiting for someone to take him home. He'd like a biscuit but he'll have to wait till after lunch or she'll tell him off.

Or worse.

Ten days later the house is full of people talking quietly, eating sandwiches and saying nice things about Daddy. Karl didn't want to go to the funeral – it meant missing *Danger Mouse* – but she made him.

– *This is all your fault.*

The last words she said to him.

Not a word since.

Not one word.

And now she's put the Guy Fawkes tin of biscuits – *his birthday biscuits* – on the kitchen table so *everyone can help themselves*.

First no fireworks, then no *Danger Mouse*, now no biscuits.

Not fair.

NOT FAIR AT ALL.

Seven

The police station sits on a busy London high street and serves two parallel universes: old-school Hackney with its blue-collar population, and Stoke Newington, otherwise known as 'Stokey', the spiritual home of brunch, cupcake cafés and sharp-elbowed yummy mummies queuing for quinoa or asserting the divine right of the double buggy.

Morgan and Lissa are cramped into the small interview suite, opposite Detective Inspector Brett Tucker. Dapper. Early fifties. Sporting a tan from a belated summer holiday. Judging by the ring of pale flesh where a wedding band has been, he's recently divorced, or perhaps bereaved. So far his idea of hospitality has extended to a polystyrene cup of water. He has ostentatiously checked his watch three times in fifteen minutes but Morgan has no intention of allowing him to give her the brush-off, not after the effort it took to secure what he insists on calling 'face time'.

Four days since the man in the white camper van sped away into the night, she has taken the precaution of moving herself and Lissa out of their isolated home and into the Dungeness Beach Inn. She has also launched a salvo of calls requesting an urgent meeting with the SIO in charge of the enquiry into Karl

Savage's murder, the prime mover behind the prosecution of Anjelica Fry. When DI Tucker ignored Morgan's messages, she hand-delivered a letter to the Police and Crime Commissioner. Her burgeoning reputation as a relentless pain in the arse did the trick. She received an email the next morning. *This case is closed but I have asked Detective Inspector Tucker if he can find time to meet with you as soon as possible.*

'Forgive me labouring the point,' says Tucker, elbows on the table, steepling his fingers, 'but just to be clear, it was night-time, there was no moon, no street lighting?'

'Correct,' says Morgan.

'And you saw the van driver's face at a distance of approximately fifteen yards, for no longer than two or three seconds?'

'Yes.'

'And this happened immediately after you'd been looking at photos of Karl Savage on the internet?'

'Yes,' says Morgan, shifting in her chair.

'And not long after you'd consumed sleeping pills, painkillers and half a bottle of wine.'

'Two glasses.'

'Large or small?'

'I don't have small glasses.'

A pause. The police officer winces and adjusts his position in the chair, rearranging the lumbar support cushion he'd brought into the room. He gives a thin smile.

'I have a bad back, Ms Vine. When it gets agonising I take painkillers. They knock me for six. I can't work, can't sleep, can't concentrate.'

'I know what I saw.'

'So you say. And you want me to reopen a murder enquiry?'

'Yes.'

'A review of a month-long, painstaking investigation, following which the arsonist was tried by a jury of her peers. And is now behind bars. Where she belongs.'

'Are you sure about the last part?'

A muscle twitches in Tucker's cheek.

'Absolutely. And thanks to the post-mortem I'm also sure she cracked the victim's skull and knocked him out. Then she set fire to the flat, trying to cover her tracks. Karl Savage may have been a nasty piece of work, Ms Vine, and he may have been unconscious, but the man burned alive. So tell me, just how convinced are you that you saw him outside your house?'

Morgan can't afford to betray a flicker of doubt, but for the sake of credibility it's vital to be honest. She thinks back to the man in the van. For how long did she glimpse his bearded face? Two seconds? Three?

'Ninety-nine per cent,' she says.

'OK,' says Tucker, wincing as he shifts position once again. 'I trump your ninety-nine with my hundred per cent. I don't just believe he's dead, I *know* it.' Without giving Morgan a chance to reply, he turns towards Lissa. 'What happened to your face?'

Morgan listens as her daughter explains how she came by the bruises: the cliff-top attack, her summer fling with 'Pablo'. She doesn't mention being persuaded into co-opting her mother to act as his unwitting mule.

'You believe the man on the cliffs was Pablo?'

'Looks like it,' says Lissa.

'Because he used a Zippo? Like the man in the van?'

'No, because Mum says the man in the van was the same as the man in this photo.'

She reaches into her pocket and produces a printout of the newspaper clipping. Tucker examines the photo and sighs. A thought strikes Morgan.

'Was Karl Savage a smoker?'

'I believe so' says Tucker.

'Did he have a Zippo?'

'I have no idea. We didn't find one in his flat.'

He turns his gaze on Lissa.

'Why would Pablo attack you?'

'He was angry with me. He wanted me to do something. I refused. Looking back, I think the attack on the cliffs was a warning. A taste of things to come.'

'What did he want you to do?'

Lissa avoids her mother's eye. They have agreed not to disclose more than strictly necessary.

'It doesn't matter.'

'Can I be the judge of that?'

'No.'

'OK. But as far as you're concerned, Karl Savage and "Pablo" are one and the same?'

'Yep.'

The DI presses his point again.

'Even though you didn't see the bloke in the van?'

'My mother doesn't make things up.'

'Does she ever make mistakes?'

Morgan struggles to keep her irritation from showing. It's not simply what the man is saying, it's how he's saying it. Smug. Patronising. He's giving them 'face time' because she went over his head and threatened to create a stink in the press. He steals another glance at his watch and sighs.

'Look, I don't doubt that you *believe* you saw Karl Savage. But unless he has an identical twin – and he doesn't, I know his backstory like I know my face in the mirror – what you're saying is simply not possible. I *personally* attended the aftermath of the fire. I *personally* saw the state of his . . .' He tails off, eyes flickering towards Lissa.

'Go ahead,' she says. 'I'm not a kid.'

'I saw his body,' continues Tucker. 'Or what was left of it. Black, charred like something out of the worst horror movie ever. As for the smell . . .' Morgan opens her mouth to protest but he beats her to it. 'Yes, it's *conceivable* that someone else was in his flat that night, and that Savage didn't die. But what's not conceivable, frankly, is that a world-renowned forensic dentist failed to correctly identify Savage's unique – I repeat for emphasis – *unique* dental make-up. And this isn't some high street quack, Ms Vine. He's got letters after his name like alphabetti spaghetti. He subjected Savage's dental records to detailed analysis. Teeth. Jawbone. Fillings. They're like fingerprints. Unique.'

Smirking, Lissa turns to her mother.

'I think he's saying they're unique.'

Tucker ignores the sarcasm and continues.

'The jury took less than two hours to reach a verdict. Anjelica Fry's motive was beyond dispute. Karl had threatened to take her baby. Traces of petrol identified by an experienced fire scene investigator match the brand in her can.' He pauses for breath before delivering the *coup de grâce*. 'Then we need to consider the Anjelica matches in her kitchen. An obscure Spanish brand they haven't manufactured for years and which have never been exported to the UK.'

'Were they *unique*?' deadpans Lissa.

The muscle in Tucker's cheek twitches again.

'Is this funny to you?'

'No.'

'Good. When it comes to murder I tend to have a sense of humour failure.'

Chastened, Lissa folds her arms, shifting in her chair as he continues. 'OK,' says Tucker, 'the matches were not *unique*, but they were as rare as hen's teeth.' He cracks his knuckles, still in full flow. 'And finally, we come to the "hoodie video". Anjelica Fry was caught on CCTV not two hundred yards from Savage's flat, a mere seven minutes before the fire started—'

Morgan interrupts.

'The defence demolished the CCTV evidence. You couldn't see the person's face. Same brand of hoodie, yes, and roughly the same build, and OK, the timing fits, but that doesn't *prove* it was Anjelica.'

DI Tucker sighs and spreads his hands, a gesture of exasperation.

'Off the record?'

'Go ahead.'

'I work half a dozen murders at any one time, doing my best for families desperate for answers. This isn't box-ticking, Ms Vine. It's about victims' mums, their nans, their kids.' He gets to his feet. 'I'm sorry, but I've got work to do.' The muscle in his cheek twitches again as frustration leaks from his lips. 'Some people like to believe the worst of the police,' he mutters. 'Frankly, it sticks in the craw.'

He gives Morgan a defiant stare. For a second she feels on the back foot. This isn't the first time she's encountered blatant hostility from the forces of law and order, but she's still taken aback by the extent to which *Trial and Error* has made her an object of suspicion, an enemy. Perhaps she should have known better. Brett Tucker is clearly going through the motions, tolerating what he sees as her drink-and-pill-fuelled, sleep-deprived stupidity. Moronic impertinence. Waste of time. Waste of space.

'Can you let me have contact details for the fire scene investigator and forensic dentist?' says Morgan.

'Are you asking me to do your job as well as mine?'

'I'm asking for help.'

He shrugs.

'I'll see what I can do.'

For a moment she thinks the man is softening, but his next question knocks her for six.

'How do you sleep at night?'

She narrows her eyes.

'Excuse me?'

'We all know the system messes up occasionally,' says Tucker. 'Once in a while some nutjob copper goes rogue or fits up some poor bastard for something they didn't do. And it makes me sick to the stomach. But do you have any idea how hard people like *you* make life for *us*? Undermining public confidence, raking over the past.'

Morgan's gaze is unflinching.

'It's not the past for Anjelica Fry,' she says. 'Or her baby.'

Outside, the meter has expired and the Mini has been clamped. Leaning against the bonnet, Morgan starts to roll a cigarette, wondering how this day could possibly get worse.

'You OK?' says Lissa.

'Terrific.'

'Me neither.'

Morgan raises a foot and nudges an empty Coke can into the gutter.

'You do believe me?' she says. 'That I saw Karl in the van?'

Her daughter's hesitation is telling.

'I guess so.'

Morgan frowns.

'But you're not sure?'

Lissa sighs.

'It just doesn't make sense, Mum. Are you saying he escaped a massive inferno then reinvented himself as a whole new person called Pablo?'

'Got a better explanation?'

Lissa sighs and shakes her head.

'So whose was the body in Karl's flat?' she says. 'And what did Pablo make you smuggle into prison?'

'I've no idea.'

They fall silent. It starts to drizzle. Morgan snatches the parking ticket from the windscreen and stuffs it into her pocket. She zaps the fob then gets into the car. Lissa follows suit, chewing on her lip, the way she does when feeling antsy. Morgan knows her daughter. Tears are not far away.

'Want to talk about it?' she says, settling behind the wheel and fumbling for her lighter.

'About what?'

'The whole Pablo thing.'

A sigh.

'Are you going to tell me I've got crap taste in men? If so: pot meet kettle.'

Morgan opens the window and lights her cigarette.

'Einstein said the definition of insanity is doing the same thing over and over again and expecting a different outcome.'

'Einstein?' Lissa is incredulous. 'A philandering egomaniac who dumped wife number one so he could marry his cousin? *He's* your go-to guy for advice on relationships?'

'All I'm suggesting is—'

'I know what you're suggesting,' says Lissa. 'I screwed up *again*, and I'm sorry. But he seemed like a nice guy, and he said stuff it was nice to hear.'

'Such as?'

'Such as, meeting me was the best thing ever, a sign he was on the right path, doing the right thing.'

Morgan plucks a strand of tobacco from her tongue.

'What did he mean by "on the right path"?'

'I don't know,' says Lissa. 'But if all men are like my last couple of picks, I give up.'

Morgan opens her mouth to speak but her daughter holds up a hand.

'Don't say it.'

She reaches for Morgan's pouch of tobacco and points to the lettering on the side. 'What does that say?'

'Smoking Kills.'

'Exactly,' says Lissa. 'We all mess up in our own way. And when it comes to self-destructive behaviour – smoking, driving fast, falling in love with the wrong sort of people – all advice is useless.'

Morgan puts her cigarette between her lips, wondering how her daughter can be so wise one minute, so idiotic the next.

'I'm starving,' says Lissa.

'There's a bagel place down the road.'

'You promised proper lunch.'

'That was before we got clamped.' Morgan drags on her cigarette. 'And before the world went bat-shit crazy.'

Eight

After settling the extortionate fee to get the clamp removed, 'proper lunch' feels like an extravagance, but a visit to an upmarket hair salon on Stoke Newington Church Street is essential. Lissa has been stoical about the attack on the cliffs. Time to help her feel better.

The ache in Morgan's ribs is easing but she hasn't discounted the possibility of delayed shock striking out of nowhere. Sitting next to Lissa, trying to tune out the hairdresser's cheerful banter, her phone vibrates. An email from D.I. Tucker.

Subject: Anjelica Fry/Karl Savage

The message contains email addresses for fire scene investigator Ben Gaminara and forensic odontologist Jatinder Singh Dip. F. Od. No greeting, no sign-off. Tucker has kept his word, but will cooperate no further.

The hairdresser goes to make coffee.

'So,' says Lissa, 'now what?'

'I need to find enough evidence to submit Anjelica's case to the Criminal Cases Review Commission.'

Her daughter studies her new fringe in the mirror.

'You keep saying "I". How about "we"? Pablo was *my* boyfriend.'

'This isn't a "we" kind of thing.'

Lissa plucks the phone from Morgan's hand, her fingers dancing over the keyboard.

'What are you doing?'

'Checking out this Criminal Cases Review thing.'

She logs on to the Commission's website and reads aloud.

'In order for the Commission to refer a case back to the appeal court we must be able to present a new piece of evidence or legal argument, not identified at the time of the trial, that might have changed the outcome if the jury had been given a chance to consider it. We look into all cases thoroughly, independently and objectively but legal rules governing the work of the Commission mean we can only refer a case if we find there is a real possibility that an appeal court would quash the conviction.'

She looks at her mother.

'A real possibility? How about, Karl is still alive?'

Morgan raises an eyebrow.

'So you do believe me?'

Lissa thinks for a moment.

'I believe *you* believe you saw him.'

Her fingers tap at the phone.

'Now what are you doing?'

'Finding the name of Anjelica's lawyer.'

The barrister who conducted Anjelica Fry's defence turns out to have died five months ago: a heart attack while playing squash. The next best thing is the legal aid solicitor saddled with a case way above his pay grade. His office is above a Turkish restaurant on bustling Green Lanes in north London. The aroma of roasting lamb wafting up the gloomy staircase is making Morgan hungry, but the smell of whisky on the man's breath is causing her to feel queasy. She can see the bottle of Bell's on the floor behind a stack of files, out of sight – or so Grahame Millar thinks. Finishing a greasy bacon roll, he leans back in a creaky chair that threatens to give way under his weight.

'You went to see Anjelica in prison?'

Morgan nods.

'She sent me a letter. Powerful. Persuasive.'

The man casts a doubtful look in her direction, adjusting his girth in the chair. His shirt is missing a button; a tuft of gingery chest hair pokes through the gap.

'She's good at pushing the "poor little me" button,' he says, using a fingernail to prise a morsel of bacon from his teeth. 'Much good it did her.'

'Is there anything you can tell us?' says Morgan. 'Something overlooked during the trial? A piece of evidence that's come to light since? A technicality that might get her case to the appeal court?'

Millar frowns.

'Not that I can think of.'

'Why did she choose you as her solicitor?' says Lissa.

'She didn't. I get a call from the local nick and deal with whatever comes in. Or should I say, "dealt".'

Lissa frowns.

'Why "dealt"?'

'They've slashed legal aid budgets, sweetheart. From now on, people like Anjelica will be lucky to get people like me.'

Morgan takes stock of the shabby office with its stained ceiling, ancient computer and teetering stacks of files. She wonders just how lucky Anjelica felt, finding herself on a murder charge, her fate in the hands of Grahame Millar. His mobile beeps. He glances at the text.

'Two more minutes, then I need to go and bail out the third toerag of the day.'

Morgan wonders if Anjelica was written off as another 'toerag', but manages to keep her smile in place.

'I've read the case reports,' she says. 'I spoke to Anjelica about her defence. She says you told her that the evidence against her was purely circumstantial, that no jury would convict, that the CPS should never have brought the case to trial.'

A shrug.

'I say a lot of things. Makes people feel better.'

'Wow,' says Lissa. 'Cynical much?'

Morgan shoots her daughter a glare but the man behind the desk doesn't seem to notice the jibe, rifling through a pile of papers, looking for a file.

'What if I said you were right?' says Morgan, trying to strike an emollient tone. 'That the case should never have gone to trial.'

A shrug.

'I'd say, win some, lose some.'

Lissa narrows her eyes.

'So, you give, like, zero fucks?'

'Did I say that?'

'Doesn't it bother you that she's banged up?' says Lissa.

'I do my job. I sleep like a baby.'

'Because you think she was guilty?'

Millar is getting testy.

'I try not to have opinions about my clients, sweetheart. They get in the way. And it doesn't matter what I think.'

'It matters to us,' says Morgan. 'And Anjelica.'

She watches his eyes flicker towards the whisky bottle. She can see him working out how to get rid of them so he can have a drink before he leaves.

'Gun to my head,' he says, sucking bacon grease from his fingers, 'I'd say the jury got it right.'

Lissa's eyes widen, her voice brimming with indignation.

'I don't understand,' she says. 'If you thought she was guilty of murdering the father of her child how could you help with her defence?'

Millar's look is laden with disdain.

'It's not my job to teach you how the legal system works. Now, if you'll excuse me . . .'

Finding the file he's been looking for, he gets to his feet. Morgan follows suit, making a last bid for the solicitor's attention.

'What would you say if I told you that Karl Savage is still alive?'

A smile spreads across the man's pasty face as he ushers Morgan and her daughter towards the door.

'That's easy, sweetheart.' He opens the door. 'I'd say you were out of your tiny mind.'

Darkness is falling as they near Dungeness, Lissa driving as Morgan dials the editor of *Pro Bono*. The new webzine was announced months ago, launched on an ocean of champagne at the Mandarin Oriental Hotel in Knightsbridge. Its mission: 'to lift the rock of the British legal system and shine a light on the miscarriages of justice festering beneath'. The party was a glitzy affair, filled with sharp-suited lawyers and dead-eyed ladies who lunch, but the venture has yet to appear online. A year ago, editor/publisher/proprietor Jocelyn de Freitas (Lissa calls her Cruella de Vil) received a gazillion-pound divorce settlement from her philandering husband, a lawyer specialising in mergers and acquisitions. In a *Tatler* profile, she promised to plough some of the spoils into what Morgan worries may prove no more than an expensive form of revenge, a vanity project of the worst kind. What's bad for the image of her much-hated ex-husband and his profession is good for Jocelyn de Freitas.

But things are worse than Morgan feared. Her potential patron's number is unobtainable and a Google search confirms that the *Pro Bono* website has been taken down. A search for Jocelyn's name unearths recent photos of her at a fancy dress party on a billionaire's yacht. She's dressed as a Nazi, complete with Hitler moustache, and accompanied by a brace of dwarves.

It's true what they say: the rich *are* different.

Morgan pockets her mobile, breaks the news to her daughter and peers out into the darkness. Drumming her fingers on the steering wheel, Lissa sighs and steers the Mini off the main road, onto the tarmac path that leads towards the beach and the hotel that is their temporary sanctuary.

'This just keeps getting better,' she says. 'No help from the only media outlet that might put resources into the case, or from the lawyer or the police.'

'In a nutshell, nope.'

'So it's you and me against the world?'

Morgan turns to look at her daughter, taking stock of her new pixie-ish hairstyle. Eighteen months ago Lissa was a spoilt brat, interested only in hanging out at her father's Malibu house or developing a 'career' as a celebutante. A brief dalliance with her mother's old flame ended in disaster, the leaking of a sex tape leading to a brush with the wrong sort of fame. Now she's a lost soul – one day brimming with enthusiasm for training as a nurse (never going to happen), or a barista (more likely), the next enthusing about becoming a YouTuber. Whatever that is. On the plus side, she seems to have stopped talking about getting breast implants.

Morgan is trying not to meddle. Her own choices have never been the smartest. Besides, Lissa is right: Pablo was *her* boyfriend. Whatever the truth about Karl, like it or not, Lissa *is* involved.

'Yes,' says Morgan. 'You and me against the world.'

Her daughter sounds pleased.

'At least you're OK for cash.'

Morgan decides not to mention her dwindling resources. Her status as a bestselling author sounds impressive, but it will be some time before her book earns out its advance, and the money is long gone.

Meanwhile, a young mother is in prison for a murder she didn't commit.

'So now what?' says Lissa.

Morgan makes a decision. It's time to commit. Take things to the next level. She scrolls to the email from DI Brett Tucker.

'Now we track down the arson investigator. If Anjelica didn't start the fire, we need to find out who did. And if Karl didn't die, whose was the body in his flat?'

Lissa pulls up outside the Dungeness Beach Inn, a Y-shape of three clapboard shacks linking to a central hub. Judging by shafts of light spilling from the windows, at least four of the twelve rooms are occupied. Stepping out of the car, Morgan listens to the waves on the shoreline. Then comes another sound in the distance – barely audible.

'Can you hear that?' says Morgan.

'Hear what?'

'The baby, crying.'

'What baby?'

'Shhh. Listen.'

They stand still, straining to hear, but there is nothing except the *whoosh* of the waves. Lissa heads inside, muttering under her breath.

'Perfect. Now she's hearing things.'

Waking just after 3 a.m., a groggy Morgan wonders if she's *hearing things* again: the distant cries of the baby?

Or maybe she's dreaming. The two Zopiclone she washed down with wine make it hard to tell. Within minutes, the powerful sleeping pills are dragging her back to sleep and she's drifting off to the sound of waves crashing on the shore.

Nine

The sun is high in the sky as Morgan braves the icy waves, swimming against the current while keeping the inn in sight. According to Sawday's guide, 'this quirky new boutique hotel is comprised of twelve individually themed rooms, each named after the wildlife for which Dungeness Nature Reserve is justly famous around the world'. Lissa is in 'Dragonfly', Morgan is in 'Falcon'. 'Wheatear' is across the corridor, between 'Badger' and 'Stoat'.

The inn opened too late to catch the summer trade and is seldom more than half-full. Its owner-manager is Eric Sweet, a shy, pony-tailed giant in his fifties. Softly spoken, he reminds Morgan of someone you might see at a party, pretending to browse bookshelves while trying not to look lonely. Needing sanctuary after glimpsing Karl Savage outside her house, widower Eric was the first person Morgan thought of. His offer of a reduced room rate was irresistible. 'Mate's rates', he called it, even though he had met Morgan just once, at the inn's launch party. Morgan was the only local to attend, apart from a rowdy gang of lads lured by the promise of free alcohol.

Returning from her swim, there's no sign of life at the polished refectory table that serves as the reception desk. A posh candle flickers, infusing the air with the dense musk of wild fig and cassis. Clad in bathrobe and flip-flops, hair wet from her swim, Morgan reaches for her key, brushing past a set of wind chimes, then freezing as she hears the sound of a crying baby. Following the noise, padding down the corridor, she pauses outside Lissa's room. The wailing is coming from inside. She raps on the door.

'*Hold on.*'

The crying intensifies as the door is opened by Lissa, looking harassed. On the bed is a baby boy, kicking his chubby legs in the air, face contorted with fury. Morgan feels a flicker of relief.

'So I wasn't hearing things.'

'No,' says Lissa. 'Remember how to change a nappy?'

Morgan nods. 'It's like riding a bike.'

'Maybe that's where I'm going wrong.'

Stepping into the room, Morgan closes the door then deftly tends to the soiled nappy. The crying subsides, dwindling to a contented gurgle.

'His mum's the new cleaner,' says Lissa, wrinkling her nose at the sight of the nappy's contents. 'Eric felt sorry for her and gave her a job. She's got nowhere to leave the sprog so I'm babysitting.'

'All day?'

'Maybe. It's not a permanent job; he's just being nice to her. Poor man'll be broke by Christmas.'

'Why is he so sorry for her?'

'She just got out of prison,' says Lissa. 'Her hostel chucked her out for smoking a spliff so she's got nowhere to go. Eric found her scavenging for food. She'd turned a wheelie bin on its side and was trying to kip inside, with the baby, so he gave her a room and a job.'

Morgan has come perilously close to skid row but she's never been reduced to sleeping in a wheelie bin.

'Why was she in prison?'

'I googled her,' says Lissa. 'Her name's Kiki McNeil. She served three and a half years for texting while driving.'

'They put you behind bars for that?'

'They do if the car's stolen and you kill a sixteen-year-old kid by knocking him off his bike.'

Morgan blows out her cheeks.

'What's she like?'

'Thin. Spiky. Scared.'

'Of what?'

'Life.'

Morgan gazes at the baby, taking stock of a tiny, heart-shaped mole on his chubby forearm. A thought strikes.

'He can't be more than six months old.'

'So?'

'So how did his mother get pregnant while she was in prison?'

Before her daughter can answer, there's a rat-a-tat on the door. Lissa opens it.

'Hey, Kiki.'

Morgan masks her surprise. The new arrival is Port Wine Stain, one of the inmates she encountered at HMP Dungeness. Painfully thin, early twenties with cropped black hair, she's wielding a mop and bucket. Morgan recalls the whispered conversation between her and her fellow prisoner, the inmate with pink hair – their plan to attack Anjelica.

I'll hold the bitch down, you kick her tits.

'Kiki, meet Mum.'

'Hiya,' says the baby's mother, flashing a nervous smile.

Morgan can't bring herself to smile back. 'I saw you the other day,' she says. 'In the Mother and Baby Unit.'

Kiki's eyes flicker over Morgan's face. No sign of recognition.

'I was visiting Anjelica Fry,' she says.

The woman's face darkens.

'Oh. Her.'

'Mum says she's innocent,' says Lissa. 'She's trying to get the case reopened, take it to the Criminal Cases Review.'

'Oh-kay.'

Kiki sounds sceptical, but Morgan is in no mood to try and persuade yet another cynic of the merits of Anjelica's case, especially one whose own purchase on the moral high ground is far from secure. She focuses on the nappy.

'Shall I do it?' says Kiki.

'It's no bother,' says Morgan. 'What's his name?'

'Charlie.'

'He's beautiful.'

'Cheers.'

Morgan resists the temptation to ask about Charlie's father. Nappy sorted, she picks up the baby.

'Mind if I hold him?'

'Be my guest.'

Cradling Charlie in her arms, Morgan feels a rare sense of peace. The baby stares into her eyes, his mouth forming a perfect O. Smiling, Morgan recalls the tsunami of dopamine-fuelled emotion that surged through every fibre of her being as she held Lissa for the first time. She tried Ecstasy once – a boyfriend promised it was guaranteed to recreate the feeling. Not even close. Love is the drug.

Charlie is smiling now, staring up at Morgan, his tiny hand fastening around her little finger.

'Should I worry about his mole?' says Kiki.

The question comes out of the blue. Morgan peers at the tiny, heart-shaped blemish.

'I doubt it. But if you're concerned, ask the doctor.'

Kiki nods, turning back to the window, eyes roving the beach.

'Lissa says you were a single mum.'

'Yes.'

'Was it hard?'

You have no idea.

'Sometimes.'

'But you coped?'

'What choice is there?'

Kiki nods emphatically.

'Exactly.' She turns from the window and bends to whisper in her baby's ear. 'So he can piss off and leave us alone.'

'Who can?' says Lissa.

'Overshare,' says Kiki, straightening up and looking Morgan in the eye. 'Lissa says you write books.'

'Just one so far.'

'Well, if you want a good story you know where to find me.'

Footsteps in the corridor. Eric Sweet appears in the doorway, clutching a smoke alarm and an electric screwdriver. His barrel chest swells under a pink T-shirt emblazoned with the slogan *This Is What a Feminist Looks Like*. He frowns at Kiki.

'On *another* break?'

The woman casts another nervous look out of the window. She seems in no rush to kowtow to her benefactor. Perhaps prison has hardened her, or maybe she's always been like this. Stroppy. Defiant.

'Just checking on the kid,' she says. Finally satisfied there is no one on the beach, she smiles for Morgan's benefit.

'Thanks, Mummy Bear.'

She picks up the bucket and leaves. The pail has left a wet ring on the carpet.

'Sorry,' says Eric, giving a bemused shrug. 'I told her she could stay a couple of nights, make a few bob, give herself a chance. They chuck these kids out with fifty quid and leave them to fend for themselves.'

Morgan keeps her doubts about Kiki to herself. The man means well. And then there's Charlie – an innocent, like Anjelica's baby, Marlon, taking his first steps behind prison walls.

Eric brandishes the smoke alarm.

'Mind if I put this up? I can come back if it's inconvenient.'

Lissa shrugs. 'Fine by me.' As Eric sets to work, she takes Charlie from Morgan's arms, cooing in his ear. 'This little cutie and I will go for a walk on the beach.'

Morgan looks on as her daughter wraps the baby in a blanket. She smiles.

'What?' says Lissa.

'Nothing,' says Morgan. 'You're just full of surprises.'

Back in her room, Morgan showers and dresses: T-shirt, skinny-fit jeans, high tops. Sitting cross-legged on her bed, underneath a bad 'hotel art' painting of a peregrine falcon, she boots up her MacBook and composes an email to fire scene investigator Ben Gaminara.

I'm a journalist and author keen to discuss the investigation you conducted into the Dalston arson attack that killed Karl Savage. I'd be grateful if you could spare an hour to talk. Anytime, anywhere.

No point in mentioning the fact that Karl is still alive. Morgan doesn't want to be dismissed as a member of the green ink brigade. She sends a similar email to Jatinder Singh, the forensic dental expert whose testimony was crucial in the identification of Savage's body. Again, she omits to mention the possibility that he might have made a mistake.

After lunch (goat's cheese and beetroot salad made by Eric and served in the half-empty restaurant) Lissa declares herself eager to look after Charlie for the rest of the afternoon, much to Morgan's amusement and Kiki's obvious relief.

Holed up in 'Falcon', Morgan calls DI Rook to ask if there's any trace of the man in the white camper van. She decides not to divulge her conviction that Pablo and Karl are one and the same. No need to muddy the waters, or make the policeman think she's losing her grip on reality. Rook has nothing to report but promises to call with any news. He keeps her on the line longer than expected, making a couple of comments clearly intended to be flirtatious. Morgan plays along but wonders if the man might have had a lunchtime pint too many.

A search of newspaper websites reveals more of Karl's backstory. Morgan knows about the man's control-freak behaviour, his bullying of Anjelica, and what sounds like borderline personality disorder, but this is the first she's read of his history of impregnating women then conning them out of their life savings.

One particular tale captures the imagination. Nancy Sixsmith, mother of two of Savage's children (he seems to have fathered five, at least) gave an interview to the *Daily Mail* a week after his body was found in the burnt-out Dalston flat.

Red-eyed, the thirty-six-year-old ex-teacher keeps one eye on her six-year-old twins, Jack and Karl Junior, while lighting another cigarette, her third in twenty minutes. 'I can't believe I'm still so upset,' says Nancy, who lives on the sixteenth floor of a Canterbury high-rise. 'He took me for every penny. I hate how he manipulated me, but part of me still loves him.'

Morgan thinks back to her conversation with Anjelica. Although the woman was candid about the ways in which Savage abused her – the stalking, the bullying, the threat to kidnap her baby – she seems to harbour a residual affection for her tormentor, just as Lissa appears to still feel something for the man who set fire to her hair. The ache in Morgan's ribs is a reminder of what men can do.

Some men, she reminds herself. There are exceptions. Like Eric Sweet.

In the days that follow, Lissa takes to spending a lot of time with Kiki and her baby. Morgan has mixed feelings. On the one hand, her daughter has been too withdrawn from the world, spending all her time at home, almost exclusively in her mother's company. But becoming BFFs with Kiki McNeil? Someone whose idiocy and carelessness cost the life of a teenager?

She checks herself.

If liberal-minded *Guardianistas* like her dismiss the idea of redemption – of second chances – what hope is there?

One evening, sharing a bottle of wine, Lissa reveals that her new friend is riven with guilt over the boy's death. His parents visited her in prison – part of an initiative in restorative justice. They told her they would never forget their son but that he would have wanted Kiki to get on with her life and, above all, do something useful. Filled with remorse, grateful for a second chance, she is trying to work out what that 'something' might be. Perhaps spearheading a campaign to spread awareness of the dangers of texting while driving, visiting schools and telling her story to kids, so they don't make the same mistake.

Meanwhile, she has shamefacedly confessed to being barely able to read or write. Lissa is giving her lessons in literacy.

'She's had a crap life,' says Lissa. 'Her mum was a sex worker, hooked on crack. She started pimping Kiki out when she was thirteen. The kids at school called her 'Elephant Girl' because of the birthmark on her face.'

As for the mystery of how the woman managed to get pregnant while in HMP Dungeness, the subject has yet to arise. Lissa is hoping Kiki will confide in her.

Could be a long wait.

Morgan's emails to Ben Gaminara and Jatinder Singh go unanswered. She sends reminders but decides not to hassle the men too much. There's a fine line between being persistent and being a pest. Sometimes the right thing to do is *nothing*.

Just after five o'clock on an unseasonably balmy late-October afternoon, Kiki finishes her shift and reclaims Charlie from Lissa's care, leaving Morgan and her daughter to go for a walk. Strolling on the deserted beach, they talk about Lissa's recent Skype session with her father, an Oscar-nominated screenwriter living in California with his Ukrainian girlfriend, Kristina, a pianist-actress-model who even twenty-year-old Lissa deems 'of foetal age'.

Dusk is closing in as they reach an outlying expanse of shingle. Not another soul in sight. This is the glory of Dungeness, thinks Morgan. The landscape is never the same. Weird, eerie, beautiful. Heading for the lighthouse, they pass the converted railway carriage that was home until a week ago.

'When can we go back?' says Lissa.

Morgan considers the question.

'Soon. We're better off at the inn for now. Safety in numbers.'

Early the following morning, Morgan is woken from a Zopiclone sleep by Eric rapping on the door.

'The police just called. The coastguard found a body down by the cliffs at St Mary's Bay.'

Morgan blinks. Her mouth is dry, her brain fogged by chemicals.

'Whose body?'

'Kiki McNeil.'

Morgan's eyes widen.

'Are they sure?'

He nods.

'She had ID on her, and one of these.'

He fishes a Dungeness Beach Inn card from his shirt pocket.

'What about Charlie?'

'No sign of him,' says Eric. 'I thought you'd want to tell Lissa.'

Reeling from the news, Morgan goes into the bathroom to splash water on her face. Knocking on her daughter's door, she finds Lissa already awake, dark circles under her eyes.

'Are you OK?'

'Up all night. Bloody food poisoning,' says Lissa. Her voice is feeble, her face pale. 'What's going on?'

Morgan closes the door, leads her daughter to the bed and sits down.

'Bad news. About Kiki.'

'What about her?'

'She's dead.'

Lissa's eyes widen in disbelief.

'Oh my God . . .'

'Apparently the coastguard found her body at the foot of the cliffs in St Mary's Bay.'

'So . . . she jumped?'

Morgan shrugs.

'That's all I know.'

'Is Charlie OK?'

'I don't know. I'm going there now. Want to come?'

Tears spring to Lissa's eyes. She shakes her head.

'What is *happening* to us?'

'Us?'

'Feels that way,' says Lissa, reaching for a Kleenex. 'First Pablo. Now this. What the fuck is going on?'

The body has been removed by the time Morgan arrives. Despite the efforts of the police, the scene is compromised by the rising tide before a thorough analysis can be completed. By 10 a.m. the incident tent is rendered useless by seawater. Even at a distance, gazing down from the cliffs, Morgan can see the head-scratching frustration of two boiler-suited SOCOs.

Up on the cliff top, Neville Rook is one of the officers working the case, supervising a fingertip search of the cordoned-off area and taking statements from the coastguard and Morgan. To her relief, the DI behaves with impeccable professionalism – no stolen glances at her cleavage, no flirtatious remarks.

A couple of local hacks are sniffing around, along with a TV news crew, but despite the missing baby at the heart of the tragedy, the death of 'just another jumper' doesn't seem to merit the attention of the national press. Following the reporters to the pub, she overhears one of them mentioning titbits gleaned from a SOCO.

Bruising on her arm. Fresh. Time of death: just after midnight. Her wristwatch was smashed in the fall.

It's midday before Morgan gets back to the inn. Lissa doesn't answer her knock, still recuperating from her bout of food poisoning and catching up on sleep. Sitting on her bed, Morgan feels desolate, her head brimming with questions.

Did Kiki jump or was she pushed?

How did she get pregnant in prison?

Where is her baby?

And what did she mean by, '*if you want a good story you know where to find me*'?

PART TWO

PART TWO

Ten

Five days after the death of Kiki O'Neil, the Indian summer has returned, ushering in a freak heatwave, and Morgan is back at HMP Dungeness. She and Lissa have assisted the police as far as possible but neither has a clue how Kiki met her lonely end or where her baby might be. Morgan is hoping that Anjelica will be able to fill in some of the blanks but the visit is not going well. The oppressive heat in the Mother and Baby Unit isn't helping.

'What was Kiki like?'

'A total See You Next Tuesday,' says Anjelica, a sheen of sweat glistening on her upper lip.

'Sorry?'

Anjelica leans back and rolls her eyes.

'I'm not a potty mouth like everyone in here but that's what she was: a See You Next Tuesday.'

Realisation dawns.

'Ah. OK.'

Morgan recalls the whispered conversation between Kiki and the prisoner with pink hair.

I'll hold the bitch down, you kick her tits.

No wonder Anjelica has nothing nice to say about her erstwhile tormentor. Morgan cranes her neck, peering out of the side room and into the open-plan unit but her view is obscured by the female officer stationed outside, fanning herself with a clipboard.

'Who was the big woman with the pink hair?' says Morgan. 'I saw her with Kiki.'

Anjelica sucks air through her teeth.

'Stacey Brown. Kiki's BFF. Got out the day after Kiki.'

'Was she also a "See You Next Tuesday"?'

'The worst.' Anjelica wipes her forehead with the back of her hand. 'Swear to God they need air conditioning in here or things are going to kick off.'

Morgan looks at the bandage on the woman's forearm, the only visible sign of her suicide bid. The crucifix is gone from round her neck. She tries a smile.

'How's Marlon?'

Anjelica shrugs, nodding towards the cubicles.

'Sleeping.'

No let-up in the frostiness. Time for a firmer tone.

'Did Nigel Cundy give you my message last week, Anjelica?'

A frown spreads across the woman's face. She seems to be struggling to focus, once again fighting her way through a haze of antidepressants.

'Nigel who?'

'The prison psychologist. I asked him to let you know that I'm doing all I can to investigate your case, to get it to the Criminal Cases Review Commission.'

'He mentioned it when he came to see me in the hospital wing.'

'You don't sound too happy about it.'

Anjelica sniffs.

'You're more interested in Kiki and Stacey than me. One's dead, one's out. I'm still here.'

Chastened, Morgan painstakingly takes Anjelica through the progress she has made: her conversations with Detective Inspector Brett Tucker and the whisky-soaked solicitor, Grahame Millar. She doesn't mention the fact that both men remain convinced of Anjelica's guilt, nor does she bring up her appointments with the fire scene investigator and forensic odontoloist. Both have finally answered her emails.

Crucially, she omits to mention her own sighting of Karl Savage. Prison can drive a person to despair even if they're guilty; for an innocent, it's the ninth circle of hell. Aside from Morgan (and Lissa on a good day) the world believes that Karl is dead: police, press, public, even Anjelica herself. Everyone 'knows' he died in the fire. Offering a ray of hope that may prove false is worse than no hope at all. Before Morgan discloses what she knows, she needs incontrovertible proof that Savage is alive. Meanwhile, she needs to find out more about the body found at the base of the cliffs.

'You heard how Kiki died?'

Anjelica nods, fanning her face with her hand. 'But I don't believe it was suicide.'

'Because?'

'She was always talking about getting out, how she and Charlie were going to have a fresh start. And she was tougher than me.

She had everything to live for. So jump off a cliff? Kiki? Not in a million years.'

'Maybe guilt over killing a sixteen-year-old boy was overwhelming,' says Morgan. 'Perhaps getting out of prison was too much to handle. Maybe she was scared of what lay ahead.'

A shrug.

'I heard her talking to Stacey, making plans. Didn't sound scared to me.'

'What plans?'

'Move to the country, start a new life.'

Morgan holds the woman's gaze.

'What are you not telling me?'

Anjelica shifts in her chair, eyes flickering towards the door. The officer is outside, pretending to study her clipboard.

'Nothing,' says Anjelica.

'Kiki had bruises on her arm. Know anything about that?'

A shrug.

'Maybe she got into a fight before she got out.'

'Maybe?'

A sigh.

'Fine,' says Anjelica. 'She got into a fight.'

'With you?'

'You seriously expect me to answer that?'

The heat in the airless room is growing more oppressive by the minute. Morgan can feel the dampness under her arms. She remembers a playground mantra: *pigs sweat, men perspire, ladies feel the heat.*

Time for the crucial question.

'How did Kiki get pregnant while she was inside?'

Anjelica stiffens and shoots another glance at the heavyset woman in the doorway. Morgan sees their eyes meet. The officer draws breath to intervene but a cry goes up from the far side of the MBU.

'*Fucking BITCH!*'

A fight is kicking off. The officer shoots a warning glare at Anjelica before lumbering off in the direction of the fracas. Morgan must make the most of the guard's absence. She leans forward. Keeps her voice low.

'I'm doing all I can to help you but this has to be a two-way street. I need to know you're being open with me, that you trust me the way I trust you.'

Anjelica cranes her neck to peer out onto the unit. Morgan follows her gaze and catches a glimpse of a woman with tattoos on her shaved skull. Three officers are kettling her, separating her from another prisoner, trying to calm things down.

'It's just you and me,' says Morgan. 'Tell me how Kiki got pregnant while she was locked up for three and a half years.'

The woman picks at the frayed edge of her bandage, a nervous tic.

'You never heard this from me.'

'I promise,' says Morgan.

Anjelica leans closer, her voice barely a whisper. Morgan can smell her sweat.

'This isn't a prison,' she says. 'It's a baby farm.'

'What do you mean?'

'You think Kiki was the first to get knocked up in here?' says Anjelica. 'Some of these girls, they've got nothing except the clothes they stand up in. Literally. No family, no home, no hope. So when a bloke pays some attention, offers a future, they listen.'

'What kind of future?'

'Get pregnant, get paid. Five grand. Might not sound a lot to someone like you, but for them it's like winning the lottery.'

Morgan remembers Kiki's attempt to sleep in the inn's wheelie bin.

'Who's this "bloke"?'

Anjelica purses her lips. Morgan perseveres.

'Someone in here, on the men's wing?'

'Let's just say, he's the inside man.'

'He has sex with women in prison?'

Anjelica shakes her head.

'No sex. No physical contact.'

'So he's a sperm donor?'

Another shake of the head.

'Not his own, in case he gets caught down the line. DNA testing, you get me? This is a man with a plan.'

'Clearly,' says Morgan. 'This "baby farm", how does it work? What happens to the babies?'

But Anjelica shakes her head. Morgan is pushing too far, too fast.

'All I'm saying is, Kiki was one of two girls getting out this month, all set to collect her five grand and make a fresh start.'

'Who else?'

'Stacey Brown,' says Anjelica. She casts a nervous glance towards the tattooed woman still scuffling with staff on the far side of the unit. 'No one will talk to you about this stuff. Everyone knows what's going on, including the screws. But no one wants to lose their job.'

'How does the inside man work?' says Morgan. The answer makes the blood thump in her ears.

'He's got someone outside – the sperm donor. But the *inside* man can't bring it in, not since they stepped up searches for staff as well as visitors. So the *outside* man plants, like, a little test tube on an unsuspecting visitor, then the *inside* man takes care of things in here and—'

She stops mid-sentence, sitting bolt upright and staring at the door.

A man's voice.

'Time's up, Miss.'

Morgan turns to see Trevor Jukes in the doorway, arms folded. She feels a rush of blood to the head as she recalls her last visit: the bull-necked officer's insistence on placing her jacket in a locker; the ripped lining into which Lissa had sewn the plastic pouch.

What was in the pouch, Lissa?

Something hard, like a glass tube. It felt cold. I think it had, like, ice in it?

How long do sperm live? An hour? Two? Longer packed in ice? Morgan isn't sure but she knows beyond any doubt that she is looking at *the inside man*, and that his sperm donor accomplice is 'Pablo', otherwise known as Karl Savage.

Anjelica is saying something to Jukes but Morgan can't take it in, her head feels as if it might explode.

Focus.

'We're talking about my appeal,' Anjelica tells the bald-headed officer.

He fakes a half-smile and turns to Morgan.

'I'll take you back to the gate, Miss.'

'We're not done,' says Anjelica.

'Yes, you are,' says Jukes. He nods towards the fracas. 'Can't put visitors at risk.' He holds the door open. 'After you, Miss. Wouldn't want to make visiting orders hard to come by, would we?'

Cheeks burning, Morgan considers her options, then turns to Anjelica.

'I'll be in touch. I promise.'

She follows Jukes along the corridors. There's no small talk, the silence broken only by the jangle of keys on his belt. How much did he hear of the conversation with Anjelica? If he *is* the inside man, he's not to be messed with. Did he have something to do with Kiki McNeil's death? Or is Morgan's imagination as overheated as the prison?

Reaching the main block, Jukes unlocks the final gate, ushering her into the reception area, scrupulously polite.

'Take care of yourself,' he says, holding her gaze a beat too long. 'And your lovely daughter.'

Only when he's walking away, whistling the theme from *The Archers*, only as she steps through the gates into the cool of the shaded prison yard does Morgan realise how much she is trembling.

Eleven

Back at the Beach Inn, mouth dry, heart racing, Morgan goes into her room and boots up her MacBook.

Google search: penalty for smuggling drugs into prison
3,760,000 results (0.49 seconds)
Possession: up to seven years in prison and unlimited fine
Supply and production: life in prison and unlimited fine

She's ninety-five per cent certain the pouch contained sperm, not drugs. Is that enough to risk shopping Jukes to the prison governor? Or to the police? To risk a prison sentence? There are plenty of results for 'smuggling sperm *out* of prison' – accounts of inmates desperate to impregnate wives and girlfriends – but a search for 'smuggling sperm *into* prison' produces nothing. Who would do such a thing?

And what if she's wrong? What if it *was* drugs? She tries to imagine the conversation with the police.

– *A prison officer called Trevor Jukes is involved in a baby farm racket.*
– *What makes you so sure?*

- *I can't say* (not without incriminating myself and my daughter) *but there may be a link to Kiki McNeil's murder.*
- *Kiki McNeil jumped off a cliff.*
- *I don't believe that. She had everything to live for. I think Karl Savage is involved.*

Pause.

- *Karl Savage?*
- *Yes.*

Pause.

- *The Karl Savage who died in an arson attack? The Karl Savage who was murdered by the mother of his baby?*
- *He's alive. Which makes Anjelica innocent. He's called Pablo now, by the way.*
- *You're saying he's a 'dead man walking'? Literally?*
- *If you want to put it like that, yes. He had a fling with my daughter and beat us both up but now he's disappeared. He's probably living in a stolen camper van with dodgy number plates so he can avoid the ANPR cameras.*

Pause.

- *Are you the Morgan Vine who wrote the book on miscarriages of justice?*
- *Yes.*
- *The woman who believes we lock up innocent people for the hell of it?*
- *That's not what I believe. That's not what the book's about. Hello? Hello?*

A demoralising prospect. But a baby is missing and a woman is dead. A single mother, like Morgan.

No, not like her.

A million times worse off. Dubbed 'Elephant Girl'. Pimped out by her own mother from the age of thirteen. God knows what horrors she endured before ending up behind bars. Prison was probably a welcome relief.

Then there's her baby.

Charlie.

Morgan remembers holding him. The smell of his skin. His impossibly tiny fingers. His heart-shaped mole.

She picks up the phone.

The conversation with Rook goes according to expectations. The DI gives short shrift to any suggestion that Karl Savage is still alive, but after much badgering (and a shameful amount of flirtation on Morgan's part) he agrees to question Trevor Jukes. He also promises not to identify his source. But Morgan knows the die is cast. Jukes will have little trouble working out her involvement. She recalls the threat implied by his parting shot.

Take care of yourself. And your lovely daughter.

Dressing quickly, she goes in search of Lissa. She finds her hunched on an old leather sofa in the inn's lounge, escaping the stifling heat of her room. Still pale, she's barefoot, wearing cut-offs that accentuate her long legs and draw the eye to her ankle tattoo: a red devil, complete with horns. She's scrolling through a newspaper report on the death of Kiki McNeil. When she looks up from her iPad, her eyes shine with tears.

'I'm sorry you lost your friend,' says Morgan.

Lissa says nothing. She reaches for a Kleenex.

'Are you OK?'

Lissa blows her nose. 'When did everything get so fucked up?'

Morgan tries to strike a nonchalant tone.

'Why don't you go and see your dad for a few weeks?'

'Er, maybe because I can't afford the flight to LA?'

'My treat.'

Lissa stays silent for a moment. When she speaks again her voice is barely audible.

'I don't deserve a treat.'

Morgan leans against the door jamb and waits for a couple to pass.

'Go and stay with your dad for a while, figure out what you want to do with your life. I'll sub you for a month but then you need to find a job.'

Lissa blows her nose again.

'Where did this come from?'

'Just helping you back on track.' Morgan hates lying by omission. 'Still want to be a reality TV star? And get a boob job?'

'Nope.'

Thank God.

'So what's Plan B?'

Lissa screws up her eyes.

'I'm thinking of becoming an expert in, like, body language?' She fixes her gaze on her mother's face. 'You're chewing your lip, the way you do when you're trying not to say what you're really thinking.'

'How did you turn into such a smart-arse?'

'Just lucky, I guess.'

Morgan appraises her daughter. The bruises are almost gone, the hairstyle is *gamine*, but the circles under her eyes speak of sleepless nights. Kiki's death has hit her hard. But that doesn't mean she'll do her mother's bidding.

Stubbornness is in the genes. Morgan was the same at twenty – *is* the same today. She has a choice: to persevere with her attempt to convince Lissa she's simply feeling generous, or bow to the inevitable and tell the truth.

Truth wins.

She sits on the sofa and describes her latest visit to HMP Dungeness and the menacing encounter with Jukes.

Lissa remains quiet for a long moment then gets to her feet and heads for her room. Morgan follows her along the corridor, brushing past the wind chimes.

'No way am I going to LA,' says Lissa.

'I'd be happier if you went till this is over.'

'And leave you with all the crazies? Not going to happen.' Morgan draws breath to protest but her daughter is in full flow. 'I'm not a kid, Mum. I should never have let Pablo bully me into planting stuff in your jacket. It's my fault you're mixed up in this. I'm not going anywhere.' She lets herself into her room, flops on the bed and gives her mother a defiant stare. 'Unless you come too.'

'Not an option,' says Morgan, standing in the doorway and folding her arms. 'I made a promise to Anjelica. I intend to keep it.'

'So we're agreed,' says Lissa. 'We see this through. Together.' She ticks off a list on her fingers. 'Figure out who was the body in Karl's flat; get Anjelica to the appeal court; expose the baby farm. Piece of cake.'

But her voice lacks conviction. She's putting on a show, trying to sound more confident than she feels. Morgan opens the window, letting air into the stiflingly hot room while trying – and failing – to figure out how to force her daughter onto a plane.

'OK,' she says, surrendering to the inevitable. 'But this isn't a game. Understood?'

Lissa nods and chews on a fingernail. Her eyes look watery. Once again, she seems on edge, on the verge of tears. Her voice is hoarse.

'So now what do we do?'

The call to Nigel Cundy doesn't go well.

'What do you know about a baby farm in the prison?'

Clutching her iPhone, Morgan is standing on the porch outside Lissa's room, smoking a roll-up while looking out to sea.

'What have you heard?' says the shrink.

'Why are you answering my question with a question?'

'If I knew about a baby farm why would I tell a journalist?'

'Are staff scared they'll lose their jobs, Nigel?' Another pause. Morgan perseveres. 'I read about a new Home Office initiative. Prison disciplinary panels. They can sack people for bringing a prison into disrepute.'

'So?'

'Might such a panel have anything to do with the last governor taking early retirement for "personal reasons"? Some kind of cover-up? Before "Genghis" Carne arrived?'

'I'm hanging up now,' says Nigel.

'One more thing: where did Stacey Brown go after her release?'

'Goodbye, Morgan.'

'Come on Nigel, be a mensch.'

A sigh.

'Like all prisoners, Stacey Brown has an offender management supervisor. She's on a mentoring scheme. She'll have gone to a hostel.'

'Where?'

'I don't know.'

'Don't know or can't say?'

'Both.'

'Last question: do you believe Kiki McNeil committed suicide?'

'Again, I don't know.'

'I'm asking what you believe.'

'What do *you* believe?'

Morgan considers the question.

'I think someone pushed her.'

'Why would anyone do that?'

'I've no idea. Yet.'

'I'm hanging up now.'

'Bye, Nigel. Always a pleasure.'

Ending the call, she hears sobbing coming from Lissa's room. Entering, she finds her daughter weeping copiously while watching a news report on the search for Charlie and the death of Kiki McNeil. She sits on the bed, gently stroking Lissa's hair. They hear the official police verdict: a tragic suicide, no suspicious circumstances.

But fears are growing for baby Charlie, still missing after a week.

The report into the woman's conviction and death – the only public recognition of a brief, miserable existence – lasts forty seconds. Morgan is overwhelmed by a sense of outrage on Kiki's behalf. Cruelly treated as a child, what kind of example had she been set? What chance did she have? True, she was responsible for a boy's death – accidental, perhaps, but caused by carelessness. She took a life. Destroyed a family. Unforgivable? The boy's parents didn't seem to think so, so who is Morgan to judge?

And is she so different?

If she hadn't had a 'decent upbringing' (blighted by her mother's death, but 'decent' nonetheless), who was to say she wouldn't have turned out like Kiki? Both were members of the single mothers' sisterhood – a club unlike any other. Had Morgan been in Kiki's shoes, it could have been her mangled body at the base of the cliffs; the missing baby could have been Lissa.

Innocent. Defenceless.

The TV news ends with a jaunty sign-off from the presenter.

Time for the weather.

Heavy rain is on the way.

The Indian summer is over.

Twelve

KARL

The cellar is cold. Dark. Smells of damp. She locked him in as soon as he got home from school, just as she does every Friday, releasing him on Sunday night in time for his bath. When he goes to school on Monday no one will guess how he spent the weekend.

He has no idea of the time. The house has been silent for ages. She's probably been in the pub. Spending all her benefits.

But now she's back. He can hear her upstairs, laughing with someone – a man, as usual. It's never the same man but there's always laughing at first, followed by other sounds.

Kissing.

Panting.

Moaning.

Then shouting.

Karl doesn't like the shouting. He's not used to voices at all, not in the house. It's three years since Daddy died and she still hasn't spoken to him – not once – not since those five last words.

– *This is all your fault.*

He switches on his torch. Not for long – he can't afford to waste the batteries – just long enough to put cornflakes in the bowl and pour milk on top. The milk is warm and doesn't taste nice but it's better than the water she left last week.

Happy birthday, Karl.

Upstairs, the shouting stops. The front door slams.

Silence descends. No TV, no music, no voices. Just footsteps above his head. He visualises her shuffling around the kitchen, getting something to eat. She eats a lot these days. Takeaways, mainly. She's getting fat.

Later comes the faint sound of fireworks from the garden next door. Rockets. Bangers. Catherine wheels.

Laughter.

Ooohs and *aaahs*

Karl eats his cornflakes while listening to the whizzes and bangs, imagining the colours exploding against the night sky. Then he pulls the blanket around his shoulders and runs his hands over the lid of the biscuit tin, feeling the raised outline of Guy Fawkes's face – his hat, his beard, the bonfire, the flames.

Closing his eyes, shivering, Karl conjures up the memory of Daddy's voice on that last morning, before he ran into the road.

– *Happy birthday, son. Your special day. And remember, remember, you need to go up like a rocket even if you come down like a stick.*

Thirteen

The weather breaks as Morgan and Lissa arrive at the tower block on the outskirts of Canterbury. Inside, rain lashes the windows of the sixteenth-floor flat, home to Nancy Sixsmith, mother of Karl's twins, both currently at school. Perched on a red leather sofa, sitting next to Lissa, Morgan watches Nancy light one cigarette from the stub of another. With the windows closed, the flat smells like an ashtray, the air is hard to breathe.

'If you had to sum Karl up?' says Morgan.

'Sociopath,' says the woman without hesitation. 'Narcissist. Con man.' She drags on her cigarette and scratches a patch of eczema on her arm. Her flesh is raw and red, reminding Morgan of the port wine stain on Kiki's face. 'Which paper did you say you're from?'

'I'm not,' says Morgan. 'I'm just looking into the case against Anjelica Fry.'

'Open and shut, if you ask me.'

'So people say,' says Morgan. 'I'm not so sure.'

Nancy turns her bleary-eyed gaze to Morgan's wan-looking daughter. It's 11 a.m. and the woman reeks of alcohol.

'I used to read about you,' she tells Lissa, waggling a pudgy finger at a stack of celebrity magazines, all primary colours and salacious shout lines. 'You shagged your mum's old flame. Made a sex tape. Tried to cash in. Nice.'

Lissa looks stricken but says nothing. Morgan intervenes.

'Mind if we stick to Karl?'

The woman doesn't seem to mind at all. She's glad of the attention. Hers is a familiar tale, reminiscent of Anjelica's version of her early days with Karl. A chance meeting with a handsome, honey-tongued charmer then a brief honeymoon period followed by the emergence of controlling, obsessive behaviour.

'I've read up on psychos since,' says Nancy. Another nod towards the magazines. 'Wish I'd known before I met him.' She flicks ash in the direction of the ashtray, missing by several inches. 'I used to have a life. Job, house, money in the bank. Now I'm stuck with two ADHD kids and I can't work 'cause of my nerves. I can't do the school run, so my neighbour does it – when she's not off her face on White Lightning – and I have to get my shopping delivered by Asda. I'm a prisoner in my own home.' She breaks off to give a hacking cough then continues. 'But the worst part? I let him do this to me. I let it happen.'

The self-pity is unedifying until Morgan remembers the *Mail*'s reference to a nervous breakdown. Torn between sympathy and irritation she watches Nancy suck on her cigarette.

'I used to be a teacher. But the idea of a class full of rowdy kids makes me break out in hives. I tried to go back to work, a year ago. Lasted two days.'

Morgan hasn't mentioned the fact that Karl is alive, nor that Lissa also fell for the man's charms, allowing herself to be seduced and manipulated.

'Did he tell you he loved you?' says Lissa in a quiet voice. Morgan has no trouble filling in the rest of the sentence. *Like he told me.*

The woman nods.

'That's how he got you.' The cigarette is burning low. Time to prise the next one from the packet. 'He reeled you in then cut you dead, leaving you not knowing if you were madly in love or just mad.' She fiddles with a hangnail. 'If you want to know about Karl Savage, watch *Batman*. The one with the Joker? Heath Ledger in all that make-up?'

'That's *so* how he is,' says Lissa, leaning forward in her chair. 'Just like the Joker.'

'Same OTT behaviour,' says Nancy, too self-absorbed to ask how Lissa knows what Karl is like. 'Same charisma, same manic energy, same grandiose, sensation-seeking behaviour.' One last drag on the cigarette. 'You know when the Joker sets fire to that massive pile of cash?' Lissa nods. 'That was Karl,' says Nancy. 'It was never about money, always about the game.' She picks up her mobile, scrolling through the contents. 'He once phoned at two in the morning, told me to look out the window. Said he had a surprise. So I looked and he was in the driveway, standing next to a car.'

She holds up the mobile. Morgan sees a night-time photo of Karl leaning against a red Porsche.

'I said, "Where the hell did you get that?" He said, "I bought it for you." But he'd done no such thing; he'd stolen it.' A sigh. 'I was in love so I told him to get rid of it and never do anything so stupid again.'

She breaks off to light the fresh cigarette.

'He went ballistic. How *dare* I disrespect him, after all he'd done for me? He refused to get rid of the car, so I said, "Right, it's over. I can't be with a bloody thief." She's scrolling through her mobile. 'That's when he sent this.'

She presses play and holds up the phone. Karl appears in a video filmed at night. He's standing on a piece of wasteland, the red Porsche behind him.

'You don't want this, Nancy? This car? This man? Fine.'

He steps aside. Flames are visible inside the Porsche. A burning rag is stuffed into the petrol tank. Now the camera jerks wildly, keeping pace with Savage as he breaks into a run. Morgan can hear him panting. After a hundred yards, he stops, the blazing Porsche still visible in the background. Morgan can hear the excitement in his voice.

'Burn, baby, burn!'

The fireball is not like a Hollywood explosion; it's quieter, a cracking noise rather than a bang. The flames are vivid orange, flickering against the night sky. Then comes the sound of whooping, Karl's voice bursting with excitement.

'See this, Nancy? All for you.'

The clip continues for several seconds then cuts out.

'Who took the video?' says Morgan.

'Spike,' says Nancy.

Karl's drug-dealing crony.

'Where can I find him?'

A shrug. 'No idea.'

'Do you know his full name?'

The woman shakes her head. 'He was always just "Spike".'

Lissa's voice is barely a whisper.

'What happened after Karl set fire to the car?'

'I said I never wanted to see him again,' says Nancy. 'But then I had to tell him I was pregnant. He was like a kid at Christmas. Swore he'd get a job, see a doctor, calm down. And for a while, he was lovely – the old Karl. Sweet, funny.' Her lips twitch into a smile. 'Top marks in the sack.'

Morgan resists the urge to glance at her daughter.

'How long did the good times last?'

'Couple of months, maybe three. He started making plans. "You and me, Nancy, and six kids – *at least*." He was going to start a classic car business. All he needed was seed money for two cars and a posh suit. Hugo Boss.'

'How much did you give him?'

Nancy studies the back of her hand.

'Nearly a hundred grand. Every penny Gran left me.'

'Cash?'

A nod.

'Said he was negotiating with a car dealer up north. Went off to do the business and that was the last I saw of him.'

She eyes her visitors and takes a slurp of tea. 'I blame his mum, Pearl. She hated kids, especially boys. Got knocked up by accident. She was a *serious* Catholic, so abortion was out of the question. On Karl's fourth birthday, he ran in front of a van. His dad – Marlon – pushed him to safety but got run over and died two days later.' The woman pauses for effect. 'Pearl never forgave Karl, never spoke to him again. You think I'm exaggerating, but I'm not.'

Lissa's eyes widen.

'Never?'

'Not one word. She used to lock him in the cellar after school on a Friday with a bucket – and his precious bonfire night biscuit tin – and not let him out till Monday.'

As the woman says *bonfire night biscuit tin* she uses her forefingers to mime quotation marks in the air. Morgan frowns.

'What was special about the tin?'

'God knows. It was sealed with duct tape. He wouldn't let it out of his sight. It had a picture of Guy Fawkes on it. The way he looked after it, took it everywhere, you'd think it was the Holy Grail.' She takes a sip of tea as another memory surfaces. 'Once, Pearl forgot to leave water. He had to drink his own urine. No wonder he hated women.'

Lissa frowns.

'He hated women?'

Nancy shoots her a pitying look.

'Yes, he loved *screwing* us then screwing us *up*. But sex was never about love, not for Karl. It was all about power. And revenge. Reclaiming the power *she* took from him. And he never wanted to be powerless again.'

Lissa falls silent, chewing on a fingernail. Morgan can almost hear her daughter's brain working overtime as she looks at a photo of Nancy's twins, Jack and Karl Junior.

'They'll be home for lunch soon,' says Nancy. 'Half day.'

Lissa's eyes are still on the photo. She clears her throat.

'I assume you *wanted* to get pregnant?'

'Christ, no,' says Nancy. 'Faulty condoms. Karl was thrilled. "One in a billion", he said.'

The phrase chills Morgan's blood.

'He used those words? 'One in a billion'?'

'Yes. Why?'

Because he used the same phrase when Anjelica told him she was pregnant.

Twenty minutes later, Morgan and her daughter are getting into the Mini outside the tower block. Lissa's recent behaviour is starting to make sense. The moodiness. The insomnia. The tears. Up all night with 'food poisoning'.

Or could there be another explanation?

Morgan feigns nonchalance.

'Early lunch?'

Lissa shrinks into the passenger seat, arms folded, hugging herself for comfort.

'Not hungry.'

They see a woman in a red parka hurrying through the rain, followed by Karl Junior and Jack. Even at a distance there's no mistaking the identity of the twins. The boys' resemblance to their father is uncanny.

As Morgan drives away, Lissa makes a bid to avoid the elephant in the room, mimicking Nancy's way of miming quotation marks with her fingers.

'So . . . what was in the "bonfire night biscuit tin"?'

But Morgan's mind is elsewhere. Matters closer to home.

'Are you OK?' she says.

Lissa looks away.

'Yep.' Then another conversational swerve. 'Are we going to see the fire scene investigator?'

'I said, are you OK?'

'And I said *I'm fine.*'

A hissy fit is not far away. Perhaps more tears. Morgan cuts through the evasiveness. Time for plain talking.

'When is your period due, Lissa?'

Her daughter can't meet her eye. She shrugs, affecting a non-chalance that Morgan knows is part of the act. A combination of bravado and denial.

'Two or three days,' says Lissa. 'Maybe four.'

Morgan's craving for a cigarette shoots to new levels.

'Tell me how you met him.'

'Who?'

Morgan's turn to roll her eyes.

'Pablo or Karl, or whatever we're supposed to call him.'

'What difference does it make?'

'I want to know if he targeted you deliberately or if it was pure coincidence he hooked up with a girl whose mother was about to help the woman he framed.'

Lissa runs her fingers through her hair.

'If anyone "targeted" anyone it was me.'

'Meaning?'

'I saw his van on the beach one night. He was skinny-dipping and seriously fit. I'd had a drink or two. I asked if I could join him.'

'He said yes? To a gorgeous young blonde? What a shocker.'

'Actually, he said no,' says Lissa, suddenly po-faced and prim. 'He said he didn't want people thinking he was some kind of paedo. So I told him, 'I'm twenty. I don't need anyone's permission to go swimming'. But he stuck to his guns. Wouldn't even give me a drink. So I thought sod him and came home.'

'When did you see him again?'

'A week later. Different part of the beach. He was parking up for the night. I took him a bottle of vodka.'

'And one thing led to another?'

'Not that night. He wasn't up for it. Said he was old enough to be my father.'

'But you were? Up for it?'

Lissa looks away.

'You know me. Never miss a chance to mess things up, especially with a fit bloke.'

Morgan knows her smile is unconvincing but it's the best she can manage.

'Go on.'

'We started hanging out and yes, one thing led to another. Then one night I mentioned your book and how you were going to see someone at the prison. He gave me a weird look and asked who. So I told him it was Anjelica Fry.'

'What did he say?'

'Not much. But it was *definitely* coincidence, not conspiracy.'

'What makes you so sure?'

Lissa's tone grows testy.

'I remember the look on his face. Total surprise. It was obvious the whole Anjelica thing had come out of the blue.'

'OK,' says Morgan. 'I'll go with the coincidence theory. Then what happened?'

Lissa fumbles in her pocket for a tissue before continuing.

'The next time I saw him he wanted me to give you that pouch to take inside. I said no way. He kept pushing and pushing. But

I said it wasn't going to happen, not now, not ever. And he was like, "OK, that's it – we're done". Next thing I know, he's vanished off the face of the earth and I'm like, ohmygod, my life is over. But *then* the bastard sneaks up on us, on the cliffs, and does *this*.' She points to her cropped hair, her eyes glazing with tears. 'He fucked with my head, Mum. He burned my hair off. He made me involve you in all this crap. He turned my life to shit. So *please can we stop talking about him now*?'

A single tear courses down her cheek. Morgan reaches out and gives her hand a comforting squeeze.

'It's going to be OK,' she says, trying to sound more confident than she feels. Blowing her nose, Lissa turns to look out of the window, not buying the blithe attempt at reassurance. Her voice is filled with despair.

'No, it's not. Nothing's ever going to be OK again.'

She falls silent for a moment. Morgan follows suit, concentrating on the road ahead while groping for the words to reassure her daughter. But suddenly, Lissa is gasping for air, trying to unbuckle her seatbelt. To anyone watching, it might seem as if she is having a fit. Morgan knows better. Steering the car into a side street, she keeps her voice steady.

'It's OK, Lissa. It's just a panic attack.'

She guides the car to a halt and opens both windows. Lissa is making a rasping sound, her breathing worsening.

'I'm here. Mum's here. Nothing bad will happen.'

She unbuckles her daughter's seatbelt, loosening the straps. She knows Lissa can't hear her but she keeps talking, her voice low, steady, soothing.

'You'll be fine. Everything is going to be OK.'

The first time Morgan saw her daughter's eyes roll into the back of her head, the way they are now, she dialled 999. The operator made her describe Lissa's symptoms, diagnosed a panic attack then dispatched an ambulance, just in case. Now, Morgan knows better. No need for paramedics, just TLC and patience. That her daughter is in a state of shock comes as no surprise. Kiki's death. Karl's machinations. And now the possibility she might be pregnant. By a sociopath.

'I'm here, sweetheart. Mum's here.'

After almost ten minutes, Lissa's breathing is still laboured but starting to ease. Morgan strokes her daughter's hair. Soft, gentle, reassuring.

'Shall I take you home?'

Lissa shakes her head and steps out of the car, her breathing slowly beginning to return to normal. Morgan joins her on the pavement and waits, biding her time until her daughter can finally speak.

'I'm OK,' says Lissa. Her voice is shaky. 'Let's see this through.'

'You sure?'

A nod.

Getting back behind the wheel of the Mini, an image springs to Morgan's mind. Karl Savage, aka Pablo, hunched over a pile of condoms, pricking holes with a pin.

One in a billion.

Fourteen

Watching Lissa turn heads in the bustling streets around Canterbury Cathedral, Morgan recalls the day she found out about her own pregnancy. Estranged from her father, her mother long dead, the shock had come during her first term at university. It was to be her last. The baby's father, a budding screenwriter, had come to address the Film Society. Twelve years Morgan's senior, Cameron was confident, good-looking and witty.

A 'quick drink' led to a Chinese takeaway.

Dinner led to breakfast.

Weeks later, realising her period was late, Morgan recalled the screenwriter's favourite Woody Allen line.

If you want to make God laugh, tell him your plans.

Cameron had left the decision to her, but made it clear he felt an abortion would be in her own best interests. Her university friends agreed – all of them. No doubt about it, it was the sensible thing to do. On the appointed day, Morgan made it as far as the clinic's door before deciding there were more important things in life than being sensible. Never – not for one second – has she blamed any woman for making a different choice, but on that lonely December morning it seemed the right – the only – decision for her.

Twenty years later, Morgan has been bracing herself for 'empty nest syndrome' (part dreading, part longing), while Cameron remains a feature of her life, thanks to occasional Skype calls from his Malibu beach house. She wouldn't dream of telling him that their daughter might be pregnant. This is Lissa's news. Lissa's life. Lissa's decision. Morgan will be supportive, no matter how rocky the road ahead.

But *a grandmother?* At *thirty-nine?*

She shakes her head, trying to dismiss the thought from her mind. As Lissa would say, this is *so* not about her.

Passing a chemist's, she once again considers buying a pregnancy test. They could pop into a pub loo and discover the truth before they finish their lattes. Or she could let Lissa handle the situation in her own way but be here for her, however things turn out.

Yes.

Better.

The panic attack has subsided, leaving Lissa pale and subdued. Exiting the shopping precinct and crossing the bridge that spans the small river, Morgan accompanies her daughter into a side street lined with timber-framed mock Tudor cottages. Lissa consults a piece of paper, searching for an address. She stops at a door and looks up at the first-floor window. The curtains are closed.

'He's expecting us?'

'Hope so.'

Morgan checks her watch. Exactly 4 p.m., the time the fire scene investigator confirmed by email. A busy man, hard to pin down. She rings the doorbell then steps back, looking up at the window. The curtains remain closed. She rings again. Sounds emanate from inside the house, footsteps clumping down a flight of stairs. The door is opened by a tall, muscular man in his late thirties. He's *GQ* handsome and naked except for white boxer shorts. Bed hair. Blinking at the daylight.

'Yes?'

Morgan does her best to sound casual but it's not easy. The man is drop-dead gorgeous.

'Ben Gaminara?'

'Yes?'

'I'm Morgan Vine. This is my daughter, Lissa.' The man seems none the wiser. 'We had an appointment? About Anjelica Fry?'

'Ah. Sorry. Come in.'

The kitchen is in chaos, recalling the aftermath of a teenagers' all-nighter. Beer cans, glasses, plates, pizza cartons. In the cluttered sitting room, a black cat is half-asleep on the table, blinking at the newcomers, cheerfully unaware that it's lying on a pink bra.

'Wow,' says Morgan. 'Looks like quite a party.'

The man scratches his stubble and surveys the carnage.

'I wish,' he says. 'I've been working flat out. First day off in months.' He heads for the staircase and gestures towards the kitchen. 'Put the kettle on. Give me five minutes.'

Morgan does as directed then catches Lissa's knowing smile.

'What?' she says.

The smile widens.

'Try not to drool, Mum. It's not a good look.'

Morgan ignores her daughter, moving away to the sitting room to scan the bookshelves. Hardbacks on military history vie for space with scores of DVDs, all romantic comedies. Ben

Gaminara seems an unlikely romcom fan; perhaps they belong to the owner of the pink bra.

Three shelves are devoted to a collection of Motown vinyl arranged alphabetically, from The Four Tops and Marvin Gaye to Diana Ross and Stevie Wonder.

By the time Ben returns, smelling of shower gel, barefoot in a polo shirt and jeans, the kettle has boiled. He makes coffee (the real thing, Morgan notes, with freshly ground beans) while avoiding eye contact with his visitors.

'I googled you,' he says. 'Both of you. You're trouble. I like that.' He pours coffee from a cafetière, then turns and hands Morgan a mug. 'Tell me why I should talk to you.'

No trace of a smile, but his eyes are kind. And Morgan notes that he's not directing his question to Lissa, not focusing his entire attention on the lissom twenty-year-old. Men do. Morgan doesn't blame them – they're simple creatures – but she's always on sleazebag alert. Perhaps she'll learn to trust again at some point, to drop her guard. But not yet.

Sipping his coffee, Ben listens as she explains her rationale for reinvestigating the case against Anjelica Fry. She hasn't planned on going over the entire story – the cliff-top attack, the vial she unwittingly smuggled into HMP Dungeness, the baby farm – but there's something about the quiet intensity of Ben Gaminara's gaze that makes her open up. When she reaches the part about seeing Karl outside her house, his eyes widen.

'You're saying he didn't die in the fire?'

'Exactly,' says Morgan.

He scratches his jaw, a rasp of bristle.

'How do you account for the fact they identified his body?'

'I can't.'

'But you've told the police what you saw?'

'Of course. I saw DI Tucker.'

'And?'

'He thinks I'm crazy,' says Morgan. 'Or a bleeding-heart liberal with a grudge against the system. Or both.'

'Which is it?'

'Neither.'

Ben nods slowly.

'Do you know how many cases the Review Commission refers to the appeal court?'

'Just over two per cent.'

'Not great odds.'

Morgan smiles.

'The woman is innocent. That's all that matters.'

He turns towards Morgan's daughter.

'Did you see the guy in the van?'

'No, but if Mum says she saw him, she saw him.'

'And you think he's the man you know as Pablo?'

'Looks like it.'

'So he groomed you'

'I hate that word. I'm not a kid.'

'What would you call it?' Ben raises an eyebrow. 'Seduced? Scammed? Conned?'

Lissa's jaw tightens.

'Whatever.'

'So,' says Morgan, keen to keep things on an even keel, 'does all this sound crazy?'

His answer takes her by surprise.

'Not to me.'

Lissa leans forward in her chair.

'But you gave evidence against Anjelica.'

Ben shakes his head.

'That's not how the system works. My role is to determine how the fire started, not who started it. That's down to the police. I located the seat of the fire; I established that an accelerant had been used; my colleagues identified the type of petrol and the brand of matches.'

'How is that even possible?' says Lissa.

Ben takes a match from a box on the coffee table. Morgan's gaze strays to his hand. Long, elegant fingers. No sign of a ring.

'You strike a match. You toss it onto a petrol-soaked towel. What happens?'

'Whole place goes up in smoke,' says Lissa.

'Including the match?'

'Obviously.'

Ben shakes his head. He points to the match-head.

'The shell contains single-cell organisms called diatoms. They can survive incredibly high temperatures. They vary from manufacturer to manufacturer. Identify the diatoms and you stand a good chance of identifying the brand.'

'The Anjelica matches?' says Morgan.

'So they said,' says Ben.

'You're not convinced?'

He sips his coffee.

'They got the right matches. But did they get the right person?'

Morgan feels a flicker of relief. Finally, someone is taking her seriously.

'You're saying they made a mistake?'

'I don't know.' Ben reaches for his laptop. 'But one thing struck me as odd.' He clicks on a file of photos showing a blackened, burnt-out room. 'This is Karl's flat after the fire.' He scrolls to another photo: Savage giving a thumbs-up to camera. 'This is the same room *before* the fire.' Another click places both pictures side by side. 'See the photos on the wall? In metal frames?'

Morgan peers at the 'before' picture. Karl is giving a thumbs-up. Behind his head are two photographs. One shows him grinning, standing beside a gold Ferrari parked outside Harrods; in the other he's at the wheel of a black Bentley coupé, the type driven by Premier League footballers.

'Where did this come from?' says Morgan.

'Anjelica kept the photo after they split,' says Ben. 'He never had money for cars like these, he just loved posing with them.' He leans forward in his chair. 'Look at the "after" picture.'

Morgan studies the photo: charred remains of furniture, the contents of a room, remnants of a life. Ben points to the wall.

'See the two tiny specks?'

'What are they?'

'Metal picture hooks,' says Ben. 'That's where the photos were hanging.'

'So?' says Lissa.

'The pictures weren't at the fire scene,' says Ben. 'We'd have found remnants of the frames.'

'Is that a big deal?' says Morgan.

'Could be,' says Ben. 'Before an arsonist torches a place it's not uncommon to remove things that have sentimental value. In this case, the hooks are still there but the photos have gone.'

Moran feels a stirring of hope, like a chink of light seeping into a darkened room. She can smell shower gel on the man's skin.

'So it's possible that Karl was the arsonist?' she says. 'That he took down his photos then set fire to his own flat?'

'It's a big leap,' says Ben. 'But possible.'

'Did you tell the police about the hooks?'

'Of course. But it didn't fit their narrative. Right from the start, they were convinced Anjelica was the fire-starter, that she was determined to make sure Savage couldn't take her baby. They found evidence to support that theory. End of story.'

'Until now,' says Morgan.

Ben nods.

'One thing I don't get,' he says. 'There's no way Karl is still alive. Dental records don't lie.'

'The dentist who made the identification is next on my list.'

'Forensic odontology is an exact science,' says Ben. 'Jatinder Singh is the best.'

'We'll see,' says Morgan. 'He hasn't answered my email but I'll doorstep him if I have to.'

He notes the steel in her voice. Smiles.

'Want me to chivvy him?'

'I'd appreciate it.'

The phone in his pocket chirrups. He glances at the text.

'I need to get going.'

He stands up. Morgan follows suit. She wants to ask about the owner of the pink bra, but there's no way to do so without sounding like she's fishing.

'Thanks for your time.'

'No problem,' says Ben. 'I'm overdue a lot of leave. They're making me take it but I don't really do holiday.'

Morgan heads for the door, dawdling, playing for time, trying to think of a subtle way to find out if he's single. She passes the shelf filled with romcoms.

'Quite a collection.'

'Yep.'

Damn. Nothing to suggest to whom the films belong. In the kitchen, the cat is asleep on the table, still lying on the pink bra.

'What's the cat's name?'

'Good question.'

'Isn't he yours?'

'Long story.'

He clearly has no intention of elaborating. They've reached the front door. He's holding it open. 'Keep me posted,' he says. 'Let me know if I can help.'

'You bet,' says Morgan. 'Thanks for the coffee.'

She steps out onto the street. Lissa follows. Ben closes the door. Morgan turns quickly and heads in the direction of the car park. Lissa keeps pace, grinning.

'You *so* fancy him,' she says.

Morgan rolls her eyes.

'I'm giving up men,' she says. 'In fact, I'm joining a convent.'

Her daughter's smile fades, her mood darkening

'That makes two of us.'

Approaching a parade of shops, Morgan plucks up courage to voice what's been on her mind since the conversation with Nancy Sixsmith. She doesn't want to trigger another panic attack but sooner or later the truth will out. Reality will have to be faced.

'We could go to a chemist's. Buy a pregnancy test.'

Lissa shakes her head.

'Might put you out of your misery,' says Morgan.

'Or be the start.'

Yet again, Morgan tries to think of something reassuring to say. She comes up short so remains silent, for now. Linking arms with her daughter, she heads along the street, turning up her collar against the sudden chill in the air.

Fifteen

Temperatures plummet the next day as autumn settles in. Tempted to skip her swim, Morgan forces herself to plunge into the freezing water, enduring just five minutes before the cold drives her back to the inn.

An email is waiting.

Subject: Karl Savage.

Apologies for the delay in replying to your query. I've been addressing a conference in Geneva. I'm happy to answer questions about my identification of the late Karl Savage but I leave London tomorrow for a lecture tour. I will be at my office between noon and 4 p.m. today should you wish to speak to me in person.

Jatinder Singh, Dip. F. Od

PS: I am reading your book. Most interesting.

Morgan phones the odontologist secretary to make an appointment then raps on Lissa's door.

'Come in.'

The room is in darkness, curtains drawn. Her daughter is sitting up in bed, her face illuminated by the glow from her mobile. Her cheeks are stained with tears.

'You OK?' says Morgan.

A shrug.

'Anything I should know?'

Lissa blows her nose.

'If you mean, has my period started, then no.'

'Just asking.'

Lissa scrolls on her phone.

'What's the difference between a sociopath and a psychopath?'

Morgan sits on the bed.

'They're different labels for antisocial personality disorder. Some people think psychopathy is down to nature whereas sociopathy is more to do with nurture. Sociopaths are reckless, like loose cannons; psychopaths tend to be more cunning. They can also be charming and charismatic.'

'Like Pablo? Or Karl? Or whatever his fucking name is?'

Morgan sidesteps the question.

'Are you OK, sweetheart?'

Lissa's eyes glisten with tears. Her voice is hot with anger and frustration.

'Apart from the fact I might be pregnant by the fucking Joker?'

Morgan strokes her daughter's hand.

My bones, my blood.

'I'm here,' she says. 'No matter what.'

Lissa prises her eyes away from the phone. Meets her mother's gaze.

'We used a condom, Mum. Always. If I'm pregnant it won't be my fault.'

'I know. We'll get through this.'

Her daughter nods, trying to put on a brave face. Morgan feels a pang of sympathy so sharp it twists her gut. She squeezes her daughter's hand and remembers the first time she held her in her arms. Those tiny fingers – perfect, like Charlie's.

As if reading her mind, Lissa says, 'What do you think happened to Kiki's baby?'

'I wish I knew. The police haven't said anything for days.'

'Do you think Kiki jumped?'

'Anjelica doesn't think so. What about you? You knew her better than I did.'

'Definitely possible,' says Lissa. 'She seemed pretty unstable. Up one minute, down the next. I'd say she was seriously depressed.'

Morgan frowns.

'You didn't mention this before.'

A shrug.

'I've been thinking about it. Going over stuff she said. Depression is definitely a possibility.'

Morgan gets to her feet, feeling in her pocket for her keys.

'I'm going to London, to see the forensic dentist. Want to come?'

Lissa shakes her head.

'I need a duvet day.'

'Want me to stay with you?'

'No, I'll be OK.'

'What will you do?'

'Sleep. Eat ice cream.'

'Good plan.' Morgan pauses at the door. 'Stay here,' she says. 'All day.'

'Got it.'

'Promise?'

A sigh.

'Promise.'

Morgan asks Eric Sweet to keep an eye on Lissa then drives to London, listening to a Mozart symphony on Classic FM, a bid to calm her growing anxiety. She lucks into a parking bay a few doors from Jatinder Singh's Harley Street office. Sitting in the lobby, she declines the receptionist's offer of green tea then scans the array of framed diplomas and press cuttings on the walls. Singh is a man at the top of his game: lecture tours, a successful private practice, forensic work on the side.

Ushered into his immaculate office on the dot of one o'clock, Morgan is struck by the emphasis on symmetry. Two white leather chairs are positioned at right angles to the white laminated desk on top of which sits a sleek iMac. Nothing else. The high-ceilinged room is dominated by a large oil painting of what Morgan takes to be Singh's wife and teenage daughters. All three wear white saris. The portrait occupies the entire wall facing the desk.

The man himself sports a neatly trimmed goatee and a charcoal-grey suit with a pristine white shirt. The only flash of colour is his turquoise tie, the sole sign of imperfection his fingernails, bitten to the quick. Rising from his chair, he extends a solid handshake and a dazzling white smile, the kind sported by movie stars. He gestures for his visitor to take a seat.

'May I call you Morgan?' A mellifluous voice, soft and soothing.

'Of course.'

He resumes his seat, shooting his cuffs.

'Ben Gaminara emailed me,' he says. 'Apparently you believe Anjelica Fry is the victim of a miscarriage of justice.'

'Yes,' says Morgan.

Singh's eyes search her face.

'I finished your book,' he says, taking her by surprise. 'Very readable, highly persuasive.'

'Thanks. I'm flattered.'

The man glances at his Cartier watch, removes it from his wrist and sets it on the desk.

'Will twenty minutes do?'

Morgan nods and outlines the reasons for her visit. The man behind the desk listens attentively, asking occasional questions then furrowing his brow as she reaches the part about Karl Savage being alive.

'Do you mind if I speak frankly, Ms Vine?'

'Of course not.'

He flicks a non-existent piece of fluff from his sleeve and speaks in formal sentences, as if addressing a public enquiry.

'I've reviewed my findings in the case, in preparation for this meeting. I understand why someone might feel a modicum of sympathy for the woman convicted of Savage's murder. It's not for me to judge Ms Fry guilty or otherwise. What I can say, without fear of contradiction, and with the benefit of twenty-four years' experience, is this: the man whose dental records I examined was Karl Savage. Those records were incontrovertibly a perfect match for the man who died in the arson attack on his flat.'

'No room for doubt?'

'None whatsoever.'

'But surely teeth aren't like fingerprints,' says Morgan. 'They're not unique from birth.'

'True,' says Singh. 'But unique nevertheless. And every bit as reliable as fingerprints.' He leans forward in his chair. 'Tooth enamel is the hardest substance in the human body. Teeth can withstand temperatures of over 2,000 degrees Fahrenheit, much hotter than a domestic house fire. In this instance, I worked on the cadaver in the morgue, exposing the jaws surgically. I then compared a series of ante-mortem radiographs with their post-mortem counterparts, not just with the naked eye but with 3D computer imaging.'

He turns the iMac screen to face her. A series of clicks brings up the image of a dental X-ray.

'Teeth grow differently in each individual. Over the years, wear and tear produce unique patterns: crowding of teeth, broken teeth, missing teeth, tooth morphology, rotations, fillings, crowns and so on.' Producing a Mont Blanc pen, he points to the X-ray. 'This is a radiograph of Savage's teeth, ante-mortem, taken by his own dentist.'

A tap of the pen draws Morgan's eye to a small arch-shaped groove at the base of one of the front teeth.

'This particular notching of the mandibular and maxillary left central incisors is characteristic of someone regularly using their teeth to strip plastic coating from electrical wire.'

'And Karl worked as an electrician.'

'So I understand.'

Another click conjures a second image, splitting the screen in two.

'This is his post-mortem radiograph, taken by me.'

Morgan scrutinises the images side by side. Even to an untrained eye they are identical.

'It was helpful that the subject had visited his dentist eleven days before he died,' says Singh. 'His X-rays were up to date. As you can see, there can be no doubt that the radiographs are identical.'

Morgan peers closer.

'Is it possible to do DNA tests from teeth?'

Singh nods. 'Even when body tissues have been burned, the structure of the enamel and pulp complex persist. We extract DNA from calcified tissues, taking, say, a molar. Then we cryogenically grind it in a mill using liquid nitrogen. The powder can be used for DNA extraction.'

'Was that done in this case?'

He shakes his head.

'The enquiry didn't progress as far as DNA testing. These radiographs told the police all they needed to know.' He taps the screen with the pen, indicating the first X-ray. 'This is Karl

Savage *ante*-mortem.' He taps the second image. 'This is Karl Savage *post*-mortem. The man died in that fire, Ms Vine – end of, as my daughters would say.' He gestures towards the two girls in the portrait on the wall. 'And this isn't opinion, it's scientific fact.'

'So how do you explain the fact that I saw Karl outside my house?'

'A doppelganger? A twin?'

'He didn't have a twin.'

'Then forgive me, but is it possible that you were mistaken?'

Not for the first time, Morgan considers the question, casting her mind back to the man in the camper van, his face illuminated by the flame of the Zippo lighter.

Click, rasp.

A fleeting glimpse, three seconds at most, after powerful sleeping pills.

And painkillers.

And wine.

Has she got it wrong?

Jatinder Singh is rising from his desk, refastening his watch on his wrist. The meeting is over.

'I'm sorry to hurry you but—'

'Thank you for your time.'

Standing, she turns to go, her eyes scanning the portrait on the wall. The three serious-looking females in white saris.

'I associate saris with bright colours,' says Morgan.

'White symbolises holiness and purity,' says Singh. 'A little pompous, perhaps, but my wife insisted. And as she never ceases to remind me, "happy wife, happy life". He ushers her towards the door and into the reception. 'I'm sorry if you're disappointed by what I've told you.'

'Not disappointed,' says Morgan. 'Just confused.'

The man extends a valedictory handshake, firm but friendly, like his greeting.

'I have a saying: people lie through their teeth, but the teeth never lie.'

Once again, he flashes that dazzling white smile, then goes back into his office, closing the door behind him. Firmly.

The Dungeness Beach Inn is wreathed in late afternoon mist as Morgan guides the Mini to a halt on the shingle. To the west, distant lights from the prison are clearly visible; to the east, she can make out the red glow from the power station. As she slams the car door, a flock of birds takes to the air, circling the hotel before heading out to sea. Morgan goes inside, walking through the deserted reception to the corridor that leads to Lissa's room.

She raps on the door.

'Lissa?'

No answer. A second knock is greeted by silence. Heading into the lounge, Morgan finds Eric Sweet balancing on a stepladder, installing another smoke alarm. His sweatshirt slogan is emblazoned with a familiar quote from Gandhi: *Be the Change You Wish to See in the World.*

'Have you seen Lissa?' says Morgan.

'Not since I brought her back.'

'From where?'

'Town. She asked for a lift, said she needed to buy something important.'

'Did she say what?'

'No.'

'When did you get back?'

He checks his watch.

'About an hour ago.'

Morgan frowns.

'Can you let me into her room?'

'Of course.'

Climbing down from the stepladder, Eric leads the way to 'Dragonfly' and unlocks the door. The room is empty, the bed unmade.

'You didn't see her leave?'

He shakes his head.

'Maybe she's gone for a walk.'

'Maybe,' says Morgan, trying to recall her parting words to her daughter.

Stay here. All day.

Yup. Got it.

Promise?

Promise.

An hour later, as darkness falls, Morgan is roving the beach, dialling Lissa's mobile for the third time and leaving yet another message.

'It's Mum. *Again.* Call me.'

Back at the inn, she sits on her daughter's bed, trying to banish from her mind's eye an image of Kiki McNeil's lifeless body at the foot of the cliffs.

Lissa's room contains no clue to her whereabouts. No note, no text, no email.

A thought strikes: Eric's trip to town.

She needed to buy something important.

Morgan hurries into the bathroom. She raises the lid of the pedal bin. Inside is packaging from a DIY pregnancy test. No sign of the kit itself. No card. No stick. No digital readout. No way of knowing if her daughter is carrying the child of a sociopath. A man universally believed to be dead.

Sixteen

By midnight Morgan is getting desperate. For hours she's combed the roads that bisect the beach, first in her car, now on foot. The mist has been rolling in fast, thickening into a swirling fog. Clutching a torch from Eric's toolbox, she approaches the outlying expanse of shingle. The tide is receding, allowing the shoreline to reveal its secrets. Slowing her pace, she can feel the blood thudding in her ears as she directs the beam of the torch over the shallow ripples, stones and mud. Out at sea, the lights of a tanker are dimly visible through the fog, but there is no sign of life.

Morgan takes her mobile from the pocket of her leather jacket. She would have heard it ring or chirrup with a text but that doesn't stop her double-checking, just as she did five minutes earlier, just as she will five minutes from now.

Or two minutes. Or ten seconds.

'Lissa!'

Her voice echoes far and wide, muffled by the fog, but the only response is the sound of the waves.

'*Lissa!*'

The cry is a forlorn hope and she knows it. Time to go back to the inn. Turning, she retraces her steps, passing an abandoned fishing boat beached outside a ramshackle house. Light shines from the window.

A face appears.

A man.

He stares at Morgan for a moment, then steps away from the window, disappearing from view. Seconds later he appears at the front door, silhouetted by soft yellow light spilling from within. He calls across the beach.

'Are you lost?'

'I'm looking for my daughter.'

Morgan sees a dog emerge from the shack, standing next to the man, ears cocked. There is something curious about the animal's gait. Drawing nearer, she can make out the breed – a border terrier – and the fact that it's missing a front leg. She's seen the dog before, scavenging in the beach café's bins, but has assumed it's a stray.

'Can I help you?' says the man. He's walking towards her, face coming into focus. Tall. Fifties. Jeans and a fisherman's jumper. Already on edge, Morgan wants to ignore him, to hurry back to the safety of the inn, but the sight of the three-legged dog's wagging tail is reassuring. Like the glow from the shack.

'Do you live here?'

'Yes.' He extends a handshake. 'Joe Cassidy.'

'Morgan Vine.'

'You're a local too?'

'Over there.' She gestures vaguely in the direction of her house. 'In the converted railway carriage, by the lighthouse.'

He nods, watching the dog move off, picking up some kind of scent.

'How old is your daughter?'

'Twenty. Her name's Lissa.'

'How long has she been missing?'

'A few hours. I'm not sure I can call it *missing*.'

The man gives a sympathetic nod. 'But after the other day . . .' He tails off.

Morgan raises an eyebrow. 'You mean, the woman on the cliffs? Kiki McNeil?'

He nods. 'Did you know her?'

'Yes. Did you?'

'No. But I was over there the night she died. Went to a pub nearby. Passed her after closing time.'

'Did you tell the police?'

A smile.

'Of course. I used to be a copper.'

'Was she alone?'

He shakes his head. 'With two other people – a woman and a man. The man wore a hoodie.'

'You didn't see their faces?'

He shakes his head.

'Just Kiki's. The other woman wore a denim jacket with big red metal buttons. Hard to miss, even after a couple of pints. But her face was in the shadows.'

'Did Kiki seem OK?'

A shrug.

'Hard to say. I just remember her face – the port wine stain was very distinctive.' The dog returns to his side. He gazes around the beach. 'Would you like some help?'

'No,' says Morgan. 'Thanks all the same.'

He smiles.

'Want to give me your number?'

She hesitates. Is he hitting on her or being nice?

'In case I see your daughter,' he says, as if reading her mind. He fishes a biro from his pocket and raises an expectant eyebrow. She tells him her number. He writes it on the palm of his hand.

'Any news, I'll let you know.'

'Thank you.'

She watches the man return to his shack, the three-legged dog at his side. Heading away, into the fog, she makes a mental note to ask DI Rook about Joe Cassidy. Ex-cop or not, the man in the fisherman's jumper needs checking out.

Nearing the inn, she glances at her watch. Just past twelve thirty, more than seven hours since Lissa was last seen by Eric. Casting a final look around the beach, Morgan walks towards the front door, freezing as she sees a figure slumped in the doorway. Quickening her pace, she can make out a familiar pair of Doc Martens and – *thank God!* – the outline of her daughter's face.

'Lissa?'

No response. She crouches down, reaching out to touch her daughter's cheek.

'Lissa?'

No reply, no sign of life. For a heart-stopping moment Morgan is certain her daughter is dead. But she's flooded with relief as Lissa's eyes flicker open.

'Mum . . .?'

Morgan can smell alcohol on her daughter's breath. Recalling the vodka bottle stashed under the bed, she sees a pool of vomit by the door. Relief gives way to anger.

Binge drinking? Seriously?

The reprimand dies on her lips as Lissa's next words change everything.

'I'm pregnant.'

As the grey light of dawn seeps through the curtains, Morgan is awake, staring at the ceiling. Lying beside her, Lissa snores softly, the hollows of her cheeks stained with tears.

Morgan dresses, donning a towelling robe over her swimming costume, then slips out to the corridor and pads barefoot into the dining room. Eric is laying tables for breakfast. Today's sweat-shirt slogan is a wearisome reminder that *If You're Not Part of the Solution, You're Part of the Problem*. He pours coffee from a large cafetière and hands Morgan a cup.

'Is she OK?'

'Not really.'

The man has the sensitivity not to press the subject.

'Would a bacon sandwich help?' he says.

'With ketchup?'

'Is there any other kind?'

He smiles and lumbers towards the kitchen, leaving Morgan to sip her coffee while watching the sun rise over the horizon. A radio burbles in the background, the local news broadcasting the latest on the hunt for Kiki McNeil's baby.

. . . although the search of the Dungeness area has yielded no results, Detective Inspector Neville Rook of Kent Police told a

press conference that his team is continuing to follow all lines of enquiry.

The newsreader's authoritative voice gives way to the familiar tones of the police officer.

We remain hopeful that someone knows the whereabouts of baby Charlie. If that person is listening, in the light of the mother's tragic death I urge you to come forward as soon as possible, so the baby can be properly cared for.

Morgan eats her bacon sandwich while sitting on the balcony overlooking the sea. Her thoughts turn to that early encounter with Kiki. The way the woman with the birthmark had stared out of the hotel window, scanning the beach for signs of life.

Nervous.

Looking for someone.

The way she'd whispered in her baby's ear.

'He can piss off and leave us alone.'

Lissa's voice: *'Who can?'*

The woman – a single mum who never stood a chance in life – had evaded the question. Now she's dead.

Morgan feels a surge of anger.

There but for the grace of God . . .

As for Charlie, what chance does he have – assuming he's still alive? If the police won't even take his mother's death seriously, how much effort will they invest in a search for a missing baby? Are they assuming the worst and quietly moving on? Overstretched and under-resourced, it's no wonder DIs like Neville Rook and Brett Tucker are keen to focus on cases that offer the possibility of resolution. But where does that leave Kiki?

Who will find justice for her?

Who will find her child?

Rising from her chair, Morgan walks to the water's edge. Gasping at the cold, she relishes the sensation of the mud oozing between her toes. A few more yards and the water is up to her waist. She plunges in, striking out with strong, confident strokes and feeling the pull of the current. Turning to face the beach, swimming backstroke, she sees Eric on the balcony, looking out to sea. She raises an arm to wave but he doesn't wave back. Perhaps he hasn't seen her. When she looks again, he has disappeared. Five minutes later, as she emerges from the icy water and makes her way back to the timbered deck, he has cleared away her plate and cup.

Morgan checks on Lissa – still asleep – then dresses quickly and returns to the balcony. She makes a roll-up while drinking her second coffee of the day. At precisely eight o'clock she dials DI Rook's mobile.

'Off the record, is there any news on Kiki's baby?'

'As soon as there's news you'll hear along with everyone else.'

'Did you talk to Trevor Jukes? About the baby farm?'

'Yes.'

'And?

'You know I can't comment on an investigation.'

'But you can tell me if there's something to investigate.'

'What part of "no comment" do you not understand?'

Morgan sighs.

'You need to find out what happened to Kiki, Neville. We can't have a world where lives are snuffed out and no one cares.'

'Brilliant. I must write that down.'

He's right. She's hectoring him. Time to turn on the charm.

'Maybe I could buy you a drink sometime?'

'I don't think my fiancée would approve.'

'She's not invited.'

Morgan hates pulling the oldest trick in the book but there are times when it's the only way.

'I'll think about it,' he says.

'Will you be talking to Jukes again?'

A pause is followed by a guarded response in the kind of overblown 'police speak' that makes Morgan roll her eyes.

'We have no plans to ask Mr Jukes for further assistance at this moment in time.'

'I'm guessing he denied having anything to do with a baby farm or smuggling sperm into prison,' says Morgan. 'I'm guessing he told you he doesn't know Karl Savage, or anyone called Pablo. I'm also guessing you're happy to let it drop because it looks like a dead end and you've got enough on your plate.'

'The last part is certainly true.'

'Final question?'

'If you must.'

'Do you know Joe Cassidy? Ex-police officer? Lives in a shack on the beach?'

It turns out that everyone knows Joe Cassidy – at least, everyone in the Kent Police. The man in the fisherman's jumper suffered a breakdown after heading an investigation into a grisly double murder, then took early retirement when his marriage broke down.

Reassured (partly), Morgan relays what Cassidy told her about seeing Kiki in St Mary's Bay, accompanied by a man and a woman.

'He mentioned the woman's jacket,' says Morgan. 'Denim. Big red metal buttons. Pretty distinctive.'

'Joe Cassidy is free to say what he likes,' sighs Rook. 'His career is over. Mine's not.'

Giving up, Morgan ends the call and stares out to sea. She wonders if she should rouse Lissa or allow her to sleep. She remembers only too well the sickening lurch in the stomach her daughter will experience on waking, as the reality of her situation sets in. Morgan's own pregnancy came as a shock, but unlike Lissa she had no one to blame but herself. Her careless-ness was her own fault.

And if she could have her time over, she wouldn't change a thing.

But what sort of man pricks holes in condoms? What sort of man tricks women into getting pregnant? Anjelica Fry. Nancy Sixsmith. Now Lissa, or so it seems.

Why are you doing this, Karl?

Where are you?

Where is Spike?

The shrill of Morgan's mobile breaks her reverie. An unknown number.

'Hello?'

'It's Ben Gaminara. Wondering how you got on with Jatinder Singh.'

Morgan sits up in her chair, a hand involuntarily – *absurdly* – straying to tidy her hair. For a moment she's unsure how to respond to the fire investigator's query. It takes a second to realise why she is so discombobulated.

Someone is taking her seriously.

'He was helpful,' she says.

'Did he convince you that Karl Savage is dead?'

Morgan considers the question.

'I think he believes Karl died in the fire.'

'Like the police,' says Ben.

'Yes.'

'And the rest of the world.'

'Apparently.'

'Except you.'

And maybe you?

Wishful thinking, but it's clear the man is troubled by doubts.

'I can't stop wondering about those picture hooks,' he says.

'Me neither.'

'Two specks on a photo. Not much to go on.'

Morgan seizes on the seed of uncertainty.

'But if you're right – if Karl *did* take down the photos before the flat was set on fire – the question is, why?'

'Could be a dozen explanations.'

'One might be that he was planning to fake his own death. Falsify evidence against Anjelica. Stop her testifying against his drug dealing.'

'How could he falsify evidence?' says Ben. 'And if he did, whose was the body in the flat? The one with the cracked skull?'

'No idea,' says Morgan. 'But if I'm right, Anjelica should be at home with her baby, not behind bars.'

She breaks off as she hears a voice.

'Mum?'

She turns. Her daughter is shuffling onto the balcony, wearing a too-big white bathrobe, her hair tousled, her tear-stained face puffy and pale.

'I need to go,' says Morgan. Hanging up, she turns to Lissa.

'How are you feeling?'

'How do you think?'

Morgan pats her thigh. Still half-asleep, Lissa curls onto her mother's lap, draping an arm around her neck. She smells of alcohol and vomit.

'You need to brush your teeth, your breath stinks.'

'Least of my problems.'

Morgan strokes her daughter's hair. Her voice is low and soothing.

'If you disappear like that *ever again* I will tie you in a sack and drown you.'

'Sorry.'

Morgan sighs, curling her fingers around strands of Lissa's silky hair.

'Don't be. I get it. You did the pregnancy test, you freaked out, then tried to drown your sorrows.'

Her daughter reaches for the coffee cup and drains the dregs.

'What am I going to do?'

Morgan squeezes her daughter's hand.

'Think. Talk. All day and all night, if necessary. Whatever you decide, your decision will be the right one. And I will hold your hand every step of the way.'

Lissa's eyes glaze with tears.

'What's the worst thing you've ever done?' she says.

'Made you eat spinach?'

'I'm serious.'

Morgan frowns, her worries returning.

'You know you can tell me anything, right?'

A nod. Lissa's voice is a whisper.

'I'm glad you're my mum.'

'That makes two of us. Now go and brush your teeth.'

Seventeen

The talking begins straight away. All day and into the early evening Lissa quizzes her mother about life as a single parent. Morgan is careful not to tell the whole truth (she doesn't want to terrify her daughter) but neither does she gloss over the never-ending anxiety, exhaustion and financial hardship.

'People think the child is created by the parents,' she tells Lissa during a sunset walk along the coastline. 'It's the other way round: the child creates the parent.'

'What about Dad?'

'What about him?'

'Does he still feel like part of your life?'

Morgan knows what the question means.

If I keep this baby am I tied to its father for ever?

She chooses her words carefully.

'I wouldn't change a thing. I'm sure your dad feels the same way.'

The rest of the outing passes in silence, Lissa lost in thought as she accompanies her mother back to the inn. A hundred yards from the entrance, they see a solitary figure waiting outside. Lissa stops in her tracks.

'Who's that?'

Morgan peers at the figure, a solidly built woman with a baby strapped to her back in a papoose. She sports biker boots, blue dungarees, an Arsenal scarf, the vivid red clashing with her pink hair. Frowning, Morgan recalls the first time she saw the woman in the Mother and Baby Unit, about to join forces with Kiki McNeil and launch an attack on Anjelica Fry.

I'll hold the bitch down, you kick her in the tits.

'Stacey Brown,' she tells Lissa. 'Kiki's best friend.'

She walks on. Lissa hangs back, rooted to the spot.

'What's the matter?' says Morgan.

'I've got a bad feeling about her.'

'Because she supports Arsenal?'

Lissa doesn't return her mother's smile, falling into step as they approach the woman with pink hair.

'Remember me?' says Morgan.

Stacey scrutinises her face.

'You work at the prison?'

'No, just a visitor.'

A flicker of recognition.

'Anjelica Fry's mate?'

'I wouldn't go that far,' says Morgan.

The woman casts a disdainful glare in her direction then swigs from a can of Red Bull. Morgan looks at the baby in the papoose – a black-haired boy, six months old, fast asleep.

'When did you get out?'

'Few days ago,' says Stacey. 'Been at a hostel. Right shithole.' She jerks her head towards the inn's door. 'My friend worked here but she snuffed it.'

'Kiki?'

A nod. 'Thought the owner might give me her job but he's out.' She glances in Lissa's direction. 'Who's this?'

'My daughter – Lissa.'

'Hiya,' says Stacey.

Lissa says nothing, keeping her distance, a wary look on her face. Stacey smiles at Morgan.

'Don't suppose you could lend us a fiver? I'd kill for some KFC.'

'My treat,' says Morgan, seizing the opportunity to pick the woman's brains. She nods towards the car park. 'I'll give you a lift.'

Lissa frowns.

'Since when do you like fried chicken?'

'First time for everything. Coming?'

The frown deepens. 'No way.'

'Not hungry?' says Stacey.

'No,' says Lissa.

She walks off, entering the hotel. Stacey watches her go.

'What's up with her?'

'Lot on her plate.'

The new arrival sighs.

'Haven't we all?'

Forty-five minutes later Morgan watches the woman with pink hair scrape the scraps from a bucket of fried chicken, finger them into her mouth then lean back in her chair. The fast food joint's strip light is flickering, the table littered with smears of ketchup, greasy bones and coleslaw.

Stacey swigs her supersized Coke, wipes her mouth with a napkin then unfastens the straps that hold her dungarees in place. Throughout the meal her baby has barely made a sound. Now, adjusting her T-shirt and tugging down her bra to reveal a blue-veined breast, she guides her son's mouth to her nipple.

'Just one thing missing,' she says as the baby begins to suckle. 'Got a fag?'

Producing her pouch of tobacco, Morgan makes a roll-up.

'Can I ask a question?'

Stacey burps then nods.

'Why were you in prison?'

The woman doesn't miss a beat.

'I stabbed the bastard. Section eighteen: inflicting a serious wound with malice aforethought.'

'Who's "the bastard"?'

'Santa Claus.' Stacey slurps her Coke then smiles. 'I'm serious. His name's Mickey but I called him Santa. Know why?' She leans forward. ''Cause he only comes once a year.' She laughs at her own joke then resettles the baby at her breast.

'Why did you stab him?'

'He smacked me about. Every payday, after the pub. One time, he threatened to drill my eye sockets with his Black & Decker. Shall I go on?'

Morgan shakes her head.

'Is the baby his?'

'None of your business.'

Morgan smiles, taking the rebuff in her stride.

'How long do you get for GBH?'

'Maximum twenty-five years. I got six, served three.'

'And your baby's six months old?'

'Seven. Pisces. His name's Ryan.'

'So, if you've been in prison for three years . . .' Morgan tails off, letting the question finish itself.

'How did I get pregnant?'

'Yes.'

'Immaculate conception.'

'Is that what you told the governor?'

A wink. 'What happens in prison stays in prison. Bit like Vegas, only with shitty food.'

'Is "Genghis" involved? In the baby farm?'

Stacey slurps her Coke. Morgan senses she's playing for time. 'I appreciate the food but let's not pretend we're friends. I don't owe you an explanation about anything.'

'Fair enough,' says Morgan. 'When did you last see Kiki?'

'The day she got out. We'd planned to meet up but I didn't have the bus money and she was working flat out.'

'Did you talk on the phone?'

A nod.

'She told me about the inn. The job. I'm hoping Eric will help me, like he helped her.'

Morgan searches Stacey's eyes.

'What do you think happened to her?'

The woman's expression darkens. She looks away, casting a glance towards the door. 'She jumped off a cliff.'

'Jumped? You're sure she wasn't pushed?'

'How should I know? I wasn't there.'

'But it's possible?'

'Guess so.'

'Was she depressed?'

'We were in prison,' says Stacey, enunciating clearly, as if talking to a dim-witted child. 'Of course she was bloody depressed.' She strokes the cheek of the baby at her breast. 'My turn to ask a question?'

'OK.'

'Why waste time on a bitch like Anjelica Fry?'

'I'm not wasting time. She's innocent.'

A frown.

'Believe in the tooth fairy too?'

Morgan keeps her tone light.

'I believe she was set up.'

'Who by?'

'That's what I need to find out,' says Morgan. She fixes her eyes on the woman's face, searching for clues as to how much she knows. 'Heard of Karl Savage?'

'The bloke Anjelica killed? Of course.'

'Is that the only context in which you know his name?'

'What *are* you on about?'

The puzzlement seems genuine.

'Never mind,' says Morgan. Then swiftly changing tack, 'What do you think happened to Kiki's baby?'

A scowl.

'Do I look like I'm psychic?'

Morgan senses she has touched a nerve, but now is not the moment to press the subject or push for more about the baby farm. The conversation turns to Stacey's life before prison, before the man with the Black & Decker. As with Kiki's story, it's a harrowing saga of childhood neglect and horrifying abuse. A series of predatory 'uncles' and 'stepdads' who persuaded Stacey's mother that the girl was safe in their hands. Teenage years in care. No wonder she's hard-boiled.

'Where's your hostel?' says Morgan.

'Folkestone. And I'm *so* done with that dump.'

'Won't you get in trouble if you don't go back?'

'Like I give a shit.'

But the relentless bravado is at odds with the scene being played out in front of Morgan. For all her tough talking, the woman is cradling her baby with tenderness and love. Morgan places the roll-up on the table.

'Want me to have a word with Eric?'

'About the job?'

'Maybe the room too.'

The woman brightens. 'Seriously?'

'Worth a go,' says Morgan.

Stacey nods. Places the roll-up between her lips.

'This bloke Eric,' she says, 'what does he get out of it?'

'He's not like that.'

The woman rolls her eyes. 'And I'm Queen Victoria.'

Eighteen

The possibility that Eric Sweet had something to do with Kiki's death has occurred to Morgan before (any local is a potential suspect) but Stacey's cynicism prompts her to double-check that the police are investigating every possibility. The following morning, while the innkeeper is showing his new cleaner how to vacuum to professional standards, Morgan takes her coffee onto the balcony and calls Neville Rook.

'Did you check out Eric Sweet?'

The DI sighs, choosing his words with care.

'We've made thorough enquiries among the local community and are continuing to do so.'

'Do they include determining his alibi for the time of Kiki's death?'

'I said, "thorough". Off the record, there's nothing to suggest anything other than suicide.'

'So you're not considering other possibilities?'

'Was there anything else, Morgan?'

'Any news on Charlie?'

'When there is, you'll find out along with everyone else.'

No mistaking the man's irritation.

'You'll miss me when I'm gone,' says Morgan.

'If you say so.'

Stacey and her baby, Ryan, are allocated 'Badger', the twin-bedded room once occupied by Kiki and Charlie. With the weather worsening the inn is all but empty, but Morgan still feels safer here than at home. Besides, Lissa seems to have overcome her hostility to Stacey, at least enough to babysit Ryan while his mother performs her duties around the inn.

At lunchtime Morgan volunteers to relieve her daughter, but Lissa shakes her head.

'He's cute,' she says, fumbling with the baby's nappy. 'Besides, I've got to learn sometime.'

Morgan decides not to ask if this means her daughter has made a final decision about her pregnancy. Lissa will confide in her in her own good time.

Alone in 'Falcon', she boots up her laptop and writes a summary of everything she's learned about Anjelica Fry and Karl Savage. Amid the catalogue of dead ends (Nigel Cundy's refusal to discuss the baby farm, dismissive police officers, the sleazy solicitor, the oleaginous Harley Street odontologist, the disappearance of 'Spike') there shines one glimmer of hope: the seed of doubt in the mind of Ben Gaminara. Morgan is tempted to text the fire scene investigator to request another meeting, but as she taps out a message she stops mid-sentence.

Does she really want help? Or is she looking for an excuse to flirt? Even if he returns the compliment, is she ready to trust again? To risk another soul-crushing disappointment? Another broken heart? Recalling the pet-with-no-name snoozing on the pink bra, she decides to let sleeping cats lie.

As a week of late October rain sets in, a pattern emerges. Each day, Morgan closets herself in her room, poring over the cache of online court reports and articles on Anjelica's trial, scrutinising every detail. She emails DI Tucker, asking if he knows the whereabouts of Karl's drug-dealing pal, Spike. The police officer's three-word reply is terse, bordering on rude.

Not a clue.

Without a surname, Morgan has no idea how to begin looking for Karl's crony. Lissa never met the man, or any of her ex's friends. Is Spike even his real name? Are he and Karl on the lam together? Or does he have a roof over his head? Is he giving Karl shelter? Is the drug-dealing duo still in business? Have they expanded their operation to include a baby farm operating behind bars?

As Morgan's research continues, Lissa busies herself by babysitting Ryan while Stacey works long hours. An unlikely bond seems to be growing between the two young women. On more than one occasion Morgan sees them locked in earnest conversation, once half-hearing what sounds like a heated argument. When asked what the row was about, Lissa shrugs.

'Arsenal, probably.'

An obvious lie – Lissa hates football – but Morgan decides not to press the point.

'What do you find to talk about?'

'Pregnancy stuff: morning sickness, episiotomies, breast-feeding.'

On the one hand, Morgan feels jealous that this charmless, stroppy stranger seems to have usurped her role as Lissa's confidante; on the other, she knows that any advice a mother offers is likely to be ignored or, worse, backfire. She would happily listen to her daughter's ruminations over the pregnancy and play devil's advocate for as long as it takes, but this must be Lissa's decision.

Returning to her room, fresh from a Friday morning swim, Morgan finds Stacey tidying the notes and press clippings littering her bed. The cleaner points to a handwritten heading in a Moleskine notebook. *How did Kiki die?*

'Says here you think someone pushed her off the cliff.'

No apology for snooping. Morgan lets it pass.

'It's one possibility.'

Stacey starts making the bed.

'I reckon she jumped.'

'Maybe. It's important to consider all angles.'

'Why would anyone push her?'

'Good question.'

The woman strips the sheets from the bed, still focused on the notebook.

'You put Trevor Jukes's name top of the list.'

'Yes.'

'Are these all suspects? People with motives to murder Kiki?'

'Possibly.'

'So why've you written Karl Savage? He's dead.'

Morgan picks up the notebook and closes the cover.

'I find it helps to think on paper,' she says. 'I'm determined to find out what happened to your friend and her baby. Isn't that what you want?'

''Course I do. But you're barking up the wrong tree.'

'You sound very sure.'

The woman stares at her. She seems on the verge of saying something but the conversation is interrupted by the arrival of Lissa, holding a bawling Ryan in her arms.

'He's been sick twice and he won't stop crying.'

Stacey frowns.

'Can't you see I'm working?'

'Er, yes,' says Lissa. 'But he's your baby.'

Rolling her eyes, the woman takes her son in her arms and stomps out of the room like a sulky teenager. The baby's cries slowly recede into the distance.

'What were you talking about?' says Lissa.

'Kiki.'

'Any news?'

'No,' says Morgan. 'But I can't help wondering if Stacey knows more than she's letting on. Has she said anything to you?'

'No,' says Lissa, picking up the Moleskine notebook. 'Can I look at your notes?'

'Of course.'

Lissa sits on the bed and begins to flick through the pages. Morgan hears the baby's cries dying away. She closes the door

Cavalry Barracks Reading Group, J

Reserved Item

Branch: Deal Library

Date: 16/03/2023   Time: 12:04 PM

Name: Cavalry Barracks Reading
         Group, Janet Goodings

ID: ...0346

Item: Kill me twice
         C334128767

Expires:06 Apr 2023

Instruction: Please process item

then goes into the bathroom to take a shower, trying to suppress a feeling of gathering gloom.

Eight days into Stacey Brown's new life 'on the out', a van deliv- ers a package by registered post. Morgan happens to be walking through reception when the pink-haired woman opens the Jiffy bag. She catches a glimpse of what looks like two passports.

That evening, she treats Lissa to supper at the local chippy, There's a Plaice for Us. She makes it clear that she's expecting a heart-to-heart – just her and her daughter – but it's not long before the conversation turns to Stacey.

'Can we lend her some cash?' says Lissa.

'Who's "we"?'

A sigh.

'Can *you* lend her some?'

'What for?'

'She needs to get to Cornwall so she can leave Ryan with her mum while she gets her life back on track.'

Morgan considers the request while sprinkling vinegar on her haddock.

'Can't you lend her some money? Out of your allowance from your dad?'

'I already have. She's cleaned me out.'

Morgan frowns.

'How much have you lent her?'

'Over three hundred. She's got lots of debts.'

Picking up a chip, Morgan studies her daughter's face.

'How long would the loan be for?'

'Not long. She just needs to look for another job, find somewhere to live.'

'Isn't Eric paying her?'

'Only minimum wage. And her mum's on benefits so Stacey needs to give *her* some dosh *and* pay the train fare.'

Morgan is struck by a thought.

'If she's going to Cornwall, why does she need a passport?'

Lissa rolls her eyes. 'I literally have no idea what you're talking about.'

That night, unable to sleep, Morgan braves torrential rain, driving to the petrol station and withdrawing £250 from the ATM.

'Thanks,' says Stacey on being presented with the cash the following morning, while polishing the reception's refectory table.

'What part of Cornwall?' says Morgan.

'Sorry?'

'Where does your mother live?'

The woman looks away, tucking the cash into the pocket of her dungarees.

'Ilfracombe.'

'Lovely,' says Morgan. 'Have a good time.'

'Cheers.'

The rain shows no sign of letting up. After an early supper, Morgan overhears Stacey asking Eric for directions to Ashford station.

'I can give you a lift,' she says.

'No need,' says Stacey. 'I'll get a taxi.'

'Save your money. What time's your train?'

'Nine in the morning.'

'We'll leave at eight,' says Morgan. 'Just to be on the safe side.'

She watches as Stacey goes into her room, then she knocks softly on the door of 'Dragonfly'.

'Lissa?'

Her daughter emerges, pale and drawn.

'I'm watching *EastEnders*.'

Morgan enters the room and closes the door. 'We need to have a conversation.'

'About?'

'Ilfracombe isn't in Cornwall,' says Morgan. 'It's in Devon.'

Her daughter frowns.

'So?'

'So why is Stacey lying about where she's going?'

For half an hour Morgan grills her daughter on Stacey's true intentions. Lissa insists she knows nothing beyond what she has already told her mother. Morgan decides to give her the benefit of the doubt.

'Come to the station in the morning. Let's see what happens.'

Overnight, the rain eases, leaving a misty start to the day. As the Radio 4 pips signal eight o'clock, Morgan loads Stacey's holdall into the boot while her daughter cradles Ryan in her arms.

'No baby seat. Can I hold him till Ashford?'

Stacey shrugs, tying her Arsenal scarf around her neck.

'Whatever.'

The drive takes forty-five minutes and passes almost entirely in strained silence.

'When are you coming back?' says Morgan.

'Depends.'

'On what?'

'How things go.'

'In Ilfracombe?'

'Yep.'

Pulling up outside the station, Morgan watches the woman strap the baby into the papoose. She's expecting Stacey to hug Lissa goodbye but there is no display of affection, merely a curt goodbye. No eye contact. Like lovers after a row.

'Now what?' sighs Lissa as they watch Stacey head for the ticket office. Morgan steers the Mini in the direction of the car park.

'We follow her. Thank God for the pink hair.'

Minutes later, Morgan and Lissa peer out from the crowded platform café, watching Stacey jostle with commuters boarding the train to St Pancras. They watch as she takes a table seat, facing the direction of travel. Sneaking onto the adjoining carriage, careful to stay out of sight of their quarry, Morgan steers her daughter to a seat facing the rear of the train. Peering through the connecting doors, she sees Stacey in the next carriage, snapping open a can of Red Bull.

'What if she sees us?' says Lissa.

'We'll make sure she doesn't.'

The journey takes just over half an hour. Morgan gazes out of the window as dormitory towns flash by. Lissa closes her eyes, leaning against the headrest, but Morgan can tell she's not asleep.

'Are you OK, Lissa?'

No reply.

As the train pulls into London, they wait for the woman in the red and white scarf to disembark. Keeping their distance, they follow her along the platform, through the ticket barrier and down an escalator. They hang back as she stops to scan a cluster of signs. The Underground is straight ahead but Stacey heads in the opposite direction. Morgan and Lissa continue their pursuit, trailing their quarry past Marks & Spencer and Boots.

Ignoring signs for the toilets, Stacey heads for the left luggage office. Morgan takes cover behind a pillar, watching her quarry reach the counter. Stacey looks around, eyes roving the busy concourse. She checks her watch then blows out her cheeks and lets the holdall fall to the ground. Casting another glance at her watch, she checks it against the station clock, her gaze almost landing in Lissa's direction.

Morgan darts behind the pillar, pulling her daughter close. When she looks again, Stacey is talking to a man. Bald, stocky. He has his back to Morgan. She can't see his face. She watches as he fishes something from his pocket – a slip of paper. He's saying something, wagging a finger at Stacey. She snatches the piece of paper from his hand. The man pats Ryan on the head then turns towards the exit. As he walks away, Morgan catches a glimpse of his profile and gasps.

'What?' says Lissa.

'Trevor Jukes. From the prison.'

They watch Stacey hand the slip of paper to the attendant at the left luggage counter then fumble in her dungarees for her passport. The man scans her ID then walks into the back of the office, reappearing moments later with two Tesco bags. Pulling Lissa back behind the pillar, Morgan watches Stacey delve into the bags and produce two large cans. The labels look familiar. Baby formula.

Morgan frowns, thinking aloud.

'But she's breastfeeding.'

They watch the woman transfer the tins from the Tesco bag to her holdall then walk in the direction of the Underground. Following at a steady pace, they join the swarm of commuters streaming towards King's Cross. Emerging from St Pancras, they follow her into the adjoining station and towards the Tube.

'Piccadilly line,' says Morgan. 'My guess? We're heading for Heathrow.'

Stacey passes through the barrier, swiping her Oyster card then heading down the escalator. Morgan and Lissa follow suit. Hanging back at the far end of the platform, jostling with the crowds, they watch as the woman with the papoose squeezes her way onto the first train that pulls in.

They board the adjoining carriage, Morgan keeping tabs on Stacey through the linking door. The carriage is hot and crowded. Standing room only. Lissa stares into the middle distance, face flushed.

'Are you feeling OK?'

'Fuck's sake, Mum, stop asking if I'm OK.'

At each stop commuters get off, heading for offices and shops. It's not long before the train is half empty, then almost deserted, apart from Morgan, Lissa and their quarry in the next carriage. Morgan flicks through a tattered copy of *Metro*. Lissa dozes.

An hour later the train pulls in at Heathrow. Morgan and Lissa trail Stacey as she follows signs for 'Departures'. They join the throng gliding upwards on a series of escalators, maintaining a safe distance as Stacey scans a monitor then joins a check-in queue.

Morgan squints at the illuminated logo above the desk.

Turkish Airlines.

A flight number.

Destination: Istanbul.

Nineteen

KARL

He lets the beam from his torch range over the dank cellar. His books, his supply of chocolate, the picture of Guy Fawkes on the lid of the tin. He can hear the distant sound of the fireworks party in the garden next door.

Whoosh . . . Bang . . .

Ooooh . . . Aaaah . . ..

Same as last birthday. And the birthday before. The cellar is still cold, still damp, but better than it used to be. He's made sure of that, little by little over the years: a cushion for his head, a duvet instead of a blanket and a plentiful supply of batteries for his torch, so he can read.

Sci-fi, mainly. Any world is better than this one.

At least it's only weekends – after school on Friday until bath time on Sunday evening. The rest of the week she lets him have the run of the house. He's not clear why, because she still won't talk to him.

Not a single word in the five years since Dad died.

Not.

One.

Word.

That's the hardest part. Not the cellar, not the cold – the silence.

He hears her talking to other people. Men she brings back from the pub on a Friday night – one man in particular, the man Karl calls The Whistler. But she never talks to him. Never to her son.

Maybe she finds having him around on weekdays easier because he's at school most of the day. Yes, that must be it, because during the holidays he has to spend more time down here. Or maybe she just doesn't want him getting in her way on weekends, when she brings men home.

He has protested, on more than one occasion, but not for long. She has ways of making her displeasure known. Ways he doesn't want to think about. Better to just go along with it.

Besides, he's used to it now. You can get used to anything. This is normal – for him, at least. He knows it's not the case for other people. He's been to friends' houses. Birthday parties, things like that.

The mother of a school friend asked if everything was OK at home. Karl said yes. Simpler that way.

She comes to school when she has no choice. Parents' meetings, that sort of thing. She takes him to the dentist or doctor when necessary. Pretends to be interested, puts on a good show. No one would know.

But now she's pregnant. Presumably by The Whistler or one of the other blokes from the pub. She's grown so bloody fat it's impossible for anyone to tell she's going to have a baby. Karl wouldn't have known if he hadn't chanced upon the pregnancy test in the bin.

He hasn't mentioned it. What would be the point? She won't tell him anything. A baby is almost certainly not what she had in mind, but he can't be sure if it counts as good news or bad news.

He closes his eyes, *wishing* it could be good news.

So she'll be in a better mood. Maybe talk to him.

But he hears Dad's voice in his head.

If wishes were horses then beggars would ride . . .

Twenty

Thirty-six hours after Stacey flies to Istanbul, dusk falls over Dungeness beach as Morgan parks around the corner from the prison. In the distance, the black and white lighthouse, built in 1904, is a quaint reminder of another era, a time long gone, a time of lost innocence. The old-style café that sits alongside the Romney Hythe and Dymchurch Railway still offers iced buns and tea from an urn. Today more than ever, the wind singing eerily in the telegraph wires sounds like music from a horror movie, and the bleak, windswept landscape feels like the land that time forgot. Inside the prison languishes a woman forgotten by the world. Meanwhile a baby is missing, a woman has lost her life, and a psychopath is back from the dead, impregnating women without their knowledge or consent. If Morgan feels overwhelmed, it's hardly surprising.

Waiting for Jukes to finish his shift, she kills time by googling *surveillance techniques*. Tailing Stacey and her baby was one thing; keeping tabs on the prison officer may not be so straightforward. But the websites offer little she doesn't already know or can't figure out for herself.

Study your target's habits and routines.

If following a car at night, put a small strip of reflective tape on the rear bumper.

Two-vehicle surveillance increases the chances of success.

Lissa is confined to her room at the inn, pole-axed by a bout of morning sickness that shows no sign of letting up. If she doesn't recover by tonight, Morgan will take her to a doctor. She searches the web for articles on *nausea in pregnancy* but wishes she hadn't. Severe morning sickness can be a predictor of twins; hormone levels are higher than when expecting a single baby.

Twins?

Fathered by Karl Savage?

Like Nancy Sixmith's?

She pushes the thought from her mind, forcing herself to focus on Trevor Jukes and his thinly veiled threat.

Take care of yourself. And your lovely daughter.

She silently chastises Neville Rook for not being more rigorous in his questioning of the prison officer, but without new evidence, without something concrete, there's little point in contacting the DI again.

As Morgan begins to make another roll-up, the sight of Jukes rounding the corner causes her to spill the tobacco onto her lap. Sinking low in her seat, she watches as he walks towards the staff car park, oblivious to her presence, whistling the tune from *The Archers*. Under his arm is a helmet. Donning it, he stops beside an old Yamaha motorcycle, clambers aboard and fires up the engine. Morgan waits until he reaches the exit and then she begins her pursuit.

With no other vehicles in sight, following the motorbike is almost too easy. Jukes drives at a steady 40 mph, navigating the tarmac road that snakes past the quarry pits and cuts through the huge expanse of shingle. Crossing the railway track, the landscape gives way to another road that leads towards rows of pebbledash bungalows facing out to sea.

Now, as cars whiz past, heading away from Romney Marsh, Morgan begins to feel less conspicuous. Careful to keep her distance, she follows Jukes along the road that hugs the seafront. After a mile and a half, she sees him indicating a left turn. Pausing at the junction, she steers the Mini into a side street, passing a row of lock-up garages. The Yamaha is now a hundred yards ahead, indicating another turn. For a moment, Morgan wonders if he's spotted her. Perhaps he saw her outside the prison? Is he doubling back, trying to shake her off? Or luring her to an isolated spot?

Should she have brought a weapon?

A knife?

A baseball bat?

Too late now.

Slowing the Mini, she reaches out to lock both doors, then follows the motorcycle as it makes a right turn. The side street is potholed and lined with bungalows, smaller and shabbier than those with sea views. Up ahead, the Yamaha pulls onto a concrete driveway outside a dilapidated bungalow. A weed-filled front yard. A gate hanging from its hinges. A green wheelie bin crammed with bulging black bags.

Morgan sees a seagull pecking at the garbage, foraging for scraps. She watches Jukes clap his hands to scare the bird away. Then he dismounts from the motorcycle, passing an abandoned sofa on his way to the door of number six. Morgan drives past, taking a right turn and pulling to a halt by a corner shop. She counts to ten before climbing out of the car and walking to the corner, peering at the squat, ugly house.

There's no sign of Jukes, but light shines through the rippled glass of the front door. Morgan takes a tentative step towards the yard then stops as a familiar piece of music – the theme from *The Archers* – blares from a downstairs window.

Tum-de-dum-de-dum-de-dum, tum-de-dum-de-dah-dah.

The irrepressibly jaunty music shatters the silence. Next door at number five a curtain twitches, but there's no other sign of life.

She imagines the scene inside the house: Jukes chucking his keys on the kitchen table and setting the kettle to boil, or maybe opening a beer while listening to his favourite soap opera. She considers her options. Knocking on the door is out of the question. What would she say to the man who knows she tried to alert the police to the existence of the baby farm?

A few doors down, three young men are emerging from another house. They wear hoodies and trainers. As they lope towards Morgan, she averts her gaze, feigning interest in her mobile, but they slow their pace.

''S'up?' says one, casting a glance at Morgan's phone. She meets his gaze. She was mistaken. They're not men, but teenagers – seventeen, maybe eighteen. One sports a small gold earring, another has a skull tattoo on his neck. The third – the one checking out her mobile – has a gap between his front teeth.

Pocketing her phone, Morgan smiles. 'Not much,' she says.

Gap-tooth narrows his eyes. 'You think we want your phone?'

'Of course not.' Morgan does her best to maintain a friendly tone.

'So why put it away?'

She refuses to be cowed, answering his question with a question. 'Why are you interested in my phone?'

'I ain't.'

'That makes two of us.'

'Leave it, man,' says Earring. 'I'm hungry.'

Gap-tooth glares at Morgan.

'Ain't no thief, you get me?'

'I get you,' says Morgan.

Neck Tattoo tugs at Gap-tooth's arm.

'We getting chips or what?'

Gap-tooth doesn't reply but walks away, keeping his steely gaze on Morgan as he follows his friends, rounding the corner and disappearing from view.

Relieved, Morgan turns to leave, then ducks to avoid the seagull as it swoops low, returning to the wheelie bin. She watches the scavenger peck at Jukes's bin bag, widening a hole in the plastic. The yard is a mess of potato peelings, eggshells

and tea bags the colour of rust. Morgan is about to head back
to her car when she sees a fragment of packaging among the
rubbish.

Bright colours. A familiar logo. Pampers nappies.

She feels a rush of blood to the head. She has no idea of the
man's circumstances. Perhaps he has a new baby. But this is not
a house occupied by a woman – at least not one who takes pride
in her surroundings.

Rooted to the spot, Morgan's eye is drawn by movement
outside the shop. An elderly man emerges clutching a can of
dog food and a newspaper. Morgan thinks for a moment then
crosses the road and enters the shop, jangling the old-fashioned
bell above the door. The woman behind the counter is refilling
racks of cigarettes. Morgan feigns interest in the meagre display
of wine, selecting two bottles of the most expensive red, a Shiraz.

'That the lot?' says the woman.

Morgan tries to ingratiate herself by splashing out.

'Make it six.'

The woman brightens, ringing up the total as Morgan places
four more bottles on the counter.

'I'm new here. What are your opening hours?'

'Seven till ten, seven days a week.'

Producing her wallet, Morgan is about to hand over her Visa
card, but the woman purses her lips, prompting her to fumble
for cash.

'What are the neighbours like?'

A shrug.

'All sorts.'

'Who's the guy at number six? The one with the motorcycle.'

The woman frowns.

'Who wants to know?'

Morgan gives a coy smile.

'Always had a thing for baldies.' She hands over the cash. 'Does he have a wife? Girlfriend? Kids?'

The woman rings up the sale and shakes her head.

'Trevor's a loner.' She glances out of the window. 'Anyway, what woman would live in a dump like that?'

Leaving the shop, Morgan casts another look at the nappy packaging in Jukes's wheelie bin. She scans the bungalow. How can she scope out the house? Breaking in seems a high-risk strategy.

Maybe there's another way.

She spots the gaggle of male police officers the moment she enters the pub. Bad haircuts, crumpled suits, shiny shoes. The Anchor is renowned as the coppers' watering hole. Many Dungeness locals (eccentrics, recluses, people with something to hide) won't venture inside for fear of attracting the wrong kind of attention.

DI Rook is at the bar, ordering drinks while joking with the barmaid. His smile withers as he catches sight of Morgan.

'Don't I get a night off?'

His voice is slurred. Morgan fishes cash from her pocket.

'What are you drinking, Neville?'

'Hemlock. Make it a double.' He waves her money away. 'My round. You do the next one.'

Morgan smiles, meeting his eye while lowering her head, Princess Diana-style.

'Red wine, please. Shiraz for preference but Merlot will do.'

Rook doesn't introduce her to his colleagues. He distributes the round of drinks then follows her outside into the pub garden. She sits at a table, sipping her wine and rolling a cigarette.

'Make one for me?'

She obliges, making small talk before steering the conversation to the Pampers in Jukes's bin. The DI rolls his eyes.

'Are you trying to take advantage of the fact I've had a drink?'

'No, I'm reporting suspicious behaviour. Doing my civic duty.'

He gives a snort of derision then sips his pint.

'Who says the nappies belong to Jukes?'

'They're in his bin.'

'Maybe he's got a friend with a baby. Maybe he's a weirdo who gets a kick out of dressing up as a baby. Maybe the neighbours dump their rubbish in his bin.'

'Or maybe he's got Kiki's baby.'

Morgan hands him the cigarette. She lights her own then holds out the lighter. He cups his hands around the flame. Draws the smoke into his lungs. Meets her gaze.

'Are you single, Morgan?'

The question comes out of the blue.

'Yes, I'm single.'

'Happy that way?'

'Most of the time. There's a high price to pay for being able to say "we".'

He sips his pint.

'So why do people get married?'

'Being alone is hard.'

He nods, dragging on his cigarette. 'Way I look at it, marriage was invented when people died at forty. Now it's eighty or ninety. Fifty years with the same bloody person, maybe more. You'd get less for murder.'

Morgan manages a smile.

'Speaking of which . . .'

Another roll of the eyes.

'Not Kiki McNeil again.'

'I'm not a relationship counsellor, Neville, I'm a journalist trying to right a miscarriage of justice. I'm doing you the courtesy of coming to you first.'

'First?'

'Before I write something for the papers. About what happened to Kiki. About the lack of progress in the search for Charlie. About an innocent woman banged up for a murder she didn't commit.'

He frowns.

'I can't help what you write.'

'No, but you can follow up a lead handed to you on a plate.'

He sighs. 'There's a word for women like you.'

'Don't tell me. Begins with C.'

He shakes his head. 'R. For relentless.'

She smiles. 'Charmer.'

The following day, on the dot of 7 a.m., Morgan is back in Jukes's road, parked at a discreet distance and watching as Rook and two uniformed officers work their way along the row of pebble-dash bungalows. 'Routine house-to-house' is how the PCs have been told to explain this phase of the search for the missing baby. A brief conversation on Jukes's doorstep will prove nothing, but it's an effective opening gambit, a way to get a feel for the situation without revealing suspicions.

Morgan watches Neville ring the bell of number six. Seconds later the door is opened by Jukes. In uniform. Ready for work. He listens to Rook then follows the policeman's gaze as he points towards the wheelie bin. The Pampers packaging is clearly visible amid the rubbish spilling from the bin bag. Morgan sees Jukes saying something to Rook. To her surprise, the prison officer waves an expansive hand, ushering the DI and one of the PCs into his house, then closing the door.

Wishing she'd brought coffee, Morgan settles down to wait. Across the road, the corner shop is opening for business. The elderly dog owner emerges from his house with an ancient black Labrador hobbling in his wake. They set off for the sea-front, passing the Mini without registering Morgan's presence. She's tempted to roll a cigarette, but it's too early, even for her. Lissa was barely awake when she left the inn, complaining of sore breasts and exhausted by yesterday's vomiting marathon. Another duvet day.

And now Jukes's front door is opening. The police officers emerge. Rook shakes the householder's hand, then walks away followed by the PC. How long were they inside? Two minutes? Three? Just long enough to scope out the bungalow. Morgan watches as Jukes locks the front door then dons his helmet and climbs aboard his motorcycle. A couple of revs of the engine and he's gone, rounding the corner and disappearing from view.

Craning her neck, she sees Rook directing his colleagues to a police car at the end of the street. The officers head for the car. The door-to-door charade is over.

Morgan reaches for her mobile and dials Rook's number. She watches him fish his phone from his pocket and answer the call.

'Hi, Neville.'

He scans the street.

'Where are you?'

'In the Mini.'

The DI turns, sees the car then heads in her direction, his phone still clamped to his ear. 'He was helpful,' he says. 'Invited us in, showed us round.'

'And?'

'No baby, no sign of a baby.'

'How did he explain the nappies?'

'His sister had a little girl. Couple of months ago. They came to stay at the weekend.'

'Do you believe him?'

The man has reached her car. He pockets his phone as she lowers the window. He's missed a spot shaving, his eyes are bloodshot.

'He showed us a selfie,' he says. 'Him, the sister and the baby.'

'Which proves nothing. Could have been taken any time.'

'He said it was taken this weekend.'

'And you believe him.'

'No reason not to.'

Morgan sighs.

'So we're none the wiser.'

'Speak for yourself.'

Resisting the urge to press her case, Morgan opens the car door, climbs out and stretches her arms above her head. The DS has done her a good turn, going out on a limb on her behalf.

'Can I buy you breakfast, Neville?'

The man looks away for a moment. When he turns to her, his response takes her by surprise.

'Why don't I buy you dinner instead?'

Morgan arches an eyebrow.

'Is your fiancée coming?'

A pause. He clears his throat.

'We had a row. She's gone to her mum's.'

'Oh. I'm sorry.'

His eyes search hers.

'Are you?'

'Of course.'

'Right,' says Rook. He scratches his neck and clears this throat. 'I thought you liked me.'

'I do.'

'I mean . . .'

'I know what you mean,' says Morgan. 'I'm sorry if I gave you the wrong impression.'

The man blows out his cheeks and looks away.

'Why are we doing this, Morgan?'

She chooses her words carefully.

'I'm "doing this" because I believe Jukes is involved in a baby farm racket. And possibly the murder of Kiki O'Neil. And the abduction of her baby.'

She doesn't mention the prison officer's link to the man who got her daughter pregnant. As far as Rook is concerned, the fact that Pablo and Karl Savage are one and the same – Morgan's unshakeable belief that Savage is alive – makes her what his pals at the Anchor would doubtless call a 'nutjob'.

'This needs to stop,' he says, sighing. 'Flirting, playing detective – it all needs to stop.'

'I'm not "playing" at anything,' says Morgan, feeling a stir of anger. 'I'm trying to get to the truth. And justice for Angelica Fry.'

He gives her a sideways look.

'I spoke to DI Tucker in London,' he says. 'About you.'

'Let me guess, he said I'm a troublemaker, mad as a box of frogs.'

'Wouldn't go that far,' says Rook. 'But he and I are on the same page.' He buttons his jacket and holds himself erect. 'I'm serious. No more "Let me buy you breakfast". And no more Mr Nice Guy.'

Turning on his heel, he walks towards the police car where the PCs are waiting. Morgan watches them drive away.

Turning her collar against the wind, she casts a final look at the litter-strewn yard of number six. The Pampers packaging protrudes from the tattered bin bag. As she heads for the Mini, the seagull circles overhead, then swoops onto the bungalow's roof, its cries echoing along the deserted street. Morgan turns towards the corner as she hears the rumble of a lorry.

No, a dustcart.

Brakes squealing, the vehicle shudders to a halt at the end of the road. Two bin men jump down from the cab. They work their way along the road, shifting wheelie bins from front yards to kerb.

Acting on impulse, Morgan darts back to number six. Reaches over the gate. Grabs the bag jutting from Jukes's bin. Tugging hard, she prises it loose, dropping it onto the pavement at her feet. She leans over to grab the second bag. Hauls it from the bin.

The dustmen draw nearer. One points in her direction, shouting something she can't make out. She ignores him. The bag is leaking its contents. Cramming sheets of spilled paper into her pocket, she takes off her jacket and wraps it over the hole to prevent further spillage. Clutching the first bag, she grabs the second with her free hand and heads for the Mini. She shoves the bags onto the back seat.

Trying not to gag at the stench, she gets behind the wheel and drives away with her booty, the mocking jeers of the dustmen ringing in her ears.

Twenty-One

Searching for a place to sift through Jukes's rubbish, Morgan settles for the deserted car park of the Beach Inn. She empties both bin bags, creating two piles: one of cans, bottles and food, the other of cardboard and paper. Crouched on her haunches, she sees two empty Pampers packages but no soiled nappies. Dozens of lager cans and polystyrene food containers suggest that the prison officer's diet would not please his doctor. His reading habits seem limited to *TV Times*. A flick through the pages reveals a selection of programmes circled in red. The man is an ardent sports fan with a subscription to Sky and an interest in Formula One. He also likes nature programmes and *Coronation Street*. Last Thursday he watched (or intended to watch) *Off the Grid*, a reality show following a group of survivalists attempting to stay hidden from society. His fondness for *The Archers* is already a known factor.

Morgan separates the paper from the cardboard: a cornflakes box, Rizla packets and tubes from three toilet rolls. She's left with a pile of tea bag-stained paper including receipts, pizza flyers and payslips from HMP Dungeness. Not surprisingly, Jukes is poorly paid, topping up his wages with regular overtime. Two brochures suggest the man has aspirations beyond his means. The first showcases top-of-the-range Harley-Davidsons; the second features a two-bedroom villa in Malaga, on the market for €90,000.

On the verge of giving up, it's the final scrap of paper that raises hairs on the back of Morgan's neck. An invoice on headed paper.

River Marsh Farm, Romney Marsh, TN99 8QT
For the attention of Mr T. Jukes
Annual houseboat mooring fees for Wandering Star: £200.

'Mum? What the actual fuck?'

Morgan looks up to see Lissa approaching. She's wearing her outsize towelling robe and Doc Martens.

'Feel better?'

Her daughter pulls a face.

'I'm not throwing up. That's progress.' She points at the mound of rubbish. 'Since when are you a bag lady?'

Morgan gets to her feet.

'The noble science of garbology. I'm going through Jukes's rubbish.'

'And?'

'I'll tell you over a bacon sandwich.'

Lissa closes her eyes.

'Don't mention food.'

She remains silent for a moment, then her face crumples. When she opens her eyes, they're glistening with tears.

Morgan tenses.

Her daughter has made a decision.

Life comes down to a few key moments. This is one of them.

'Time to talk?'

Lissa nods, then bites her lip as tears well in her eyes.

'I keep thinking about what Pablo said.' She fumbles for a tissue. 'He asked me what was the worst thing you could do to a woman, I said, "Kill her, rape her?" He said that would be too easy, too ordinary.'

Morgan blinks.

'So what was his "worst thing"?'

Her daughter's gaze remains fixed on the horizon. Her hands tremble, her voice is shaky.

'The worst thing would be to sentence her to a life with a child she'd never wanted, fathered by a man she despised.'

Morgan lets the words sink in.

What kind of person would *think* this way?

She recalls the video of the man setting fire to the Porsche.

The Joker.

'But I'm *so* going to prove him wrong,' says Lissa, her lips quivering. Morgan holds her breath. She knows what's coming.

'I've researched this psychopath bullshit,' says Lissa. 'There's no concrete evidence to prove it's hereditary. And even if it *is*, lots of people say that nurture trumps nature.' She draws breath. 'So I'm going to keep my baby, Mum. And I'm going to love it to within an inch of its life.'

Exhaling slowly, Morgan does her best to make her smile tender and reassuring. After all the talking, no explanation is required. The decision seems inevitable – already the new normal. For more than a year Lissa has been a lost soul, struggling to find her way in the world, but now there is purpose, something larger than herself, something to get out of bed for every day. It's not the *raison d'être* Morgan would have chosen for her daughter – life will be hard – but John Lennon's observation remains as true as ever.

Life is what happens while we're making other plans.

'Will you help?' says Lissa.

Morgan hugs her daughter close.

'Try and stop me.'

Lissa is shaking, her body heaving with sobs.

'I'm sorry,' she says. 'I'm *so* sorry . . .'

'We'll be fine,' says Morgan. The 'we' is crucial.

Lissa blows her nose, then tucks the tissue into her sleeve, turning her face to the sun and breathing out slowly. Crouching down, Morgan stuffs the rubbish back into the bags.

'Find anything?' says Lissa.

'Not unless you want a Harley-Davidson or a villa in Spain.'

Turning away, Morgan surreptitiously slips the mooring invoice into her pocket, then gets to her feet. Linking arms with her daughter, she leads her towards the hotel. She will check out the houseboat soon – without involving Lissa.

From now on, there are three lives to consider.

The world feels a colder, darker place.

It's seventy-two hours before Morgan manages to get away to visit River Marsh Farm. The second half of the week passes in a flurry of activity: a visit to the GP; appointments with the midwife; stocking up on folic acid; buying new bras and baby books; deciding when to break the news to Lissa's father in LA.

'He'll be hurt if you don't tell him soon,' says Morgan, driving back from a shopping trip to Canterbury. But Lissa has made up her mind.

'Not till the second trimester.'

Having prevaricated for so long, she now seems decisive about what lies ahead. There's no debate about home birthing; her child will be born in hospital with every available form of pain relief. Rebecca for a girl; Jake for a boy.

There's no mention of how Lissa intends to provide for her child (Morgan maintains a diplomatic silence on the subject), nor any further discussion of the baby's father – at least, not until suppertime on the second day after the decision to proceed with the pregnancy. The inn's small restaurant is almost full, a harassed-looking Eric Sweet acting as both waiter and chef.

'Will he have any legal rights?' says Lissa, looking gloomy.

Morgan lays down her fork and takes a sip of wine. Her daughter is barely eating, and sticking to water. The drunken binge was a one-off, and there have been no more vodka bottles stashed under the bed. From now on, no alcohol, no caffeine. Morgan has considered trying to quit smoking – again – in a show of solidarity, but there's too much going on. As a compromise, she'll smoke only when Lissa isn't around.

'Legally, Karl is dead,' says Morgan. 'How can he claim rights unless he surfaces and gives himself away?'

A shrug. Lissa pushes a cherry tomato around her plate.

'Am I like Dad?'

The question takes Morgan by surprise.

'In some ways.'

Bolshie. Self-absorbed. A fan of the three-day sulk.

'So what happens if my baby *is* like Pablo?'

The certainties of the other day have evaporated.

'You mean, tall, dark and handsome?'

Her daughter is in no mood for levity.

'I mean, what if it's a psychopath?'

'That's not how it works.'

'You don't know that.'

Morgan reaches across the table, taking her daughter's hand.

'You are going to have a gorgeous, healthy baby. And meet a lovely man, if that's what you want. And have a great life.'

Her daughter's eyes fill with tears.

'Can we change the subject?'

'What would you like to talk about?'

'Anything to take my mind off how I've fucked up. How about you and the fire scene investigator? The fit bloke with the nice arse.'

'And the romcom-loving girlfriend?'

'Have you heard from him?' Lissa wipes her nose. 'Texted? Called?'

'I am *so* not having this conversation.'

Her daughter shrugs, swallowing the tomato then laying down her fork with a clatter. She seems scattered, unable to focus. She switches to another topic. 'What about the baby farm?'

'I've written to the prison governor.

'And?'

'He'll deny all knowledge. At best, he'll launch an internal enquiry, which will uncover nothing.'

'So that's that?'

'Unless I can persuade someone at the prison to go on the record, which isn't going to happen.' Nigel Cundy's face flashes briefly into Morgan's mind. 'Everyone has something to hide or something to lose.'

Lissa blows out her cheeks, a picture of misery.

'When did everything get so complicated?'

The following morning, while her daughter is walking on the beach, Morgan sits on the balcony, trying to imagine what she might say in a text to Ben Gaminara.

My daughter is pregnant by a sociopath who faked his own death. I'm thirty-eight and sick of doing everything on my own. I hate romcoms except The Apartment *and* When Harry Met Sally. *Drink?*

She composes a number of variations but deletes them.

He's in a relationship. Focus on your daughter. And finding out what happened to Kiki and Charlie. And helping Anjelica and Marlon. Isn't that enough?

Pocketing her phone, she lights a roll-up then stares out to sea, eyes fixed on the horizon until she falls asleep, the cigarette dropping onto the deck.

In her dream, a baby boy with a heart-shaped mole on his forearm is locked in an adjoining hotel room. She can hear him but can't reach him. She smells smoke, hears the crackle of flames . . .

And wakes with a start.

Sits bolt upright.

Heart pounding, she takes a moment to recover her composure, then goes inside to check on her daughter. Lissa has taken to bed with a pile of pregnancy books and her iPad.

'I'm going out,' says Morgan, poking her head around the door. 'Will you be OK?'

Her daughter doesn't look up from the screen. Her voice sounds thick with cold.

'Did you know that callous and unemotional traits associated with psychopaths can now be detected in infants?'

Morgan ignores the question.

'Do you need anything, Lissa?'

A brisk shake of the head, then she is dismissed.

Twenty minutes later Morgan is driving past a wind farm on the road to Romney Marsh. Mile after mile of bleak but beautiful wetlands. Aside from flocks of birds and sheep there is no sign of life. The landscape is deserted, a bitterly cold wind blowing in from the sea. This used to be smugglers' terrain. The seventeenth-century gangs were known as owlers because of the owl-like noises they made when signalling at night. During the Second World War the government drew up plans in case of invasion. The marsh was to be flooded, then drenched with oil and set ablaze. Now there is a wide variety of wildlife, the Royal Military Canal and huge fenced-off tracts of land, designated as Ministry of Defence training areas.

River Marsh Farm is not easy to find. A succession of villages and lanes with no signposts builds an impression of an inbred community wary of outsiders. If it weren't for Google Maps, Morgan would be lost. Instead, reaching her destination, she pulls to a halt on a verge opposite a muddy, rutted track leading to the farm. She glances at the invoice in her hand.

For the attention of Mr T Jukes
Annual houseboat mooring fees for Wandering Star: £200

Half a mile along the lane she comes to a disused track overhung with sycamore trees. She overshoots, then reverses, squeezing the Mini alongside the hedgerow. Stepping out of the car, she grabs her wellingtons from the boot, donning them while straining to catch the slightest sound. The sea-salted wind is gaining force, but there is no birdsong, no traffic, no farm machinery.

She listens, savouring the silence.

How the world used to sound.

She walks along the lane until she comes to a dilapidated fence. Climbing over, she drops down into the wheat field, stalks bristling from the harvest. The landscape is flat. She sees the farmhouse in the distance, surrounded by outbuildings. No sign of life, no dogs in the yard, no smoke rising from the chimney. Staying low, keeping to the edge of the field, she heads for the river. It's further than she thought, requiring her to cross another field and negotiate a barbed wire fence that borders a hedgerow on one side, a thicket of trees on the other.

Emerging into a clearing, she can see the river up ahead: a sliver of still water, green with algae and barely broader than the width of a houseboat. The banks are overgrown with ferns and reeds; the water smells brackish and stale.

No sign of a path. No choice but to trample along the bank, feeling the dried-out reeds crunch underfoot. Rounding a bend, the river curves away from the direction of the farmhouse, broadening to a stretch rendered gloomy by overhanging trees.

And there it is. The houseboat. Or what's left of it. Wedged between the banks of the river. Its name, *Wandering Star*, was daubed on the side long ago. The faded paint is the only decoration. Years of neglect have reduced the vessel to little more than a wreck: one cabin window is boarded up, the weather-beaten door is sealed with a rusty padlock.

Morgan inches forward. Her eyes dart everywhere, searching for signs of activity – broken reeds, flattened ferns – but there is no indication that anyone has been here recently. A few more steps bring her alongside the houseboat. Cupping her hands over a porthole, she peers inside, but the darkness is total.

Then she hears it in the distance.

Faint but unmistakable.

Someone whistling.

The theme from *The Archers*.

Blood pounding in her ears, she scans the riverbank. There is no sign of life. The whistling grows louder, coming from the opposite direction, further along the river. Hastily retracing her steps, wincing as reeds crunch underfoot, Morgan retreats, pausing as she reaches a clump of bushes.

The whistling stops.

Craning her neck, she glimpses movement in the distance. Someone is heading her way. Making for the houseboat. She backs into the bushes. Crouching low. Pulling the branches around her.

Two figures are approaching. The whistling starts again.

She sees Trevor Jukes clutching a holdall and drawing alongside *Wandering Star*. The second figure follows close behind. Morgan can't make out a face. She watches Jukes clamber aboard the houseboat. He moves aside, revealing his companion.

Stacey Brown.

Holding her baby.

Twenty-Two

Speeding back to Dungeness, Morgan considers telling Neville Rook about Stacey's return from Istanbul but dismisses the idea. The DI couldn't have been more clear.

No more Mr Nice Guy.

Next time she tries to tip off the police she needs hard evidence that someone is breaking the law.

By the time she gets back to the inn, the beach is in darkness apart from the beam from the lighthouse and the distant lights of the power station. Lissa is still confined to bed, nursing her cold, her face illuminated by the glow from her iPad, her cheeks streaked with tears.

'What's up?'

Her daughter points to a photo on a news website. It shows a boatload of refugees in a flimsy dinghy.

'The traffickers make extra cash selling lifejackets to the refugees,' Lissa says, sniffing. 'Parents buy them for babies. But they're fake, just foam and plastic. And the traffickers *know*.' Tears rolling down her cheeks, she shakes her head in disbelief. 'How can anyone do that? To a *baby*?'

Morgan says nothing. She takes her daughter's hand, letting the seconds tick by.

'Have you eaten?'

A sniff and a nod.

'Eric made scrambled eggs.'

'How's the vomiting?'

'Just once since this morning.'

'Taken your vitamins?'

Lissa closes her eyes, leaning back against the pillow.

'Fuck's sake, Mum. People are killing babies and you're worried about folic acid?'

Morgan has been wondering whether to tell her daughter about Stacey and her baby. The decision is made. Now is not the time.

'Need anything?'

Lissa shakes her head.

'Where have you been?'

'Driving, walking, thinking,' says Morgan, lying by omission, but all in a good cause. She takes the iPad from her daughter's hand and places it on the bedside table. Lissa's face crumples, a bubble of snot forming in her nostril.

'You know the weirdest thing? Part of me actually *wants* him to call.'

Morgan frowns.

'Pablo?'

A nod.

'Does that make me crazy?'

Yes.

'It makes you pregnant. And hormonal. And normal.'

Her daughter blows her nose and looks out of the window. Out at sea, the lights from a tanker are visible on the horizon.

'What do you think Anjelica Fry is doing?' she says.

'Looking after her baby,' says Morgan. 'Like you need to look after yours.

She hands Lissa the vitamins.

'Pregnancy Nazi.'

'Get used to it.'

Alone after supper, Morgan sits on her bed, eating an apple while scrolling through contacts on her mobile. Her parents are dead, her friends have moved away or disappeared onto Planet Marriage, and life as a single mum was never conducive to forging new friendships – at least, that's how it seemed.

Cameron's name flashes by but once again the idea of calling a man she knew twenty years ago evaporates as quickly as it appears. They have only one thing in common: their daughter. If Morgan is going to open up, it needs to be to someone who understands the situation she's in, someone who *gets* her.

Reaching the XYZs, she scrolls back to the Bs, her finger hovering over *Ben Gaminara*. She hesitates, questioning her motivation for phoning the arson investigator, then thinks *fuck it*. She taps his name. The phone rings once, twice, three times. On the verge of cancelling the call, she lets the phone ring one final time.

'Hello?'

'It's Morgan Vine. Are you in the middle of something?'

'Does feeding the cat count?'

'I thought you worked all hours.'

'The cat doesn't care.'

Couldn't Pink Bra Lady feed him?

'Does he have a name yet?'

'I'm thinking of calling him Elkie.'

'Because?'

'He'll only eat elk meat. Imported from Sweden.'

'High maintenance.'

'You have no idea.'

'Can I pick your brains?' says Morgan. 'About the Karl Savage case?'

A pause.

'Have you eaten?'

'Yes,' says Morgan, regretting her reply the instant it leaves her mouth. Dinner with Ben is an appealing prospect. But it's too late.

'Never mind.' he says. 'Pick away.'

'Apart from me and Lissa, you're the only person who has doubts over Karl being dead.'

'Did I say that?'

'Not in so many words. You kept mentioning the picture hooks. The gaps where Savage took down photos before his flat was torched?'

'That's all you've got?'

'Bear with me.'

She tells him about the baby farm inside HMP Dungeness. He listens attentively, asking pertinent questions. Then he falls silent. The seconds tick by.

'Are you still there?' says Morgan.

'I'm thinking.'

Another pause. When he speaks again, his words raise hairs on the back of her neck.

'It's not much to go on, but I called the trainee I worked with during the Karl Savage investigation. He updated me on something I didn't know – something DI Tucker mentioned about Anjelica's cot catching fire when she was a baby. Her dad was a chain-smoker, apparently. Anjelica nearly died.'

'And?'

'Not surprisingly, she's a pyrophobe. I assume you know what that means?'

'She's scared of fire.'

'Not scared. Terrified.'

Under normal circumstances it takes at least two days to arrange a visitor's order, but Nigel Cundy has a word in the right ear and cuts the delay to twenty-four hours. While waiting, Morgan pays two further visits to the *Wandering Star* – one early in the morning, the other at midnight. There's no sign of Jukes, or Stacey, or her baby, only trampled reeds and a scattering of litter suggest the houseboat might be occupied.

Now, sitting in the neon-lit side room of the Mother and Baby Unit, Morgan takes stock of the dark circles under the woman's eyes.

'Where's Marlon?'

'Having a nap,' says Anjelica, staring dully at her visitor and moistening her lips with her tongue. 'Any news?'

Morgan shakes her head.

'Why didn't you tell me you're scared of fire?'

Anjelica blinks slowly. Medication is still addling her brain.

'Why would I?'

'It makes the idea of you being an arsonist absurd.'

'That's what I told the lawyers,' says Anjelica. 'They said it was "immaterial and inadmissible". Told me to let it drop.'

Morgan sighs.

'I don't think you've always had the best advice.'

She glances towards the doorway. The obese prison officer is sitting outside, feigning interest in her nails while eavesdropping on their conversation. The woman sits bolt upright, suddenly on the alert, lifting her gaze towards the door. Someone arriving?

'Spot check bull*shit*,' mutters the officer under her breath. Getting to her feet, she shoots a glare in Anjelica's direction, then lumbers away. Morgan leans forward in her chair, taking advantage of the woman's absence to ram her message home.

'Getting a case to the appeal court is like pushing boulders up a mountain. If we're to stand a chance I need you to tell me *everything* you know about the baby farm and Kiki McNeil.'

Anjelica leans back in her chair and cracks her knuckles. Once again, her movements are in slow motion; she seems oblivious to the flurry of activity in the corridor outside.

'Here we go again,' she says. 'You tell me you want to help me and Marlon but you concentrate on everyone else.'

'Because everything is connected,' says Morgan. 'The baby farm, Stacey, Karl, Jukes, Kiki – they're all *part of the same thing*.'

Anjelica blinks again, weighing Morgan's words, but before she can speak, a bearded man enters, followed by Trevor Jukes and a woman clutching a clipboard.

'Sorry to interrupt,' says the new arrival, addressing Morgan. His suit is ill fitting, his voice thin and reedy. 'Ian Carne, governor. Just a routine visit.'

His hands are clasped behind his back, reminding Morgan of members of the royal family. He flashes a thin smile at Anjelica.

'How's it going?'

Anjelica's eyes flicker towards Jukes then back to the governor. 'Like I've said a hundred times, the pillows are rock hard, the showers are freezing and I wouldn't give the food to a pig.'

A muscle twitches in the governor's cheek.

'Noted.'

'I shouldn't even be here in the first place.'

The governor's sidekick blows out her cheeks and scribbles on her clipboard. Her boss turns to Morgan.

'You are?'

'Morgan Vine. I'm visiting Anjelica. I wrote to you.'

'About?'

'The baby farm in this prison.'

A sharp intake of breath from Anjelica. Idly scratching his beard, Carne responds with an indulgent smile. He turns to the woman with the clipboard.

'Has the letter gone out?'

'Last week.'

'I haven't received it,' says Morgan.

Carne spreads his hands.

'I'm responsible for many things, but not the efficiency of the Royal Mail.'

Morgan hasn't been home in a while. The letter is probably on the doormat.

'Care to tell me what it said?'

'I can't recall the detail,' says the governor, still smiling. 'Suffice to say, I'm sure it will put your mind at rest.' He turns to go. 'Don't let me interrupt your visit.'

But Anjelica is getting to her feet, studiously avoiding Morgan's eye.

'We're done,' she says.

Morgan opens her mouth to protest, then thinks better of it. The woman has good reason for clamming up in front of authority. Best not to interfere. She watches Carne usher Anjelica towards the door.

'Anjelica?' she says. The woman turns. 'Do you know what Karl kept in the biscuit tin? The one with Guy Fawkes on the lid?'

Anjelica blinks twice in quick succession, then looks away.

'I don't remember a tin.'

A lie? Or is she being discreet in front of the governor?

'Never mind,' says Morgan.

Anjelica turns and exits, followed by the governor and the woman with the clipboard. Morgan is left alone with Jukes. Unsmiling. Poker-faced.

'I'll show you out, Miss.'

The walk to the gate seems to take for ever. It passes in silence.

The letter from the governor is no more than a series of bland reassurances.

Such allegations are taken very seriously. However, despite an extensive internal enquiry, no evidence of a so-called 'baby farm' has come to light, either during my tenure or that of my predecessor. Even so, I am grateful for your interest in HMP Dungeness.

What happens in prison stays in prison.

Morgan flicks through the rest of her mail, then sinks onto the sofa and looks around her home. The place is cold and smells of damp, but she misses the familiarity, the reassurance of being surrounded by her own belongings, the feel of her own bed. Walking into her bedroom, she takes off her shoes and lies down, relishing the comforting creak of the iron bedstead.

She glances at the bedside clock. Just after 3 p.m. Lissa is at the inn, confined to bed, increasingly weepy, and not just because of the plight of refugees. This morning she was reduced to tears by a YouTube video of an elderly dog that had adopted four orphaned kittens, covering them with a protective paw as they slept in his basket. Closing her eyes, Morgan tries to summon memories of her own pregnancy. Had raging hormones played havoc with her emotions? She doesn't recall crying, but remembers devouring huge quantities of butterscotch Angel Delight and a week during which she ate nothing but anchovies.

Focusing on the sound of the waves crashing onto the shingle beach, she slides under the quilted bedcover. Just a quick nap – half an hour at most. Then she'll head back to the hotel.

The shrill of her mobile wakes her with a start. Peering at the screen, she sees Lissa's name.

'Mum? Where are you?'

The room is in darkness apart from the blood-red digits of the bedside clock: 7.04 p.m. Her daughter is crying. Morgan sits up, snapping on the light.

'What's the matter?'

'He phoned.'

'Who did?'

'Pablo.'

Throwing the quilt aside, Morgan gets out of bed, instantly alert.

'What did he say?' Her daughter is sobbing too hard to speak. 'Take a breath and tell me what he said.'

'He asked how I liked his surprise.'

'Meaning the baby?'

'Obviously!'

'What else?'

'I asked why he was doing this. He said, "It makes life interesting".'

'What else?'

'I told him he was a bastard. He laughed. I asked if this was some kind of vendetta, if he'd deliberately pricked the condoms, like he did with Anjelica and Nancy and God knows who else.'

'And?'

'He kept laughing.'

Putting her daughter on speakerphone, Morgan sits on the bed, pulling on her shoes.

'I asked why he hated women,' says Lissa. 'Was it because of what his mother did to him when he was a kid? He told me to stop being a psychobabble bitch.' Getting to her feet, Morgan grabs her phone and heads out of the bedroom. Her daughter is still talking. 'So I told him what I'd done.'

Morgan freezes.

'What do you mean?'

Lissa is sobbing again.

'What did you tell him?' says Morgan.

'It was the only way I could think of to get him out of my life. I can't keep this baby and spend every minute worrying he might show up.'

Morgan is struggling to remain calm. She moves her lips closer to the mouthpiece.

'Tell me what you said to him, Lissa.'

A pause.

'I lied. I said I'd had an abortion.'

Morgan closes her eyes. Her heart is pounding.

'What did he say?'

'He started yelling. Said I'd made the biggest mistake of my life. I'd killed his baby so he was going to kill me.'

Striding across the room, Morgan tosses sofa cushions onto the floor, searching for her keys.

'When was this?'

'Twenty minutes ago. I wanted to call you but I was having a panic attack, I couldn't speak.

'I'll be there in five minutes. Find Eric. Do not move from the hotel.'

'OK.'

Morgan ends the call. She bends down to snatch her keys from beneath the sofa. As she straightens up, about to dial Neville Rook's number, she catches sight of the curtain fluttering in the breeze. The window is broken. Shards of glass lie on the floor. She glances outside, her eyes roving the darkness.

Parked yards away is the white camper van.

Behind her, a floorboard creaks.

Then oblivion.

Twenty-Three

It's not like in the movies. No blinding light, no blur of concerned faces slowly coming into focus. Instead, the sharp pain in her head is accompanied by an all-enveloping darkness and the sound of an engine. There is also the sensation of being in a moving vehicle, and, as she surfaces into consciousness, the realisation that she has been blindfolded. And gagged. Her hands tied behind her back. She's lying on a mattress. Cheap, thin, barely separating her bones from the floor of the van.

The camper van on the beach.

It's all coming back.

The fluttering curtain.

The broken window.

The creak of the floorboard.

Now this: the smell of diesel, the shuddering engine. And another sound.

Clink-rasp.

The familiar noise of the Zippo is followed by the smell of cigarette smoke. She raises her head and tries to free her arms, but the rope is too tight. No wriggle room.

'Hey, Morgan.' The driver must have glimpsed movement in his rear-view mirror. 'Sorry about the sore head.'

'Aside from the "Joker" video, it's the first time she's heard his voice. She can't be totally sure the speaker is Karl (or Pablo) but she'd bet her life on it.

'I know you're scared,' he says. 'Let me set your mind at rest. Everything's cool. We're cool, Lissa's cool. She's still at the inn.'

Her mouth is parched, she can barely swallow. But she feels a spark of hope. A flicker of relief.

'Lissa's cool'.

Thank God.

Assuming he's telling the truth.

Now another voice. A woman?

But it's only a newsreader on the radio warning of heavy rain sweeping the country.

'In case you're wondering,' says the driver, dragging on the cigarette, 'I've been keeping tabs on you. And Lissa. Saw her buy the pregnancy test. I couldn't resist calling to say congratulations. Crazy, but hey, a baby's a big deal, right?'

She hears the window being opened and feels the air rush in as he raises his voice to make himself heard above the engine. No sound of other traffic. Morgan guesses they're on a country road.

'I tailed you from prison today,' he says. 'Had a drink – more than one, to be honest – then I sat outside your place and called Lissa. I knew she'd get on to you so I thought I'd pop in, ask a couple of questions.'

The van slows and makes a sharp turn, jolting Morgan from the mattress. The man drives another few hundred yards, then makes another turn before pulling to a halt. The engine dies. She hears him dragging on his cigarette, then feels a series of jerky movements as he clambers from the driver's seat into the rear of the van.

'We're somewhere nice and quiet,' he says. She can smell alcohol on his breath. Stale cigarettes on his clothes. 'Just you and me. Need a little chat.'

Blood thudding in her ears, she winces as his fingers peel the tape from her mouth. She takes a lungful of air, then another, feeling his hands untying the blindfold.

The interior of the van is in darkness but there's no mistaking his identity. Morgan is looking at the man believed to have died in the fire started by Anjelica Fry.

The man known to Lissa as Pablo.

Real name: Karl Savage.

Handsome. Soulful brown eyes. Full beard. Shaved head. He's wearing a white boiler suit and paper overshoes, the kind sported by crime scene SOCOs.

'Did you plan to have Lissa?' he asks.

The out-of-the-blue question catches her off guard.

'No.'

'Ever regretted having her?'

'No.'

He smiles and spreads his hands.

'Welcome to my world.'

He drags on his cigarette, then holds the stub to her lips.

'Smoke?'

She shakes her head. Her voice is a croak.

'Water.'

A shrug.

'Can't help, sorry.'

She makes a decision. She will act like this is normal. She will survive. For Lissa's sake. A litany of questions forms in her head.

Is Lissa OK? Why am I here? Who killed Kiki? Where's her baby? What happens to the children from the baby farm? And their mothers? How did you convince Tucker and Singh you were dead?

One question above all.

'Is Lissa OK?'

'Don't make me repeat myself. She's fine.' He frowns. 'You know who I am?'

'Yes.' Her head is throbbing. 'Did you target her to get to me?'

'Wow,' he says, 'and they accuse *me* of having a big ego.'

'*They?*'

'This isn't about you,' he says. 'We had a thing. She mentioned her mum was visiting someone in prison. Turned out it was someone I knew.'

No mention of the fact that Anjelica is the mother of his child. Or that Morgan is doing all she can to prove the woman's innocence. Surely he must know about their correspondence? About her visits? A tip-off from Trevor Jukes? Is that what this is about? Is that why she's here?

'So it's just coincidence?' she says. 'You "happened" to be having a "thing" with Lissa, I "happened" to be visiting Anjelica and you saw a chance to smuggle stuff into the MBU.'

He smiles at what he takes to be her attempt at delicacy.

'You mean sperm?'

'Sperm, spunk, jizz,' says Morgan, refusing to be cowed. 'Call it what you like. I want to know if you planned this.'

'I'm not interested in what you want.'

Morgan lets it go. Her throat is dry, her tongue sticking to the roof of her mouth.

'Can I sit up?'

A look of concern crosses his face.

'Of course.' He shifts to create space in the rear of the van. 'You must be very uncomfortable.'

He takes a final drag on his cigarette, pinches it out with his fingers then pockets the stub.

'How about some fresh air?' He produces a Swiss Army knife and begins to saw through the rope that binds her wrists. 'Stretch those lovely long legs?'

His hand caresses her knee. She stiffens, determined not to flinch. Her eyes stray over his shoulder. Lying on the floor of the van is an old square biscuit tin. Sealed with duct tape. Larger than she'd imagined.

On its lid is an image of Guy Fawkes burning at the stake.

'What's in the tin, Karl?'

His eyes follow her gaze.

'That's for me to know and you to wonder.'

Nancy Sixsmith's observation comes to mind.

He had all these stupid sayings.

'Is your head OK, Morgan?'

The concern seems genuine. She nods, rubbing her wrists.

'Fine.

'Good,' he says. 'You're a clever woman. I know you're not going to do anything silly.'

She manages a nod.

'Good girl.'

As he turns away to pocket the knife she sees a cigarette tucked behind his ear. Reaching towards the rear of the van, he releases the catch to open the doors then peers outside, into the darkness. Satisfied no one is around, he raises the hood on his boiler suit. Then he gets out and motions for her to follow. Sliding past the biscuit tin and stepping down from the van, she takes stock of her surroundings.

The van is parked on a track that runs through a cemetery. Gravestones border the path, stretching into the distance on both sides. There are no lights on the horizon, no moon, no sign of life. Rain is falling. In the distance, she hears a faint hum of motorway traffic.

'Why are we here?'

She knows she sounds stroppy but she doesn't care. Determined not to show fear. Stuffing his hands into his pockets, Karl turns and walks along the path. Morgan falls into step.

'What is the worst thing a person can do?' he says, like a teacher posing a rhetorical question.

'I don't know what you mean.'

He sighs.

'The worst thing is to harm children,' he says patiently. 'Am I right or am I right?'

'Let's say you're right.'

They reach the end of the track, arriving at a T-junction. He takes the path to the left. She follows. The motorway is still audible in the distance, the rain falling harder now. The graveyard is bordered by trees swaying in the breeze. Up ahead, a church looms out of the darkness.

'Is it true?' says Karl. 'Did Lissa have an abortion?'

He stops and turns, producing the Zippo from his pocket.

Clink-rasp.

He holds the flame close to Morgan's face, scrutinising her reaction to his words.

'When she told me, I went ape-shit,' he says. 'She tried to backtrack, said she was lying, trying to get me off her back. So now I'm confused.' He steps closer. *The heat of the flame. The smell of lighter fuel.* 'I need to know: did she or didn't she get rid of my baby?'

Morgan's heart is hammering, the pain in her head is getting worse. A kaleidoscope of images runs through her mind: *the attack. . . Lissa's burning hair . . . Kiki's body at the foot of the cliffs . . .*

She looks him in the eye. These next seconds are critical.

'No,' she says, meeting his gaze. 'She lied because she's scared. She wants you out of her life. But she's keeping the baby.'

His eyes search her face. A pause. When he speaks again he sounds wounded and weary.

'I don't believe you.'

Try harder. Make him believe.

'It's the truth.'

He shakes his head, puffing out his cheeks and sighing heavily.

'You're all the same.'

'You mean women?'

He takes the cigarette from behind his ear, lights it, then pockets the Zippo. He walks on. She falls into step. Listening intently. Trying to think of a way to reach him.

'I had a lot of time on my own when I was a kid,' he says. 'Did a lot of thinking. Came to the conclusion that women are not to be trusted.'

Morgan's mind flashes to Nancy, the mother of his twins, chain-smoking in her high-rise flat.

His mum, Pearl, hated kids, especially boys. She used to lock him in the cellar after school on a Friday, leave cornflakes, water and a bucket, and not let him out until Monday. One time, she forgot the water so he had to drink his own urine. No wonder he hates us.

'Have you heard of Pablo Escobar?' says Karl.

Morgan frowns, puzzled by the non sequitur.

'Yes.'

'A hero for a lot of people. He started out wanting to make money, but things grew. Then they grew some more. At a certain point, it stopped being about the money and became about the game.'

This is a game?

'I don't think creating a narco-state made Escobar a hero, Karl. And I'm pretty sure he didn't live in a camper van.'

He stares. For a moment she thinks he's angry, but he throws back his head and laughs.

'I see where Lissa gets it from,' he says. 'And I know what you're thinking.'

'Tell me.'

'Textbook sociopath. Delusions of grandeur. Risk-taker. Obsessed with games.' The cigarette glows as he takes a drag. 'I read the books, I know the score.' He exhales slowly.

'You got Lissa pregnant. Deliberately.'

'True.'

'How many children have you fathered?'

'A few.'

'What happens to the babies?'

'They have a great life. The best. *That's the point*.'

'All of them? Or just the boys?'

He grins.

'There are only boys – so far.'

'What if one turns out to be a girl?'

He meets her gaze, grin fading. His answer chills Morgan's blood.

'I'll jump off that bridge when I come to it.'

Stopping by a headstone, he proffers the cigarette and takes two mobiles from the pocket of his boiler suit.

'Hold these.'

If Morgan feels a flicker of hope it's dashed by his next words.

'Your battery's flat. Don't get ideas.'

She takes the phones and the cigarette. He rolls up his sleeves, exposing the soft white flesh on his forearm. She glimpses his tattoo.

Rather die on my feet than live on my knees.

He turns away, unzipping his fly, directing a stream of piss at the grave. Morgan sneaks a look at her phone. He's right: no juice in the battery. For a second she considers using the tip of the cigarette as a weapon. She could stab him in the neck . . . Make a run for it . . .

But he's bigger. Stronger. Faster.

'You need to understand: I don't do fear,' he says, as if reading her mind. He arcs a stream of urine towards the gravestone. 'That's the thing about dead people: we don't scare easy.'

He zips up. Turns to face her. The grin is back. Taking his mobile, he thumbs it to life and plays the phone's light over the grave. A cloud of steam rises from the piss trickling down the headstone. Morgan's eyes widen. The stone is chiselled with the dates of the deceased.

14 June 1971 – 5 November 1997.

The name makes her catch her breath.

Pearl Savage.

Out of the corner of her eye she can see Karl studying her reaction.

'May she rot in peace.'

He takes back Morgan's phone and the cigarette, sucks down a final lungful of smoke and grinds the stub under the heel of his overshoe. She watches as he picks it up. Places it in his pocket.

'Actions have consequences,' he says, staring at the headstone. 'People need to understand that.'

'Are you talking about your mother or my daughter?'

'Both.'

Morgan shivers, whether from cold or fear it's hard to tell.

'Was she ill?' she says, gesturing towards the gravestone.

'Only in the head. She always said she'd never make old bones.' A smile plays on his lips. 'Like mother, like son.'

'Meaning?'

'Meaning we're a long time dead. So we'd better go up like a rocket even if we come down like a stick.'

She watches as he circles the grave.

'How did she die?'

'Fell down the steps. Hit her head on concrete. On my birthday.'

'Anjelica says she hated you.'

'Like I give a shit.'

Morgan can't keep the scorn from her voice.

'Is that why you're doing all this? To get back at Mummy?'

His jaw tightens. Morgan ploughs on.

'Are you going to let Anjelica rot too? The mother of your baby?'

No response.

'What about Marlon? He's your son—'

He cuts her dead, a flash of anger. 'Shut the fuck up.'

She looks around the cemetery, hoping someone will come – a mourner, a dog walker – but there is no sign of life.

'Where's Spike?'

He frowns.

'What's he got to do with anything?'

'That's what I want to know,' says Morgan. 'Are you in this together?'

'Fuck Spike. This isn't about him.'

'So what is it about? Why are we here?'

He steps forward, bringing his face close to hers. She can smell his beery breath.

'I need the truth,' he says. 'About Lissa.'

The blood thumps in her ears. She stares into his eyes. Not blinking. Refusing to show fear. Third time lucky.

'She's keeping the baby.'

But the man has made up his mind.

'Lying bitch.'

Grabbing her arm, he yanks her away from Pearl's grave, heading towards the van.

'All the fucking same – *all of you*!'

He's dragging her behind him. She stumbles and falls to her knees.

'Get up.'

He pulls her to her feet. Moves behind her. Grabs her shoulders. Propelling her forward. And then she sees it. An open grave, dug in readiness for a burial. A tarpaulin covers the earth. A spade juts from the mound of upturned soil.

This isn't just about Lissa.

He's brought her here to silence her.

To stop her proving he's alive.

He'll cover her with earth.

The burial will take place.

The coffin will hide her body for ever.

Survival instinct kicks in. She brings her elbow forward then jerks it back, into his face, loosening his grip for a second, long enough to break free from his grasp. Swivelling on her heel, she raises her leg and lashes out with all her strength, landing a powerful kick to his groin. He staggers, winded. She springs forward, grabbing the spade, raising it above her head then bringing it down on his body. He lets out a cry. She tosses the spade away.

And suddenly she's racing along the path. Away from the van. Towards the distant sound of traffic. She can hear him behind her, heavy boots thudding on the ground. Adrenaline coursing through her veins, she strains every sinew, leaving the path and weaving among the gravestones then bursting through the churchyard gate onto the deserted country lane. She doesn't look back. She can hear him chasing behind her, *running, running, running* . . .

The rain stings her face. Her leg muscles are protesting. The sound of the traffic grows louder. Ahead, an orange glow. Lights from the motorway. The road slopes down, towards the slip road.

He's gaining on her. The rain is falling harder now, slicking the tarmac beneath her feet. Just a few yards separate her from her pursuer. The slip road is empty – no vehicles, no sign of life – but further down the slope it's a different story, with three lanes of Friday night traffic. Cars, lorries and vans speed by, headlights ablaze.

Darting to her left, Morgan leaves the slip road and leaps onto the verge that slopes down to the hard shoulder. She steals a look behind her. He's closing the gap. Eyes bulging, face contorted with effort and fury.

The rain is falling harder, the grass slope slippery and treacherous. She slips, losing her balance, then straightening up as her feet thud onto the tarmac. She faces the speeding traffic, waving her hands.

'Stop! *Help!*'

A lorry approaches, followed by a car. After that, a let-up in the flow of traffic. She risks another glance over her shoulder. He's closing in. The lorry speeds past. Then the car. The gap opens up.

She jerks to her left, sprinting across the three lanes. Horns blare. But she's made it onto the central reservation. Her body slams into the barrier. Panting, she turns to look behind her. He's on the far side of the motorway, the traffic separating him from his quarry. Now he's yelling but she can't hear above the blaring horns. Catching her breath, she watches as he turns in the direction of the oncoming cars, making the same calculation she made.

Dare he risk it?

A van zips past, spraying her with rainwater. Another gap in the traffic flow. Karl hesitates. As he starts to make his way across the motorway, placing a tentative foot in the slow lane, he's clipped by a car. Jerking crazily, he spins around and falls to the ground, clutching his leg. Horns blare but no one slows, no one stops. Morgan waves her arms at the oncoming traffic. A cacophony of horns. Up ahead, a convoy of lorries is approaching. Four? Five? She stands motionless, watching as the HGVs thunder past, one by one, clearing her line of sight to reveal another gap in the traffic flow. She looks across the lanes, scanning the hard shoulder.

Karl has disappeared.

Her eyes scan the verge, the grass slope leading down from the slip road. No sign of him. Not on the motorway. Not on the verge. He has vanished.

And now another sound above the blaring horns. A siren. In the distance, a flashing blue light. Shielding her eyes from glaring headlamps, she watches the police car drawing nearer, moving into the slow lane, then pulling to a halt on the hard shoulder. The driver jumps out, gesturing to Morgan with outstretched hands. He wants her to stay where she is. A second police officer runs to the rear of the car. He takes something from the boot – a megaphone. He calls across the lanes of traffic.

'*Do not move. Do not try to cross the motorway. Stay where you are.*'

Morgan gives a thumbs-up. Her heart is still hammering. Turning her face to the torrential rain, she gives silent thanks.

The police will stop the traffic. Bring her to safety. Take her home. Maybe they'll charge her with breaking traffic laws, but she doesn't care.

As long as they listen.

As long as Lissa is OK.

As long as they find Karl Savage.

Twenty-Four

KARL

He hears her footsteps overhead, moving around the kitchen, dragging her feet, shuffling in her slippers. He knows she's not been well. It's been going on for months. On weekdays, when he's allowed to roam the rest of the house, she stays in bed all day, curtains closed. The house is silent.

He wonders if her illness is anything to do with being pregnant this time last year.

He wonders if she's depressed.

Above all, he wonders what happened to the baby.

He overheard the dinner ladies talking about the head teacher.

Leave of absence . . . post-natal depression . . . post-partum psychosis . . .

Maybe the same is true of his mum. If he hadn't stumbled upon the pregnancy test in the bathroom, he'd never have known she was having a baby.

And because she'd grown so fat, neither would anyone else.

The Whistler is a regular fixture these days. Weekends only. Seemed an OK bloke, at first. Cooked a nice beef stew, brought it down to the cellar. Watched Karl eat every morsel.

- *Nice?*
- *Not bad. Thanks.*

A grin.

- *You know it was dog food, right?*
- *Seriously?*
- *Yeah. And stop snivelling. Boys don't cry. Your dad sounds like a right poof. We've got to toughen you up, kiddo. You need to learn to take a joke.*

Karl shudders, trying to banish the memory of the dog food.

He's doing his best to forget the game too. The one The Whistler makes him play when he comes down into the cellar at night, while she's sleeping.

- *Our special game.*

Another shudder.

Karl closes his eyes, trying to block the image from his mind. But he can't.

He opens his eyes. Switching on his torch, he stares at the old biscuit tin, letting the light play over the image on the lid: Guy Fawkes burning at the stake.

She took the tin away for a long time.

Yesterday she brought it back.

It's been empty for as long as he can remember – ever since the people at Dad's funeral ate all the biscuits.

But now there's something inside.

Before bringing it back to the cellar, she sealed it with duct tape. Then she did something she hasn't done since the day Dad died.

She spoke to him.

Just two words.

No peeking.

Twenty-Five

If there was any doubt in Morgan's mind that Karl is alive, the graveyard encounter has dispelled it for good. Which makes Jatinder Singh either incompetent or dishonest. Morgan will call the forensic odontologist as soon as his office opens, but right now, sitting in Neville Rook's car, she has other things on her mind. The DI arrived at her house shortly after 9 a.m. accompanied by the SOCO team, who even now are searching for evidence to nail the identity of the intruder once and for all. The rain has died away (a newsreader dubbed it a 'mini-monsoon') but the Dungeness skies are blanketed by thick cloud. As they talk, Morgan watches the policeman take notes. Their last conversation was awkward, to say the least. She considered insisting on someone else – a fresh start with another DI – but changed her mind.

Better the Neville you know . . .

'Did you get the van's registration number?'

She shakes her head.

'Other things on my mind.'

'Pity. Missed a trick.'

Morgan says nothing, glancing across the beach towards the Mini where Lissa is slumped in the passenger seat, feet on the dashboard, scrolling through her phone.

Rolling a cigarette, Morgan becomes aware of a tremor in her hand. The encounter with Karl has left her shaken. A sleepless night hasn't helped, the throbbing in her temples a reminder of the blow to her head.

Savage by name . . .

Not wishing to alarm her daughter more than necessary, she has played down the extent of her ordeal.

'I haven't told Lissa everything I'm telling you,' she says to Rook. 'Nothing about being knocked out or tied up.'

Or the open grave.

'Understood,' says Neville. He consults his notebook. 'Uniform say there was no sign of the camper van.'

She nods.

'I took them to the churchyard but he'd disappeared. Taken the spade too. They found tyre tracks, said they'd check the motorway ANPR cameras. I told them he was probably sticking to back roads.'

A nod.

'How's your head?'

Painful.

'A & E said the X-ray was fine.'

He casts a look around the bleak, windswept landscape, the glowering clouds, the vast power station looming in the distance.

'Tell me you're not sticking around this godforsaken place, not after last night.'

'No,' says Morgan.

'Where will you go?'

'Good question.' She fishes her lighter from her pocket. 'OK if I smoke?'

'If you must.'

Lighting the cigarette, she sucks the smoke into her lungs.

'You believe me? That it was Karl Savage?'

She can see him choose his words with care.

'It's not that *I* don't believe you, but when it comes to getting the criminal justice system to admit it's made a mistake . . .'

He tails off, giving a shrug that suggests utter powerlessness and defeat. She fights the urge to punch him. Or yell in his face.

'Can you offer us protection? Me and my daughter?'

An apologetic shake of head.

'That's not how the system works.'

'Fuck the system.' She waves a hand around the beach. 'He's out there, gunning for me and Lissa.'

'If you stay in Kent the best we can offer is increased patrols.'

'That's your advice? Run?'

'That's my advice.'

She can feel her anger growing.

'Don't make me go over your head, Neville.'

To her surprise, instead of looking affronted, the DI meets her gaze.

'I beat you to it. Called my guv on the way here.'

'And?'

'Like I said, increased patrols is the best she can do.'

Morgan frowns.

'Did you tell her what happened?'

He nods. 'She was very clear. She said, "I've fewer staff than three years ago. Smaller budgets. There was a thorough Met investigation into Savage's murder, followed by a trial. The perpetrator is in prison. But you want me to believe the victim has risen from the dead, like Jesus sodding Christ? To sanction twenty-four-hour protection against a bloody *zombie*?"'

Morgan's mood is taking a dive – a combination of delayed shock and rising frustration. Losing her temper will not help. She needs this man on her side.

'At least send SOCOs to the graveyard, check for traces of his urine, do a DNA search.'

'After seven hours of rain?'

Morgan says nothing, letting the silence do its work.

'OK,' he says, sighing. 'It's worth a shot. Assuming his DNA is in the system.'

A thought bubbles to the surface of Morgan's weary brain.

'What about the baby farm? If you find babies conceived *after* he's supposed to have died, and if they match his DNA, surely that proves he's alive.'

'Not if they used frozen sperm.'

'But what if it wasn't frozen?'

The policeman chews the inside of his lip, thinking.

'OK, I'll talk to the prison, ask about mums who've been released recently.'

'Like Kiki McNeil?' Morgan's voice is full of reproach.

His jaw tightens. 'We're doing all we can to find Charlie.'

Another thought struggles to fight its way through the fog in her brain. She tells the DI about Stacey Brown and her baby. The flight to Istanbul. The woman's return. The houseboat registered in Jukes's name. He listens, jotting in his notebook.

'I'll check the houseboat. I'll talk to Jukes again – and the governor. But you need to understand the reality of this situation. Prisons are a world apart: normal rules don't apply.'

'They keep records, don't they? Names, dates, a log of where prisoners go after release.'

'Don't hold your breath. If they want to drag things out, hide behind "prison protocol", they can take for ever.'

Morgan stubs her cigarette out in the ashtray and glances towards the Mini. Lissa is blowing her nose, talking on her mobile.

The idea strikes with the force of a fist.

'What about a prenatal DNA test?'

Neville follows her gaze, arching an eyebrow.

'On Lissa's baby?'

'Why not?'

He thinks for a moment, scratching the side of his nose.

'The law stipulates that prenatal DNA tests can only be done with the consent of the man presumed to be the father.'

'Assuming he's alive,' says Morgan.

'Obviously.'

Morgan allows a pause before playing her trump card.

'But if Karl's dead – at least from a legal perspective – then the law can "stipulate" till it's blue in the face. If the father's dead then the problem of consent can't exist.'

He nods, weighing her words.

'I'll talk to Tucker at the Met,' he says, sighing. 'Check they've got Karl's DNA on the database.'

No mistaking the defeatism in his voice. Morgan sighs.

'Work with me, Neville. The baby farm, Stacey, Kiki, Jukes, Karl – they're all connected. Meanwhile a woman is banged up for a murder she didn't commit, my daughter's pregnant by a sociopath and I'm terrified.'

An exaggeration. She's scared, God knows, but mostly angry. No, *furious.*

'OK,' says Rook, pocketing his notebook. 'Looks like I've got my work cut out.'

He looks up. She follows his gaze. Lissa is approaching, crunching across the shingle.

'We're sorted,' she says, her voice thick with cold. 'I called Ben. We can stay in his spare room.'

'Who's Ben?' says Neville, quickly adding, 'Sorry, none of my business.'

'Ben Gaminara.' says Lissa, cocking a knowing smile at her mother. But Morgan frowns.

'We barely know the guy.'

'Got a better idea?'

Morgan *does* have a better idea – a Plan B that came to her at 5 a.m. while she was nursing her head and soothing her worried daughter back to sleep. But now is not the time to broach it. She steps out of the car, watching as Rook walks towards the house. One of the SOCOs is waiting for him.

Morgan puts her arm around her daughter.

'We're not damsels in distress, Lissa. We can look after ourselves.'

Lissa pulls away, eyes flashing with anger.

'Why do you make everything so *fucking difficult*?'

Morgan counts to three, takes her daughter's hand and leads her towards the Mini.

'Where are we going?' Lissa's voice is sulky, like a petulant teenager.

'To check out of the inn.'

A pleading tone enters her daughter's voice.

'And then we go to Ben's?'

'All right.' Morgan keeps her tone gentle. 'If it makes you feel better.'

Lissa blows her nose.

'When are you going to tell me what really happened last night?'

'I already have,' says Morgan.

'You seriously expect me to believe he just took you for a ride in the country?'

Morgan forces a smile. The temptation to tell the unvarnished truth is trumped by maternal instinct, the overwhelming need to protect her daughter.

One day Lissa will understand. But not today.

'Trust me, I'm fine,' she says. 'Let's go and pack.'

Twenty-Six

Ben is out most of the time, confirming his reputation as a work-aholic, returning merely to sleep and shower. The spare room of the Canterbury house is small but cosy. Twin beds. Crisp, clean sheets. The black cat is still in residence, but there's no sign of the pink bra or its owner.

On the second morning of her stay, Morgan is woken by the distant sound of the cathedral bells, followed by an 8 a.m. call from DI Rook.

'Want the good news or the bad news?'

Morgan yawns and stretches. She can hear Lissa snoring softly in the next bed.

'Too early for games, Neville. I haven't had coffee.'

'Karl Savage was never arrested. His DNA isn't on the database.'

The cat with no name jumps on the bed.

'And the good news?'

'Tucker says the Met kept Karl's teeth. They're in storage.'

Morgan sighs, reaching out to stroke the cat.

'That's no use. They're not *his* teeth; they belong to whoever died in the fire.'

'So you say. But if so, they may match someone else on the database. Which would prove the body *wasn't* Karl's. Which would be a start.'

Brightening, Morgan sits up in bed.

'Any luck with Jatinder Singh?' Like the DI, she's been trying to reach the elusive odontologist, but with no success.

'He's still in the US,' says Rook. 'I keep leaving voicemails, but he hasn't called back.'

'Do you think he's giving you the runaround?'

'His secretary says he's just busy. Big lecture tour. Seven cities in five days.'

'Do you believe her?'

'No reason not to.'

Morgan recalls her meeting in the all-white Harley Street office.

Is it possible to do DNA tests from teeth?

Yes.

Was that done in this case?

No. The police enquiry didn't need to go as far as DNA testing. The radiographs told them all they needed to know.

The cat is purring.

'What's the next step?'

'I'll liaise with the Met, apply to log the teeth out of the storage facility.'

'How long will that take?'

'How long is a piece of string?'

'Not helpful.'

'They're busy, Morgan. We're all bloody busy.'

She continues to refine Plan B, discussing the details with Lissa's father in California, but only when their daughter is out of earshot. Although still unaware of Lissa's pregnancy, it's a relief that Cameron is willing to cooperate with Morgan's scheme, quickly grasping the urgency of the situation. The absence of Karl's DNA on the police database means there is no need for Lissa to undergo an amniocentesis, which is probably just as well, for the sake of the baby.

Lissa has confined herself to bed, emerging to sip an occasional bowl of Heinz tomato soup or eat half a Weetabix. She spends her waking hours in bed, trying to reassure herself by compulsively reading about sociopaths on her iPad. If this goes on much longer Morgan will force her daughter to go to the doctor, to find out which anti-depressants are compatible with pregnancy.

Seventy-two hours into their stay in Canterbury, DI Rook calls again: another update. As promised, he's checked out the *Wandering Star* houseboat. No sign of life, no trace of Stacey or her baby. A check with the UK Border Agency has confirmed she flew to Istanbul, returning three days later, since when she seems to have gone off the radar.

Rook has also interviewed Trevor Jukes for a second time, but the prison officer continues to deny knowing the whereabouts of the former inmate or her baby. Turns out he bought the *Wandering Star* eighteen months ago and plans to use it for holidays as soon as he carries out the necessary renovations. Meanwhile the vessel is legally berthed at the bottom of a farmer's field and remains empty, or so Jukes insists.

'He's lying,' says Morgan. 'I'm positive Stacey stayed there with the baby.'

'Your word against his,' says Rook. 'You need to do better.'

'Makes two of us,' says Morgan. 'What about the prison governor?'

A sigh.

'Carne's hard to pin down. I'm working on him.'

'Work harder.'

On the fourth morning – the day when all hell breaks loose – Morgan is woken by a noise from downstairs. It's shortly after eight o'clock. Since the encounter with Karl Savage she has slept with a knife under her pillow. Now, barefoot and clad in knickers and T-shirt, she creeps downstairs and finds herself brandishing the blade at her startled host. Hollow-eyed and gaunt, Ben is returning from an all-night job investigating a suspicious lorry fire on the M20 outside Dover. Exhausted, his voice is barely a whisper.

'Sixteen adults. Four kids. Locked inside a refrigerated lorry. Someone set fire to it.'

Following him into the kitchen, Morgan remains silent for a long moment. When she speaks, her voice is low.

'Refugees? Migrants?'

'I don't know. Either way, they were desperate.'

He places a Sainsbury's bag on the table then stares out of the window.

'My guess: they died of carbon monoxide poisoning and the driver panicked. He torched the lorry, trying to hide the evidence, and now he's disappeared.'

Blowing out her cheeks, Morgan stands at the sink, gazing at the grey light of morning. Taking a breath, she sets the kettle to boil. Ben clears his throat, making an effort to leave the night's harrowing events at the door.

'It's weird coming home to someone,' he says softly, watching her set mugs on the table. 'Good weird,' he adds.

Morgan smiles.

'We won't stay long, I promise. You know what they say about fish and guests.'

'No?'

'After three days they both start to stink.'

His smile is weak, but there is warmth in his tired eyes.

'Is Lissa asleep?'

Morgan nods, busying herself with the cafetière. He notes a tremor in her hand.

'You're shivering.'

'Heating hasn't come on yet.'

'Hang on a sec.'

He goes upstairs, returning moments later with a red and black lumberjack shirt. She slips it on like a dressing gown, rolling up the sleeves. It dwarfs her body.

'Suits you.'

They take their coffee into the sitting room. He sits in the armchair; she perches on the leather sofa. During their brief encounters over the last few days she has updated him on the events that prompted Lissa to ask for help from a virtual stranger. The man is a good listener. Time to return the compliment.

'Want to talk about it?' says Morgan. 'The people in the lorry?'

His expression darkens. He shakes his head.

'Not much of a talker.' He sips his coffee, staring into the middle distance before offering half a smile.

'Can I ask a question?' says Morgan.

A nod.

'How would you go about finding an arsonist?'

'Are we talking generally or someone specific?'

'Generally.'

She watches his Adam's apple move as he swallows another sip of coffee.

'A first step could be to check out the scene of the crime. Some pyromaniacs get a kick out of gawking at their "work". They can't resist watching people trying to work out how they set the fire. It makes them feel superior because most of them are inadequate.' He stretches out his long legs. 'Can we change the subject? Tell me how you and Lissa are getting on.'

'As well as can be expected – isn't that the phrase?' Morgan nods towards her laptop. 'I've been digging into Karl's background.'

'And?'

'He grew up in the East End of London. The local paper ran a story about his mum's death. She sounds like a nasty piece of work. Locked him in the cellar every weekend. God knows what else.'

Ben warms his hands on the mug.

'What's that Jesuit saying? Give me the child until he is seven and I will give you the man.'

'You believe that?'

'I'm living proof. My parents died when I was nine, along with my kid brother. A Boxing Day fire. My Christmas present was a spaceship. There was no battery so Dad took the one from the smoke alarm. I remember him scribbling a Post-it note to replace it as soon as the shops reopened, but our Christmas tree lights were cheap crap, from a stall in the market . . .'

He tails off, letting the sentence finish itself.

Lost for words, Morgan says nothing. Puts a hand on his shoulder.

He doesn't react, sitting in silence for a moment. Getting to his feet, he heads for the staircase, avoiding her eye while calling over his shoulder.

'I need a shower,' he says, nodding towards the Sainsbury's bag. 'If you feel like rustling up bacon and eggs I'll be fifteen minutes.'

Watching him go, she boots up her laptop and scans the news websites for any mention of the search for Kiki's baby, but the story has slipped off the agenda. The official version – just another depressed woman ending her own life – has become an accepted truth. The waters have closed over Kiki's head.

In the kitchen, Morgan grills the bacon and poaches the eggs. There's no point in cooking for Lissa. Left undisturbed she'll sleep till lunchtime. Her cold has cleared up but her mood is changeable, to say the least. Morgan has caught her crying on more than one occasion but the girl insists she's just tired and emotional, a mass of raging hormones. Morgan knows there's something else, something preying on her daughter's mind, but Lissa is in no mood to be challenged.

As Morgan sets a fresh pot of coffee on the table, the doorbell rings. She calls upstairs.

'Ben?'

No reply. She slips the chain on the door, then opens it a crack. Neville Rook is outside.

'Your mobile's off.'

Unhooking the chain, she ushers him inside. She can see him taking stock of the lumberjack shirt, but he makes no mention of it.

'The SOCOs checked out the churchyard,' he says. 'No trace of the man's urine. Not surprising after that rain.'

'Did they find anything at my place?'

He shakes his head.

'So why are you here?'

She turns at the sound of Ben coming down the stairs, naked except for the bath towel around his waist.

'Do you two know each other?' says Morgan.

Ben extends a handshake.

'Ben Gaminara.'

'DI Rook.'

The police officer glances at his watch, then gives Ben a quick smile.

'Mind giving us a moment?'

'No problem,' says Ben. He grabs a plate of bacon and eggs, along with a knife and fork, then heads into the sitting room and closes the door.

Rook can't resist a dig.

'Very cosy.'

Morgan fights the temptation to roll her eyes.

Men . . .

Sitting at the table, she gestures for the DI to follow suit.

'Coffee?'

'No, thanks.'

He's trying not to look at her legs.

'So?' she says.

'I had a call last night. From the prison governor. Turns out he *has* been investigating the baby farm.'

Morgan frowns.

'Why did he tell me there was nothing to investigate?'

A shrug. 'Prison's a closed world. Think North Korea with "Genghis" Carne as Kim Jong-un. They don't tell us anything unless they have to.'

'But there *is* a baby farm?'

'There's an investigation. Big difference.' He straightens his tie, then gets to the nub of the matter. 'He called to tell me his main informant was attacked last night. Slashed across the face with a razor blade melted into a toothbrush.'

Suddenly, Morgan's heart is racing. 'Anjelica Fry?'

Rook nods.

'She needs specialist care. They've taken her to Ashford hospital. Which means the prison can't guarantee to keep a lid on what happened and there's likely to be a leak. Which is why Carne called. To keep me "in the loop".

'Why are you telling me?'

'He asked me to.'

'Because?'

'He knows you have a special interest in her case. He's trying to put his finger in the dyke, to stop any leaks spiralling out of control. He thinks the attack on Anjelica is tied to the baby farm investigation. But he doesn't want you splashing it all over the papers while it's ongoing. He'd rather have you inside the tent than outside pissing in.'

Morgan nods, sipping her coffee.

'How is she?'

'She'll recover, but the wounds sound severe.'

'Does Carne know who did it?'

Rook shakes his head.

'Usual prison crap – no one saw a thing. They're looking for the weapon but he's not holding out much hope.'

'It was Jukes,' says Morgan. 'Either he did it, or he made it happen.'

'There's no proof,' says Carne. 'But Carne has suspended him, "pending further enquiries".'

'On what grounds?'

'His name was mentioned in connection with the baby farm.'

'Mentioned by Anjelica?'

A nod.

'Which is why Jukes wanted to shut her up,' says Morgan. 'At best it's a warning, at worst attempted murder.'

'Either way, it's an internal matter,' says Rook. 'That's how it's going to stay.'

'What happens when she goes back inside?'

'Under normal circumstances, she'd be moved to the vulnerable prisoners' unit, but she has a baby, so things are . . . complicated.'

He looks away. Morgan doesn't like how this is shaping up.

'You mean they're going to take her son?'

The policeman doesn't meet her eye.

'The governor's first responsibility is safety. If he believes Anjelica can be best protected on VPU, without her baby, then that's how it'll have to be.'

Morgan feels a wave of anger and despair.

'What will happen to Marlon?'

'He'll be placed in care.'

'You mean, tossed on the scrapheap.'

'It's not that bad.'

'It's worse.' Morgan puts down her mug. 'Anjelica tried to kill herself once already, Neville. Taking Marlon will be the final straw.'

'You don't know that.'

'Yes, I do.'

His mobile rings. Morgan gets to her feet and leaves him to take the call. Walking into the sitting room, she finds Ben watching the news. A report on the people who died in the lorry. Twenty lost souls in the back of a refrigerated HGV filled with imported fish. His plate sits on the coffee table, the food untouched. His eyes are red.

'You OK?'

A nod. He holds up a hand, blocking more questions.

Morgan closes the door softly, walking back to the kitchen as Rook ends his call and pockets his phone.

'That was the Met's storage facility, calling about my request for Karl Savage's teeth.' He clears his throat, embarrassed. 'They're missing.'

Morgan's eyes widen in disbelief.

'Lost?'

A shrug. 'Things get moved around, reorganised, misplaced. Bottom line: they're not there. The computer's crashed so they can't be sure who signed them out. They've referred me to the SIO.'

'DI Tucker?'

'Yes.'

Morgan sighs. She can hear Lissa's phone ringing upstairs. Glancing at his watch, Rook heads into the hall. Morgan follows. He turns, eyes filled with concern.

'Are you OK, Morgan?'

She manages a smile. She seems to be back in favour. Perhaps her graveyard ordeal has earned some sympathy.

'Never better.'

She manages to keep the smile in place until he's gone. Upstairs, Lissa's phone is ringing again, the sound vibrating through the floor. Morgan goes back into the kitchen to clear the table and stack the dishwasher. Mission accomplished, she heads upstairs and goes into the room she shares with her daughter.

Lissa is lying on the floor.

Gasping for air.

Eyes rolling back in her head.

Another panic attack.

Morgan falls to her knees.

'Lissa? Can you hear me?'

No response. The breathing becomes increasingly laboured.

'I'm here, Lissa . . . Mum's here . . . Try and breathe slowly . . .'
The gasping continues. Lissa is staring at the ceiling, her eyes wide
open. 'You're not in any danger. I'm here. I will stay with you.'

Her daughter's breathing is starting to calm down, just a little, but enough to give hope that the worst is over. Morgan takes
Lissa's hand, gently stroking her wrist, speaking softly, repeat-
ing comforting words designed to soothe, over and over, until
finally her daughter is able to stop gasping for breath.

'It's OK,' says Morgan. 'Take your time. I'm here.'

Lissa shakes her head, pointing at something on the bed. Her
mobile. Morgan picks it up.

'Was it the phone call? Is that what triggered the attack?'

A nod.

'Who was it? Who called?'

Another gasp, then two words uttered in between gulps of air.

'He. Did.'

'Karl?'

A nod.

'What did he say?'

Lissa shakes her head.

'Did he threaten you?'

Another shake of the head.

'He didn't. Say. Anything.'

'How do you know it was him? Did you recognise his number?'

A shake of the head. Another gulp of air.

'Voicemail.'

Morgan wakes Lissa's phone then taps the voicemail icon and holds the phone to her ear. For a moment there is silence on the line. Then the sound of someone breathing.

'How can you be sure it was him?'

Lissa holds a finger to her lips, urging her mother to hold the phone closer to her ear.

'Listen,' she whispers.

Morgan strains to hear but there is only silence on the line.

Then she catches it. The sound that haunts her dreams, turning them into nightmares.

Clink-rasp.

She lowers the phone.

Makes a decision.

It's time for Plan B.

Twenty-Seven

The following morning, Morgan accepts Ben's offer of a lift to Heathrow. The rush-hour drive from Kent passes in bleary-eyed silence apart from Lissa's occasional sulky questions.

'Where are we going?'

'I told you. It's a surprise.'

'Since when do I like surprises?'

'Everyone likes surprises.'

'Why are you treating me like a five-year-old?'

'You'll understand when we get there.'

If the police can't protect us, we need to protect ourselves.

Morgan hasn't bothered asking Rook to trace the call that triggered her daughter's latest panic attack. What would be the point? Karl is 'off the grid', most likely in the company of Spike. His phone will doubtless turn out to be a pay-as-you-go mobile – totally untraceable – and as far as the DI is concerned Morgan is already overdrawn at the bank of goodwill.

Clink-rasp.

The menacing sound has been playing inside her head throughout the last twenty-four hours, while she was making the arrangements that will set Plan B in motion. She has secretly packed a suitcase for her daughter, concealing it in the boot of Ben's Range Rover. Under normal circumstances, she would have explained her thinking to Lissa, but these are not normal circumstances. What matters is getting her daughter out of harm's way. If that involves subterfuge, then so be it.

Morgan has confided in Ben but sworn him to secrecy. She's hoping he will prove a calming influence if things get tense.

Her phone beeps with a text.

'Who's that?' says Lissa, briefly raising her eyes from her own mobile.

'Neville Rook,' says Morgan. 'He's trying to find out what happened to the teeth from the body in Karl's flat.'

'And?'

'No luck so far. But at least he's on the case and keeping me posted.'

'Only because he fancies you,' says Lissa.

Morgan says nothing. Ben clears his throat. Silence falls.

Glancing in the wing mirror, Morgan's attention is drawn to a Yamaha motorcycle swerving into the fast lane, then ducking back into the line of rush-hour traffic and disappearing behind a van. She wonders briefly if the biker might be Jukes. The thought doesn't last long but keeps resurfacing as the miles flash by, niggling at her weary brain. An old joke bubbles to the surface.

Just because you're paranoid doesn't mean they're not out to get you.

Ben steers the Range Rover into the airport's multi-storey car park. Lissa frowns.

'Why are we going to arrivals not departures?'

'All part of the surprise,' says Morgan.

Her daughter mutters something under her breath.

Inside the car park, Morgan opens the boot and takes out the suitcase.

'Why the luggage?' says Lissa.

'Can you stop asking questions?'

'Can you stop being so annoying?'

In the arrivals hall Ben leads the way as the two women follow. Checking her watch, Morgan is relieved to discover they're bang on schedule. She feels a surge of gratitude towards Ben.

Punctual Ben. Dependable Ben. Straightforward Ben.

All the things she used to find dull and unsexy.

Not any more.

Scanning the monitors, she sees the flight has landed ten minutes ahead of schedule.

Baggage in hall.

A cluster of minicab drivers and chauffeurs are grouped by the doors leading from the customs hall. And suddenly, there he is – a familiar, lanky figure loping through the doors with a group of trolley-wheeling passengers.

'Surprise,' says Morgan quietly. Lissa follows her gaze. Her eyes widen in disbelief.

'Dad?'

It's years since Morgan last saw her ex in the flesh. Discussions about their daughter are generally conducted via email or Skype. Cameron is not as tall as she remembers, but he's still in good shape – lean and sporting a tan, an expensive haircut and what Californians insist on calling 'leisure wear'.

London born and bred, he's now a denizen of Malibu, an award-winning Hollywood screenwriter whose lifestyle couldn't be more at odds with Morgan's. They've had many differences (not least over whether or not she should go ahead with the pregnancy) but right now she's flooded with relief that he has dropped everything to fly in from Los Angeles.

Of course I'll come. I'm glad you asked.

She watches as he spreads his arms, embracing his bewildered daughter. Lissa wriggles free of the hug, bestowing a wary look on her parents.

'Is this some crappy romcom where you tell me you're getting back together?'

'Let's find somewhere to talk and get coffee,' says Cameron, scanning the departures hall.

'Fuck coffee,' says Lissa. 'Tell me what's going on.'

Morgan does her best to keep her smile in place. Time to come clean.

'I asked your dad to come. I need to know you're safe.'

Lissa scowls.

'What does that even *mean*?'

Cameron smiles.

'It means you and me get some father–daughter time together, in the countryside.'

The scowl shows no sign of fading. 'Are you *serious*?'

Cameron blinks, taken back by the ferocity of the response. 'You love the countryside.'

Lissa looks at her parents, shaking her head in disbelief. 'When will you get it? I'm NOT A FUCKING CHILD!'

Her voice echoes throughout the arrivals hall. Heads turn. Ben clears his throat.

'Can I say something?' He extends a handshake to Cameron, who appears to notice him for the first time.

'Ben. Pleased to meet you.'

'Likewise.'

For the second time in forty-eight hours Morgan looks on as two men size each other up. Ben turns to Lissa. His face is grave.

'Your mum needs to put an end to the Karl Savage situation *and* get Anjelica out of prison. But you're her first priority. She needs to know you're safe so she called your dad.' He pauses. 'Don't take this the wrong way – I know you're going through a crappy time – but you *really* need to give her a break and stop behaving like a brat.' He smiles. 'I mean that in the nicest possible way.'

Lissa stares at him. Her father blinks again, then turns to Morgan. His expression says *Who the fuck is this guy?* Morgan smiles at her daughter, determined to see this through

'I need to know you're somewhere Karl can't get at you.'

'What about getting at *you*? I thought we were a *team*.'

Morgan nods. 'But I'm the captain.' Lissa rolls her eyes as her mother continues. 'Don't make me go through all the "every crisis is an opportunity" crap. Have some time with your dad and let me do what I need to do.' She pauses. 'Besides, you've got stuff to talk about.'

Cameron raises an eyebrow. 'Stuff?'

Morgan and Lissa exchange a look. Cameron doesn't know his daughter is pregnant, let alone the identity of the father. Lissa will break the news in her own time. A series of long walks in the countryside will provide the perfect opportunity.

Lissa scowls. 'I'll tell you later.' She puts her hands on her hips and turns to Ben. 'You knew about this?'

'Afraid so.'

'Fuck's sake.'

She falls silent for a moment, shaking her head from side to side, taking a moment to absorb this latest turn of events.

'I've booked a five-star hotel,' says Cameron, his tone switching to emollient. 'Saunas, massage, facials.'

Lissa remains unimpressed. 'Jesus . . . you sound like Elton John.' Despite the bravado, her eyes brim with tears. She turns to Morgan. 'Who'll look after you?'

'I'm a big girl,' says Morgan, sounding braver than she feels. 'I don't need looking after.'

Ben clears his throat.

'I'll be around. Your mum can stay with me as long as she likes.'

Morgan feels a mixture of gratitude and irritation but says nothing. The man doesn't mean to be patronising, and anything to persuade Lissa to go with her father. Her daughter chews on the inside of her lip.

'OK,' she says, resignation entering her voice. She grabs the handle of her suitcase, glaring at Ben as she takes revenge on her mother. 'Mum fancies you. Look after her or I'll kill you.'

Morgan rolls her eyes but says nothing. Ben swallows a smile then raises an eyebrow in Lissa's direction.

'Shall we give your mum and dad a couple of minutes?'

Lissa nods, then hugs her mother and whispers in her ear.

'How did you get to be so devious?'

Morgan whispers back, echoing one of her daughter's favourite phrases.

'Just lucky, I guess.'

They break the clinch. Lissa turns and wheels the suitcase towards the coffee shop, Ben following in her wake. Morgan turns to Cameron. Only now does she notice flecks of grey in his hair, the lines on his forehead and the circles under his eyes.

'Thank you,' she says. 'It was a big ask.'

He shrugs. 'My new movie fell through. The timing was perfect.'

So not such a selfless gesture after all.

She keeps her smile in place. He came when asked. That's what counts.

'How's Hollywood?'

'Same old same old. They screw you around, mess up your script, crush your spirit and what do you get for it? Millions of dollars.' He has the grace to smile. 'And now Kristina wants a baby.'

'And you?'

'I'd rather have a Lamborghini.' He scratches his stubble and gestures towards Ben. 'Seems a nice guy.'

Morgan nods.

'Just a friend.'

Cameron gives her a knowing look. His face grows serious.

'This Karl guy sounds crazy. Sure you know what you're doing?'

Morgan considers the question.

'Yes,' she says. 'Absolutely positive.'

A barefaced lie, but it's the best she can do.

Twenty-Eight

'Sorry I'm such a slob,' says Morgan.

Sprawled on Ben's sofa, she takes stock of the mess she and Lissa have made of his house. Clothes are strewn on the floor, mugs and plates litter every surface and the dining table has disappeared beneath transcripts of Anjelica's trial.

He answers from the kitchen, raising his voice above the sound of clam shells clattering into a pan.

'You've a lot on your plate. Besides, I'm never here.'

She gets to her feet, crosses the room and leans against the kitchen doorpost.

'You work like crazy. Do you ever sleep?'

He shakes his head.

'Not my strong suit.'

Taking a bottle of Shiraz from the wine rack, he inserts the corkscrew and tugs hard. The wooden handle breaks in his hands, rendering the device useless.

'Shit.'

Morgan suppresses a smile.

'Do you know the shoe trick?'

He raises an eyebrow.

'Show me.'

She takes the bottle from his hand.

'Take off one of your shoes.'

He obliges. Inserting the base of the bottle into the heel, Morgan places the shoe flat against the wall. She thumps the bottle against the inside of the leather sole, several times in quick succession. By the sixth thump, the cork is protruding halfway from the bottle. Relieved the trick worked (it doesn't always) she twists the cork, tugs it out, then pours two glasses of wine, raising hers in a toast.

'Cheers.'

They clink glasses. He smiles.

'What do you do for an encore?'

Enjoying her small triumph, she returns the smile, watching as he splashes vermouth onto the garlic, olive oil and chilli frying in the pan. Adding the pasta, he puts the lid on the pan, swirls the clamshells around then adds a handful of chopped parsley. 'If this is edible, I'll take the credit,' he says, dividing the *spaghetti alle vongole* onto two plates. 'If not, blame Nigella.'

They eat side by side on the sofa, watching *Off the Grid*, the reality show in which survivalists in the wilderness try to avoid being caught by experts based in the studio. It's Jukes's favourite, the programme he'd ringed in the TV listings guide. Morgan wonders if Karl and Spike are watching too, skulking in their hideout and gathering tips on how to evade capture.

Grateful for a respite from her worries, she's diverted by the tactics of the contestants (one sleeps in a ditch, concealed under piles of roadside litter) but Ben is more interested in Lissa and Cameron.

'Will she be OK?'

Morgan sips her wine.

'Hard to say. She's complicated. And she's keeping something from me.'

'Like?'

'No idea.'

'Maybe she'll confide in her father.'

'I'm not holding my breath.'

'Did he help when she was a kid? With money, at least?'

Swallowing a mouthful of pasta, Morgan considers her response.

'Eventually.'

She leaves it there, not wanting to criticise the man who has responded to her SOS and jumped on a plane from the US. Truth is, it was years before Cameron stepped up to his responsibilities, leaving Morgan to juggle the trials of single parenthood with the demands of freelance journalism. No wonder her career nose-dived and her friends melted away.

As he said when she broke the news, a baby wasn't on his 'to-do list'. If Morgan wanted to proceed with the pregnancy then fine, but if the decision was hers then so was the responsibility.

She'd never taken him to court, hoping there was a decent man in there somewhere, a man who would come to understand that writing romantic comedies didn't make you a *mensch* whereas doing your imperfect best as a parent was your one shot at making sense of your time on the planet.

Romcoms . . .

She glances at Ben's bookshelves. The Motown LPs and books on military history are still there but the DVDs have disappeared.

'What happened to the romantic comedies?'

'My sister took them when she moved back in with her girl-friend.'

His sister.

'Was the cat hers too?'

And the pink bra?

Ben nods. 'They have a bust-up every few months, she crashes here, cries a lot, then goes back and swears she's never been so happy.'

'So you're close?'

Another nod, eyes firmly on the TV.

'We're the only ones left.'

Morgan can smell the soap on his skin. Or is it Nivea? Could she trust a man who moisturises? She puts her plate on the coffee table and picks up her glass of wine. Tempted to ask about his family, about the Boxing Day fire that claimed the lives of his parents and brother, she senses the subject is closed – for now, at least.

Besides, with Lissa in the care of her father, Morgan has a rare opportunity to think about other things.

Like how Ben's stubble would feel against her skin.

'Delicious pasta,' she says. 'Thank you.'

'I never cook for myself. Makes a change.'

He puts his plate on top of hers, knocking a clamshell to the floor. They reach for it at the same time, hands touching briefly. She picks up the shell, places it on the plate, then licks her fingers while holding his gaze a beat too long.

His face creases into a smile.

'More wine?'

She nods, watching as he pours a glass. His hands are strong, his fingers long and elegant, his nails immaculate. He reaches for the remote and turns off the TV. When he speaks again, his voice is low.

'You know that moment when you're about to kiss someone for the first time? And both of you know it's going to happen? And it feels *so* intense?'

She nods.

'I know that moment.'

'How would it be to prolong that feeling? To keep prolonging it till you both think you might go mad?'

'How long?'

His eyes search hers. 'As long as possible.'

'Sounds good.' Her voice is husky. 'Up to a point.'

She's holding his gaze, feeling her heart rate quicken.

'There's a thing I'd like to do,' he says.

'What kind of thing?'

'It's a little weird.'

'Try me.'

'Good weird, not bad weird.'

'*Try me.*'

'OK.' He sips his wine, sets his glass on the table, then turns to face her. 'I want you to touch yourself.'

'Now?'

'Now.'

'OK. I can do that.' She reaches for her belt buckle. 'Is that it?' she says. 'Is that the "thing"?'

'That's the beginning.'

'OK, what else?'

She's slowly unfastening the button on her jeans. Can't decide if he's sexy or sleazy. Maybe both. She'll think about it later.

'I want to kiss your neck,' he says.

'While I'm touching myself?'

'Yes.'

'I thought kissing was going to wait.'

'That was a stupid idea,' says Ben.

'Shut up and kiss me.'

He moves closer, raising his hand to her mouth, gently caressing her lower lip with his thumb. She can feel his breath on her cheek. Their lips meet – softly at first – then she feels the tip of his tongue gently teasing her mouth. Her heart is racing. Her hands creep between her legs.

'Is this what you want, Ben?'

'Yes.' His voice is a whisper. 'Make yourself wet.'

'Not going to be a problem.'

His eyes flicker towards her mouth.

'While your fingers are wet I want you to trace them around the rim of my glass, so every time I take a sip of wine I can taste you.'

Breathing hard, heart racing, Morgan closes her eyes and slips her fingers inside her knickers. He leans forward, kissing her neck, tracing feather-light kisses over her skin.

Her phone rings.

Her eyes snap open.

'Sorry. Might be Lissa.'

He pulls away, leaning against the sofa, smiling his slow, sexy smile.

'It's fine,' he says. 'We've got all night.'

Morgan reaches for her mobile. A number she doesn't recognise.

'Hello?'

'It's Joe Cassidy.'

Joe Cassidy?

'We met the other night, on the beach? You were looking for your daughter?'

The guy in the fisherman's jumper.

'I found her, thanks.'

'That's not why I'm calling.'

'Oh?'

'I just drove past your place. I think you'd better get over here.'

She sits up straight.

'Why?'

'Your bed's on the beach. Someone set it on fire.'

By the time they reach Dungeness, Eric Sweet has arrived and is standing alongside Joe Cassidy, watching the mattress burn. Flames flicker around the iron bed frame, the intensity of the blaze throwing shadows over the clusters of kale and the abandoned fishing boat a hundred yards from Morgan's house. Hands in her pockets, she watches Ben shine a torch over the back door. The lock is broken, the wooden panel splintered. Shattered by kicks? An axe?

'Did either of you see anyone?' says Morgan.

Eric shakes his head. The man in the fisherman's jumper follows suit.

'I'd have put the fire out myself,' he says, 'but the SOCOs wouldn't have thanked me.'

'No point calling the police,' says Morgan. 'They're sick of hearing my name.'

'How did he get the bed out of the house?' says Eric. 'It's wider than the door.'

'Must have dismantled it inside then reassembled it out here,' says Ben.

'And risk being seen?'

Morgan scans the deserted beach.

'Hardly Piccadilly Circus.' She digs her hands into her pockets. 'Besides, he loves risks. They make him feel alive.' She turns to Joe. 'Thanks for the call.'

'No problem,' says Joe. He gestures towards the broken sitting-room window, where Karl broke in the night he took Morgan to the cemetery. The shards of glass have been removed. A large sheet of cardboard packaging is taped to the window frame.

'I patched it up,' he said. 'A bodge job, but it'll hold till you get it fixed properly.'

'Thanks,' says Morgan.

Cassidy nods towards Ben and Eric. 'Mind if I leave you to it? I'm supposed to be meeting my son for a drink.'

'Of course,' says Morgan.

'Let me know if you need anything,' says Joe, turning and heading for his car. Ben watches him drive away, frowning.

'Is he kosher?'

'According to Rook, yes,' says Morgan. 'He's an ex-copper.'

Ben doesn't look convinced but says nothing. Eric gestures towards the broken door.

'Sure about not calling the police? It's a crime scene.'

'But not much of a crime,' says Morgan. She recalls Karl's white boiler suit, and the scrupulously careful manner in which he picked up the cigarette stub in the cemetery. 'He knows how to run rings around SOCOs.'

Eric raises an eyebrow.

'You know who did this?'

'I've an idea,' says Morgan. 'I pissed him off by taking Lissa out of his clutches, so he's sending me a message. He's smart but not as smart as he thinks.'

Her mind flashes back to the man pissing on his mother's grave. OK, so the rain washed away the urine before the SOCOs could collect it for analysis, but sooner or later he'll make a slip-up that will prove to be his undoing. In the meantime, she'll focus on bringing that day closer.

'I'll check inside,' says Ben, heading into the house.

Sitting in the passenger seat of the Range Rover, Morgan tries to roll a cigarette but her hands are trembling. She stuffs her tobacco pouch back in her pocket then stares at the house while listening to the waves on the shoreline. Eric leans against the car, saying nothing. Out at sea, a fishing trawler is crawling across the horizon, its white light a warning to other vessels. After two minutes of companionable silence, the mattress fire has dwindled to ashes and Ben is back, making his way across the shingle.

'He used white spirit to start the fire.'

Morgan nods. 'I could use a drink.'

Eric gestures in the direction of the inn.

'On the house.'

Getting into his car, he leads the way. Ben and Morgan follow close behind.

'If this *is* down to Savage,' says Ben, steering the Range Rover onto the tarmac road, 'he's made a fool of the police, the courts and me.'

If . . .

The word suggests he still can't bring himself to accept the man is alive – not one hundred per cent – there's still a scintilla of doubt. Morgan is too tired to argue. She falls silent, wondering how it's possible to feel so alone.

'You OK?' Ben steers the car over the shingle and onto the tarmac road.

She doesn't answer, peering at distant pinpricks of light from HMP Dungeness. She thinks of Anjelica Fry recovering in hospital, her face slashed on the order of Savage or his crony, Jukes.

She thinks of her daughter, pregnant by a man suffering unfathomable childhood wounds.

She thinks of the impotence of the police – no, not impotence – their *refusal* to help find Karl, to challenge the status quo, to admit the system screwed up. And why? Is it because they can't keep pace with criminals who are still alive, let alone search for someone they 'know' to be dead?

Or because a woman wrote a book suggesting they're less than perfect?

'No,' she says, turning to face Ben. 'I'm not OK.'

Not long ago she was looking forward to spending the night with a man with strong hands and a sexy smile. Now she wants to drink till she passes out.

In the deserted bar, Eric sets glasses on a table and uncorks a bottle of red wine. Ben covers his glass with a hand.

'Just Coke. I'm driving.'

Eric obliges, then goes into the kitchen. Ben watches him go, waiting until he's out of earshot.

'Why would anyone open a hotel here?'

'What's wrong with Dungeness?'

'Nothing, unless you want a business that makes actual money.' He sips his drink. 'I presume the police checked his alibi? For the day Kiki died?'

Morgan nods but the question makes her doubt her own certainty. Her stomach gives a lurch.

Had they?

She remembers quizzing Rook about Eric. The DI had reassured her that he was very 'thorough' with his enquiries. But had he specifically told her Eric was in the clear? She sips her wine.

'When it comes to men, I have no idea who to trust any more. Neville, Eric, Joe Cassidy, Cameron, you . . . who knows what you're all *really* like, what you all *really* want?'

He meets her gaze.

'I googled your old flame,' he says. 'I'm sorry he was such a bastard.'

She responds with what she hopes is a nonchalant shrug. Her childhood sweetheart, Danny, had found himself behind bars, victim of a miscarriage of justice. Morgan was a lone voice protesting his innocence. She'd fought to clear his name and her campaign had been a success. On his release, he'd repaid his champion by behaving like a shit. Learning to trust again won't be easy.

She turns to face Ben. 'If you're a bastard, do me a favour and tell me now.'

His voice is serious, his smile sincere.

'I'm no bastard,' he says. 'But I'm far from perfect.'

She searches his eyes.

'Makes two of us.'

He's no longer looking at her, his eyes straying towards the ceiling. She follows his gaze. He's looking at the smoke alarm, frowning.

'Odd.'

He cranes his neck for a closer look.

'That's a not real smoke alarm. It's a spy cam.'

Morgan frowns.

'Are you sure?'

He nods.

'Probably linked to his computer so he can keep tabs on what's going on.'

Morgan's heart is racing. An image comes to mind of Eric balancing on a stepladder, installing a smoke alarm in Lissa's hotel room. Another in the lounge.

'They're all over the hotel.'

'Even the bedrooms?'

Morgan is suddenly queasy. Struck by a thought.

'Stay here.'

Slipping down from her stool, she heads for the Ladies. Scrutinising the ceiling, she can see a smoke alarm – or what looks like one – directly over the cubicle. It's identical to the one in the bar, so not an alarm at all, but another spy cam, part of Eric's private CCTV system.

Suddenly self-conscious in case he's watching, she washes her hands, then returns to the bar.

Eric is on his feet, topping up her glass. Ben is scrolling through his phone, doing a good job of avoiding the innkeeper's eye.

'Hungry?' says Eric, proffering a menu.

'No,' says Morgan. She shoots a look in Ben's direction. 'We need to get going.'

Ben reaches for his wallet.

'On the house,' says Eric.

But Ben remains stony-faced, saying nothing as he slaps a ten-pound note on the bar. Eric frowns, puzzled by the change in atmosphere.

'Everything OK?'

'Long day,' says Morgan, avoiding the man's eye. 'I need to get home.'

Outside, climbing into the Range Rover, she is quivering with anger.

'Why didn't you say anything?' says Ben.

'He'd dismantle the spy cams. If he's a peeping Tom, the police need to catch him red-handed.'

Another thought strikes with the force of a speeding truck: Kiki's brief stint as a cleaner. Had she stumbled upon Eric's secret?

Had he silenced her?

Morgan checks her watch. Nearly 11 p.m. Reaching for her mobile, she composes a message.

'Who are you texting?'

'Rook. He needs to know about this.'

Ben says nothing, peering out at the road ahead. The journey passes in silence, driver and passenger lost in thought.

By the time they reach Canterbury, her mood has taken a dive. Inside the house the heating is off, the coffee table littered with dirty plates and glasses. She's grateful to Ben for not trying to pick up where they left off. The moment has gone.

'Thanks for not being a dick.'

'Best compliment ever.' He takes her hand. 'We've got unfinished business. But not tonight.'

She smiles and plants a kiss on his cheek.

'Always leave 'em wanting more.'

Then she goes up to her room and closes the door.

The blazing bed features in her dreams, along with Lissa, her belly swollen as she dances on a burning beach with Anjelica and two babies, Marlon and Charlie. Both wear fisherman's jumpers.

Waking with a start just before seven, Morgan is slick with sweat, her throat dry, her mouth parched. Going downstairs, she finds the house has been tidied and the dishwasher is humming. No sign of Ben.

Downing a glass of water, she sets the kettle to boil then sees a note on the table.

See you tonight? x

It's not the message that makes her smile, or the *x*, it's the PS.

I believe you're right. Karl Savage is alive.

Twenty-Nine

Forty-eight hours after the incident with the burning bed, Morgan is back in Dungeness, driving past her house. The iron bedstead is still on the beach, an absurd-looking addition to the piles of scrap littering the landscape. A locksmith has installed new deadbolts and the back door has been repaired, but the sitting-room window is still boarded up with cardboard. Joe Cassidy's 'bodge job' will do for now.

A mile further on, she passes the Beach Inn. No sign of life. A *Closed* sign on the door. A police car in the car park. Frowning, she pulls to a halt next to a silver Ford she recognises as Neville Rook's. As she climbs out of the Mini, feeling the late-October chill, her mobile beeps.

A text from Ben.

Sorry to sound like your mum but let me know you're OK?

She taps out a quick reply. There has been no mention of what nearly happened two nights ago. The arson investigator has been absent most of the time, working with the police team probing the burnt-out lorry.

Brief encounters in the kitchen have been short, almost monosyllabic, but Morgan doesn't take it personally. They're both under pressure. There will come a time for conversation, laughter and, she hopes, sex, but not now.

Passing Neville's car she catches sight of the *Kent Courier* on the passenger seat. A photo of Eric Sweet alongside a headline.

Police Quiz Hotel 'Peeping Tom'.

The paper has latched on to the story fast, its front-page splash the work of a reporter with good contacts or a leak by the police, perhaps a combination of the two.

Morgan feels a pang of sympathy for the hotel owner – he was kind and supportive during a difficult time – but the sentiment doesn't last long. There's nothing kind about spy cams in bedrooms and toilets, and there can be no innocent explanation. Eric will most likely go out of business. Perhaps to prison. But he has no one but himself to blame.

The question remains: is he simply another sleazebag?

Or something more sinister?

As Morgan approaches the hotel, two uniformed police officers emerge carrying see-through plastic evidence bags containing the dismantled 'smoke alarms'. Neville follows, face falling as he catches sight of her.

'What are you doing here?'

'I'm on my way to the prison.'

'To see Ian Carne?'

She shakes her head. 'Anjelica Fry.'

'How is she?'

'Traumatised. But out of hospital.'

'What about you?' says Rook, buttoning his jacket. 'Joe Cassidy called me about the burning bed.'

'Do you think Eric had something to do with it?'

'No idea. But you should have called us.'

She shrugs. 'Small fry compared to everything else going on. I'm trying not to waste your time.'

He gives a wan smile. Time to change the subject. She nods towards the hotel.

'Is Eric inside?'

'No.'

'Mind if I ask where he is?'

'Staying with friends, I believe.'

'Does he have an alibi for the time of Kiki's death?'

Rook looks away, avoiding her gaze.

'I can't talk about an ongoing enquiry.'

'But there *is* an enquiry?' says Morgan, undeterred. 'You're no longer taking the suicide scenario at face value?'

Blowing out his cheeks, the DI ignores the question and heads towards his car. She follows, crunching over the shingle.

'I assume there's no news on Charlie?'

'No comment.'

'How about Stacey and her baby?'

'No comment.'

'At least tell me about Jukes. I drove past his house. He's disappeared.'

'Says who?'

'I looked through his letterbox. Pile of junk mail on the doormat. He's gone.'

She remembers the journey to Heathrow, the Yamaha motorcycle following Ben's Range Rover. Was she right to dismiss the possibility of being tailed by Jukes?

'Have you checked his houseboat?' says Rook.

'Not lately. Have you?'

'Yes.'

'And?'

They've reached his car. He zaps the fob. 'Nothing – nada, zip, zilch.' He opens the door, watching the uniformed officers drive away. 'You were right to tell us about the spy cams – but the other stuff? Leave it to us. You're out of your depth.'

'Which is why I keep asking for help.'

'From Fireman Sam?'

'Who?'

'Ben Gaminara. You looked pretty cosy the other day.'

Morgan raises an eyebrow.

'Do I detect the green-eyed monster?'

He gives her a look filled with disdain.

'This isn't personal. I'm just trying to do my job.'

He gets into his car and sits behind the wheel. She tries one last question.

'What happened to the teeth from Karl's so-called corpse Are they still "missing" from storage?'

A sigh. 'No. DI Tucker signed them out.'

Morgan frowns. 'Why?'

A pained smile.

'My psychic powers don't extend as far as the Met.'

'Can't you ask him?'

'Maybe. When he gets out of hospital.' He starts the engine. 'He's having a back operation.'

Morgan remembers the Hackney DI adjusting his lumbar support cushion and wincing in pain.

'Have you got his mobile number?'

'No.'

'Which hospital is he in?'

Rook rolls his eyes.

'Don't you ever give up?'

Without waiting for an answer he closes the door and drives away. Morgan watches him go then walks back to the Mini, leaning against the bonnet. Rolling a cigarette, she stares out to sea, gazing at a flock of seagulls circling a fishing boat on the horizon. The low sun hurts her eyes. She lights the cigarette, sucking the smoke deep into her lungs. Her phone rings.

Cameron. Not happy. Straight to the point.

'Why didn't you tell me she's pregnant?'

'It's her news, not mine.'

'Jesus, Morgan, she's practically a kid.'

'I hope you're not giving her a hard time. She's been through a lot.'

A pause. A sigh. He softens his tone.

'Maybe that's why she's always in tears.'

Morgan frowns.

'What do you mean?'

'I can hear her at night, in the next room. I ask what's wrong, but she says, "just hormones". Says she's happy about the baby. What am I supposed to do?'

'Don't *do* anything. Listen. Be supportive. Tell her you love her.'

He sighs. 'What kind of man pricks holes in condoms?'

'He's deeply messed-up,' says Morgan. 'His father died saving him from a speeding lorry, and his mother was sick in the head.'

But Cameron isn't interested in the roots of Karl's behaviour, only the consequences. The rest of the conversation is brief, ending with his promise not to give Lissa a lecture.

Ending the call, Morgan takes a walk along the beach, breathing in the briny air, her mind fizzing with questions. How long before she can return home? Will Lissa and the baby live there too? How will they all manage?

In the distance, a plume of smoke rises from the engine that tows the Romney Hythe and Dymchurch Express through the wide-open spaces of Romney Sands. On board the narrow-gauge railway are day-trippers and train buffs, sipping their takeaway coffees and eating sandwiches while enjoying a morning of old-fashioned fun. Over by the black and white lighthouse, two teenage girls are wrestling with a kite, trying to catch the wind and send it soaring into the sky. Normal people, doing ordinary things. Morgan finds it hard to imagine life ever being normal again.

Her phone beeps with a message: a selfie of Lissa in the upmarket spa hotel, grinning from ear to ear. A pillow shoved up her shirt makes her look nine months pregnant. The text reads *I'm having a BABY! SO excited!*

Morgan frowns. Her daughter's moods seem more unpredictable than ever. But she's safe. One less thing to worry about.

So why the feeling of impending doom?

Turning, she retraces her steps to the car. Then she starts the engine and heads for HMP Dungeness.

Anjelica's face is bandaged. Seated across from Morgan in the main visitors' room, her eyes are glazed, her voice slurred. The strong medication is continuing to take its toll.

'They moved me out of MBU. Took my baby.'

'I'm so sorry,' says Morgan.

She pushes a Kit Kat across the table, bought from the prison vending machine. Anjelica ignores it, fingering a stray thread on the sleeve of her fleece.

'Tell me you have good news?'

'I'm working on it,' says Morgan, aware of the lameness of her reply. She looks around the room, taking stock of other prisoners' friends and families before bringing her gaze to rest on Anjelica's face. She dreads to think what horrors lie beneath the bandages. The woman looks demoralised. Close to defeat.

Until now, Morgan has decided against revealing that Karl is still alive, reluctant to encourage what might prove to be false optimism. What had the woman said?

This is the one place you can die of hope.

But things have changed. Since the encounter in the graveyard there can no longer be the slightest doubt that Karl Savage faked his own death, that he framed Anjelica for his murder. The 'why' is clear. She'd exposed his drug-dealing activities to the police. The question now is how?

Morgan has spent two days holed up in Ben's house, sustained by coffee and cigarettes while poring over trial transcripts and notes of her meetings with Anjelica. According to the woman's original testimony, the father of her child was selling class A drugs for years, working with a long-time crony, Spike. Morgan vividly recalls the video of 'Joker' Karl setting fire to the Porsche. According to Nancy Sixsmith, mother of his twins, the video was shot by Spike.

'What can you tell me about Karl's second-in-command?' says Morgan.

Anjelica frowns.

'Spike? What about him?'

'He may be one of the missing pieces of the puzzle. When did you last see him?'

'Couple of months before Karl died, maybe more.'

'Can you describe him?'

'Not really.'

'Tall? Short? Black? White? Thin? Fat?'

'White, maybe six feet, medium build.'

Morgan can feel her heart starting to race.

'So he looked like Karl?'

Anjelica shakes her head.

'Karl was a looker, not like Spike.'

'But the same build?'

'Roughly. Why?'

Morgan ignores the question.

'Was he Karl's best friend?'

'No, they just ran the drug racket together. Karl used to say he couldn't trust Spike further than he could throw him. But the man had contacts. Clever ideas about how to move the stuff around.'

The woman moistens her cracked lips, frowning as another thought struggles to the surface.

'I remember him saying he was sure Spike was stealing from him, siphoning cash.'

'They fell out?'

'Maybe.'

'What happened to people Karl fell out with?'

Anjelica raises her gaze.

'That a serious question? To me, of all people?'

Morgan flashes an apologetic smile.

'Just trying to get to the bottom of things.'

The woman sniffs, raises her arm and scratches an armpit. Morgan catches a whiff of stale sweat.

'Why the interest in Spike?'

Morgan looks around, checking she can't be overheard by the patrolling prison officer. Time to drop the bombshell she's been avoiding.

'This will be a shock.' She leans forward in her chair. 'I need you to hear me out before you say anything. And it's best you don't tell *anyone*.'

'Tell them what?'

Morgan lowers her voice.

'Karl is alive.' She continues as Anjelica's eyes widen in disbelief. 'I've seen him. He's behind the baby farm. He faked his own death. I'm starting to think he killed Spike, burned the body beyond recognition and passed it off as his own. He killed two birds with one stone, Anjelica – making everyone believe he's dead and silencing you.'

The frown furrowing Anjelica's brow deepens.

'Is this some kind of joke?'

Morgan shakes her head. She tells Anjelica about the churchyard encounter with Karl and the burning bed on the beach. She doesn't mention Lissa's pregnancy. One revelation at a time.

Anjelica listens in silence then leans forward, bringing her face inches from Morgan's.

'Do you know how mad you sound?'

'You're not the first to say that.'

'Karl died in that fire. The police have his teeth. They identified the body.'

'They were wrong,' says Morgan. 'I've seen him.'

The woman's eyes search hers. Desperate to believe.

'Why should I trust you?'

'Why would I lie?'

Anjelica leans back in her chair, her gaze fixed on Morgan's face.

'Who else have you told?'

'The police,' says Morgan. 'The fire investigator. Your solicitor. The forensic ondontologist who identified the body.'

'And?'

'They think I'm crazy. Except for Ben Gaminara.'

'Even my lawyer – Millar?'

'Especially Millar.' Morgan recalls the whisky-soaked solicitor's contempt for his former client. 'There's no point in trying to get the system on our side, Anjelica. Not till I prove Karl's alive.'

The woman is chewing the inside of her lip, trying to process the news that could lead to her release. 'What did Singh say?'

'He's sticking to his story. He even showed me the X-rays he used to make the ID. But I think it was Spike's body in the flat, not Karl's.'

'How did Singh get it wrong?'

'I don't know.'

Morgan can see the gamut of emotions behind the woman's eyes. Bewilderment. Disbelief. Hope. Confusion.

'If Karl is alive, why didn't you tell me before?'

'I needed to be certain,' says Morgan. She looks at the woman's bandaged face. 'And let's face it, you could use a ray of hope.'

I don't want you to kill yourself.

I don't want your death on my conscience.

Anjelica's eyes glaze with tears and the first signs of anger.

'How *could* he?'

'I can't answer that,' says Morgan. 'But I know what I know.' She takes Anjelica's hand. 'All I have to do is prove it.'

Returning to the car park, Morgan sees two familiar figures walking in the opposite direction: psychologist Nigel Cundy and prison governor Ian Carne.

'Mr Carne?'

The men turn as she approaches. Carne raises a quizzical eyebrow.

'Yes?'

'Morgan Vine. We met the other day. I was visiting Anjelica Fry.'

'Yes. I remember.'

'Thank you for your letter—'

He cuts her off, zapping the fob on a pristine black BMW. 'I'm afraid we're late for a meeting.'

'Prison Officers Association,' adds Cundy, by way of explanation.

Morgan knows there's little point in asking about the baby farm. Both men will only stonewall, like before.

'I won't keep you. I need to ask about Kiki McNeil.'

'What about her?' says Carne.

'You heard what happened to her?'

'She jumped off a cliff.'

Cundy nods.

'Depression. Terrible thing.'

'Was she clinically depressed?' asks Morgan. 'While she was in prison?'

The men exchange a look.

'We're not at liberty to discuss prisoners' medical histories,' says Cundy. 'Even when they're no longer our responsibility.'

'What if she didn't jump?' says Morgan. 'What if she was pushed?'

A muscle twitches beneath the governor's eye.

'The police seem satisfied that's not the case,' he says.

'I'm not the police.'

'So I've noticed.'

'She served three and a half years in your prison.'

'Correct,' says Carne.

He gets behind the wheel of the car. Cundy climbs into the passenger seat. Morgan perseveres.

'What if someone wanted to keep her quiet?'

'About what?' says Carne.

Morgan nods towards the prison gates. 'Secrets. Things that could ruin careers. Like how women get pregnant in your prison.'

The colour drains from the governor's face. He starts the engine.

'Tread carefully, Ms Vine.'

'Is that a threat?'

'A friendly warning. People get the wrong end of the stick; they can make fools of themselves.' He scratches his beard. 'Especially those with an axe to grind against the system.'

Morgan raises an eyebrow.

'You've read my book?'

A chilly smile.

'I'm too busy for books.'

He closes the door of the car and drives away. Morgan watches the BMW exit the car park and disappear from view. She chides herself for tackling the men on the spur of the moment. What did she expect? A confession? To what?

She recalls DI Rook's remark about the climate of secrecy at HMP Dungeness.

Think North Korea with Carne as Kim Jong-un.

Returning to her car, she smokes a cigarette while making a list of people who might have wanted to silence Kiki McNeil. She writes the governor's name next to Cundy's. Both have a vested interest in ensuring that 'what happens in prison stays in prison'. What if Kiki had threatened to blow the whistle on the baby farm?

Next on the list are Trevor Jukes and Karl Savage.

That they are partners in crime is beyond doubt.

But *what* crime? What was Kiki's involvement?

Then come the names of two men with whom Morgan knows Kiki had contact, albeit fleetingly. Innkeeper Eric Sweet and near neighbour Joe Cassidy, the man who glimpsed the woman on the night she died in St Mary's Bay.

Last on the list is Karl's crony, Spike, followed by Kiki's best friend, Stacey Brown.

Gazing at the names, Morgan's head is abuzz with questions. None the wiser, she makes a decision. To discover how the puzzle fits together – Kiki's murder, the baby farm, Anjelica's conviction – she must settle the question of how Karl faked his own death.

She will start with the man who identified his remains. The man with the bitten fingernails. The family portrait. And the Harley Street smile.

Thirty

KARL

No peeking.

That's what she told him when she returned the tin to the cellar, sealed with duct tape. For a while he resisted temptation. Sixteen weekends in a row, locked up with his books and his torch.

And the tin.

At 3 a.m. on the seventeenth Saturday he cracked.

Peeled off the tape.

Prised open the lid.

Looked inside.

Big mistake.

Did she really think he'd never look? Is the cellar her idea of a safe hiding place? Somewhere to keep her darkest secret? There's no point in asking. Having uttered those two words – 'no peeking' – she has reverted to silence.

The Whistler knows what's in the tin. No doubt about it. He came down to the cellar (after she'd gone to bed, as usual). Even said he was sorry. But he was drunk. Very drunk.

– *Fucking baby wouldn't stop crying. I kept telling him to shut up, but he wouldn't. So I snapped. I'm sorry. But it was*

his fault for crying all the time. You forgive me, don't you,
Karl?

– *Yes. I forgive you.*

What else was he supposed to say?

– *Good boy. Show me how. Show me how you forgive me. Let's*
play our game, shall we? Our special game.

After 'the game' – after The Whistler had gone – Karl opened the
tin again. Just to check. Then he sealed it up, good as new. He
won't tell her that he knows.

Won't tell her about The Whistler's 'special game' either. Too
ashamed.

But he's got to do *something*. He's ten. This has been going on
for over half his lifetime. He's been hoping she'll change if he's
a good boy. Hoping she'll talk to him. Hoping The Whistler will
leave him alone.

But one of Daddy's sayings keeps playing inside his head.

Hope is not a plan . . .

Thirty-One

Sitting at Ben's dining table, Morgan speaks softly into her mobile, doing her best not to lose her temper.

'Are you telling me Mr Singh is refusing to see me?'

The receptionist's voice – honeyed, designed to soothe the anxieties of wealthy patients – emanates from the speaker.

'Not at all, Ms Vine. He's just a busy man, which is why he starts work so early. Patients, conferences abroad, not to mention his forensic work.'

'That's what I want to talk to him about.'

'Perhaps you could email him again?'

'He's ignored two emails, why would a third make any difference?'

'It's not a question of *ignoring*, I assure you. He's just—'

'A busy man. I get it. Thanks.'

Hanging up, she resists the temptation to hurl her phone across the room. She has been awake most of the night, reviewing the evidence, and has reached a conclusion: Jatinder Singh, Dip. F. Od. may have a string of letters after his name and a Harley Street office with a portrait of his wife and daughters adorning the wall, but the man is either incompetent or dishonest.

Stepping into the courtyard garden, Morgan smokes her first cigarette of the day while gazing at the clouds scudding across the Canterbury sky. In the distance, she can hear the peals of the cathedral's oldest bell. She checks her watch: 8 a.m. She recalls her father telling her about Bell Harry. Cast in 1635, it hangs at the top of the tower to which the bell lends its name. 'Harry' strikes at eight every morning, then at nine in the evening, marking the opening and closing of the cathedral.

Although not on speaking terms with God, Morgan has always found church bells comforting. Today is different. She's weary after another semi-sleepless night, worried about her daughter and frustrated at the lack of progress in unravelling a miscarriage of justice that seems more unjust with each passing day.

In the kitchen she makes a pot of coffee, then spends half an hour googling articles about Jatinder Singh, reading up on his presentations to conferences around the world – Amsterdam, Dubai, Rome, Mexico City. A leader in his field. It seems unlikely he made a rookie mistake identifying Karl's remains. Which leaves only one explanation.

A lie.

She can find no trace of Singh's home address, but a flattering piece appears on the website of a local paper, the *Camden Examiner*. The article is a thinly disguised ad for a charity supported by Singh. The interviewer refers admiringly to the forensic odontologist *pro bono* activities in Sierra Leone and Bangladesh, operating on children with cleft palates. Accompanied by a photo of Singh's wife and daughters, the article was printed last year and references the man's current case, identifying a charred corpse found after a fire in Dalston.

Karl Savage?

About to click away, Morgan's attention is drawn to a mention of stone lions on pillars outside the man's 'pastel-coloured family home in uber-trendy Primrose Hill'.

Two and a half hours later she's roving the streets of the well-heeled north London neighbourhood, searching for Singh's house. The overpriced cafés, delis and boho-chic clothing shops denote eye-watering property prices and prosperous locals. Just the sort of place a well-off professional might raise a family if he'd established a foothold before the housing market went crazy.

After two hours of slogging around Primrose Hill with no sign of lions on pillars, Morgan is tired, hungry and despondent. She sits at a table outside a café, drinking laughably expensive coffee, eating a Parma ham baguette and smoking two roll-ups in quick succession. The sunshine is unseasonably warm for late October, the locals dressed for summer, not autumn. Paying her bill, Morgan overtips the waitress, a young black woman of Lissa's age, who maintains a smile while catering to three pinch-faced ladies debating whether or not climate change is real, and a table of sharp-suited estate agents braying about the size of their commission. Pocketing Morgan's fiver, the waitress flashes a grateful smile.

'Nice one. Thanks.'

Morgan gets to her feet, picking up her pouch of tobacco and lighter.

'Don't suppose you know a house with lions on pillars?'

A long shot but worth a try.

'Sorry,' says the waitress. 'Not my area.'

Morgan smiles.

'Nor mine.'

Turning to leave, she bumps into a woman hurrying past, laden with carrier bags.

Morgan mutters an apology – reflex politeness – but the woman doesn't hear. She has her head down and is focused on navigating a cluster of yummy mummies pushing outsized buggies and scattering pedestrians in their wake.

Morgan frowns. Has she seen the passer-by before? It takes a moment for realisation to dawn. It's not the woman's face that strikes a chord, but her distinctive dress: a white sari, like the one worn by Singh's wife in the portrait in his office.

Instantly, the woman is transformed from stranger to quarry.

Morgan follows her along the pavement. The sari makes it easy to keep her in sight, the heavy shopping bags ensuring a slow, steady pace. As the road curves around the south side of Primrose Hill, Morgan sees affluent Londoners on the slopes – walking dogs, chasing toddlers, savouring the unexpected sunshine beaming down on the spiritual home of all things cupcake.

The woman in the white sari is fifty yards ahead, walking away from the park, towards the urban sprawl of Camden. The houses facing the hill are tall and elegant, four or five storeys painted in delicate shades of blue, yellow and pink. One window displays a magnificent antique rocking horse, others feature huge floral arrangements that must cost more than the wages of the army of cleaners, gardeners, nannies and au pairs required to keep each household ticking over smoothly.

For a moment Morgan feels a pang of jealousy, but then remembers that the only thing to envy about the rich is their money. Dismissing fantasies of a lottery win, she focuses on her quarry, following the woman onto a tree-lined street. The houses are smaller than those opposite the park but well cared-for and still worth many millions. The road is lined with BMWs, Mercedes and enough 4 x 4s to suggest a community braced for severe snowdrifts.

Now a second turn, another quiet street, one that escaped Morgan's notice during her trawl of the area. She slows, lingering at the corner and watching the woman approach a set of wrought-iron gates and tap a combination onto a keypad. The gates swing open. The woman walks onto the driveway, lets herself into the house and shuts the heavy door.

Morgan counts to ten, watching the gates close then scanning the windows for any sign of life. There is none. She takes a tentative step forward. The double-fronted house is three storeys high and painted a rich shade of cream. A silver Mercedes sits in front of the garage next to a red Volvo estate and a yellow Fiat 500. But it's not the house or cars that command Morgan's attention.

It's the stone lions on pillars, perched on either side of the gates.

Her eyes rove the house, taking stock of three CCTV cameras beneath the eaves, alongside a battery of security floodlights. Closer scrutiny of the gates reveals loops of razor wire across the top.

A voice at her side: male, elderly, posh.

'Wouldn't loiter, if I were you. They'll have the police out before you can say Jack Robinson.'

Morgan turns to see a spry-looking man in his eighties. He sports a blue cashmere cardigan over a Viyella shirt, and yellow cords tucked into wellington boots. At his side is a motley pack of dogs – eight or more, all shapes and sizes. Morgan makes an instant evaluation. The man is a widower who keeps fit by acting as dog walker for his time-poor, cash-rich neighbours. He nods towards the cream house.

'They don't care for dogs,' he says, 'so I don't care for them.'

Morgan smiles.

'I take it you're a local?'

He gestures towards a house at the end of the road; it's the same size as the Singh's residence, but scruffy and dilapidated.

'Since I was a nipper,' says the man. 'You could buy a decent house for five thousand *and* have change for an Austin. Which my parents did.'

One of the dogs – a King Charles spaniel – is straining at the leash.

'Excuse us,' says the man. 'Nell's desperate for walkies.'

He heads towards the corner. Morgan acts on impulse.

'Don't suppose you'd like company?'

The man smiles.

'Can't think of anything nicer.'

His name is Edward Somebody-or-Other, a double-barrelled surname Morgan doesn't catch. Keeping the dogs under control, he leads the way towards Primrose Hill, pointing to where shops and pubs used to be 'when God was a boy and I was knee-high to a grasshopper'. Morgan is happy to let the man talk but feels shabby about her motive for keeping him company.

Still, it makes a change from flirting with Neville Rook.

Reaching the park, Edward unleashes the dogs, calling out to keep them under control but never breaking his stride while ascending the steep hill. Morgan struggles to keep up. Reaching the top, she pauses to catch her breath, panting like a marathon runner. Edward raises an eyebrow.

'Young thing like you? Out of puff? Well, I never.'

'Smoker, I'm afraid.'

The smile falters.

'So was my dear wife.'

He raises his gaze, looking across the spectacular view of London. To the east St Paul's nestles amid the City skyscrapers; to the west a glimpse of the London Eye. He points to a familiar building in the foreground, the BT Tower.

'I remember when that was the GPO tower. Bet you don't know what GPO stood for.'

'General Post Office,' says Morgan. 'There used to be a revolving restaurant at the top. My father took my mother there the night he proposed.'

Edward smiles.

'And here you are.'

'In a nutshell.'

She sits on the bench, rolling a cigarette.

'Mind if I ask about the Singhs?'

'I was wondering when you'd get round to it.'

'Am I that obvious?'

He smiles, warm and twinkle-eyed.

'I've always been a sucker for a pretty face.'

Morgan smiles back.

'How long have they lived here?'

He sits next to her, rummaging in his pocket for a spotted handkerchief.

'Thirty years? Maybe more.' He blows his nose. 'Mr Singh is a dentist, I believe. Two delightful daughters and a somewhat charmless wife, or perhaps she's just shy. I seem to recall my wife saying that it was *Mrs* Singh's family who had the wherewithal to buy the house.' He turns to face her. 'Why the interest?'

She lights the cigarette.

'Mind if I keep that under my hat?'

'Not in the least.'

Turns out that many of Edward's neighbours refer to the Singh's family home as 'Fort Knox'. The draconian security measures are as unwelcome as they are new.

'He put up the gates after the attack, about nine months ago.'

Morgan plucks a wisp of tobacco from her tongue.

'What attack?'

'Racists,' says Edward. 'At least, that was the assumption. Someone put a burning rag through the letterbox, soaked in petrol.' The mention of arson makes Morgan's pulse start to race. She focuses on the man's every word. 'Three in the morning, no one around. They were lucky the dog next door started barking, woke them up and saved their lives.' He gestures towards one of his pack, a black poodle chasing a pigeon around the slopes of the hill. 'There's their saviour – dear old Suki. You'd think they'd be grateful, but no. Still, perhaps it's a cultural difference. I know many people from India are wary of dogs.'

It's not the dogs that interest Morgan.

'Did the police catch anyone?'

Edward shakes his head.

'Not for want of trying. I sometimes have a pint with one or two of the local coppers. They took it seriously but the arsonist was too clever by half. Wore a hoodie and managed to avoid being caught on CCTV. Which is why poor Mr Singh felt it necessary to put up cameras and install those ruddy gates.' He sighs. 'Used to be such a friendly neighbourhood. Now it's all bankers and Botox. Ghastly.'

A question nags at Morgan's brain.

'If he wasn't caught on CCTV, how do they know he wore a hoodie?'

'Our local bag lady, Eileen, bumped into him two minutes before the fire was started, and asked for a light. She told police she remembered nothing about the man except his cigarette lighter.'

'A Zippo?' says Morgan.

Edward raises an eyebrow.

'How did you know?'

Morgan's mind is racing. The arson attack occurred around the time of the investigation into the fire at Karl Savage's flat. Was the arsonist Karl himself? Is the timing significant? A warning to Singh? A threat to his family? A bid to strong-arm him into lying, into furnishing the police with evidence to identify the charred body as Karl's, thus 'proving' he died in the inferno?

She recalls the conversation in the Harley Street office, the ante-mortem radiograph taken by Savage's own dentist. Singh had used his Mont Blanc pen to point to a small, arch-shaped groove at the base of one of the front teeth. What had he said? Something about *the notching of the mandibles being indicative of someone regularly using his teeth to strip plastic coating from electrical wire . . .*

And now Morgan remembers another tap of the pen, pointing to the *post*-mortem radiograph, the one taken by Singh himself.

Or so he had told her.

And the police.

And the jury at Anjelica's trial.

No doubt he'd shown the evidence to the court, just as he'd shown it to Morgan.

And they'd all believed it.

Why wouldn't they?

Who would doubt a distinguished professional?

What could he possibly have to gain by lying?

She flinches. The cigarette has burned down, singeing her fingers. She drops it on the ground, grinding the stub under her heel.

'Are you all right?' says Edward.

'Fine,' says Morgan. Getting to her feet, she sees a woman at the bottom of the hill, pushing an overloaded supermarket trolley along the path. The trolley is piled high with newspapers.

'Is that Eileen?'

Edward follows her gaze and sighs.

'Yes,' he sighs. 'I'm afraid it is.'

Ten minutes later, Morgan is back outside the overpriced café, ignoring the glares of the po-faced yummy mummies furious at the introduction of a bag lady into their gilded world. Eileen has refused to enter the café (*I can't leave my papers unattended*), instructing Morgan to commandeer a pavement table. The imperious, grey-haired woman is in her fifties, overcoated despite the heat, and holding on to her trolley's handle for dear life. Five minutes of small talk have led nowhere. Eileen blocks any attempt to elicit personal information, which is fine by Morgan. She's not here to make friends.

'Was the hoodie's lighter definitely a Zippo?'

Eileen nods, crooking her little finger as she takes a sip of camomile tea.

'I used to have one myself.'

'But you didn't see his face?'

'No.'

Morgan begins to make a roll-up. The woman stares.

'Would you like a cigarette?' says Morgan.

A sniff.

'If you insist.'

'Do you know the Singhs?'

'I know everyone, darling. This is my manor.' Another sip of tea. 'But I don't see much of the girls these days, not since they got back.'

'From where?'

The woman doesn't answer immediately, distracted by the window display of eye-wateringly expensive cakes. Morgan senses a calculation being made: information for food.

'Do you think I might have a chocolate éclair?'

'Of course.' Morgan waves at the waitress, who takes Eileen's order then goes inside the café.

'You were saying?'

The woman looks at the roll-up in Morgan's hand.

'Is that for me?'

Morgan hands the cigarette over, lights it, then watches Eileen exhale twin plumes of smoke.

'I used to see the girls all the time,' she says. 'We'd meet on top of the hill, after school, and feed the pigeons. But their father sent them away after the arson attack on the house.'

'Where to?'

'France. The wife went too. She has relatives in Paris. I believe Mr Singh's plan was to move the whole family eventually – out of harm's way. But—'

She breaks off as the waitress returns with the éclair. Morgan suppresses a flicker of irritation, watching as the woman takes her time, nibbling the chocolate coating.

'What happened in Paris?'

'It seems they had a stalker. There was another firebomb, at their apartment block.'

Morgan's eyes widen in surprise.

'You think the arsonist followed them to Paris?'

A shrug. 'I've no idea,' says Eileen. 'But it does seem quite a coincidence.'

Watching the woman take another bite of éclair, Morgan's mind is racing.

If the arsonist *was* Karl it seems unlikely that he managed to leave the country without attracting the attention of the authorities. But he could easily have commissioned one of his cronies – Jukes or Spike – to follow the Singhs. To ensure they didn't feel safe *anywhere*. To make the patriarch feel his family may as well come home, where he could at least keep them close.

What father wouldn't do the same?

And who would believe him if he tried to blow the whistle on his tormentor? To shop Karl Savage – a man known to be dead.

It had been simple enough for Morgan to discover that Singh was working to identify the corpse in the burnt-out Dalston flat. Karl could have found out just as easily.

And mounted a campaign of terror to ram the message home.

Wherever you go, I will find your family.

There is no safe place.

Unless you do as I say.

Thirty-Two

Parked outside the Harley Street consulting rooms, Morgan sits in the Mini and lights another cigarette, her fourth in less than an hour. Darkness fell a while ago. Singh's office lights are ablaze but Morgan has no idea if he's inside. There seems little point in trying to make contact via the smarmy receptionist; Morgan has been given the runaround too many times. Never at ease with doorstepping, there are occasions when it's the only option.

Her phone beeps. A text from Ben. *Back by 9. Thai takeaway? x*

Morgan taps out a reply. *Back late. Thanks anyway.*

She hesitates, deliberating over whether or not to add an *x*, then sends the text with no form of endearment. Kisses can wait.

The *Six O'Clock News* burbles on the radio, making her drowsy despite the chill in the air. The rush hour is well under-way. People hurry past, heading for the Tube at Oxford Circus. During the last hour, three women and two men – patients, presumably, or fellow medical professionals – have emerged from the elegant Georgian building that houses Singh's consulting rooms, but there has been no sign of the man himself.

Stubbing out her cigarette, Morgan stretches her aching arms as far as the roof of the car will allow, then turns off the radio.

And now she sees him. Emerging from the front door, buttoning an elegant grey overcoat with a black velvet collar, a look she associates with smug Tory MPs. He hurries along Harley Street towards Regent's Park. She climbs out of the Mini, shoving her hands in the pockets of her leather jacket and setting off in pursuit of her second quarry of the day.

Reaching the top of Harley Street the man turns onto Marylebone Road. The traffic is bumper-to-bumper, exhaust fumes and rush-hour tension filling the air. Increasing her pace, Morgan closes the gap between herself and Singh, following as he takes advantage of a red light to cross the road. He turns onto a wide street leading into the park. She falls into step.

'Mr Singh?'

Without slowing, he turns to scrutinise her face. No trace of recognition.

'Yes?'

'Morgan Vine? We met the other day?'

'Ah, yes.' He carries on walking. 'Do you live locally?'

'No. I wanted a quick word.'

'I'm in rather a hurry.'

'That's OK. I'll walk with you.'

He does nothing to alter his pace. 'If you insist.'

The tree-lined road runs alongside the park and is bordered by white stucco terraces. The street lighting is a soft pink, the traffic sparse. Once again she notices the man's fingernails: bitten to the nub.

'I need to ask about the arson attack on your house.'

A wary tone enters Singh's voice.

'How do you know about that?'

'I'm a journalist. It's my job to know things.'

'I'm not sure I can help you, so—'

Morgan interrupts. 'Do you think the attack on your home had anything to do with the Karl Savage investigation?' No response. 'The charred corpse you identified as his? The Anjelica Fry case?'

'I fail to see a connection.'

'The thing is, Mr Singh, Anjelica is a pyro*phobe*, while Karl Savage is a pyro*maniac*.'

'Was,' says Singh.

'Excuse me?'

'Savage *was* a pyromaniac. He's dead.'

'That's what I want to talk to you about.'

The man stops and turns to face her. 'Remind me who you work for.'

'No one,' says Morgan. 'I'm a freelance journalist investigating a miscarriage of justice.'

'And barking up the wrong tree.'

Morgan waits for a bickering couple to pass, then lowers her voice.

'Did Karl threaten your family? Did he try to burn down your house? Did he have someone follow your wife and daughters to Paris? Is that why you faked the X-rays? Is that why you identified the body as his? Is that why you helped him escape justice?'

A thin smile creases the man's face

'You sound like a tramp I sometimes see in the park. Always ranting about conspiracy theories and shouting at pigeons.'

Morgan swallows a small smile of satisfaction. Given the circumstances, the response is as much as she could have hoped for – what spin doctors call a non-denial denial.

'The coroner would never have questioned your professional opinion, not with your track record. Nor would the police. It must have been a simple matter to duplicate Savage's *ante*-mortem X-rays then pass them off as the ones *you* made, *post*-mortem.'

The man gives a slight shake of his head.

'I don't have time for this nonsense.'

He walks on. Morgan follows.

'Do you know who does have time, Mr Singh? Anjelica Fry. Did you know she tried to kill herself? She was attacked in prison – her face slashed – and that's not the worst part.' Morgan draws breath, pausing for effect. 'They've taken her son. An innocent baby will be flung into care and messed up for life.'

'I'm sorry to hear that.'

Not giving an inch. Time to try another tack.

'I know you're not a bad man. I know you do *pro bono* work in developing countries, fixing cleft palates for children. But good people sometimes do bad things. Maybe they have no choice. Maybe they're in an impossible position. Either way, my question is: how do they sleep at night?'

The man quickens his pace. His tone is clipped, his anger simmering beneath the civilised veneer.

'Karl Savage is dead,' he says. 'The police, the coroner, the CPS, judge, jury, the press – everyone agrees. Except you.'

'Not everyone,' says Morgan thinking of Ben, her sole supporter. She switches gear. 'Do you know about the Met's storage facility? The one that has Karl's teeth.'

'What about it?'

'Why would DI Tucker sign them out?'

'Because I asked him to.'

Morgan raises an eyebrow.

'*You* did?'

'Yes. I needed them for a presentation at NYU College of Dentistry.'

'May I ask why?'

'To demonstrate a crucial part of my lecture. The notching of the mandibular and maxillary left central incisors was exceptional. I asked Tucker if I could borrow the teeth. He was kind enough to oblige.'

'With a crucial piece of police evidence?'

'From an old case – a *closed* case – on which he was SIO.'

'Even so, isn't that unorthodox?'

'I'm Home Office-accredited, Ms Vine. He was happy to help.'

'When was this presentation?'

'Last week.'

'Where are the teeth now?'

'I mislaid them.'

Morgan can't help smiling at the man's chutzpah.

'In New York?'

A nod. 'I left my briefcase in a taxi. I doubt it will turn up, but hope springs eternal.'

'You can see how this looks.'

'No doubt you'll enlighten me.'

'A journalist asks awkward questions about Savage. A short while later the only hard evidence confirming he's dead goes missing. That's one hell of a coincidence.'

'Life is full of coincidences. We're conditioned to seek patterns in everything, but that doesn't make everything a conspiracy, despite what your silly little book would have us believe.'

Morgan is determined not to be sidetracked by the jibe, the first crack in the man's composure. Following him across the road, she makes one final appeal to his better nature.

'I can see your problem, Mr Singh. You fabricated evidence, lied to the police, lied in court and breached professional ethics. If this came out you'd be ruined, maybe go to prison. So I understand there's no going back. But when you're trying to sleep tonight – in your lovely house, with your lovely wife – think about an innocent woman in a cell, miles from home, miles from her baby.'

They've reached the gates leading to Camden Town and the tree-lined road that contains Singh's house. He doesn't break his stride.

'I've nothing more to say, Ms Vine. Don't contact me again. Unless you want to hear from my lawyers.'

Morgan feels a fresh surge of fury but knows argument is futile. She watches him walk round the corner and disappear from view. Turning to retrace her steps, she strides towards her car.

Heart hammering.

Mind racing.

Resolve stiffening.

Thirty-Three

By the time Morgan gets back to Canterbury the remains of Ben's takeaway are congealing on the kitchen table. She picks at cold noodles while listening as he unburdens himself about his day. The lorry fire that claimed the lives of twenty migrants – victims of smoke inhalation – appears to have been a tragic accident. The driver fled but has been traced by police. Ben's part of the investigation is complete, but the memory of the corpses, especially the children, is seared into his memory. He sits at the table smoking a joint and drinking beer. The smell of dope reminds Morgan of her brief stint at university: barely a term before the surprise pregnancy forced a change of plan.

She watches Ben suck smoke into his lungs.

'You can't do this job without a crutch,' he says. 'For most people it's alcohol or screwing around, for me it's weed.'

He proffers the spliff. She shakes her head, wondering if 'screwing around' is also part of his coping mechanism, then chastising herself for assuming the worst. Nothing in her recent history has given her much reason to trust men, or the police, but she must at least *try* not to spend the rest of her life in a state of permanent suspicion.

They sit in silence listening to the rain, then he rises from the table and stacks the dishwasher, padding around the kitchen barefoot.

'How did you get on in London?'

Morgan pours herself a glass of wine and tells him about her encounters with Jatinder Singh, Eileen and Edward, the Primrose Hill dog walker.

'So Singh did Karl's bidding, to protect his family?'

'Looks like it.'

Ben removes the cap from a second bottle of Corona.

'Wouldn't you do the same? If Lissa were at risk?'

Morgan considers the question.

'I hope I'd have found another way. But anyone who messes with my child messes with me.'

Ben smiles

'Never get between Mama Grizzly and her cub?'

'Exactly.'

He takes a final drag on the joint, then stubs it out and fishes in the pocket of his jeans.

'I got you a present.'

He hands her a key ring attached to a small red plastic square with a silver button. She frowns.

'Is this what I think it is?'

He nods.

'A rape alarm. Not that I think you're at particular risk, but Karl is clearly a maniac.'

Is he expecting her to be unnerved or grateful? Nonplussed, she pockets the key ring.

'Just what I always wanted.' She raises her glass. A toast. 'To a better day tomorrow.'

His face grows grave as he clinks the bottle.

'Amen.'

As he drinks, she watches his Adam's apple moving and takes stock of the stubble on his face.

'Been a long day,' he says. 'I need to go to bed.'

Morgan nods, suddenly aware of the beating of her heart.

'Alone?'

For a second, she thinks she's misjudged the moment, but his smile broadens and his eyes crinkle at the edges. He reaches out to cup her chin in his hand. Then he leans forward and kisses her cheek, his lips grazing her skin, planting a series of soft kisses as he brings his mouth to hers. She can feel his breath on her face. Their lips touch, gently at first, then with increasing urgency. His tongue finds hers. She closes her eyes, savouring the taste of him, the touch of his hands on her hair, her face, her neck. She opens her eyes. He's smiling.

He kisses her, long and slow. Then she gets to her feet as he takes her hand, and leads her out of the kitchen.

'Aren't you going to carry me to bed?'

'Is that what you want?'

She leans closer and whispers in his ear.

'That's what I want.'

It's 'first time' sex. Tentative, occasionally clumsy (her elbow in his eye triggers laughter), self-conscious opening moves giving way to a burgeoning passion that takes its time reaching a crescendo, then subsides into stroking, caressing and sleepy murmurs. For a while, into the small hours, they whisper about their first impressions of each other and their respective pasts. Drowsy murmurs give way to more kissing and then another bout of lovemaking, slower and more assured. More intense than anything Morgan can remember experiencing for a long time.

In the morning, she finds him emerging from the shower. Grinning, he pulls her into the glass cubicle, sinks to his knees and slowly kisses his way up her body, from her feet to her legs and thighs. Closing her eyes, she savours the feeling of his tongue between her legs, the water cascading over her body. He seems in no hurry, relishing the taste of her. She takes her time coming, grinding herself against his face while clutching the shower pipes for support. After a moment, Ben gets to his feet, plants a series of soft, slow kisses on her neck, then grabs a towel and disappears into the bedroom.

By the time she comes downstairs he's dressed and has made coffee and toast. Outside the rain is falling, the skies are gravestone grey.

'What are you doing today?' says Ben, handing her a cup of coffee.

'Trying to find Stacey. And her baby.'

'Why not leave it to the police?'

'She's not on their priority list. But finding her could bring me closer to tracking down Karl. It might also help me find out how Kiki died. And what happened to *her* baby.'

He sips his coffee. 'Why is Rook so helpful to you?'

'Why do you ask?'

A shrug. 'No reason.'

'Are you jealous?'

'Isn't it a bit early to be talking about jealousy?'

'Touché,' says Morgan, still smiling while swallowing a pang of disappointment. He's right. This is a one-night stand, nothing more.

Yet.

'You don't seem to have a very high opinion of the police,' says Ben.

'You read the papers. Do you blame me?'

'I think they do a tough job under difficult circumstances.'

'So do I. But they're human, which means they mess up, yet they never admit getting it wrong until forced to. Take your pal Tucker.'

'Colleague, not pal.'

'Either way, he won't admit the possibility that Anjelica is innocent, yet Rook can't get him to explain why he's in cahoots with the dentist who misidentified Karl's body.'

She's bending the truth, hoping Ben *is* jealous of Neville, that he'll be keen to get one over on his rival.

'What do you mean by "in cahoots"?'

'Tucker signed out Karl's teeth from evidence storage,' says Morgan. She tells him what she learned from Singh. 'But now Rook can't contact him. Can you?'

Ben chews on his lower lip for a moment, thinking, then picks up his mobile. Scrolling through his contacts, he taps Tucker's name and puts the call on speakerphone. Morgan hears the Hackney DI's voice. A weary croak.

''Morning, Ben.'

'You sound terrible.'

'Painkillers. I had a back operation. First day home, convalescing.'

'I'll keep it short,' says Ben. 'I'm calling on behalf of Morgan Vine.'

Tucker sighs. 'The one who wrote that bloody book?'

Ben ignores the question. 'She's keen to know about Jatinder Singh.'

'What about him?'

'His family was threatened by Karl Savage. Morgan thinks that's why he misidentified the body, so Karl could fake his own death and disappear.'

'Why would Karl do that?'

'To kibosh Anjelica's accusation that he was dealing drugs. Make a fresh start. Maybe abroad.'

A sigh. 'This is all bollocks. Singh didn't misidentify anyone. Savage is dead.'

Ben leans closer to the phone. 'Is it true you signed his teeth out of evidence storage?'

'Yes,' says Tucker evenly. 'Singh wanted them for a lecture in New York.'

'Has he told you he lost them?'

'Yes.'

'And?'

'Shit happens. The case is closed, the right person is behind bars. But if you're suggesting that Jatinder Singh lost the evidence *deliberately* . . .'

He tails off. Ben backtracks, striking an emollient note. 'I'm not suggesting anything. Just asking a question.'

A pause.

'Are you screwing Morgan Vine, Ben?'

'No, I'm having breakfast.'

A knowing laugh. 'Tell her from me that Jatinder is a decent man and Karl Savage is dead.'

'Thanks for your time.'

'Have a good day.'

Hanging up, Ben takes a sip of coffee.

'Do you believe him?' says Morgan.

'I think he believes everything he said.'

'Which doesn't make it true.'

'No.'

'So another dead end?'

He shrugs.

'Like I said, maybe you should leave the complicated stuff to the police.'

'Either they're too busy or they've given up.'

'Even so, sometimes it pays to stick to the rules.'

The man has a habit of playing it safe. Smiling, Morgan reaches for the buckle on his belt while quoting from the gospel according to Karl Savage.

'Keep all the rules, miss all the fun.'

Thirty-Four

The downpour stops by lunchtime. Morgan is back on the narrow river in Romney Marsh, checking out the houseboat belonging to Trevor Jukes. Still no sign of Stacey and her baby, or Jukes himself. Tramping through the sodden fields, Morgan returns to her car and takes the meandering drive through miles of wetlands to the prison officer's pebbledash bungalow. His motorcycle is nowhere to be seen. She peers through the letterbox. The pile of junk mail has doubled.

Sitting in her Mini, trying to decide her next move, she ducks low in her seat as three familiar figures emerge from the corner shop. The local hoodies – Earring, Neck Tattoo and Gap-tooth – lope past on the other side of the road, tussling over a bottle of cider and failing to register Morgan's presence. She watches them enter one of the bungalows and close the door.

Driving off, she pulls to a halt several streets away and smokes a cigarette while making another list of all the people she's encountered during her quest to find Karl Savage. As she writes Nancy Sixsmith, her pen runs out of ink. She stares at the woman's name, recalling her visit to the mother of Karl's twins.

If her pen were working she'd add another name to the list.

Spike.

Karl's drug-dealing crony hasn't surfaced since the Dalston blaze. Has he, too, gone *off the grid*? Is he doing Karl's bidding, like Trevor Jukes?

Or, despite's Singh's protestations, is there another possibility?

Did the corpse in the burnt-out flat belong to Spike?

Deciding her next port of call, Morgan restarts her car and makes her way through the deserted flatlands, heading towards a bleak high-rise block on the outskirts of Canterbury.

'I told you all I know last time,' says Nancy, stubbing out her cigarette.

The flat still smells like an ashtray. Once again, Morgan makes a silent vow to quit smoking, but not today, not until she gets her life back. She leans forward in her armchair, facing the woman on the sofa.

'What can you tell me about Spike?'

A shrug.

'We knocked about a bit.'

'But you don't know where he might be?'

'Not a clue.'

'Were he and Karl close?'

'They were business partners.'

'Never a cross word?'

'I didn't say that.'

'Could they have fallen out?'

A pause. Then a nod.

'Big time. And it never paid to get on the wrong side of Karl.'

'What did they fall out about?'

'Money. Karl thought Spike was stealing from him.'

'Was he?'

'What do you think?' Nancy lights her cigarette. 'They were drug dealers.'

Rummaging in her pocket, Morgan takes out her pouch of tobacco and begins to make a roll-up while glancing at two framed photos on the wall: a picture of Nancy's twins, Jack and Karl Junior, wearing school uniform, and Nancy herself with a man sporting a toothsome smile and a topknot.

'What time do your kids get home?'

Nancy sighs.

'Gotta pick 'em up soon. Doing it myself today. Bloody neighbour's ill.'

Morgan remembers the woman's agoraphobia, her reluctance to leave the flat. She gestures to the photo of the man with the topknot.

'Is that Spike?'

'Yeah.'

'Were you close?'

The woman blinks.

'Meaning?'

Morgan gives what she hopes is a friendly smile.

'I'm not trying to catch you out, Nancy.' She reaches into her bag for the wine she bought at the corner shop. 'I'm just trying to find out more about Karl.'

She places the offering on the coffee table, next to the teetering pile of celebrity magazines. Nancy stares at the bottle.

'Trying to loosen my tongue?'

Morgan ignores the question. 'I don't believe Anjelica Fry started the fire in Karl's flat.'

Nancy frowns.

'So who did?'

'That's what I'm trying to find out.'

The woman considers this for a moment, then gets to her feet and walks into the kitchen. She returns with two glasses. Outside, the rain is starting again, spattering the windows.

'I need to know everything I can about Karl,' says Morgan, lighting her cigarette. 'And the people who knew him, including Spike.'

Nancy unscrews the cap on the bottle, pours two glasses, then picks up her mobile and scrolls through its contents.

'This is Spike,' she says, tapping a video and holding up the phone.

Morgan peers at the clip. Nancy and Spike in the courtyard outside Canterbury Cathedral, larking around for the camera.

'Who took the video?'

'Karl,' says Nancy. She drags on her cigarette and stares at the screen. Spike is waving at the camera, pulling a face. Nancy pokes out her tongue.

A voice off-camera.

'*Give her a kiss.*'

'Typical Karl,' says Nancy. 'Always mucking about.'

Morgan watches as Spike plants a mock-coy kiss on Nancy's cheek.

Karl's voice again. '*Come on, Spikey, you can do better than that.*'

Spike shakes his head. '*Camera shy.*'

Nancy turns to peck him on the cheek. Then she does something that makes Morgan hold her breath. She reaches out to pluck something from the sleeve of his fleece. The clip shows a few more seconds of horseplay then cuts out.

'Nice-looking guy,' says Morgan, trying to sound casual.

'Not as nice-looking as Karl' says Nancy. 'But he's OK, if you like that sort of thing.'

A smile.

'And did you?'

The woman reaches for her wine.

'Spike and I were friends.'

'Friends with benefits?'

'What does that mean?'

'You know what it means.'

Nancy says nothing. She takes a drag on her cigarette.

'Do you remember Princess Margaret, Nancy?'

'What about her?'

'When she was young she had a secret love affair. With a man called Captain Peter Townsend. But he was divorced, so they couldn't get married. It was another era, the world was a different place.'

'And you're giving me a history lesson because . . .?'

'They managed to keep their relationship under wraps until a *Daily Mirror* journalist noticed Margaret brushing something from his lapel – a piece of lint. The editor refused to run the story but the American press printed it and it became a huge scandal.' Morgan flicks her cigarette into the overflowing ashtray. 'The

British public were still reeling from the abdication and Margaret was under huge pressure to "do the right thing". So she ended the relationship with the man she loved.' She pauses for effect. 'But without that tiny, intimate gesture, the journalist would never have cottoned on and the world might never have known. Just a woman plucking fluff from a man's lapel, that's all it took.'

Nancy says nothing, taking another drag on her cigarette. Morgan presses the point home.

'Did Karl know? About you and Spike?'

The woman exhales slowly.

'You're relentless.'

'So I'm told.'

Morgan allows the silence to do its work.

'OK,' sighs Nancy. 'Spike was on his uppers. No friends, no family. He crashed on our sofa for a while. Karl came home early one day, caught us at it. Not a happy bunny.' She gulps her wine. 'He kicked the crap out of Spike. But he never laid a finger on me. Said he was good at playing the long game.'

'Meaning?'

'He had something else in mind.'

'Something worse?'

Nancy nods, gesturing towards the photo of her twins.

'Said he'd take the kids off me. I said, "Good luck, pal. A drug dealer? The courts are going to love you."' Another drag on the cigarette. 'Know what he said?'

'Tell me.'

'"*You have no idea who you're dealing with.*" He said he'd wait. For ever, if necessary. But he'd get what he wanted.'

'He told Anjelica the exact same thing,' says Morgan. 'He threatened to take her baby away.'

The woman leans forward. 'Which gives her a solid motive to want him dead. And you *still* think she's Little Bo Peep?'

Morgan refrains from mentioning the glaringly obvious – that Nancy herself had an identical motive. She considers telling the woman that the father of her twins faked his own death, but the thought is interrupted by what sounds like distant gunfire.

'Kids chucking fireworks,' says Nancy. 'Same every year. Makes me think of Karl.'

'Why?'

'His birthday: fifth of November. His dad told him they were in *his* honour, to celebrate *his* birthday.' She sucks on her cigarette. 'One way to create a bloody pyromaniac.'

Morgan tops up both glasses, trying to sound nonchalant. 'What was in the biscuit tin, Nancy?'

The woman arches an eyebrow, thrown by a question that seems to come out of the blue.

'What do you know about the tin?'

I saw it in his van. The night he took me to the graveyard.

'You mentioned it before. What was in it?'

She's careful to speak in the past tense. Like everyone else, Nancy believes Karl is dead. Nothing Morgan can say will change her mind.

'There was no mention of it after he died,' says Nancy. 'The papers never wrote about it.'

Morgan keeps still. A poacher waiting to pounce.

'Why would they mention a tin?'

Nancy falls silent, flicking ash from her cigarette, considering her response. Then she leans back against the sofa cushions. Something seems to settle inside her. A decision made.

'Did you know his mother was clinically obese? The size of a house. She trained as a midwife. The irony was, when *she* got knocked up, no one knew. Her clothes hid it.' She takes a last drag on the cigarette and stubs it out. 'Karl never said who the father was but I know he hated the man's guts.' A cough. 'And I've no idea if it was accidental or deliberate.'

The ash on Morgan's cigarette is about to drop. She doesn't stir.

'If what was accidental or deliberate?'

Nancy raises her gaze, looking Morgan in the eye.

'The baby died.'

'But you don't know how?'

The woman shakes her head.

'Karl never said. Either Pearl or the dad put the body in the tin. Hid it in the cellar. No one ever found out. Except Karl.'

The ash drops. Morgan ignores it. 'He opened the tin?'

Nancy nods.

'But he never told Pearl he knew. She kept locking him up, every Friday night for years. No company. Just the tin.' She takes another gulp of wine. 'I told him it was no wonder he hated women. Tried to get him to see a shrink.'

'And?'

'He said knowing *why* we do stuff doesn't stop us doing it, so what was the point? Hurt people *hurt people*.'

Morgan looks at the photo of the twins. 'Do the kids miss him?'

'Junior does. He told me he saw Karl not long ago, driving past. I explained it was something called wishful thinking. Jack doesn't seem bothered. He's an old soul, more mature.'

Morgan can feel her pulse racing.

'Where did Junior think he'd seen his dad?'

'Outside school, in a van.' The woman glances at her watch. 'I need to get going. Bloody neighbour. Says she's ill but she's probably pissed. And just when the Asda man's due.'

'Can I help?' says Morgan, trying not to sound too eager. 'You could call ahead, tell the school I'm picking up the boys.' She gestures to the photo. 'I know what they look like.'

The woman hesitates, then looks out at the driving rain.

'You wouldn't mind?'

Morgan dons her most trustworthy smile.

'Not in the least.'

The parents assembled outside the school are huddled under a forest of umbrellas. There are one or two dads sporting tracksuits but the crowd is mostly comprised of mums and grandparents. Leaning against her car, Morgan immediately spots Karl Junior and Jack, hoods raised against the rain and early-November chill. The six-year-old twins are the image of their father, and are being ushered through the gates by a red-haired teacher, her eyes roving the parked cars. Morgan waves and dons her friendliest smile.

'Morgan Vine?' says the teacher.

'That's me.' She proffers her driving licence.

The woman scrutinises the card, then bends down to address Jack.

'This is the lady your mum sent to collect you. OK, Jack?'

The boy nods and takes his brother's hand, leading him towards the Mini.

'He's Junior,' he tells Morgan. 'My little brother.'

'I thought you were twins.'

'I'm nine minutes older. That's why he's Junior.'

Morgan nods gravely, then exchanges a smile with the teacher. She watches the woman scurry back inside, escaping the rain.

'*I'm* in front,' Jack tells his brother. 'You're in the back.'

Morgan watches as the boy does his brother's bidding and clambers into the back seat.

'Seat belt,' says Jack.

Karl Junior obeys without protest. Morgan sits behind the wheel, watching Jack settle in the passenger seat and buckle his own belt.

'OK,' he says. 'We can go.'

His face is serious, an earnest little boy. Morgan stifles a smile and starts the engine.

'Did Asda come?' says Jack.

'Not yet. That's why your mum sent me.'

A voice from the back. Karl Junior.

'Are you the special lady?'

'Shut up,' says Jack.

The vehemence in his voice is startling.

'But he told us—'

'Shut up, Karl!'

'No, *you* shut up!' The boy's face is contorted with anger. 'He said she's coming before his birthday!'

Jack turns to face him in the rear seat.

'It's a secret!'

'Not if this is the special lady!'

Jack turns to Morgan, glowering.

'*Are* you?'

Morgan chooses her words with care.

'Is that what Daddy says?'

'*See?*' says Junior. 'She *knows* him.'

His brother isn't convinced.

'Stop it or I'll bite you!'

Morgan glances in the rear-view mirror. The little boy looks close to tears.

'Did Daddy tell you what the special lady is going to do?'

'Don't say!' says Jack.

His brother refuses to be cowed. 'She's taking us to the house in the sunshine.'

'That's right,' says Morgan.

Junior's face lights up. 'Are we going now?'

'No. Not today.'

'Told you!' says Jack. 'She's *not* the special lady.' He turns to glare at Morgan. 'Are you?'

'No,' admits Morgan. 'I'm not the special lady.'

The rest of the journey passes in subdued silence, the flare-up seemingly forgotten by the time she delivers the twins to their mother.

'Thank you,' says Nancy, greeting her boys at the front door. Once again, Morgan considers revealing the truth about Karl, but knows she won't be believed.

'Keep an eye on the twins,' she says. 'Lot of dodgy people out there.' It's the best she can do without sounding crazy.

Nancy frowns. She seems on the verge of asking a question, but the doors to the second lift open. The Asda man emerges, laden with bags. He nods to Morgan as she heads for the lift. Turning, she sees Nancy usher him into the flat. Jack stands in the doorway, fixing Morgan with a look. He places a finger to his lips.

'Shhhh.'

He turns and goes inside.

Morgan hesitates, searching for a way to convince the woman to heed her warning. She returns to the door and raps on the flimsy plywood. Nancy reappears, eyebrows arched.

'Thought you'd gone.'

'What would you say if I told you Karl is alive? Still playing the long game? Still coming after your kids?'

Nancy stares at Morgan as if she's lost her mind.

'Any idea who killed JFK? Got any pictures of the Loch Ness Monster?'

Morgan manages half a smile.

'Fair enough.' Turning away, she calls over her shoulder. 'Enjoy the rest of the wine.'

Nancy goes back into the flat. From the courtyard below comes the rat-a-tat-tat of exploding fireworks. As Morgan heads for the lift, her mobile rings.

Cameron.

She answers the call.

'How's the countryside?'

His voice is shaky.

'There's been an accident.'

Morgan's stomach lurches.

'Is Lissa OK?'

'It's complicated . . .'

'Fuck's sake, Cameron. *Is she OK?*'

He takes a breath.

'Someone ran us off the road. Lissa lost the baby.'

Thirty-Five

An hour since darkness fell. The temperature has plummeted. Slewing to a halt in the car park, Morgan climbs out of the Mini and hurries into the cottage hospital on the outskirts of town. Cameron is in the deserted reception. He looks up from his mobile. Haggard. In shock.

'How is she?' says Morgan.

'OK.' He corrects himself. 'All things considered.'

'She definitely lost the baby?'

A nod.

'They've done an ultrasound. "No pregnancy remaining within the uterus".'

Morgan closes her eyes for a moment. She's been hoping for better news, a miracle. Now all hope is gone. Opening her eyes, she takes stock of cuts and grazes to Cameron's face.

'And you?'

'I'm OK.' He pockets his phone. 'Lucky, I guess. I forgot to fasten my seatbelt. Thank God she's smarter.'

He gets to his feet and leads Morgan through swing doors, along an empty corridor.

'Tell me what happened.'

'We were driving along a country road. Guy comes out of nowhere, zooms up behind us in a van. He rear-ends us, twice, then rams us off the road, into a ditch. Airbags explode. Car's a write-off. Guy drives away.'

'So it was no accident?'

'No. He picked his moment. No cars, no witnesses. One piece of good news, though. Lissa was taking a selfie, just before he hit us the first time.'

Morgan feels her pulse quickening.

'So there's a photo of the driver?'

He shakes his head.

'Just a partial registration.'

'Was it a white camper van?'

'She said you'd ask that. It was red. That's all I saw, the rest was a blur. The police are checking the registration now.'

Morgan's mind has been working overtime. That the crash was no accident comes as little surprise. The driver's identity remains a mystery, but Morgan recalls the journey she and Lissa made to meet Cameron's flight at Heathrow.

Ben at the wheel of his Range Rover. Glimpses of a Yamaha motorcycle in the mirror. An instinct that they were being followed.

She'd dismissed it as paranoia. Not any more. She can't prove the motorcyclist was Jukes, acting on Karl's instructions – that he'd tailed Cameron and Lissa, stolen a van and picked his moment – but Morgan knows this to be true, just as she knows what she will do if they come face to face.

Fighting to keep a lid on her rage, she follows Cameron around a corner, heading along another corridor.

'What do the doctors say?'

'There was extensive bleeding. The pregnancy sac was expelled shortly after the car went off the road. They also say a miscarriage is not uncommon during the first twelve weeks, but the physical and emotional trauma of the crash could have been the cause.' He slows to a halt outside a ward. 'I'm sorry it happened on my watch. She'll be OK. She's a tough cookie. Takes after you.'

They exchange a rueful look. Two semi-strangers bound together for life because of a one-night-stand in a university bedsit twenty years ago. Morgan remembers the selfie her daughter sent from the posh hotel, a pillow stuffed under her shirt, making her look heavily pregnant.

I'm having a BABY! SO excited!

Cameron clears his throat.

'Ready?'

Morgan takes a breath, steadying herself. She needs to stay calm for Lissa's sake. This is the second time her daughter has been hospitalised in recent weeks.

'Ready.'

The ward is small. Four curtained-off cubicles, two empty. An elderly woman dozes in the bed by the window. Lissa, too, is asleep, or so it seems, but her eyes flicker open as Morgan draws near. She keeps her voice even.

'Hi, sweetheart.'

Her daughter's eyes glisten with tears. Morgan takes her hand.

'I'm so sorry,' she says.

Lissa manages a nod. Her voice is hoarse with emotion.

'Is it because I made him think I'd had an abortion?'

Yes.

'Maybe,' says Morgan.

Lissa closes her eyes. Morgan allows the silence to stretch, taking her daughter's hand and squeezing it gently. When Lissa looks at her again, the tears are gone. Her voice is full of anger and frustration.

'How long do I have to stay in this dump?'

'We're trying to find out,' says Cameron. He turns to Morgan. 'The guy's a maniac. I've told the police. He needs to be stopped.'

You think?

Morgan feels another surge of frustration. Before she can reply, her attention is taken by a flurry of movement outside the door. Two police officers are visible through the pane of glass, heading for the ward. Entering, they introduce themselves. PC Golding is a stocky man with a rugby player's nose. PC Williams is a slight woman with a hint of a lisp. Both are in their early twenties. Neither inspires confidence.

'I know who did this,' says Morgan. Her appetite for small talk is limited at the best of times. These are not the best of times.

PC Williams takes out her notebook.

'Your daughter gave us a name.' She flicks through the pages and raises an eyebrow. 'Karl Savage?'

Morgan feels overwhelmed by a wave of hopelessness and fatigue.

'I know what you're going to tell me,' she says. 'But you're wrong, he's alive.' The police officers exchange a look. Morgan can feel her jaw tightening.

'Have you checked the van's registration?'

Golding nods.

'Reported stolen just after seven this morning,' he says. 'From Folkestone. A Ford Transit.'

'It'll be in a crusher by now,' says Morgan. 'Or at the bottom of a lake.'

Williams clears her throat and checks her notepad.

'Pity the selfie didn't catch the driver's face.'

Morgan feels her face redden. 'Is that the best you can do? Criticise my daughter for not being a better witness?'

In the silence that follows, she's dimly aware of Cameron placing a hand on her arm. Placatory. Patronising. She shrugs him off and turns to her daughter.

'Back in a moment.'

Lissa frowns.

'Don't keep stuff from me, Mum.'

Morgan gives a reassuring smile.

'You've been through a lot. You need rest. Back in two minutes.'

Lissa nods, then closes her eyes. Morgan heads out into the corridor, gesturing for Cameron and the police officers to follow.

'I'm sorry,' she tells them. 'I'm upset.'

PC Williams nods.

'We've taken statements. We're doing all we can. Finding the van is a priority, but without witnesses we've not a lot to go on.'

'Understood,' says Morgan. Her smile is unconvincing but it's the best she can do. 'Thanks for your help.'

She watches the police officers retrace their steps along the corridor, crossing with an exhausted-looking doctor who introduces himself as Dr Patel. He accompanies Morgan and Cameron back onto the ward. Gathered around the bedside, it's established that the patient is to be discharged. Lissa can expect vaginal bleeding for the next five to seven days and should ring the gynaecology ward if it becomes heavy or clotted.

'Best to use contraception for three months before trying for another baby,' finishes Patel.

Lissa's eyes widen in disbelief. 'Are you kidding? I'm never having sex again.'

Gallows humour. Morgan feels a lump in her throat. Once again, her daughter is being brave. She thanks Dr Patel for his help. As he leaves and Cameron waits outside she helps her daughter get dressed while listening to her account of the crash.

All the while, her mind is whirring.

I will find you, Karl Savage.

You will rue the day you met my daughter.

You will regret knowing my name.

An hour later, they're at a window table in an empty seafront café, gazing at the glow of Calais's lights across the Channel. Coffees for Morgan and Cameron; hot chocolate for Lissa. And Marmite toast. Comfort food. Morgan suggested going straight to Ben's, so Lissa could rest, but her daughter insisted on doing something normal.

Right now, Morgan is resisting the urge to reach out and brush Lissa's hair – long, slow strokes, the way she loved as a little girl – but her hair is too short.

Another casualty of Karl's Savage's vicious streak.

Clink-rasp.

Cameron is glued to his mobile (or cellphone, as he calls it these days). The *tap tap tap* as he sends emails grates on Morgan's nerves, but she's trying to stay on an even keel.

Conversation has faltered. They've exchanged commiserations over the miscarriage, dissected every aspect of the crash and agreed that the police will make little effort to find the red Transit – and none to find Karl Savage.

Lissa's face is etched with misery, her voice morose.

'It's like we're in a zombie movie. He's the living dead.'

Tap tap tap.

Morgan rolls her eyes.

'Can't that wait?'

Cameron doesn't look up.

'Only if I want to get fired from this movie.'

'I thought it fell through.'

'That was last week. Welcome to my world.'

Lissa's eyes blaze with anger.

'Hasn't the world had enough shitty romcoms?'

'No, thank God.'

He sips his coffee, then puts his phone on the table, face down, and launches into an explanation.

'It's 11 a.m. in Hollywood: peak bullshit hour. The producers read the latest draft of my script overnight. Now they're bombarding me with demands. They all want different changes. The director's in rehab in Arizona, something two of the four producers are keeping from the other two, in case they pull their funding, which would bring the whole project crashing down. For the bazillionth time.' He sighs. 'It's not called development hell for nothing.'

Morgan can only guess how much Oscar-nominated Cameron is paid per screenplay. Half a million? More? The Malibu house, the cars, the twenty-something baby-hungry Ukrainian girlfriend – none of his lifestyle comes cheap.

'When are you going back to LA?'

'Tomorrow.'

His phone vibrates. She can tell he's desperate to check the message.

'You need to take her with you.'

Lissa looks up from her hot chocolate.

'Who's her?'

'Who do you think?'

Morgan can see Cameron thinking, weighing up the suggestion.

'OK,' he says.

The speed of his decision takes Morgan by surprise, but it reminds her, briefly, of what she once saw in him.

Lissa folds her arms.

'No way.'

'This isn't up for discussion,' says Morgan. 'It's happening.'

'Only if you come too.'

'I can't go anywhere.'

'Then *I* can't either.'

Cameron frowns.

'Why not?'

'I'm not leaving Mum on her own.'

'I'm not on my own. Ben's very supportive.'

Only half true, but if it makes her daughter feel better about getting out of harm's way . . .

'Are you and he a thing?' says Lissa.

'Irrelevant.'

A shrug.

'Either way, I'm not going.'

Cameron's phone vibrates again. He doesn't move. He's staring at Morgan.

'Why are you so obsessed with this Karl guy?' he says. 'I know about Anjelica Fry and all the rest of it, but why are you so determined to take him on?'

Morgan sips her coffee, choosing her words with care. Her answer will determine Lissa's decision.

'I'm scared of him. But I refuse to live that way. No matter what happens, I refuse to be frightened any more. I don't want Lissa to be scared either. So I need to do what needs to be done. But first, I need to know she's safe.'

Moved, Lissa's eyes glaze with tears. When she speaks, her voice is a whisper.

'OK, I'll go with Dad.'

'Thank you.'

'On one condition. You let Ben help. And don't do anything stupid.'

'That's two conditions.'

'Fuck's sake, Mum.'

'OK, it's a deal.'

Cameron signals for the bill. Morgan finishes her coffee, gripped by a sense of foreboding. She smiles for her daughter's benefit, trying to sound more cheerful than she feels.

'Will you just look at us?' she says brightly. 'One big happy family.'

Lissa rolls her eyes. Cameron coughs, then picks up his phone.

'I'm booking you a flight,' he tells Lissa.

Tap tap tap . . .

Morgan studies her daughter.

'Am I allowed to ask how you're feeling?'

A shrug.

'I'm OK.'

Her daughter's eyes fill with tears. Not for the first time, Morgan has the feeling she's keeping something back.

'Is there something you need to say, Lissa?'

A shake of the head.

'I'm fine.'

'Promise?'

'Promise.'

Morgan manages a smile.

But she doesn't believe a word.

Thirty-Six

KARL

Hope is not a plan.

That's what Daddy used to say.

Karl's been thinking about *the plan* for months.

Years.

Hoping things will change. But they never will. Apart from 'no peeking', she hasn't said a word, not since the funeral.

This is all your fault.

He's eleven today. Getting bigger every week. Stronger. He needs strength if he's to carry out *the plan*.

The Whistler has become a permanent fixture, staying every weekend. The 'special game' happens on Saturday nights, while Pearl is asleep.

Or pretending to be.

Karl tried saying no.

Once was more than enough.

He had to take ten days off school, until the bruises faded. Ten days, alone in the cellar.

He's been thinking about taking the tin to the police, perhaps one day after school, but has decided against it. They'd only put her away, give her three meals a day, put a roof over her head. Which is more than she deserves. Much more.

So her secret is safe. If nobody knew she'd had the baby, it stands to reason nobody will report him missing. Ever.

No one knows what The Whistler did.

Except Pearl.

And Karl.

He's got the letter to prove it. A snivelling apology, clearly written when drunk. Karl found it in the kitchen bin, torn in two, but taped it back together. Written in red ink, the handwriting is distinctive.

Karl is keeping the letter safe, tucked inside his trouser pocket.

You never know when something like that might be useful.

He's not sure if The Whistler is aware of what's inside the tin. Maybe that's *her* secret. He wouldn't put it past her. She's not normal. Not like the mums who pick up their kids from school. Help with homework. Cheer on sports day. If she were a normal mum she wouldn't turn a blind eye to what The Whistler does.

And she would never have helped him cover up what happened.

Even so, what happened to Guy was The Whistler's fault.

Guy.

Karl decided on the name when he looked inside the tin and saw the baby was a boy. He remembers the man's hot, beery breath.

Fucking baby wouldn't stop crying. I kept telling him to shut up, but he wouldn't. So I snapped.

If Karl does it – *when* he does it – it'll be as much for Guy as for himself.

Today's the day. A birthday present to himself. The only one he'll get.

He'd have done it ages ago but didn't have everything he needed.

Now he does.

He knows every single thing that's down here, every piece of piping, every brick, every crack in the concrete floor. There's nothing he can use as a weapon. Which is why he brought the poker from upstairs and hid it under the mattress.

The Whistler sometimes makes log fires, like Daddy used to. But he never roasts chestnuts in winter. Or marshmallows. Never leaves a stocking on Christmas Eve.

Hiding under the duvet, Karl hears the key in the padlock. Waiting for the familiar jaunty whistle, his fingers tighten around the heavy iron poker. He doesn't move, biding his time until the man moves closer.

No whistling. Not yet. But it will come. The Whistler knows the cellar is in darkness. He never turns on the torch. Not till after the special game.

Heart pounding, Karl feels a hand groping towards his leg.

NOW!

He throws back the duvet. Jumps up. Raises his arm. Brings the poker crashing down. A single blow to the head. His aim is perfect. The figure crumples and lies still.

Panting, Karl backs away from the body on the floor. He grabs his torch. Poised to land a second blow if necessary. But there's no need. Hands shaking, he switches on the torch and lets the beam play over the concrete floor

He gasps.

The motionless figure bleeding from the head is not The Whistler.

It's Pearl.

Thirty-Seven

The morning after Cameron and Lissa fly to LA, Morgan wakes to feel Ben planting soft kisses along the length of her back. She lies motionless, savouring the sensation of his lips on her skin and listening to the rain outside until a wave of intrusive thoughts (*Lissa's miscarriage . . . clink-rasp . . . red van*) make it impossible to lie still.

She sits up in bed. 'Mind if we save this for later?'

A grin.

'Now that's what I call foreplay.'

He kisses her shoulder.

'Coffee coming up,' he says, slipping out of bed. Lying back against the pillow, stretching luxuriantly, she watches as he heads into the bathroom. Broad back. Long legs. Perfect bum. She calls after him.

'What's the catch, Gaminara?'

But her voice is drowned out by the sound of water running in the shower.

Twenty minutes later, over coffee and scrambled eggs, he tells her about the day ahead. A backlog of paperwork, if he gets the chance, but it's more than likely he'll be called to the scene of at least one suspected arson attack – probably more.

'Around Bonfire Night I tend to get mega-busy. People think they can torch their home or car or warehouse and blame it on a rocket gone astray.'

'Not with you on the case?'

That grin again.

'No chance.'

He watches as she begins to roll a cigarette.

'What are your plans?'

'Same as yesterday and the day before,' says Morgan. 'Try to find the invisible man.'

He nods, suddenly grave.

'Can I do anything?'

Morgan briefly considers her promise to Lissa, then sets it aside.

'You already have,' she says, spreading tobacco along the cigarette paper. 'And telling me I'm not insane helps. But I can't expect you to do the legwork. You've already got a job.'

He checks his watch and gets up from the table.

'Speaking of which . . .'

He slips his laptop into a rucksack and grabs his keys from the table. Pausing at the door, he turns.

'I did judo when I was a kid,' he says. 'The instructor talked about rule number one: use your opponent's strength to defeat him. What's his superpower?'

'That he's the invisible man?'

'Be serious.'

She ponders the question.

'Is being relentless a superpower? Because I don't think he'll stop till he gets what he wants – whatever that is. And you could say he takes huge risks, so he's brave – sort of – in a way that's borderline crazy.'

Ben smiles.

'There you go. Be brave. Be relentless. Be borderline crazy.' He steps towards her, cups her chin in his hand and plants a kiss on her lips. 'But leave the risks to him.'

Another kiss and he's gone, leaving Morgan to finish her coffee, smoke a cigarette and wonder if she might have found a man worth her trust.

Rain sweeps across Romney Marsh as she tramps through sodden fields, making her way to the decrepit houseboat moored in a remote outpost of River Marsh Farm. She's not optimistic about finding Trevor Jukes, but there's no sign of the motorcycle outside his bungalow and the search must continue.

Approaching the *Wandering Star*, she takes cover behind a cluster of bushes, scanning the area for signs of life. She waits until satisfied there is no one around, then creeps up to the houseboat and peers through the porthole.

She steps back, heart pounding.

Someone is inside.

A dark-haired woman.

Her back to the porthole.

Morgan is sure she hasn't been seen but is taking no chances. Retracing her steps, she scurries back to the safety of the bushes, crouching low while focusing her gaze on the houseboat and considering her next move.

Is the woman Stacey? Has she changed her hair, removed the pink dye? Is she alone?

And then Morgan hears it.

A baby crying.

The sound is coming from the houseboat.

She feels blood thudding in her ears, her pulse racing. She checks her phone – a reflex action – but there's no signal. Besides, whom would she call? The police? And say what?

There's a woman! On a houseboat! Come quick!

Staying low, she emerges from the bushes and creeps back towards the vessel, eyes fixed on the porthole. Reaching the houseboat, she crouches down, out of sight, then straightens up and peers inside.

Stacey is staring at her. She's holding the baby to her breast. Her voice is barely audible through the grimy glass.

'Morgan?'

Morgan retreats, stepping back. Seconds later, the door is yanked open. Stacey appears, no longer holding the baby. Her face is pale and wan. She glares down from the deck but her voice is full of surprise, not anger.

'What are you doing here?'

'Looking for you,' says Morgan.

'Why?'

'Long story. Can I come in?'

The woman is wary.

'I'm not well. And I'm supposed to be feeding the baby. He's crying his bloody head off.'

Morgan clambers aboard, then follows Stacey inside, closing the door against the rain and descending into the cramped interior. The damp cabin smells of paraffin. She sees an old heater in the corner. A rickety Formica table is littered with jars of baby food, pre-packaged sandwiches and bars of chocolate. Nothing requires cooking, which is just as well because there's no sign of kitchen equipment, just a single bed and a cardboard box. Inside, a pink blanket and the baby, who continues to cry.

'What do you mean, "not feeling well"?'

'Something I ate,' says Stacey. 'Been throwing up all morning.'

Which explains the stench emanating from the chemical toilet. The baby's wailing intensifies.

'Can I pick him up?'

A shrug.

Morgan lifts the infant from the box, cradling him in her arms.

She feels goosebumps on her arm and her heart races as she sees the baby's chubby forearm.

A heart-shaped mole.

She stares at Stacey.

'This is Charlie . . . Kiki's baby . . .'

No response, just a sullen glare. But Morgan knows she's right.

'Talk to me, Stacey.'

'I . . . don't know.'

'Yes, you do.'

The baby stops crying and stares up at Morgan. She softens her tone.

'Kiki was your best friend. It would make sense for you to look after her baby when she died.'

The woman averts her gaze, studying a stain on the hardboard ceiling. Playing for time. Close to tears.

'If you're in trouble, I can help,' says Morgan. 'We can go to the police together . . .'

Stacey's eyes blaze.

'No police.'

'Then tell me what's going on. Otherwise . . .'

She tails off, letting the sentence finish itself.

The woman's voice is small, almost a whisper.

'I can't say.'

'Is it Jukes?' says Morgan. 'Is he making you do this?'

A nod, barely imperceptible, but something to build on.

The baby has fallen asleep. Morgan lowers him into the cardboard box, carefully arranging the pink blanket.

'Why don't you start by telling me what was in the cans?'

Stacey looks startled.

'What cans?'

'The baby formula you picked up from the luggage office at King's Cross and took to Istanbul.'

The woman's eyes widen in disbelief.

'Who told you?'

'No one. We followed you.'

'We?'

'Me and Lissa. We saw you meet Jukes. We tailed you to Heathrow. Saw you check in. I know Jukes gave you something to take to Istanbul. I'm guessing it was drugs.' The woman stares but says nothing. 'Is he using you as a mule? Is that what the baby farm is all about? Getting women pregnant then using their babies as a cover for smuggling drugs?'

Stacey's voice is hoarse.

'I can't say anything.'

'You need help, Stacey. Whatever's going on, whatever mess you're in, this is a chance to get out of it. *I'm* your chance.'

She sits on the bed. Stacey looks at the stain on the ceiling for a long moment, then sits beside her. She sighs. A decision made.

'The cans were full of cash,' she says. 'They buy baby formula, chuck away the powder then reseal the cans, so they're airtight. Don't ask me how – some kind of soldering iron, I guess. I took them to Istanbul – me and Ryan – we went to a flat and I handed them over.'

'Who to?'

'We didn't do names.'

Morgan nods.

'Then what happened?'

Stacey's eyes fill with tears.

'I left Ryan.'

'In Istanbul?'

A nod. 'That was the deal, right from the start, when I was in prison. Take my baby to Istanbul, with the cans, then leave him with . . . the people.'

'Baby traffickers?'

Stacey looks affronted.

'Not traffickers, no. Decent people. They sort out adoptions for rich couples who can't have kids of their own, people who have reasons for avoiding red tape.'

Traffickers by any other name.

'What reasons?' says Morgan.

A shrug.

'Criminal records? Maybe they got rich illegally.' She sniffs. 'There was one bloke I heard them talking about – one of these oligarchs? Happily married but he has a mistress. She's desperate for a baby. Thing is, he doesn't want her to have *his* kid, in case he dumps her and has a big paternity hassle which would make his wife leave him and take him to the cleaners. So he bought a baby.'

Morgan's craving for a cigarette is growing stronger by the second.

'Is that it? You take the cash to Istanbul, you leave the baby, end of story?'

Stacey shakes her head.

'Jukes told me I wasn't finished. Said I had to bring cans back to the UK.'

'More money?'

The woman shakes her head.

'Drugs. Sealed inside. The cans are airtight so the sniffer dogs can't detect a thing.'

'OK,' says Morgan. 'So you use the baby as a cover story, you take the cash *out* of the country then you bring drugs *in*?'

A nod.

'What's in it for you?'

'Five grand.' Stacey sniffs. 'Not much to you maybe, but a fortune to me. The most important thing is that Ryan goes to people who'll love him and look after him, give him all the stuff I never could. So everyone's a winner.'

Morgan wonders if these are Stacey's true feelings or merely a second-hand rationale designed to assuage consciences and passed along the chain. From Karl Savage to Trevor Jukes. From Jukes to the vulnerable, impoverished women he recruits as mules.

'What do you say when people ask where Ryan is?'

'I tell them he's gone to live with his dad.'

Morgan studies the woman's face.

'Was Kiki involved?'

Stacey clears her throat.

'She was supposed to be,' says Stacey. 'Got knocked up while she was in prison but they kept it quiet, like they did with me. Jukes doesn't use his own sperm, in case they do DNA tests on the babies. He smuggles it in, or gets people to do it for him.'

Morgan nods, recalling the pouch Lissa sewed into her jacket.

'Whose sperm?'

She knows the answer but she wants Stacey's version.

A shrug.

'Does it matter?'

'No. Go on. What happened to Kiki?'

'She changed her mind. After Charlie was born. Said she couldn't give him up. Tried to back out.'

Morgan's eyes widen.

'So Jukes killed her? Pushed her off the cliff?'

The woman looks away.

'I don't know if it was Jukes.'

'Who else could it be?'

A shrug. 'Maybe the other bloke.'

'What other bloke?'

'I don't know his name. I never met him, I just heard Jukes talking on the phone.'

'Could it have been Karl Savage?'

Stacey frowns.

'He's dead.'

Morgan lets it pass. The woman is holding something back – she can feel it – but she doesn't want to scare her into clamming up.

'Tell me what happened when you got back from Istanbul.'

'Jukes said I had to look after Charlie. Keep him hidden.'

'Where?'

'His sister's in Ramsgate. She'd been looking after Charlie since Kiki died. I had to pretend I'd been released from prison and couldn't cope on the out. Then, when I got back from Istanbul, I had to say I was better and needed a place to stay.'

'The sister put you up? You and Charlie?'

A nod.

'But she couldn't hack it. She's got her own baby; she couldn't handle the stress, so she chucked us out. That's when he dumped me here, with him.'

She gestures to the sleeping baby.

'What happens next?' says Morgan.

'I'm supposed to take him on the ferry. With more cash. Give it to a bloke in Calais. But he hasn't got a passport so I have to hide him in that.'

She points to a holdall in the corner. The opening is covered by plastic mesh, to allow the baby to breathe.

'What if he cries?'

'He'll give him pills, to make him sleep.'

Pills? A baby?

'And if you don't cooperate?'

Stacey turns to face her.

'Doesn't bear thinking about.'

'After what happened to Kiki?'

The woman gives a sheepish nod but can't meet Morgan's eye.

'What are you not telling me, Stacey? What did you and Lissa talk about, on your breaks at the inn?'

A shrug.

'Baby stuff.'

'Bullshit. I heard you arguing. What about?'

Another shrug.

'Can't remember.'

Morgan decides against pushing harder. She leans forward.

'Is there anything else?'

Stacey sighs.

'I'm supposed to pick up two other kids and take them to Jukes.'

'What kids?'

'Twins. He hasn't told me names. It's a custody battle. The dad wants to smuggle them out of the country so his ex can't get at them. Start a new life with money from the drugs racket.' The woman has the grace to look ashamed. 'He's primed them to expect me to pick them up from school. I just have to give the teacher a note, supposedly from their mum.'

Morgan joins the dots. The 'kids' are Karl Junior and Jack. Stacey is 'the special lady'.

'When are you picking them up?'

'Tomorrow.'

Remember, remember the fifth of November . . .

Stacey gets to her feet, clutching her stomach. The colour has drained from her face.

'Sorry . . .'

She heads for the far end of the houseboat. Morgan watches her disappear into a cubicle. The door closes. Then comes the sound of retching.

Morgan has given no thought to her next step, but the plan seems to arrive in her head almost fully formed. She will never find Karl on her own. Forget needles and haystacks – this is a thousand times harder.

What had Ben said?

Be brave. Be relentless. Be borderline crazy.

The only way to lure Karl out of hiding is to turn the tables, to make *him* come after *her*. A strange sense of calm takes hold. She reaches for her wallet. Ninety-five pounds. She places the cash on the table, then scribbles a note.

Run. Hide. Good luck.

The retching sound worsens. Morgan picks up the box containing the sleeping baby. She climbs the steps leading to the door. Opening it, she steps out into the rain. Holding the box, she jumps down from the deck and heads towards the trees that border the field. Careful not to look back.

It's a full minute before she's safely on the other side of the tree line and hears Stacey's angry cry.

'Morgan? *Morgan!*'

She quickens her pace. The rain is easing. Hugging the edge of the field, she makes her way towards the gap between the trees. The gate is in sight.

Stacey's voice in the distance.

'*Morgan!*'

Hurrying to the gate, she hoists herself up then lowers the box to the other side. It slips from her grasp, hitting the ground with a jolt. The baby begins to wail.

'*Morgan!*'

Stacey's voice is closer; she's heading for the trees. Morgan clambers over the fence and drops to the other side, landing in mud. She can see the Mini a hundred yards away, parked alongside the hedgerow bordering the lay-by.

Picking up the box, she stumbles towards the car, splashing through puddles on the rutted track. The baby's cries grow louder. She reaches the car. Places the box on the roof. Fumbles for her keys. Zaps the fob. Opens the passenger door. Puts the box on the seat. Runs around to the driver's door. Clambers behind the wheel.

And then she hears it.

A motorcycle in the distance. Drawing closer.

Jukes?

Starting the ignition, her foot hovers over the accelerator. The motorbike is approaching the bend. It will pass at any second.

Three . . .

Two . . .

She ducks, bending over the box on the passenger seat, bringing her face close to Charlie's.

One . . .

The motorcycle rounds the corner. The baby's crying grows louder. His eyes are scrunched up, his tiny hands jerk in the air.

The biker roars past, heading for the lane that leads to the farmhouse and houseboat. Heart thumping, pulse racing, Morgan counts a full ten seconds, holding her breath as the sound of the engine recedes into the distance and silence descends.

Was it Jukes?

Did he recognise her car?

Will he come back?

She peers through the windscreen, scanning the road. No sign of life. She releases the handbrake and presses her foot on the accelerator, easing the car forward. The rain-slicked road is empty. Tyres squealing, she drives away, the car filled with the sound of the wailing baby.

The bait in the trap.

Thirty-Eight

The shopping mall car park is half empty but she is taking no chances. The likelihood that Stacey will alert police to the missing baby is minuscule, but anything is possible.

Especially where Karl Savage is concerned.

Rummaging in the boot, Morgan dons a hooded top left by Lissa. Raising the hood, she walks around to the passenger seat, lifts Charlie from the cardboard box and hoists him under her arm. The crying has stopped. The baby is placid and smiling but a telltale odour is emanating from his nappy; action is required. Cradling him in her arms, Morgan walks briskly towards the mall, keeping her head low, her face hidden from the CCTV cameras.

Entering the shopping centre, her anxiety levels soar. The feeling of low-level panic is similar to the sensation when passing through customs, even with nothing to declare. She shivers, anticipating a tap on the shoulder at any moment.

Her eyes rove the lunchtime crowds. Her heart, already pulsing at twice its normal rate, threatens to burst from her chest as she sees a policeman. Clutching a sandwich, he's emerging from Marks & Spencer, listening to a voice squawking from the radio strapped to his stab vest. He says something into the radio. Morgan can't make out the gist but doesn't want to tempt fate. Feigning interest in a shop window, she waits for the PC to pass, then continues towards the escalator. She glances over her shoulder. The man is making for the exit. She takes a breath to settle her nerves, then consults the mall's store guide.

Mothercare – ground floor.

Just over three hours later she's back in Canterbury, pulling up outside Ben's house, a sweet-smelling and mercifully well-behaved Charlie asleep in the new baby seat. Installing the harness and navigating the tangle of straps and buckles has tested Morgan's patience. The infant's bawling and wriggling rendered the operation ten times harder, so she's hoping for an easier transition to the new baby carrier. Her wish is granted. Strapped to her chest, Charlie remains asleep, oblivious to his role in the unfolding drama.

Moving in slow motion, Morgan quietly unloads the bags of shopping: twelve cartons of formula; a week's supply of bottles and teats (sterilising on the run will be too complicated); sachets of purées and yoghurts, plus nappies, nappy bags, wipes and a selection of dummies in case the transition from breastfeeding to formula and solids proves not to the baby's liking.

Which is pretty much guaranteed.

Morgan feels exhausted by the very thought.

Inside the house, her fears prove well founded. On waking, Charlie immediately starts to cry, exercising his lungs at a decibel level reminiscent of Lissa as a baby at her most implacable. After ten crazy-making minutes of screeching and head turning, half a dozen spoonfuls of mush find their way into the baby's mouth, but most ends up on his cheeks or the kitchen floor. The bottle of formula is greeted with a similar lack of enthusiasm, forcing Morgan to resort to an old trick – a sugary rusk. Then, as the crying dies down, she cradles the baby in her arms. Several minutes of writhing and snuffling follow before Charlie falls silent and closes his eyes.

Gazing at the slumbering baby, Morgan is transported back twenty years, to the good-old-bad-old days. Life as a single mother. Surges of unalloyed joy mingled with tedium and terror.

She has decided against a cot, opting for another time-honoured technique: clearing out the bottom drawer of the chest in her room. Using a bath towel to line the drawer, she lowers Charlie inside, covering him with the pink blanket. She studies the sleeping baby for several minutes, then tiptoes to the landing and goes downstairs.

Stepping into the courtyard garden she sits at the wrought-iron table, rolling a cigarette. She smokes while gazing at the dwindling daylight and taking stock of what she has done.

As Lissa would say . . . *WTF?*

Does spiriting Charlie away count as kidnapping? Abduction? Morgan has little idea of the legal definitions, but the answer is almost certainly yes. The baby will come to no harm – she'll make sure of that – and he's in safer hands than a few hours ago. But is that the point?

Yes.

It must be.

As for Morgan's next move, her plan is now coming into sharper focus: she will use Charlie as bait to lure Karl out of hiding.

True, she could tip off the police about Stacey's intention to collect Jack and Karl Junior from school – her vital role in their abduction – but what good would it do? By now, Savage and Jukes will have discovered that Morgan has taken Charlie; the co-conspirators will have no choice but to rethink their plans. Taking the baby was impulsive, but there is no turning back. A line from an old Bette Davis movie bubbles to the surface of Morgan's mind.

Fasten your seatbelts – it's going to be a bumpy night . . .

She jumps.

Fireworks in the street. Bangers exploding, followed by rockets soaring over the rooftops. A burst of distant laughter – teenage boys – then silence.

Morgan stubs out her cigarette, then goes inside to make tea. She checks on the sleeping baby while the kettle boils, then runs a bath. Twenty minutes later, bathed and partially restored, she lies on the bed, listening to Charlie's breathing.

The thought strikes with the force of a punch.

Nancy.

The twins.

Jerking upright, she grabs her mobile and thumbs Nancy's number. She hears the chain-smoker's familiar rasp.

'What do you want, Morgan?'

She can hear a TV blaring in the background. Shrill music. Cartoons?

'Are your boys back from school?'

'Yes. Why?'

'This is going to sound crazy, Nancy, but I need you to keep them at home tomorrow.'

'Excuse me?'

'Trust me. Please.'

A pause.

'Is this some kind of terrorist warning?' says Nancy. 'Because I didn't have you down as a jihadi bride.'

'Nothing like that.'

'So, what is it?'

'If I tell you, you won't believe me. Just don't send them to school tomorrow.'

'Are you serious?'

'Totally.'

Another pause, followed by a hacking cough.

'I'll think about it.'

'It's just one day.'

'I said, I'll think about it.'

The woman coughs again, then hangs up.

Morgan feels a surge of guilt. Should she have told the whole story?

No.

The past few weeks have proved beyond doubt that a sure-fire way to be dismissed as a crackpot is to tell the truth about Karl Savage. She has done her best. The rest is up to Nancy.

A noise from downstairs.

Ben's key in the door.

Tingling with apprehension, she springs to her feet and steps onto the landing.

'Hi.'

He's at the foot of the stairs, looking up at her, a smile creasing his face.

'You're back early,' says Morgan, hoping he hasn't glimpsed the bags of baby food on the table, visible through the kitchen door.

The smile widens.

'Very pipe and slippers.'

She heads downstairs, following him into the sitting room.

'I need to tell you something.'

He turns, smile fading.

'Is this where you say it's been fun but you're not ready for anything serious? Because if it is . . .'

A surge of panic. Is he going to dump her? Getting his retaliation in first? If so, she doesn't want to know. Not now.

'Nothing like that.'

'OK,' he says. 'I'm listening.'

And so she tells him. About staking out the houseboat and finding Stacey. About abducting the baby. About using Charlie as bait.

Ben listens in silence, framed by the window, studying her face intently. When she finishes, he leaves a moment's silence.

'The baby's upstairs?'

'Yes.'

He nods, grimly processing the news.

'So . . . is *this* the trap?' He gestures around the room. 'Are you trying to lure Karl here?'

'No.'

'Where, then?'

'I'm working on it.'

'And what makes you sure he gives a damn about this particular child? He seems happy to act as sperm donor for God knows how many other babies, why is this one different?'

'I'm not saying he is. But Karl needs to fund his new life abroad. He's been planning this for ages. Charlie represents a lot of money – as cover for smuggling cash and drugs, and as a commodity in his own right. Plus, Karl seems to care about some of his kids. Why else would he go to such lengths to get hold of the twins?'

Ben raises an eyebrow.

'You're asking me to second-guess a sociopath?'

'No, I'm trying to answer your question.'

'So there's no guarantee he'll come after your bait?'

Morgan feels her cheeks redden.

'If you've got a better idea, now would be a good time to mention it.'

He blows out his cheeks, then walks into the kitchen. She follows, watching as he takes a beer from the fridge. Studiously ignoring the bags of baby food, he opens the can and takes a long swig.

'Can I ask a question? Are you out of your mind?'

'I'm desperate. My daughter lost her baby. She's an exile. I've fled my home. I'm scared of this man and that's no way to live.'

She pauses for breath. 'I want my life back. I want my daughter back. Bringing Karl out of hiding is the best chance I have. I'm taking it.'

And it would be nice if you could be supportive.

Upstairs, the baby starts to cry. Morgan turns to leave.

'Wait,' says Ben.

She stops. His voice is stern, his expression hard to read. 'I really like you, Morgan.'

'Good. I like you too.'

He's about to say something about their relationship – or fling, or whatever this is – but changes his mind. Takes another swig of beer. Playing for time.

'Did anyone see you arrive with the baby?'

She shakes her head.

'The street was empty when I unloaded the car.'

He wipes his mouth with the back of his hand.

'You understand the ramifications for me? My career? My life?'

A knot of disappointment tightens inside her stomach. The baby's wailing grows louder.

'I need to see to Charlie.'

He ignores her. 'Go to the police.'

'I can't—'

He interrupts, holding up a finger.

'Whatever the rights and wrongs, the police will charge you with abducting a child. That makes me an accessory. Don't tell me your plan. You have twenty-four hours. After that, if you don't go to the police, I will.'

The disappointment intensifies. But at least he's giving her a chance.

'Thank you.'

'Don't thank me. You never brought the baby here. We never had this conversation. Clear?'

'Clear.'

'Now do something about all that bloody crying before my neighbours get home.'

She turns and leaves the room, wincing at the sound of the kitchen door slamming.

Upstairs, she scoops Charlie from the drawer, cradling him in her arms. For a moment, she feels on the verge of joining in with *all that bloody crying*. She forces herself to get a grip. There will come a time for release, but not today. Today there is one priority.

The baby hiccups twice in quick succession, then the crying slowly subsides. He seems responsive to Morgan's attempts to soothe him.

Be glad of small mercies.

She changes Charlie's nappy. Hearing the shower running, she takes the baby downstairs and prepares a bottle of formula. More fireworks outside. She can't see them, but she can hear the rockets soaring into the evening sky.

Back in her room, she sits on the bed, rocking the baby in her arms for several minutes before touching the rubber teat to his rosebud lips. The baby turns his head. Morgan tries again. No response, apart from wriggling and squirming. She squirts a little of the liquid onto her forefinger then traces it over Charlie's lips. The baby writhes, his features wrinkling into a scowl.

Then a breakthrough. As she guides the bottle towards the baby's mouth, his lips close around the teat. Morgan holds her breath, gently squeezing the bottle as the baby suckles then swallows.

Once.

Twice.

Three times.

Thank God.

If Charlie will take a good quantity of formula, maybe he'll go back to sleep and allow time for Morgan to plan her next move. She can hear Ben clattering in the kitchen. The sound of his mobile ringing. He takes the call, the murmur of his voice vibrating through the floorboards.

The baby is suckling at the teat. Morgan's leg is cramping but she is determined not to move, to maintain her position until Charlie has had his fill. She tends to the dribble, then adjusts the one-piece and lowers the baby into the drawer. Tucking Charlie inside the pink blanket, she straightens up and turns.

Ben is framed in the doorway.

'Jesus, you scared me . . .'

He casts a look in the baby's direction. 'Is he OK?'

'Yes. It took months before Lissa would eat any. . .'

She breaks off. He's not listening, chewing on his lower lip.

'What's wrong?'

'Just had a work call. I need to get going. Sounds like an all-nighter.'

She frowns.

'What are you not telling me?'

He looks towards the window, still biting his lip.

'It's a weird one. A fire in a graveyard. Someone dug up a coffin. Doused the corpse in petrol. Set it on fire.'

Morgan can feel the hairs prickling along her arms.

'Whose body?'

But she already knows the answer.

He turns to meet her gaze.

'Pearl Savage.'

Thirty-Nine

Ninety minutes after Ben leaves, Morgan is still trying to suppress a sense of rising panic. Charlie has been crying for an hour, impervious to all attempts to pacify him. Before the onset of tears, Morgan had bathed him, changed his nappy and persuaded him to eat several teaspoons of banana rice. Then her luck ran out. The baby screwed up his face and launched a marathon of howling that shows no signs of abating.

Now, pacing around the dimly lit bedroom, Morgan is holding him close, gently clasping his head to her shoulder, hand on his back, rocking him from side to side while cooing in his ear, the way she remembers soothing Lissa.

'Shhh, sweet thing, shhh . . .'

The crying intensifies. Morgan starts to hum, keeping the sound to a low rumble, hoping the vibration will transmit itself to Charlie and prove calming.

Fat chance.

The baby continues to bawl.

'Shhh, baby boy, shhh . . .'

Her mobile rings.

Lissa.

Morgan hesitates. How to explain the crying infant? Her daughter's eyes stare from the screen. The phone shrills. The baby's cries grow louder. Morgan takes the call.

'Hello?'

'Mum . . .?'

'How are you?'

'OK . . .' Pause. 'Is that a baby?'

'Yep.'

Another pause. Morgan detects an instant change of mood.

'Whose?'

'It's a long story.'

'I'm in no hurry.'

'It's difficult to talk . . . there's a lot of crying . . .'

'Fuck's sake, Mum. Whose baby?'

'Sorry . . .? I can't hear you . . .'

'You can hear perfectly. *Whose baby?*'

Morgan sits on the bed. Holding Charlie to her shoulder, she lets the phone fall onto the duvet and puts Lissa on speakerphone.

'Before I tell you, I need to know how you are.'

Because when you find out what I've done you'll hang up and I can't handle more stress.

'How do you *think*? I had a miscarriage. I got on a plane. Now I'm in LA and Dad's having a meltdown over his script. His girlfriend's a bitch on wheels and I feel like ten sacks of shit. *Now, whose baby?*'

Time to come clean.

'Kiki's.'

A sharp intake of breath.

'No way . . .'

Charlie is calmer now, the crying less shrill. Morgan transfers him to her lap, wrapping him in the blanket while leaning closer to the speakerphone. Talking softly, she tells her daughter how she comes to be caring for the baby who disappeared weeks ago and whose mother's body was found at the base of a cliff. By the time she's finished, Charlie's eyes are closed and the crying has ceased. But not on the other side of the Atlantic.

'Lissa? Are you OK?'

Morgan can hear her daughter weeping.

Lissa blows her nose. Her voice sounds small.

'Who's been looking after him?'

'Stacey. And Jukes's sister.'

'Is he OK?'

'He's fine.'

'What will happen to him?'

'Adoption, I guess,' says Morgan. 'But I'm not ready to hand him over. Not tonight.' She hears the click of a lighter and frowns. 'Are you smoking?'

'Yep. And drinking beer.'

'For breakfast?'

'What are you, *my mother*?'

Morgan listens to Lissa sucking smoke into her lungs.

'Lissa?'

'Yes?'

'I keep thinking there's something you're not telling me.'

'Says the woman who kidnapped *a baby*?'

'Talk to me.'

'I *am* talking to you.'

'You know what I mean.'

A pause.

'I'm *so* sorry, Mum.'

'About what?'

'I've got to go.'

'Don't hang up on me—'

'Don't do anything stupid. Call me when it's over.'

'Lissa? *Lissa?*'

But her daughter has gone.

Ten minutes later, Morgan straps Charlie into the car seat and sets off for the cemetery. The baby sleeps throughout the drive, calling to mind Lissa's behaviour as an infant: explosive tantrums followed by merciful periods of deep sleep. Morgan is hoping Charlie will follow a similar pattern.

Just past eight o'clock. The evening rush hour is over, the motorway almost deserted. Morgan is briefly distracted by the sight of fireworks exploding against the night sky – two corner-shop rockets launched by someone unable to wait for the main event tomorrow evening.

Remember, remember . . .

Turning onto the slip road, she guides the Mini up the ramp that leads towards the churchyard. A mile or so along the road, she slows at the entrance to a single-track lane, her attention taken by bright lights visible through the trees. Last time she was here – with Karl Savage – there was precious little light. Tonight, the wooded area is a crime scene: powerful arc lamps illuminate a flurry of police activity. SOCOs in white overalls. Blue and white tape cordons the churchyard from rubberneckers undeterred by the November chill. She drives past the path that leads to the church, registering the sight of Ben's Range Rover, then pulling to a halt on a grass verge.

The baby stirs, opening his eyes. Humming softly, Morgan gives what she hopes is a reassuring smile, then steps out of the car. Two minutes later she has settled Charlie in the harness around her neck, taking care to ensure the baby is secure. He looks up, wide-eyed and smiling.

'OK, baby boy, let's go hunting.'

Hunting.

She turns the word over in her mind. The thought of Karl as prey makes her feel empowered.

Courageous.

Reckless.

She walks towards the crime scene, standing at the fringe of the crowd. Twenty or so onlookers, mostly men, a few women, a couple of teenagers. No one pays attention to Morgan. All eyes are on the team behind the tape. She glimpses Ben talking to two police officers, one plainclothes, the other in uniform. Like the SOCOs and the photographer, the fire scene investigator wears white overalls and paper overshoes.

For a moment, Morgan is seized by a powerful desire to turn and run. She has abducted a baby. The proximity to police officers makes her heart race. She forces herself to remain calm, to think clearly. As far as the police are concerned she's just another rubbernecker. And if she's brought her baby to a crime scene, so what?

Bigger fish to fry.

She watches Ben say something to the plainclothes officer. He ducks his head and enters the tent that conceals the exhumed corpse of Karl Savage's mother.

Morgan tries not to stare at the faces in the crowd, but Ben's insight into pyromaniacs is at the forefront of her mind.

Check out the scene of the crime. Some arsonists get a kick out of gawking at their 'work'.

She gives a sidelong glance to the faces in the crowd. One, a middle-aged woman in a bobble hat, notices the baby and smiles.

'My two were the same. Fresh air. Best way to send them to sleep.'

Morgan gives a non-committal smile. She nods towards the tent.

'What's going on?'

'Some sicko dug up a coffin. Set the body on fire.' She rubs her hands together, keeping the cold at bay. 'Not much to see, but it beats *Emmerdale*.'

Morgan turns away, letting her eyes rove across the other onlookers. Most faces are clearly visible, illuminated by the glow from the lamps, but a couple are obscured by hoodies. There is no sign of Karl Savage.

Stepping to one side, she cranes her neck, trying to get a line of sight on a figure standing alone at the rear of the crowd – a man in a baseball cap, hands plunged into the pockets of his leather jacket, face in the shadows. As he turns to leave, his face catches the light. She suppresses a gasp.

Jukes?

She can't be sure – it's a fleeting glimpse. And now he's walking away, quickening his pace, and the baby is starting to cry and the bloody woman in the bloody bobble hat is saying something.

'What's her name?'

The pink blanket. She thinks it's a girl.

'Lissa,' says Morgan. The man in the cap is heading into the woods. He's wearing biker boots. She starts to follow. 'Excuse me, I need to—'

'Morgan?'

A familiar voice. Neville Rook.

Morgan is dimly aware of the woman in the hat giving her a quizzical look. She doesn't want to explain why the police officer knows her name. Or answer questions about the baby. Above all, she doesn't want to lose sight of the man in the base-ball cap.

'Morgan?'

The DI is drawing closer. Morgan raises her head, scanning the woods. The man is nowhere to be seen.

Was it Jukes? Did he see her?

'Thought it was you,' Rook has reached her side.

'Hi,' says Morgan, trying to keep her tone light. 'I was driving past, saw the lights.'

He nods, peering at the baby.

'Who's this little munchkin?'

Morgan's clears her throat, playing for time. She peers over the DI's shoulder as Ben emerges from the tent. She feigns ignorance.

'Is that Ben?'

Rook turns, following her gaze.

'Yes.'

She can see the fire investigator casting a look in their direction, taking stock of the situation. He walks towards them.

'What's in the tent?' says Morgan.

'I told you,' says the woman in the bobble hat. She sounds peeved that someone could doubt her word. 'Someone dug up a body and set it on fire.' She looks to Rook for confirmation. 'Am I right?'

The DI gives a non-committal shrug. 'I can't say anything at this stage.' He gestures towards the sleeping baby. 'So?'

'So what?' Morgan plays for time, watching Ben duck beneath the crime scene tape.

'Whose baby?' says Neville.

'Her name's Lissa,' sniffs the woman.

The policeman raises an eyebrow.

'I thought Lissa was *your* daughter's name.'

'This *is* her daughter,' says Bobble Hat.

The blood thuds in Morgan's ears. She smiles.

'You misunderstood. It's a boy.'

The woman draws in her neck, affronted.

'Whose is he?' says Rook.

Morgan clears her throat, playing for time. Ben reaches the DI's side.

'My sister's,' he says. 'She's in hospital. I'm being Uncle Ben for a few days. Morgan's helping out.'

'Ah, right,' says Rook. 'What's his name?'

Morgan's mind is a blank; the one name she can think of is the one she can't say.

Charlie.

The police officer is staring at her.

'Are you OK?'

Struck dumb, Morgan looks at the baby.

'His name's Tom,' says Ben. He smiles at Morgan, but there's no warmth behind the eyes. 'Bit cold for him to be out?'

Morgan nods. 'Better get him home.' She turns to go.

'Could have sworn you said Lissa,' grumbles the woman, but no one is listening. In the distance, Morgan hears a motorcycle revving then roaring away into the night.

'See you later,' she says, feigning nonchalance. She can feel Rook's eyes on her as she turns and walks towards the car. She hears the DI addressing Ben under his breath.

'*Give us a moment, OK?*'

She carries on walking.

'Morgan?'

She stops. The DI is walking towards her. Behind him, Ben is rooted to the spot, powerless to intervene.

'Can I have a word?' says Rook.

Morgan's heart threatens to burst from her chest.

'Of course.'

He clears his throat.

'Bit of news. Me and the fiancée, we're back on. Fixed a date. Next June.'

Relief floods every fibre of Morgan's being.

'Congratulations.'

He holds her gaze. A sheepish smile.

'Just thought you should know.'

'Absolutely.'

He seems disappointed. Raises an eyebrow.

'No hard feelings?'

Despite the fact that she's talking to a police officer while holding a kidnapped baby, Morgan stiffens. What is he implying? That *she* was holding a torch for *him*?

Let it go.

'Of course not. I'm happy for you.'

'DI Rook?'

Ben's voice. The policeman turns to leave, gesturing towards the baby.

'Look after Tom,' he says.

'You bet.'

Heart pounding, Morgan walks in the direction of the Mini. Casting a look over her shoulder, she sees Neville and Ben duck under the tape and head for the tent. Ben doesn't look back, locked in conversation with the DI.

Another wave of relief is mingled with gratitude. Pausing, she strains to catch any trace of the motorcycle engine but there is none.

Jukes – if it *was* him – has vanished.

She reaches the car and straps Charlie into the baby seat. The baby is awake but mercifully quiet. Morgan gets behind the wheel and drives away.

Less than a mile down the road, her phone beeps. She pulls to a halt and scans the text. It's from Ben. His anger at being drawn into her web of lies is palpable.

Forget twenty-four hours. You have twelve.

Morgan checks her watch.

9.02 p.m.

The baby starts to cry.

It's going to be a long night.

Forty

Morgan cruises past Jukes's bungalow. She pulls to a halt at the end of the poorly lit street. No sign of the motorcycle. The pebbledash bungalow is in darkness, the road deserted. Parked cars. A wheelie bin on its side. A pair of trainers dangling from an overhead power cable.

The baby is awake, gurgling happily in the back of the car. He slept through the first half of the journey, but a nappy change precipitated a stop in a service station and was followed by an impressive helping of formula and a lot of strident crying.

Morgan turns to look at Charlie and is greeted by what might be a smile. The wailing has abated, but for how long? She considers her options. Leave him the car? Or take him on what feels like mission impossible, rifling through Jukes's rubbish in the hope of finding clues to the whereabouts of Karl Savage? As plans go, it's what Lissa would call *so lame*, but Morgan is out of ideas.

Soon she'll be out of time.

The dashboard clock shows 10.30. The *Newsnight* theme blares from one of the few bungalows showing signs of life. Most are in darkness, curtains drawn against the chill November air.

The only movement in the street is an emaciated cat foraging scraps from a fast food container in a front garden.

The thought of leaving Charlie unattended goes against every instinct in Morgan's body. Which leaves only the second option. The familiar struggle with straps ensues. Then, the baby secure in his harness, Morgan walks towards Jukes's house. She can feel Charlie snuggled against her upper body, radiating warmth.

Reaching the driveway, Morgan navigates the gate hanging from its hinges and heads for the wheelie bin. She raises the lid. The bin is empty. She mutters under her breath.

'*Idiot . . .*'

The possibility of the garbage having been recently collected hasn't occurred to her. She looks at the windows of the house. No lights, no sign of life. A side gate leads to the garden. She clicks the latch. The gate opens. Her heart races. The baby coughs and blinks. Then he closes his eyes.

Morgan turns to survey the street. Deserted. Hand on the latch, she opens the gate and steps onto a path bordered by weeds. She closes the gate behind her. The darkness is almost total. She makes her way down the path, passing a side door covered with rippled glass. The baby coughs again, twice, but his eyes remain closed.

Reaching the rear of the house, Morgan is surprised by the neatness of the garden. In contrast to the patch of ground at the front of the bungalow, the garden is orderly and well tended. The allotment is bare – unsurprising for November – but has been in recent use. The hedge is neatly trimmed, the barbecue covered with a green tarpaulin.

Morgan fishes her phone from her pocket and selects the torch app. She shines the light through a window and makes out the kitchen. About to move on, she freezes, straining to hear.

A motorcycle in the distance.

Her heart rate triples. She hurries back along the path, towards the gate. The engine noise grows louder, closer. She hesitates. If she leaves now, and if the motorbike belongs to Jukes, she won't make it to the car before he turns onto the street.

Better to let him get inside the house, then make her escape.

She hears the motorcycle drawing nearer, the rumble of the engine growing louder as it slows outside the bungalow. The sound of it driving onto the paved area at the front of the house. The engine cuts out. Silence descends. He dismounts. Walks to the front door. A jangle of keys. The door opens and closes. Then silence.

Trevor Jukes is home.

About to take the final steps towards the gate, Morgan stops in her tracks as a light is switched on inside the house, spilling from the glass door. The gate is on the far side of the door. She can't move without being seen. She freezes, rooted to the spot.

The sound of a key turning. The door judders then creaks, opening outwards. She holds her breath as she hears a match being struck. Then comes the sound of Jukes inhaling sharply, accompanied by the unmistakable smell of dope. Morgan closes her eyes. She tries to regulate her breathing, to transmit calming vibes to the baby strapped to her chest.

If Charlie cries . . .

Or coughs . . .

She hears Jukes drawing on the joint, sucking the smoke into his lungs. Then the sound of his ringtone – the theme from *The Archers*, absurdly jaunty but unmistakable. He fumbles for his mobile. Takes the call.

'Yeah? . . . No, no sign of her. What about you?'

Morgan can make out the faint voice of the caller – a man – but she can't hear what he's saying.

'How should I know?' says Jukes. 'This was your idea, not mine.' Another pull on the joint. 'OK, whatever. Phone me back at one o'clock. No later.'

The call ends. The sound of the mobile being put down. On a shelf? A table? Footsteps as Jukes walks away, into the house, leaving the door ajar. Morgan is rooted to the spot, not daring to move. Moments later, she hears the sound of running water – a shower. She counts to ten, then inches forward, peering around the open door. No sign of life.

The mobile is on a table, just inside the door.

The baby coughs.

Once

Twice.

He starts to cry.

Morgan darts through the door. Takes two quick paces inside the house. Snatches the phone from the table. The baby's cries grow louder. The shower stops. She turns to the door, retracing her steps.

'Hello?'

Jukes's voice from the other room.

She steps out onto the path. Heads for the gate. Her fingers grasp the latch. She doesn't look behind her. The baby's cries stop. Morgan opens the gate. Walks through to the front garden. Closes the gate behind her. She hears footsteps inside the house. Imagines Jukes's face as he realises his mobile is gone.

'*What the fuck?*'

Tucking the phone into the pocket of her jeans, she breaks into a run, passing the motorcycle and heading for the front gate.

He'll be here any second.

He'll see her.

She changes tack and ducks behind the motorcycle. Hears the click of the latch. Footsteps. Bare feet on concrete.

'*Who's there?*'

She holds her breath. Imagines him scanning the empty street. Naked? In a dressing gown? A towel? More footsteps. He's on the other side of the motorcycle, just yards away. The harness digs into her ribs. The baby is wriggling. Another crying jag is seconds away.

'*Give me my fucking phone!*'

The furious cry echoes down the street. She imagines veins bulging in the man's neck. His eyes combing the road as he searches for the thief in the night.

More footsteps. He's moving. Out of the garden, onto the pavement, heading along the road.

Charlie is wriggling in the sling, scrunching his face in an expression Morgan has come to dread. The baby is filling his nappy, a crying fit is seconds away. Reaching into her jacket pocket, Morgan searches for any kind of weapon. Her hands make contact with something small and hard. She draws it out.

Ben's rape alarm.

She doesn't hesitate, yanking the pin from the device. The sound is high-pitched and deafening. She draws back her arm, lobbing it like a grenade. But her aim is off. Instead of landing several houses away, distracting Jukes from her hiding place, the alarm ricochets off a telegraph pole and lands in the middle of the road, yards from where he's standing. She sees him running towards it, cupping his hands over his ears to block out the piercing sound, angry eyes scanning the empty street. He's wearing a black dressing gown. Reaching the alarm, he stoops to pick up something from the gutter – a stone? a brick? – raises it above his head and *smashes* it onto the device. The wailing stops. Silence descends. Morgan holds her breath.

Miraculously, the baby hasn't started crying. But it's only a matter of time.

Now another sound, from across the road. A rapping on glass. A voice, muffled.

'*Can't hear you,*' says Jukes. Angry. Frustrated.

Peering through the spokes of the motorcycle, Morgan sees him approach the bungalow opposite. An elderly woman stands at the window, gesticulating towards the motorbike, mouthing, like a character in a pantomime.

'*Behind you.*'

Unlike Jukes, Morgan can decipher what the woman is saying. Striding through the gate, the man in the dressing gown approaches the house, raising his voice.

'*What the hell are you on about?*'

Morgan can wait no longer. She straightens up. Runs for the gate. Out of the corner of her eye, she can see Jukes, his back to her, the woman rapping on the window.

Suddenly, he turns.

Sees her.

'Hey!'

Morgan is running running *running*, holding the baby tight, her footsteps echoing down the street as she races towards her car.

'*Hey!*'

She hears him breaking into a run. The Mini is a hundred yards away. If it weren't for the baby, she could beat him to it. But he's closing in.

Seventy yards.

Charlie starts to cry.

Jukes's angry voice.

'Bitch!'

Fifty yards.

Morgan reaches into her jacket pocket, fumbling for her keys.

Thirty yards.

The baby's cries grow louder.

Morgan zaps the fob. It doesn't work; she's too far away.

Twenty yards.

She tries again.

The lights flash as the doors unlock. She glances over her shoulder. His dressing gown is flapping open, exposing his belly and boxers.

Ten yards.

'Fucking bitch!'

She turns back to the car, hand outstretched towards the driver's door.

And drops the key.

Watches it slither into the gutter.

Slams into the car, jolting the baby, who cries louder.

Feels Jukes's meaty hands grasp her arm.

They stand there, panting, eyes wide. She can smell his tobacco breath.

'Help!' Her cry echoes along the deserted street. No sign of life. '*Help!*' Three houses away, a curtain twitches in an upstairs window. 'Help me!'

He's seen it too.

'Come inside,' he says, gasping for breath. 'I just want to talk.'

'Like you "talked" to Kiki McNeil?'

His jaw tightens, a muscle twitches in his face.

'Come in the fucking house!'

She squirms, but his grip is too tight.

'Help! *Help!*'

Turning, she sees three figures emerging from the bungalow opposite her car. She recognises them immediately. The neighbourhood lads. The one with the gold earring quickens his pace, leaving the others to bring up the rear.

'What the fuck, man?' says Earring.

'She stole my phone,' says Jukes, still panting.

Earring looks from Morgan to Jukes, weighing up the situation. Folding his arms, he plants himself in front of the Mini, blocking the driver's door.

'You steal the man's phone?'

'No,' says Morgan, raising her voice to make herself heard above the crying baby. 'He's a liar.'

'*She's* the lying bitch' says Jukes. 'Give it back.'

He grabs her wrist. She shakes him off. Turns to Earring.

'See what I put up with? Lies. Bullying. Bullshit.'

'*I'm* not the liar,' says Jukes.

The baby's cries grow louder, a stench emanating from his nappy.

'Can't you shut her up?' says Gap-tooth.

'She's a he,' says Morgan, her mind racing. 'Maybe he wouldn't be so upset if Trev didn't hit me.'

'*What?*' says Jukes. 'This is bollocks.'

'I've had enough,' says Morgan. She snatches her keys from the gutter. 'I'm going to the police.'

'Shut the fuck up,' says Earring.

Jukes smiles, tying the dressing-gown belt around his belly.

'Took the words out of my mouth.'

'Not her, bruv,' says Earring. He turns to Jukes. '*You.*'

Jukes's smile disappears.

'I don't even know the woman.'

'So how come she knows your name?' says Gap-tooth

'Because she's—'

'Shut the fuck up.'

Earring takes a step forward. Jukes spreads his hands.

'Guys, you've got this wrong.'

Earring ignores him. Turns to Morgan.

'You OK?'

The baby is bawling at the top of his lungs. Morgan clasps him tightly.

'I just need to get away from—'

'This is *bollocks*—' shouts Trev, but he breaks off as Gap-tooth's fist makes contact with his jaw, rocking him on his feet. The third youth – Neck Tattoo – slips behind the man, holding him in an armlock.

'Won't tell you again,' says Earring. He steps away from the car, tugs at the handle and opens the door. Morgan is already unclipping the harness, hoisting the baby into the rear seat.

'This is bullshit!' Jukes's face is purple with rage. '*She* stole *my* fucking phone. And that's not even her baby!'

Another blow from Gap-tooth, this time to the stomach. Morgan tries to ignore the scene unfolding behind her, focusing on strapping Charlie into the baby seat. Job done, she gets behind the wheel. Starts the engine. Earring reaches inside the car and stays her hand.

'Got a kiss for me?'

Morgan meets his gaze. He grins. 'Knight in shining armour, innit.'

She says nothing. He bends closer. Looks her in the eye.

'Truth. He hit you?'

'Yes.'

Earring shakes his head, then straightens up. Turns to Jukes.

'What the fuck, man?' He takes a step forward. Neck Tattoo and Gap-tooth follow suit, closing in on their prey.

Revving the engine, Morgan hears Jukes's protests. She pulls the door closed, then puts her foot down. The Mini jerks forward. The baby is still crying. She steers the car along the street, heart pounding, eyes flickering to the rear-view mirror. A glimpse of raised fists as Earring and Gap-tooth lay into the man in the dressing gown. Knocking him to the ground. Kicking his legs and stomach.

Morgan averts her gaze and rounds the corner, the baby's cries growing louder as she drives away into the night.

She can feel Jukes's phone in her pocket, digging into her thigh.

His last call was from her quarry.

She's sure of it.

What did Jukes say?

Call me back at one o'clock.

She checks her watch. Eleven on the dot.

She's two hours from talking to Karl Savage.

Forty-One

KARL

Lying on his lumpy bed in The Shithole, he takes the tattered newspaper article from the pocket of his fleece and reads it, just as he has every birthday since making the mistake.

Tragic Mum Dies in Cellar Fall.

Cracked her skull on the concrete, or so the paper says. No mention of the poker. Why would there be? He'd hidden it, repositioned her body, then told everyone he'd seen her trip and tumble down the steps. An eye-witness account from a grief-stricken schoolboy mourning the loss of a second parent. A convincing performance

Especially with The Whistler backing his version of events.

Karl's masterstroke had been to hide the poker, then remind the man that his fingerprints were on it too. In case he got ideas.

He's never told The Whistler who the real target was, how lucky he is to be alive. What would be the point?

As for remorse, Karl doesn't do guilt. She was a bitch. RIP. Rot in peace.

He knows where she's buried. One day, he'll piss on her grave. But for now he contents himself by rereading the article.

Pearl's tragic son, Karl, was celebrating his eleventh birthday on the day the accident happened. Local Authority sources say he's likely to be put in care.

'Care'? More like 'couldn't care less'. 'The Shithole', that's what the others call it. A cockroach-infested house in the worst part of town. But he's fifteen now. This part of his life will soon be over.

And he's put up with worse.

Much worse.

Just ask The Whistler.

When Karl becomes a dad he'll give his kids the best start possible. Especially the boys. Boys like himself. And Guy. He thinks of the biscuit tin, still sealed with tape, still in its hidey-hole, along with the poker, waiting to be reclaimed once he gets a place of his own.

Folding the article, he slips it between the pages of his book and continues to read.

Pablo Escobar, the Robin Hood of Colombia. OK, the man created a massive narco-state. OK, he was ruthless. OK, he lived like a god and had mad stuff like a private zoo and planes and submarines and Christ know what else. But he used a lot of his money – *billions* – to help people. Ordinary people. That's why thousands turned out for his funeral. That's why they loved him. That's why they *still* love him, even though he's been dead for years. He made his mark.

Karl's thinking of changing his name.

Pablo.

Sounds exotic. Girls would love it. Not that he needs much help in that direction.

A knock on the door. Karl ignores it. He knows who it is. The mousey girl who's been coming to visit her brother for the last few weeks. She's the same age as Karl – fifteen – and she's 'in care' too, just not the same shithole. He's seen the look in her eye. Knows what's on her mind. Same as his slag of a mum used to have on hers.

They can't do it here, of course, but there's always somewhere. Down by the canal or behind the bins outside the café. Maybe they'll get chips first, watch the fireworks, then wait for everyone to fuck off home.

Another knock. He calls out.

'Wait a minute'.

He reaches into his pocket and pulls out the pack of condoms. Unpinning the safety pin from his fleece, he pricks three tiny holes in the plastic. It won't bring Guy back, but it's the next best thing, the best he can do for now.

Soon he'll be master of his own destiny. Then he can show the world what he's made of. Leave something to be remembered by. Something big. Something beautiful. Who cares if life turns out to be short, so long as it's sweet?

Down in the office some middle-aged twat is listening to Radio 4. That stupid soap opera, *The Archers*. Same shit, same time every night.

Tum-de-dum-de-dum-de-dum, tum-de-dum-de-dah-dah . . .

Just the sound of the jaunty signature tune makes Karl feel nauseous.

It's the tune The Whistler used to whistle. Walking around the house. Coming down to the cellar.

And after the 'special game'.

Pearl never listened to Radio 4. The first time Karl heard the music on the radio was the day they took him into care. The *tum-de-dum* music made him sick. Physically sick. To this day, it makes him feel bad. Dirty. Filled with shame and rage. PTSD, or some bullshit like that. But he's found a way to calm himself down. The trick is to think ahead. Look forward, not back. He takes the letter from his pocket. The one he rescued from her bin and taped back together. The one The Whistler wrote in red ink when he was drunk and full of self-pity.

Dear Pearl,

    I didn't mean to kill the baby. I kept telling him to shut up, but he wouldn't. So it was his fault for crying all the fucking time. But I'm sorry. Please forgive me. Love you always.

    Trevor xxx

Karl rereads the letter for the millionth time. It's what they call a smoking gun. Something he can use in the future, to make Jukes do as he says. Not now. But one day.

A third knock.

He tucks the letter back in his pocket, next to the condoms, and gets to his feet. The jaunty music has stopped. Downstairs, the radio blares. As Karl opens the door, he returns the girl's smile, but his thoughts are miles away.

With The Whistler.

Another of Daddy's sayings plays inside his head.

Revenge is a dish best served cold.

Forty-Two

Entering her house, Morgan shivers. The place is cold and dank, the sitting-room window still boarded up. Turning on the lights, she fires up the heating, but it will be days before the place feels warm.

The kitchen clock shows 23.46. She's hoping Karl won't phone ahead of schedule. She has things to do. As for the risk of Jukes trying to contact Savage, to warn him about the stolen mobile, she's counting on the fact that people no longer remember numbers or write them down. Lose your phone, lose your world.

Top priority is Charlie, awake but no longer crying. Morgan liberates him from the harness, then fetches the rug from the hall and places him in the middle of the kitchen floor. She keeps a watchful eye on the baby while preparing a bottle of formula and a sachet of puréed vegetables.

Fifteen fractious minutes later, Charlie is wrapped in the pink blanket, sound asleep. Morgan sets the kettle to boil, then rummages in the freezer, taking out a pack of cod fillets. She places the fish in a bowl of hot water.

Glancing out of the window, she sees a distant starburst of fireworks exploding against the night sky, followed by the sound of outraged seagulls as they take to the air, their cries echoing far and wide.

Morgan bides her time, waiting for the fish to defrost. She needs to entice the birds as close as possible.

The fish are bait.

The baby is bait.

She is bait.

She craves a cigarette but there is no time. Dialling Rook's number, she paces the room while waiting for the call to connect.

'Do you know what time it is?'

He sounds sleepy but sober. A TV murmurs in the background.

'I've kidnapped a baby.'

'What . . .?'

'It's Charlie. Kiki's little boy.'

A pause. The TV is silenced.

'Is this a joke?'

As if on cue, the baby wakes and starts to cry. Morgan holds the phone close to Charlie's mouth.

'No joke,' she says. 'Come and arrest me.'

The DI doesn't sound sleepy any more.

'Have you gone crazy?'

'Two birds with one stone,' says Morgan. 'This is the only way I can get you to take me seriously *and* bring Karl out of hiding.'

'How?'

'He's Karl's son. Worth big money. I'm betting Karl will do anything to get him back.'

'You're *betting*?'

'A calculated risk,' says Morgan. 'Get over here – but not mob-handed. Nothing to scare him off.'

'Where are you?'

'My place.'

'Jesus . . . Does he know?'

'He will. But if he thinks he's being set up, he won't come. Which is why I'm going to make him guess where I am. So he thinks *he's* the smart one.'

She hears the jangle of Rook's keys.

His front door opening and closing.

His footsteps on gravel.

He's running, a breathless urgency in his voice.

'Don't do this, Morgan.'

She hears a fob being zapped. He's getting into his car.

'Morgan?'

'Don't tell me what to do. I'm doing it.'

She ends the call and pockets her phone. Then she walks into the kitchen, passing the now sleeping baby. She drains the water from the bowl and carries it outside. Making her way across the shingle, she heads for the old fishing boat beached two hundred yards from her door. Above her, the seagulls are circling, still unsettled by the fireworks.

Approaching the decrepit boat, she takes two fish fillets and hurls them high into the air. Then two more. They land on the beach, yards from where she's standing. She watches the gulls swoop low over the boat. She throws the last two fish onto the shingle. Reaching for her phone, she selects the voice app and sets it to record the cacophony of shrieks as the birds land and peck at the fish. Within seconds, the size of the flock has doubled as word spreads of the unexpected feast. The tussle triggers another frenzy of ghastly shrieking. Holding her phone aloft, she watches the gulls do battle, one bird clamping a fish in its beak, digging its feet into the pebbles while resisting the tugging of another. Suddenly, the fight is over, the victor taking to the air with its prize, the loser cawing angrily as it follows into the night. Morgan heads back inside.

Charlie is still asleep.

The clock shows 00.23.

Less than an hour until he calls.

Fighting a surge of anxiety, Morgan takes Jukes's phone from her pocket, checking the battery is charged. The status bar is half-full. Reassured, she places the phone on the table. Then she sets the kettle to boil and rummages under the sink, digging out a fleece-covered hot water bottle.

Jukes's phone rings.

She jumps. Straightens up. Checks the screen.

Karl's name appears.

He's early.

Her heart is pounding, her palms clammy. She snatches the mobile from the table. Swipes a finger across the screen and holds the phone to her ear.

Karl's voice.

'Trev?'

She says nothing.

'Trev?'

Her words come in a rush. She needs to make him understand before he can hang up.

'It's not Trev. It's Morgan Vine. I've got your baby.'

A pause. His tone switches from wary to incredulous.

'What the fuck are you talking about?'

'I took Charlie from Stacey. I want to do a deal.'

A pause.

The phone cuts out.

'Karl . . .?'

No response.

Shit!

She's blown it. Scared him away. But at least the phone is unlocked. If she moves quickly, she can call him back, before the lock kicks in . . .

The phone rings again. His name flashes on screen. Maybe he hung up in a panic. Now he's back. She answers, trying to sound calmer than she feels.

'Talk to me, Karl.'

'Fucking bitch.'

'If you don't want a conversation, I'm taking Charlie to the police.'

She holds her breath. Hears him lighting a cigarette.

Clink-rasp.

'Where are you, Morgan?'

'You expect me to answer that?'

He sucks the smoke into his lungs. She scrolls to the voice memo app on her own phone and presses play. The room fills with the sound of shrieking gulls.

'What do you want?' says Karl.

'You first.'

She hears him exhale slowly.

'A new start,' he says. 'To give my kids everything I never had. Isn't that what dads do?'

'Being a father is biology,' says Morgan. 'Being a dad is something else.' The recording of the bickering gulls grows louder. She brings her mobile closer to Jukes's phone. 'How many children have you fathered?'

'That's for me to know and you to wonder.'

'What about Jack and Karl Junior?'

A pause.

'What about them?'

'Did they show up for school today?'

He's struggling to keep his tone light, but there's no mistaking the menace in his voice.

'Was that down to you? Are you fucking with me?'

She brings her lips closer to the phone.

'You're not in charge, Karl. Not any more.'

'What do you want?'

'To feel safe,' says Morgan. 'This war needs to end.'

'War?'

'That's how it feels. Like you're the enemy. Like you're never going to surrender, never going to leave us alone. I can't live like that. Promise you'll leave us alone and I'll tell you where Charlie is.'

A pause.

'That's what you want? A *promise*?'

'That's it.'

She can hear his mind whirring.

'How do I know this isn't a trap?'

'You don't. But if we do this right we can both have what we want.' The recording of the gulls cuts out. 'If you want Charlie, call me tomorrow. Deadline midday.'

She hangs up before he can answer. Her heart feels like it will burst from her chest. Did he register the sound of the gulls?

Will he take the bait?

Pulse quickening, she lifts the sleeping baby from the rug, picks up the hot water bottle, then steps out into the night.

Forty-Three

The oven clock shows 1.17 a.m. Morgan stubs out her cigarette. She eyes the bottle on her kitchen table. She'd kill for a glass of wine, but not now. She needs to stay focused.

About to roll another cigarette, she freezes. A noise outside. She remains still. Listening to the waves. Feeling her heart race. She hears the noise again. Faint but unmistakable. Shingle crunching underfoot. She darts to the window. Peers outside. No sign of life. A single knock on the back door. She gives a start. Hears a familiar voice speaking softly.

Neville Rook.

'Morgan?'

She opens the door. He slips inside.

'Is he coming?'

'Christ, I hope so,' says Morgan.

'Where's the baby?'

'Safe.'

'What does that mean?'

She ignores the question. Peers out of the window.

'Are you alone?'

Rook shakes his head. 'You can't see them. But they're there.'

She frowns.

'Where are the cars?'

'For God's sake, Morgan. You said be discreet.' He casts a look around the kitchen, into the sitting room. 'Don't make things worse for yourself. If you've got Charlie, hand him over.'

'That's not how this is going to work.'

Her tone brooks no opposition. He sighs.

'So now what?'

She nods towards Lissa's bedroom.

'You go in there.'

'And?'

'Wait.'

2.13 a.m.

Morgan's hands are trembling. She's trying to roll a cigarette but the tobacco spills onto the table.

What if he doesn't come?

What if he decides to leave Charlie behind? To save his own skin. To start his new life tonight. She has no idea how he plans to get out of the country, but a man like Karl Savage has ways. And money. Enough to buy the right sort of help. He could hide in the boot of a car and sneak aboard a ferry. Or in a lorry or van. Or on a boat. He could cross the Channel, land in a remote spot – France, maybe, or Belgium – and disappear into the night.

Risky?

The man loves risk. Thrives on it.

2.14 a.m.

No sound from Lissa's room, not since she told Rook to keep quiet. The DI's patience won't last for ever. And how much longer can Charlie stay safe and warm? He's fine now. The hot water bottle will see to that. Morgan has taken every precaution.

But what if he doesn't come . . .?

2.15 a.m.

And then she hears it. An engine in the distance. She peers outside. No sign of movement. But she hears it drawing closer. Sees a glint of moonlight on something metallic. The bumper of a car?

No, not a car. A van.

A white camper van.

No lights.

It slows, engine idling. She can't see the driver but she imagines him behind the wheel, scanning the darkness, searching for signs of life. Cars. People. A trap.

She whispers.

'He's here.'

Rook's voice from the bedroom.

'OK.'

Retreating from the window, she moves to the sitting room. She hears the van drawing closer. The engine dies. The clunk of the door.

She can hear him now – his footsteps on the pebbles outside. Creeping closer. Circling the house.

He stops. She visualises him staring at the broken window. The sheet of cardboard taped to the frame. She holds her breath and watches as the cardboard begins to move. Hears the screech of the duct tape being peeled back. Sees his gloved hand reaching inside. Watches his fingers grasp the frame. He levers himself through the window, into the room, and straightens up.

She turns on the light. He freezes. Eyes widening in surprise. Something in his hand. Yellow. Oblong. A small, yellow can with a red spout?

'Where's Charlie?'

Before she can reply, she hears Rook yelling into his radio.

'*Go, go, go!*'

Karl's eyes bulge. 'You bitch!'

He springs forward. Rook bursts into the room but Karl's forearm is already around Morgan's neck, holding her in an armlock. He flicks the spout on the can. Sprays liquid over her. The smell is unmistakable.

Lighter fuel.

'Stay back!'

Karl reaches into his pocket. Brandishes his Zippo.

'Where's the baby?'

Morgan struggles, but his grip is too tight. The lighter fuel is seeping into her clothes, dripping down her arms, her legs. He raises the container above her head, squeezing. She feels the liquid on her hair, her head, running down her neck, her face.

Karl is dragging her towards the bedroom.

'Where's the baby?'

She says nothing.

'WHERE IS HE?'

She gasps for breath.

'My car.'

His eyes jerk to the window.

'Keys!'

She grabs them. He drags her towards the door. Looks out of the window. Morgan glimpses movement outside. Three men? Four? Some plainclothes, some uniform. Karl sees them too.

'Tell them to stay back.'

The DI hesitates.

'Do it!'

Rook reaches for his radio.

'Stand down. Repeat: stand down.'

Karl pushes Morgan towards the door.

'Open it.'

His arm is pressing on her windpipe.

'I . . . can't breathe.'

He relaxes his grip, just a fraction.

'Open it!'

She obeys. Outside, she sees the four figures rooted to the spot. Karl brandishes the Zippo and calls to Rook.

'Tell them what to do!'

Rook raises his voice, calling out.

'He'll set her on fire. Stand down.'

The figures remain still.

Rook's voice again. 'Don't do this, Karl.'

But the man is dragging Morgan towards the Mini.

'Open it!'

She zaps the fob. The lights flash, the doors unlock. His grip tightens around her neck. He peers inside the car. Sees Charlie strapped into the baby seat, swathed in the blanket. Asleep. He releases her from the armlock. Grabs her shoulder. His grip is like iron.

'Take him out.'

Morgan opens the door and reaches into the back seat, fumbling with the straps.

'I know it was Spike,' she says. 'The body in the flat. You cracked his skull, just like you cracked your mother's.'

Karl's eyes burn.

'Fuck 'em. They deserved all they got.'

The baby wakes as Morgan lifts him from the car. She can feel the hot water bottle through the blanket, still warm. Karl still has her shoulder in his grip. The baby starts to cry.

'Hold him up!'

Morgan holds the baby at arm's length. Karl raises the lighter fuel.

'No!' says Morgan.

He squirts the liquid over the blanket. The baby's cries grow louder.

Rook's voice.

'*Karl . . .!*'

'Shut up!'

Karl raises the yellow container in the air, squirting fuel over his own clothes. Holding the Zippo aloft, he shouts to Morgan.

'Give me the kid.'

Morgan hesitates.

'Now! Or we *all* fucking burn!'

She hands over the baby. Karl takes him in his arms. The hot water bottle falls to the ground. He releases Morgan from his grasp.

'Everyone stay back!'

He pockets the lighter fuel and walks towards the van.

'Karl . . . Please . . .!'

He ignores her. She hears Rook's voice.

'Not the baby, Karl . . . For the love of God, *not the baby . . .*'

'Shut up!'

He reaches the van. Morgan steps forward. She can smell fuel on his clothes, on the baby's blanket. He calls out.

'Stay back!'

But she takes another step. And another. He wrenches open the door of the van. Clasping the baby, he gets behind the wheel.

'Don't do this, Karl.' Morgan keeps her voice steady. She gestures to the police officers, standing at a distance, frozen. 'Not to Charlie.'

He meets her gaze. His eyes glaze with tears. He opens his mouth to speak but the words won't come. He tries again. But his voice is hoarse, inaudible, little more than a croak.

'Can't hear you, Karl.'

Clasping his son to his chest, the man climbs out of the van. He plants a kiss on the baby's forehead.

'Up like a rocket . . . Down like a stick . . .'

Without warning, he flings the baby towards Morgan, high in the air. The blanket falls away. She runs forward, arms outstretched, straining every muscle, every sinew. Catches the baby. Clutches him to her chest.

She hears Rook. '*Go, go, go!*' The police officers break into a run.

Karl jumps into the van and locks the door. Staring at Morgan, he flicks open the Zippo.

Perhaps it's her imagination, but even above the baby's cries she swears she can hear it: the sound that has haunted her dreams since the attack on the cliffs.

Clink-rasp.

PART THREE

Forty-Four

The MBU visitors' room is almost deserted. Just the two women in a corner. Anjelica cradles her sleeping baby in her arms. Her voice is barely audible.

'I don't know how to thank you.'

Morgan manages half a smile. She has barely slept in three days. Traumatised by the sight of a man setting himself on fire.

'Cook me supper when you get out. Bring Marlon.'

Anjelica nods. The mention of her impending freedom seems to help her voice gain strength.

'They say it'll take a while. Lots of legal stuff: confirming Karl's DNA; matching it with his kids.' She shoots a worried look in Morgan's direction. 'It will happen, won't it?'

'Yes,' says Morgan. 'It will happen.'

She sips from a plastic cup of water and takes stock of Anjelica's face. The transformation is not yet complete – the woman is still gaunt – but the dark circles under her eyes are fading, her speech is no longer slurred, her mind no longer addled by the chemical cocktail that has helped to numb the pain throughout her ordeal.

'How are you feeling?'

Anjelica considers the question.

'Relieved. Scared they'll say I'm not going home.'

Morgan takes her hand.

'You're going home. I promise.'

The woman gives a tentative smile. But it fades quickly.

'So who died in the fire?'

'Spike.'

Anjelica's eyes widen.

'For real?'

Morgan nods, recalling Karl's dismissal of his erstwhile crony, and his own mother.

Fuck 'em. They deserved all they got.

Anjelica is still trying to piece things together, taking an educated guess.

'So Karl took the matches from my flat? And he emptied the petrol from the can in my car?'

Morgan nods.

'To frame you and shut you up. To pave the way for a new life abroad.'

Anjelica shakes her head slowly, digesting the enormity of the events that have wreaked havoc in so many lives.

'Thank God it's over.'

'It's not,' says Morgan. 'Not until I find out who pushed Kiki off the cliff. There has to be some justice in this shitty world.'

Anjelica frowns.

'Surely Jukes killed her? Doing Karl's dirty work?'

Morgan shakes her head.

'He swears not.'

'You believe him?'

'I don't know. But I intend to find out.'

She takes another sip of water and studies the woman's face.

'Have you thought about what you'll do when you get out?'

A shrug.

'Get a job. Take care of Marlon. That's as far as I've got.'

'Let me know if I can help.'

A nod. Then a frown. Something is preying on Anjelica's mind.

'What will happen to Jukes?'

Morgan stares out of the barred window. Three days after Karl died from his burns, the story continues to make headlines.

Dead Again!

Murder Conviction to be Quashed.

Police under Pressure.

'Genghis' Carne has been suspended pending an enquiry, but the Dungeness rumour mill suggests he played no active part in the baby farm. At worst, he's guilty of keeping the situation under wraps.

What happens in prison stays in prison.

Jatinder Singh has been charged with perverting the course of justice, as has Jukes's sister. Meanwhile, along with Stacey Brown, Jukes has admitted to playing a key role in Karl's baby-farm-and-drug-mule operation and the abduction of Charlie. The prison officer denies murdering Kiki McNeil.

Morgan looks out at the rain falling in the exercise yard.

'Jukes might end up here. Couldn't happen to a nicer guy.'

Anjelica takes a tissue from her pocket. Clears her throat.

'The papers say there was a skeleton in Karl's tin. A baby.'

'Yes,' says Morgan. 'He'll have a proper burial.'

Anjelica blows her nose and falls silent for a moment. When she speaks again, her voice is quiet.

'What about Charlie? Is he with Social Services?'

'For now.'

The woman leans back in her chair. Something seems to settle inside her. A decision made.

'Do you think they'd let me adopt him? He's Marlon's half brother. They should be together.'

Morgan smiles.

'Yes,' she says. 'They should.'

Half an hour later, parking outside her house, Morgan sees Joe Cassidy installing a new pane of glass in her broken window. The three-legged dog sits beside him. The man in the fisherman's jumper scrapes a layer of putty from the window frame, then steps back to admire his handiwork. He casts a look around the windswept landscape. Out at sea, a fishing boat chugs across the water, surrounded by seagulls.

'How do you find the winters here?'

'Rough,' says Morgan. 'But beautiful.'

He nods.

'You're not thinking of moving?'

She considers the question.

'No.'

He smiles, holding her gaze a beat too long.

'Good.'

Feeling a blush steal across her face, Morgan watches him gather his tools and load them into his car. Instinct tells her that this is a man she could learn to trust. Not now, perhaps, but given time.

As for Ben, her feelings have cooled. The sex was good, a welcome release. But was there real intimacy? Is she capable of truly letting go? Of placing her faith in another human being?

Or is she only thinking this way because the man let her down, putting his interests first in her hour of need? His reaction to the arrival in his house of baby Charlie is fresh in her mind.

'You understand the ramifications for me? My career? My life?'

Her train of thought is interrupted by the sound of an engine. A car is approaching, Neville Rook at the wheel. He pulls to a halt, tyres crunching over the pebbles. Morgan sees a woman in the passenger seat.

Stacey Brown.

Joe frowns.

'What's she doing here?'

'I'm putting her up while she's on bail.'

'After everything she did?'

'She acted under duress,' says Morgan. 'She's a victim too.'

Joe takes a moment to absorb this. The narrowing of his eyes suggests he's not so forgiving.

'Have they charged her?'

Morgan nods, counting off the charges on her fingers.

'People trafficking. Money laundering. Drug smuggling. Child abduction. Should keep the lawyers busy.'

'She'll plead coercion,' says Joe. 'Like Singh.'

'Will it work?'

'In his case, perhaps. In hers, I doubt it.'

They watch as Neville gets out of the car followed by Stacey. She drapes her red and white Arsenal scarf around her neck and hoists her rucksack over her shoulder.

'Any news on Ryan?' says Morgan.

The woman shakes her head, gesturing towards Rook.

'He's passed everything to the Turkish police: the address in Istanbul, descriptions of the middle-men.'

The DI nods in agreement.

'Our best hope is getting info out of Jukes,' he says. 'We'll get there in the end.'

Morgan can tell he's trying to sound more confident than he feels. Stacey casts an eye over the ramshackle house.

'Do I get my own room?'

'You can have Lissa's,' says Morgan. 'She's still in LA.'

She watches her not-very-welcome houseguest go inside and close the door.

'Shouldn't be more than a couple of days,' says Rook, reading Morgan's mind. He nods a greeting to Joe.

'I take it you two know each other,' says Morgan.

''Fraid so,' says Joe, smiling. 'I'm an usher at Nev's wedding.'

Morgan raises an eyebrow.

'Am I invited?'

The DI rolls his eyes.

'Don't hold your breath.'

He walks to his car without a backward glance. Morgan watches him drive away, then turns to Joe.

'Can I buy you a drink sometime? To thank you for fixing the window?'

'Single malt?'

'A large one.'

He smiles.

'Is there any other kind?'

Followed by the dog, he makes his way across the shingle and climbs into his car. And then he's gone.

Later, as darkness descends over Dungeness, Morgan is too tired to cook. She's relieved when Stacey suggests phoning out for pizza. They eat while watching the local news – a report on Eric Sweet. The man has pleaded guilty to charges of voyeurism. He's been sentenced to nine months in prison.

'Sleazebag,' says Stacey, taking a slurp of beer.

Morgan says nothing. She's regretting her decision to offer the woman a place to stay. She yawns.

'Early night for me.'

'What are you, ninety?' says Stacey. 'Can I have a bath?'

'Of course. I'll sort out the bed.'

Morgan washes up while Stacey clatters around in the bathroom, lighting one of Lissa's scented candles, then opening a second beer and closing the door.

Morgan is relieved to be left alone but the feeling of wellbeing is short-lived. Her mobile rings. Ben's name flashes up. She hesitates before answering the call, doing her best to sound breezy.

'Hi, Ben.'

'Sorry I didn't call sooner. I've been busy.'

'Me too.'

'Did you see the news about Eric?'

'Yes.'

A pause. She lets the silence stretch.

'Are you pissed off with me?' he says.

She thinks for a moment.

'I'm in the middle of something.'

'Otherwise known as avoiding the question.'

Morgan sighs. The man may not be Mr Right but he was Mr Right-Now, at least for a while. She doesn't want to part on bad terms.

'I'm glad to have known you, Ben. Good luck out there.'

She hears a sigh, then the line goes dead.

She stares at her phone for a moment then pockets it, wondering if she should feel more upset. Her reverie is broken by the sound of splashing water emanating from the bathroom, bringing her back to the task at hand.

She fetches linen from the airing cupboard. Entering her daughter's room, she strips the sheets from the bed and wrestles with the duvet, replacing it with a fresh cover. Her foot makes contact with something under the bed – Stacey's rucksack. She picks it up, placing it on the bedside chair next to the red and white scarf. As she does so, a plastic bag falls to the floor. A denim jacket falls out.

Morgan freezes, rooted to the spot.

Her memory flashes back to Joe's account of the two people he saw with Kiki on the night she died.

A man and a woman. The man wore a hoodie. The woman had a denim jacket. Big red metal buttons.

Picking up the jacket, Morgan's heart beats triple-quick as she turns it over.

The outsize buttons are red.

Arsenal red.

'Everything all right?'

She turns to see Stacey standing in the doorway, dressed in Lissa's bathrobe, holding her can of beer.

'You were there.' The words are out of Morgan's mouth before she knows it. Her heart is pounding. 'The night Kiki died. You were on the cliffs.'

Stacey opens her mouth to reply, but Morgan cuts her off.

'Don't lie. You were seen. In this jacket.'

Stacey's stare is hard.

'You don't want to have this conversation. Trust me.'

Morgan ignores her. Blood thudding in her ears. Pulse racing.

'Did you push Kiki?'

Stacey shakes her head, but Morgan is in full flow.

'Tell me the truth. You were on the cliffs. You and a man.'

She reaches for her phone. A reflex action. Stacey sucks her teeth, shaking her head slowly.

'You are *so* not calling the police.'

'Tell me what happened.'

A sigh.

'I'm warning you—'

'No, I'm warning *you*. What happened to Kiki? Who was the man in the hoodie?'

Stacey chews on her lip, staring at Morgan for a long moment. She sighs, making a decision. Time to come clean.

'It wasn't a man.'

Morgan frowns.

'Who was it?'

Stacey smiles, relishing her moment of power.

'It was Lissa.'

The words open a sinkhole in Morgan's world. So ludicrous are they – so divorced from reality – that she is tempted to laugh. Her mind turns somersaults, flashing back to Lissa's tearful question.

What's the worst thing you've ever done?

'You're lying.'

A reflex response, but inside – deep down, where she knows fundamental truths about herself, her daughter, life – she knows Stacey is right. The thought is unbearable.

'It's a lie.'

But she knows it's true.

Lissa's panic attacks.

Sleepless nights.

Tears.

Her drunken binge.

Her insistence that Kiki was depressed, suicidal.

True, true, true.

Stacey perches on the bed. The smile has gone.

'Call me what you like. Won't change what happened.'

Morgan shakes her head, trying to blot out the flow of words, but Stacey continues, undaunted.

'Kiki changed her mind about the deal with Jukes. It was one thing at the start – all theory, nothing real. But when Charlie was born, everything changed. She *could not* give him up. You understand, right? *I* do.' She sniffs. 'I went through with it, with Ryan. Kept my part of the deal. It nearly killed me. Sobbed my eyes out for weeks, and I still cry myself to sleep every night.' She takes a breath. 'Could you have done it?'

Morgan says nothing. Her body is trembling, her head swimming as Stacey continues.

'Kiki couldn't go through with it. Refused to do the Istanbul trips. Wouldn't give up her baby. So Jukes told the bloke who was pulling the strings – Karl – and *he* went ballistic. He sent a message, through Jukes, told Kiki there were two ways out: six feet under or find a substitute mule. What choice did she have? She told Jukes she knew just the person.'

Morgan's voice is a whisper.

'Lissa?'

A nod.

'Kiki said she was taking her to a party. You were out cold, on your pills. Lissa snuck out to meet me and Kiki. I'd nicked a car and we stuck Charlie and Ryan in the back, drove to St Mary's Bay. Went up to the cliffs, the three of us, drinking, smoking weed. Started mucking about near the edge, daring each other to go near the edge. Closer and closer.' She breaks off, swigging her beer before continuing. 'Then the mucking about stopped. Me and Kiki, we dragged Lissa to the edge of the cliff, me holding one arm, Kiki the other. We told her what she had to do. She was crying and screaming, but there was no one to hear. We kept on and on till she said yes, to make it stop. Then we let her go.'

Morgan's heart is hammering. She can't bear to hear the rest, yet she must. 'Lissa lashed out,' says Stacey. 'She kicked Kiki in the stomach. Kiki doubled up. I thought she was going to collapse, fall on the grass.' Stacey leans forward, her eyes boring into Morgan's. '*But then Lissa did it again*. Your daughter kicked her. Hard. Kiki toppled back and fell.'

Morgan's voice is a croak.

'You're lying . . . That day outside the inn . . . after Kiki died . . . I was there when you met Lissa for the first time . . .'

Stacey shakes her head. 'We were putting on a show.'

'I don't believe you. *You* pushed Kiki.'

Stacey shakes her head. Her voice is filled with bitterness.

'I knew people would say that. Who'd believe me over a girl like Lissa? A jailbird who stabbed her boyfriend? Nobody.' She pauses for breath. 'I might be going back to prison, Morgan, but not for a murder I didn't commit. No fucking way. Me and Lissa – we knew we could screw each other over *unless we stuck together.*' She takes a breath, calming herself down. 'That's why we made the pact.'

'What pact?'

Stacey gives a thin smile.

'Lissa wouldn't tell lies about me. And I wouldn't tell the truth about her.'

The words hang in the air. They have the ring of truth.

And yet . . . And yet . . .

Morgan tries again.

'If it happened the way you say . . . I'm not saying I believe it . . . but *if it did* then it was an accident . . .'

Stacey interrupts again.

'The first kick, maybe. You could call it self-defence. But not the second. I was there. I saw it. It was murder.' Her eyes narrow. 'The way the system is, if you try to pin this on me you might pull it off. But send me down for something I didn't do? Is that what you want, Morgan Vine? Is that who you are?'

Morgan's eyes fill with tears. She refuses to let them fall. Shakes her head. A rushing sound in her ears.

Disbelief, denial, despair.

Something inside Stacey seems to snap. She springs to her feet and snatches the phone from Morgan's hand. Scrolling to Lissa's name, she holds out the mobile. Her eyes blaze.

'Ask her.'

Morgan hesitates, then takes the phone. Feeling Stacey's eyes on her, she leaves the room and walks to the front door.

Outside, the air is bitterly cold but she barely notices. There is no moon, no stars, the night sky is wreathed in thick cloud. Apart from the sound of waves on shingle, there is silence. Hands shaking, heart beating at twice its normal rate, Morgan scrolls to Lissa's name, tracing her thumb over the photo of her daughter's face.

She waits.

Six thousand miles away, the call connects.

'Hey, Mum. What's up?'

Morgan clears her throat.

'Stacey just told me something.'

A pause.

'About what?'

'Something she says happened on the cliffs.'

Another pause. Lissa's voice is barely audible.

'What do you mean?'

Morgan closes her eyes.

'She said she and Kiki tried to force you to take Kiki's part in Savage's plan. She said they threatened you.' She takes a breath. 'Stacey said . . .' She falters then tries again. 'She said you kicked Kiki off the cliff.'

No response. Morgan lets the silence stretch.

Then she hears it. The sound of weeping.

'Lissa?'

A sob. But no words. Morgan tries again.

'I will always love you, Lissa, no matter what. But I need to know the truth. Did you do it?'

Another sob, louder this time.

Then the whisper that changes the world.

'Yes.'

Forty-Five

Baggage in hall.

The terminal teems with travellers wheeling suitcases, greeting friends and families. Morgan watches the smiles and hugs, the knot in her stomach tightening with every second.

Catching sight of Lissa – gaunt and hollow-eyed – her heart leaps briefly before sinking like a boulder. She manages a smile, stretching out her arms in greeting. Her daughter doesn't return the smile, her bleary, red-rimmed eyes brimming with tears.

They hug. Holding on for dear life. The intensity of the embrace triggers Lissa's loss of composure. Her body is racked with sobs.

'I'm . . . sorry,' she says, gulping for air. 'I'm . . . *so* . . . sorry.'

Morgan ignores the stares of passers-by. She can't give in to her emotions. Not here. Not now. Her voice is hoarse, the lump in her throat making it hard to speak.

'We'll get through this.'

Lissa shakes her head. She whispers in her mother's ear.

'I did a terrible thing. I didn't mean to, but it happened. They'll make me pay for it.'

Morgan closes her eyes. A 'terrible thing', yes. But was Kiki blameless? Was Stacey? Surely people would understand how things had been, on the cliffs?

Fear. Survival instinct kicking in.

Literally.

Surely no jury would convict Lissa of murder? Morgan opens her eyes, trying to sound more confident than she feels.

'I'm hiring a lawyer. The best.'

'We can't afford the best.'

'Yes, we can. The money from the book.'

A lie. The advance is long gone. Thank God for overdrafts.

Lissa sniffs.

'Dad would help.'

Morgan stiffens.

'Did you tell him?'

Her daughter shakes her head.

'No.'

A flicker of relief. They have agreed to tell no one. Not even Cameron. Not until Lissa makes the biggest decision of her life. It's just the two of them. Mother and daughter against the world.

Over Lissa's shoulder, Morgan can see a brace of police officers patrolling the arrivals hall. Armed. Unsmiling. Eyes roving the crowds. She shudders.

'Let's go home.'

Wheeling the suitcase towards the exit, Morgan updates her daughter on Stacey's move to a bail hostel.

'How much did you know? The day we followed her to the airport?'

Stepping onto the moving walkway, Lissa tugs a tissue from her sleeve and blows her nose. She keeps her voice low.

'I knew she was smuggling money. I guessed drugs were involved. I didn't know about the baby trafficking, I swear.'

'I believe you.'

Lissa seems relieved.

'Is Stacey going to shop me?'

'She says not,' says Morgan. 'She feels guilty that she and Kiki drove you to it.'

A glimmer of hope on Lissa's face.

'And you believe her?'

Morgan can only shrug.

'She's in enough trouble as it is. I think there's a chance she'll let sleeping dogs lie.'

Lissa blinks.

'Only a chance?'

Morgan has no idea if Stacey will keep her promise. The woman is unreliable and unpredictable. If she can sell her own child for £5,000 . . .

She tries to strike a reassuring note.

'A good chance.'

Her mind flashes back to the scene by the lighthouse.

Dawn breaking over the deserted beach. Stacey swigging beer while watching Morgan set fire to the denim jacket, the only piece of physical evidence that ties anyone to Kiki's death.

Lissa is saying something.

'So . . . bottom line. The decision's up to me?'

No sense in trying to varnish the truth: the stakes are too high.

'I wish there were another way,' says Morgan. 'But yes, it's up to you.'

Lissa falls silent for a moment. Entering the walkway that leads to the car park, she turns to face her mother.

'Do you hate me?'

The words strike at Morgan's heart.

My bones, my blood.

She takes her daughter's hand. Holding tight.

'I love you, Lissa. I'm here for you, no matter what happens.'

'Always?'

'Always.'

Morgan manages a small smile, but her eyes glaze with tears. People talk about broken hearts. They know nothing.

Forty-Six

The rain is back. Pounding the roof of the converted railway carriage.

'I'm so sorry,' whispers Lissa. 'I took a life. I killed a mum.'

It's moments before Morgan can bring herself to speak. In spite of everything, her daughter needs comfort. She clears her throat.

'We're all better than the worst thing we've done.'

She strokes Lissa's hair, gently tracing a finger over her tear-stained cheek. They're lying on the sofa. The room is lit by a single candle.

'If I give myself up, I'll go to prison.'

Morgan nods, struck dumb.

'But if I don't, I'll be looking over my shoulder for the rest my life. Either way, I'll have to live with the guilt for ever.'

'Yes,' says Morgan, her voice little more than a croak.

Her daughter closes her eyes, trying to stem another fit of crying.

'I'm living with the guilt anyway. What's the point of wasting years behind bars? It won't bring her back. How does it make anything better?'

Morgan has no answer. She could talk about justice and atonement, but what good would it do? Sometimes, words are just words.

'What am I supposed to do?' says Lissa.

Morgan knew the question would come. There are times when the truth is unbearable. She strokes her daughter's hair.

'Turning yourself in won't bring Kiki back. It won't make anything better. But unless you do the right thing you will never be at peace. I think that might be worse than prison.'

Lissa looks stricken. Her voice is barely audible.

'Oh my God . . .'

Groping in vain for words of wisdom, Morgan freezes as she hears footsteps on shingle. Someone is outside. Getting to her feet, she crosses to the window and peers into the night. A shadowy figure is circling the house, hoodie raised against the rain.

Morgan walks to the door and tugs it open, letting in a blast of cold air.

'Who's there?'

The figure emerges from the shadows. A familiar face.

'Anjelica?'

The woman is clutching her baby in one arm, a holdall in the other.

'I didn't want to go to the hostel, not on my first night out.' Rain drips from the rim of her hoodie. 'Cundy told me where you lived.'

Morgan suppresses a flicker of annoyance. The shrink could at least have given her some warning. Tonight of all nights.

'Come in.'

'You sure?'

Morgan looks at the woman who has been through so much. The baby squirms. Mother and son are on the verge of tears.

'Of course.'

Anjelica steps inside, stamping her trainers on the mat. Morgan gestures towards Lissa, prone on the sofa.

'This is my daughter.'

'Hiya,' says Anjelica. 'Heard a lot about you.'

'Likewise,' says Lissa.

She glares at her mother.

Tell me they're not staying.

Morgan gives a small shrug, equally eloquent.

What am I supposed to do?

Sensing a chill in the atmosphere, the newcomer looks from Lissa's face to Morgan's.

'Hope this isn't a bad time.'

'Well, actually . . .' begins Morgan, but her daughter cuts her short, getting to her feet.

'It's fine. I was just going to have a bath.'

She walks into the bathroom and closes the door.

Anjelica places her baby on the sofa, dabbing moisture from his cheeks with her sleeve. She seems to have made herself at home.

'I was thinking maybe I could cook you that meal?'

'Not tonight,' says Morgan. 'Nothing in the fridge.'

Regretting the sharpness of her tone, Morgan searches for a way to get rid of her visitors (a hostel? a B & B?) but how can she turf Anjelica out, into the rainy night?

On the other hand, there's Lissa.

Her situation.

Her trauma.

Her decision.

'Mind if I change Marlon's nappy?' says Anjelica.

''Course not.'

Morgan leaves the woman to it, crossing to the bathroom and tapping on the door.

'Can I come in?'

'*Yup.*'

Morgan enters the bathroom and closes the door. Her daughter is sitting on the edge of the bath, twisting a tissue in her hands.

'Give them my room,' she says. 'I'll take the sofa.'

Morgan raises an eyebrow.

'Is that a good idea?'

Her daughter sighs, her eyes bright with tears.

'Don't give me a hard time. This might be my last night.'

As Marlon sleeps on the sofa, the reason for Lissa's change of heart becomes clear over a meagre supper of beans on toast. She wants to pick Anjelica's brains. They have discussed Karl and Jukes, and the baby in the tin, but one topic is uppermost in Lissa's mind.

'What's prison like? I've seen it on TV but what's it really like?'

Morgan pours another glass of wine, listening to the wind howl outside and watching as the visitor blows out her cheeks.

'At first, it's surreal. Like it's happening to someone else. Then reality bites.' Anjelica pauses, wiping her mouth with the back of her hand and nodding towards the front door. 'Tell me what you see.'

Lissa follows her gaze.

'The door.'

'Describe it.'

'White. A lock halfway up. And a latch.'

'That's it?'

'What do you mean?'

'Is there a handle?'

'Of course.'

'Exactly,' says Anjelica. 'The moment prison hits home is when you walk into your cell and hear that door being locked behind you. For the first time in your life you're looking at *a door with no handle*.' She sips her water. 'I stared at that door all night, listening to women yelling, crying out for their mums.' She pushes a crust of toast around her plate. 'The first few weeks were like the worst nightmare. Violence. Bullying.'

'Jesus,' whispers Lissa. 'Sounds awful.'

A thin smile.

'I could have handled "awful". Another sip of water. 'The tea tasted terrible. Kiki worked in the canteen. She used to make me tea in a special mug. Said I'd get used to it. She was right. After a few weeks, it started to taste normal. Which is when she showed her true colours. She hadn't made mine with water, she'd used her own urine.' She pauses, looking down at the beans on her plate. 'And don't get me started on the sausages.'

Lissa drops her fork with a clatter, muttering under her breath.

'Jesus Christ . . .'

Unable to take any more, she gets to her feet, chair scraping the floor.

'I need to go to bed. Jet lag. Mind if I have my own room after all?'

She avoids her mother's eye.

This might be my last night . . .

Anjelica nods towards her sleeping baby.

''Course not. We'll be fine.'

Lissa heads for her room.

'Goodnight,' says Morgan.

No answer.

She watches as her daughter opens the door to her bedroom.

Her hand lingering on the handle.

Later, on her way back from the bathroom, Morgan knocks on Lissa's door. No reply. Entering the sitting room, she hears a whisper from the sofa.

'Thanks for this.'

She sees Anjelica wrapped in a blanket, cradling her sleeping baby in her arms.

'You're welcome.'

The woman nods towards a pile of Jiffy bags stacked in the corner of the room.

'Fan mail?'

Morgan shakes her head.

'Letters from prisoners, forwarded by my publisher. They all swear they're innocent and seem to think I'm Wonder Woman.'

'You are to me.'

Morgan manages half a smile. Any triumph in securing Anjelica's release has been cast into the deepest shadow.

'Any news on what happened to Kiki?'

'Nope,' says Morgan, appalled by the ease with which the lie slips from her lips.

Anjelica sighs.

'She was a nasty piece of work. But no one deserves to die that way.'

Morgan says nothing, heading for her room.

'I'll cook you that meal another time,' says Anjelica. 'Sweet dreams.'

It's 2 a.m. before Morgan manages to snatch some sleep. But she's awake by four, mouth dry, head thumping. She lies quietly, listening to the rain on the roof and wishing there was someone she could call. Being a single mother has never been easy, but there are times when the lack of a partner feels overwhelming. Cameron has never been 'hands on' – quite the opposite – but he might share legal bills. On the other hand, Morgan wonders how seriously he'd take this latest turn of events. He views the world through the prism of a Hollywood screenwriter. She could imagine him describing Lissa's responsibility for Kiki's death as an 'interesting plot twist'.

Picking up her phone, Morgan scrolls to Ben's name.

She hesitates, then deletes his number.

Her thoughts turn to Stacey Brown, presumably asleep in her bail hostel, facing another lengthy sentence. Will the woman stay silent?

Should she?

How do people live with a secret this toxic, a burden this heavy?

Maybe it's the loneliness of the night, but Morgan feels an urgent need to confide in someone, preferably someone who knows the criminal justice system. Scrolling through her contacts, she comes to Joe Cassidy's name. She hesitates, struggling to imagine a conversation in which she picks the ex-copper's brains without giving anything away.

Not possible.

Her headache worsening, she gets out of bed and pads into the bathroom, passing Anjelica and Marlon asleep on the sofa. She rummages in the medicine cabinet, searching for the paracetamol.

No sign of the jar.

But she bought some not long ago . . .

Her mind races. She recalls her daughter's words.

This might be my last night.

Emerging from the bathroom, she hurries along the corridor and sees a light shining under Lissa's door. She knocks. No reply. She opens the door.

The bed is rumpled. The room is empty.

Grabbing her daughter's bathrobe, she dons a pair of flip-flops. Then she steps out into the night.

The rain is still falling. To the east, the beam from the old lighthouse cuts through the darkness. To the west, the lights of HMP Dungeness are visible, along with the glow of lights from the power station. But there is no sign of life.

'Lissa?'

Morgan steps onto the shingle, drawing the bathrobe around her.

'Lissa?'

Her feet crunch over the stones as she walks towards the light-house, eyes roving the darkness. Passing the Mini, she glances inside but there is no sign of her daughter.

'*Lissa!*'

The rain teems down. The bathrobe is sodden. Her feet are freezing. She hurries on, slipping and sliding on the shingle, passing the wreckage of the abandoned fishing boat. She calls her daughter's name, again and again.

No response.

Gripped by a growing panic, she turns and glimpses movement by the shoreline. A figure in white.

No, a woman.

A naked woman.

Lissa.

Morgan stumbles over the pebbles, hurrying towards her daughter, calling her name. Lissa is facing out to sea, ankle-deep in water. Lost in a world of her own, she doesn't respond to her mother's cries. Drawing closer, Morgan can hear her railing against the world.

'*Why me? . . . Why? . . . Why?*'

Sobbing, Lissa's arms are outstretched, her slim, pale body framed by the night sky. Her feet are bleeding, cut by the flint. Morgan splashes through the ice-cold water, reaching her daughter, enveloping her in her arms.

'Did you take the pills?'

Lissa continues to cry but says nothing.

'Lissa! Talk to me!'

A guttural roar emerges from her daughter's mouth. She turns. Eyes bulging. Rain cascading down her face. But she doesn't answer.

Over her shoulder, Morgan sees the plastic jar of paracetamol lying on the shingle. She darts forward and grabs the container, flipping open the cap with shaking hands. The cotton wool is still in place. The jar is full.

Flooded with relief, she turns back to her daughter, whose cries echo far and wide.

'Let's go home.'

She puts an arm around Lissa, leading her towards the house.

'I can't do it, Mum . . . I can't go to prison . . . I'd rather die.'

'Don't say that . . .'

'I'm not just *saying* it . . . I *mean* it . . . I can't go to prison. I swear to God, I'll kill myself.'

Morgan steers her distraught daughter towards the front door. In her heart, she knows Lissa means every word. The girl always speaks her mind.

Like mother, like daughter.

Forty-Seven

Morgan spends what's left of the night in Lissa's bed, holding her daughter close, stroking her hair. Slowly, the sobs subside, replaced by soft snores. Then comes the rhythmic breathing that accompanies deep slumber. Morgan's last two Zopiclone have done their job.

Her mind racing, she doesn't sleep until the first glimmers of dawn, then she dozes for what feels like minutes, waking to find her daughter still out for the count.

Merciful oblivion.

Emerging from the bedroom, Morgan discovers that Anjelica and Marlon have gone. A note on the kitchen table.

Thank you. For everything.
PS: I'll let you know how I get on with adopting Charlie.

She takes a long shower, then carries a pot of coffee outside, onto the deck, and rolls her first cigarette of the day. A long-ago exchange with Lissa flashes through her mind.

I thought you were going to quit smoking.

So did I.

The rain has died away, the sun is filtering through wisps of white cloud. Morgan scans the deserted shoreline, the only sign of life a flock of gulls circling a lone fishing trawler out at sea. There is a hint of warmth in the air and, in spite of everything, solace in the wild beauty that surrounds her house: every bird, every scrap of shingle, every clump of sea kale.

Hearing barking, she looks up to see the three-legged dog heading in her direction. Joe Cassidy follows in its wake. The ex-DI is wearing his fisherman's jumper. He raises an arm in greeting. Morgan manages a brief wave. Nothing too friendly. She needs him at arm's length for now.

Perhaps for ever.

Reaching the deck that surrounds the house, his greeting is cheery.

''Morning.'

Her response is curt.

'Hi.'

Taking a seat at the table, she focuses on finishing her roll-up. The dog scampers away, nose to the shingle, following a trail of smells.

'Did you hear from Neville Rook?' says Joe.

'About what?'

He smiles, pleased to be the bearer of news.

'Probably shouldn't shoot my mouth off, but the baby in the biscuit tin? The father was Jukes.'

Morgan raises an eyebrow.

'Definitely?'

A nod.

'Their DNA matches.'

Morgan lights her cigarette. She can see Joe eyeing the coffee pot. Senses him angling for an invitation.

'They found a letter in the tin too,' he says. 'It was singed by the heat from the fire, but still legible. It's Jukes's confession to killing the baby. In his own handwriting. Open and shut case.'

Morgan's eyes widen. She says nothing, dragging on her cigarette.

'They think he killed Kiki too,' says Joe.

Her heart rate quickens.

'Rook said that?'

A nod.

'Jukes denies it.' Joe scratches his nose and frowns. 'And I'm not convinced Neville's right.'

Morgan tries to keep her voice casual.

'Why not?'

'Those people I saw the night Kiki died? The woman in the denim jacket? The man in the hoodie?'

'What about them?'

He reaches into his pocket and pulls something out. 'The dog was sniffing around over there.' He nods towards the lighthouse. 'Found these.'

He opens his palm.

Suddenly, Morgan's heart is hammering. In Joe's hand are the remains of two buttons from Stacey's denim jacket. Charred by fire, the red paint is mostly gone, but one or two specks remain on the fragments of metal.

Joe pokes the buttons with a forefinger.

'Maybe it's just a coincidence, but something doesn't smell right.' He tucks the buttons back in his pocket. 'Once a copper, always a copper.'

Morgan says nothing. Blood thuds in her ears. Is he going to follow his instincts?

Joe studies her face. Raises an eyebrow.

'You OK, Morgan?'

'Fine.'

She daren't pick up her mug for fear her hands will tremble. She nods towards the front door. Tries to strike a cheerful note. 'My daughter came home.'

'For good?'

She considers the question.

'Looks like it.'

Joe gazes out to sea and clears his throat. He nods in the direction of the lighthouse. 'I hear the Beach Inn is under new management.'

'Is that so?'

'Would you like to try the restaurant? Dinner? Bring your daughter?'

Morgan looks into the man's grey-green eyes.

'I don't think that's a good idea.'

His smile fades.

'Oh?'

Still shaking, she daren't drag on her cigarette. Joe says nothing for a moment. The silence swells, becoming uncomfortable.

'Have I done something wrong?'

No. You're kind. Clever.

Too clever.

'Not at all,' she says. 'It's just . . .' She tails off, hoping the sentence will somehow finish itself.

'Just . . . one of those days?' he offers.

She manages half a smile.

'One of those lives.'

After the man has left, trailed by the three-legged dog, Morgan smokes two more cigarettes while watching the sun rise high in the sky. The clouds have drifted away and there is more warmth in the air, perhaps the last of the year. She finishes her coffee, staring at the prison in the distance, her mind still racing.

Back inside the house, she finds Lissa asleep, curled in a foetal ball. Gazing at her daughter's tear-stained face, she sits by the bedside for several minutes.

What now, Lissa? Your life is in two halves: before and after.

Mine too.

Her daughter gives a small cough and turns her face towards the wall, but sleeps on. Morgan can sit still no longer. She rises from the chair and walks into the kitchen.

For a moment, she considers opening a bottle of wine.

The impulse dies as quickly as it is born.

It's 9 a.m. Get a grip.

But Joe's words are still playing inside her head.

Something doesn't smell right.

Will he act on his suspicions? Does Lissa's determination to remain silent mark the end of the story? Or just the beginning?

Morgan paces the room. Anxious. Restless. Looking for something to do.

She sits at the table, rolls another cigarette and turns her attention to the mail from prisoners. She opens the first Jiffy bag and lets a pile of letters cascade onto the table. One falls to the floor. She picks it up. It's addressed to *Morgan Vine, author of Trial and Error.*

Lighting the roll-up, she slits open the envelope and begins to read.

Acknowledgements

Many thanks to Joel, Claire, Bec, Emily, Kate, Mark and the rest of the team at Bonnier Zaffre and to Caroline Michel at PFD.

Thanks also to Mark Billingham and all the other readers, bloggers, and reviewers who were kind enough to say nice things about the first Morgan Vine thriller, *Without Trace*.

A special mention to Graham Minett, Ayisha Malik, David Young, Alex Caan, Lesley Allen, Colette Dartford, Chris Whitaker, Vanessa O'Loughlin, Rebecca Thornton, Deborah O'Connor, Sophie Nicholls, Kevin Sullivan and Deborah Bee, who launched debut novels around the same time and enjoyed many laughs along the way.

In the words of the great Lily Tomlin, 'We're all in this together – *alone.*'

Above all, my love and thanks to Melanie McGrath for being delightful, delicious and de-lovely, and keeping the home fires burning.

Reading Group Questions

- To what extent is Karl Savage a victim of his upbringing? Do you feel any sympathy for him?
- Morgan's daughter Lissa is put through the mill. Morgan loves her but doesn't always find her easy to like. How do you feel about Lissa? Do your feelings change as the story progresses? Is she a spoilt brat? Victim of her own choices? Unlucky in love?
- Morgan's relationship with arson investigator Ben Gaminara ends on a bitter-sweet note. Do you feel he let her down? Was she right to ditch him?
- Does Joe Cassidy seem like a better bet as a potential love interest? Or does he pose a potential threat to Morgan and her daughter?
- Morgan is not above flirting with DI Neville Rook in order to get the information she needs. Does she lead him on unfairly or is he fair game?
- Morgan takes desperate measures to lure Karl Savage out of hiding. Was she right to take the risks she did?
- The book has a shocking twist (no spoilers!) as the identity of the killer is revealed. If you were in Morgan's shoes, what would you do with the knowledge she now has?
- If you've read the first in the Morgan Vine series (*Without Trace*) how do the two stories compare? Is it any wonder she has a hard time trusting men?